LIMERICK CITY LIBRARY

Phone: 407510
Website:
www.limerickcity.ie/library
Email: citylib@limerickcity.ie

The Granary,
Michael Street,
Limerick.

**This book is issued subject to the Rules of the Library.
The Book must be returned not later then the last date
stamped below.**

PICTURES

PICTURES

ROBERT DALEY

AN OTTO PENZLER BOOK
Quercus

First published in Great Britain in 2007 by

Quercus
21 Bloomsbury Square
London
WC1A 2NS

A CIP catalogue reference for this book is available
from the British Library

ISBN (HB) 1 84724 041 0
(978 1 84724 041 5)
ISBN (TPB) 1 84724 042 9
(978 1 84724 042 2)

10 9 8 7 6 5 4 3 2 1

Printed and bound in Great Britain by Clays Ltd, St Ives plc.

This book is for Theresa

PICTURES

CHAPTER

I

A CAR TURNED OFF THE STREET, stopped in front of the barrier, and a guard came out of the booth and pointed his flashlight in on the driver. When he saw whose face he had illuminated he flicked the light off fast, mumbled an apology, jumped backward, and raised the barrier.

It was the middle of the night. The parking lot, empty of cars, was vast. Floodlights on poles lit up the perimeter fence, together with the trailer trucks backed up against it. The rest was dark, except for a dim bulb burning over the plant's executive entrance far across the lot.

The car drove over there, stopped, and three men got out.

This was on Chicago's north side close to the lake. The night was chilly. In some places spring was far advanced, but midwestern America was not one of them. The cold wind that blew in off the lake caused one of the men, who stood beside the car and whose name was Vincent Conte, to turn up the collar of his coat.

Gazing back at the guard booth, he said: "What about the guard?"

The driver said: "What about him?"

"We drive in here at this hour, he'll tell everyone."

"I trust him," said the driver, whose name was Tinsley. "He's been with me a long time."

In a situation like this, Conte's trust didn't go far. He said: "Is there a watchman as well?"

"He patrols the perimeter. He doesn't go inside."

"Where is he now, if I might ask?"

The three men looked around.

"Probably asleep in one of the trucks," muttered Conte. "I don't think too much of your security so far."

One was not supposed to criticize clients, in this case Tinsley, principal owner of the plant. But Conte was a brusque kind of man. In addition, the case wasn't ready to break. Being here, in his opinion, was premature.

"I'm the one opens the plant," said the third man, Lonano. "I'll send them home before the workforce punches in."

Conte did not trust Lonano either. He was the plant's general manager but had come up through the ranks and was still a member of the union. If his sympathy lay with the men, he might try to warn somebody.

Tinsley unlocked the entrance, and they went inside.

The building, only one story high, measured about a hundred yards square, nearly all of it the cooler, an enormous refrigerator the size of a football field. The offices ran in a row along one of the sides of the building with a corridor in front, then a wall with windows that looked into the cooler, and a number of refrigerator doors that provided access. The doors were thick, insulated.

The three men went through one of them into the cooler.

It was very bright—Lonano had thrown a master switch somewhere—and Vince Conte was confronted by beef, tons of it. Beef piled on tables, beef hanging from hooks. A thermometer on the wall read 38 degrees. In this room at this temperature 250 butchers worked all day hacking up steers.

"We're the second biggest meat packers in Chicago," Tinsley said.

Conte was walking down aisles toward the scales. The aisles were quite broad; nonetheless, it felt like wading through meat.

"Someone is robbing us blind," Tinsley said to his back.

"Yeah, you told me."

"We sold a million and a half pounds last month. Didn't make a dime."

It was cold in here and Conte's topcoat was thin. He snuffed the air which, despite the cold, had an unpleasant metallic tang.

He was a compact man with scar tissue over one eye that was still a bit raw, meaning recent. If he had been a boxer he would have been a middleweight. He was not a boxer. He was an ex–New York cop. He was 35 years old, and until recently had been the youngest captain in the department, with a future that seemed unlimited. But that was then, not now.

Conte said: "I don't like the layout."

He looked behind him at the heavy doors leading to the offices. During working hours they would open and shut every few minutes, people in bloody smocks going in and out.

The ex-cop was a man who weighed possibilities, weighed odds. The butchers and luggers were going to watch colleagues being led through into the offices, men who did not come back. It would not take long to figure out what was happening. And without the element of surprise, which was his principal tool, almost his only one, he would have nothing.

"This case is not ready," Conte said. He had had agents working here for weeks, but they had not developed much.

Two months ago Tinsley had phoned him. Conte flew to Chicago and they had met in a conference room at the airport. Tinsley had spoken of shrinkage in his plant.

"Shrinkage?" said Conte.

Meat was going out that was not being paid for. To the tune of about $100,000 a month.

Conte had said only: "Are you sure of your figures?"

Tinsley had gone over them and over them, he said, and so had his accountants. "I went to the police. Without evidence they can't operate. The only evidence I have is the figures. The figures don't interest them. I went to the FBI. Same story."

"So you came to us."

"You're supposed to be the best."

Conte worked for Probe Consultations Inc. Already a major presence in America, Probe had begun to open offices worldwide. It employed accountants who traced laundered money, detectives who tracked down missing executives and whatever was left of what they had stolen. The recently hired Conte was in charge of the industrial theft division.

Conte had put two of his men into Tinsley's plant, a white man named Bruno into receiving, and a black man named Simmons into shipping, because shipping and receiving were the two areas most vulnerable to employee theft. Tinsley was to pay the two agents a meat packer's salary, and then stay away from them. It would be at least three weeks, perhaps longer, Conte told him, before the other employees felt comfortable with the agents, at which point they might see something, hear something. To steal as much meat as Tinsley claimed, the ring would have to be a big one, 20 or more men.

The investigation would take time, Conte warned.

Three weeks passed and Bruno in receiving had encountered nothing suspicious, whereas Simmons had overheard drivers talking about a certain supermarket that would buy hot meat.

Tinsley Meat Packers did not sell to that particular market.

Conte pulled Bruno out of the plant, and put him in a rented car in the supermarket parking lot. The agent changed cars every day, as ordered, and he watched the market's loading bay but nothing happened.

Conte reported regularly to Tinsley, reports that were always the same: nothing. Each time the client was almost in tears until finally, en route to Oklahoma on another case, Conte had had to stop in Chicago to calm him.

At the start of the sixth week one of Tinsley's trucks rolled into the supermarket lot that Agent Bruno was watching, pulled up to the loading bay, and the driver, Jack Ritinski, 32 years old, a big guy with a goatee, staggered inside under a side of beef weighing 180 pounds. He came out counting bills, which he shared with his helper, later identified as Anthony Amato.

A week later the same thing happened, except that the helper on the truck was a black man, Shawlee Summers.

Conte sent another agent to Chicago to follow other trucks. Within a week this agent observed a side of beef being delivered to a supermarket on the other side of the city. The driver was a black man, Roosevelt Kelley. The lugger and helper was again Anthony Amato.

It put Tinsley in a panic. Losses would continue for as long as the investigation lasted, the owner said. In addition he was paying for the meals, hotels, and rented cars of all those agents, not to mention their salaries. He wanted the four thieves arrested. He was insured against employee theft. He wanted whatever money the bonding company would pay him.

Conte again flew to Chicago where he urged patience. There was enough evidence to arrest the four men, he told Tinsley, probably not enough to convict them, and to arrest them now would be to leave the ring intact, or nearly so, another 15 or 20 human termites still eating into the profits. "We don't know who they are yet," Conte told him, "or how many they are, or even how the stealing is being done. Make arrests now and the leak will be stanched—temporarily. In a week or a month, as soon as the heat is off, they will start up again."

"There might never be any new evidence." Tinsley was a tall thin man with a lugubrious face. "I'm bleeding to death."

In the end, one was obliged to do what the client wanted. "All right," Conte had said, "we'll go forward with what we have."

Which now, in the middle of the night, didn't look like much.

Conte glanced at his watch. "It's going to be a short night," he told Tinsley and Lonano. "My suggestion is, we all get some sleep."

Conte and his team—he had four men with him—were staying at the Holiday Inn on North Marine Drive. Once in his room he brushed his teeth, put on pajamas, and then sat on the edge of the bed studying his notes. He had the names of the four men who had been observed delivering stolen meat, and a list of men whom Agent Simmons, based on remarks he had overheard, thought might be involved.

All of the first four names were deliverers. None worked regularly inside the plant. Would they even know how widespread the ring might be? They were tough men physically. They could sling around sides of beef weighing up to 200 pounds. Two of the four had police records and had done time, one for armed robbery, the second for burning down a synagogue. The other two were probably little better. The factories and meat plants of the country were full of such thugs. The owners hired them without investigating their backgrounds, paid them little, and then were surprised when they stole.

Tomorrow he would interrogate each of the four men, and after that the men on Agent Simmons's list. Guilt weighed more than most men supposed. The suspects had been carrying it around a long time, half fearing, half expecting to be exposed—at least that was the theory.

Their guilt had got heavier every day—in theory.

When he interrogated them—assuming he did it right—some of them should crack.

Maybe.

But the first four men, if they had any brains, would simply call his bluff, deny all involvement. If they did, Tinsley would not even be able to fire them lest the union shut down his plant. The accused might then institute lawsuits against Conte, Tinsley, and their respective companies— they might not think of this themselves, but any claims lawyer would, one or more of whom would surely pop up, the union would see to it.

So the stakes were high for Tinsley, but they were high for Conte's firm, and for himself personally as well. One doesn't get three strikes in life, it seemed to him. Especially in law enforcement a man got only one usually, and he had had his and was on his second. If he lost this job he might not find another.

By seven forty-five A.M. Vince Conte was back at the meat-packing plant. The four men with him—Agents Bruno and Simmons, plus an assistant and a polygraph operator—were put in a cubicle down the hall, and told to wait.

Conte was clean shaven and smelled of aftershave. He had dark eyes, dark curly hair, a square jaw, and big white teeth. He wore an immaculately pressed three-piece suit with a chain hanging across the vest, and a starched shirt with a somber tie, and on his nose rode wire-rimmed spectacles he didn't need. He looked like an accountant conducting a survey, or so he hoped.

Tinsley and Lonano had been waiting for him.

There was a small window in one of the refrigerator doors through which Conte watched as the butchers entered the cooler. They were men in work boots and heavy sweaters, most of the sweaters dirty and half raveled in places. They punched in at the time clock, then moved toward the row of lockers where they slipped into their bloody smocks. They did this with a good deal of laughter and conversation, and socked each other in the arm a lot, but Conte was sealed off by the heavy door and although he could see the camaraderie, he could not hear it.

"I'll use your desk, your office," Conte told the owner. He did not turn around, but bounced his voice off the glass. "Ritinski first. He's the one we have the most evidence against. Then the others one by one."

"Ritinski's a tough guy," said Lonano.

"What are our chances?" said Tinsley.

Conte continued to peer through the glass. The men had taken their places at the tables, their white smocks caked with stale blood. Most now wore heavy gloves. Except for the gloves they could almost have been surgeons after a particularly bloody operation. At eight promptly a bell went off and through the glass he saw the axes begin slamming into the meat.

Conte stepped into Tinsley's office. "All right," he said, "bring him in."

The refrigerator door closed behind Lonano. During the seconds it was open Conte heard the sounds at last, the thudding axes and whining saws, the voices, the rasping of hooks as sides of beef were slid along overhead rails.

He sat down behind Tinsley's desk.

Lonano came in with Ritinski, the refrigerator door thunking shut behind them, both men smiling, as if one or the other had just recounted a joke.

Lonano said only what Conte had told him to say. "This is Mr. Conte, Rit. He wants to talk to you."

Ritinski was built like a linebacker. He wore a bomber pilot's jacket with the sleeves cut off, and a bloody apron. Both his deltoids were tattooed. He had done two years in jail in the synagogue case, and had been arrested a number of other times. "Sit down, Rit," said Conte amiably. "Make yourself comfortable."

In the hall Lonano gnawed at his thumbnail, while Tinsley paced. From the cubicles behind them the salesmen could be heard selling meat by telephone.

Three minutes passed, then five. Through the door came the muffled voices of Conte and Ritinski. Ten minutes, fifteen.

Finally the door opened. Behind Conte, seated in front of the desk, Ritinski examined dirty fingernails.

"Would you come in please," the detective said to the executives. He had stepped out into the hall, and was not smiling. "Agent Bruno," he called down the hall.

Bruno came running.

Pointing to Ritinski, Conte said to Bruno: "Is this the man you observed delivering stolen meat to the King Supermarket on March 10 and again on March 19?"

"Yes it is."

"Thank you."

To Tinsley and Lonano, Conte said: "Rit here has been lying to me for the last ten minutes. He says my agent must be mistaken, that he never delivered anything to that supermarket, that he never stole meat, that he knows nothing about a ring of thieves in your plant. Is that right, Rit?"

"I got nothing to say to you."

To Bruno, Conte said: "Take him over to the clubroom and babysit him."

Ritinski started to protest, but Lonano shouted: "If you want to keep working here, you'll do what you're told."

I never should have started with Ritinski, Conte told himself. Hardened criminals don't crack. I should have started with someone else.

He waited until his agent and the suspect were gone, then said to Lonano: "I'll take Anthony Amato next."

Amato had been the helper during two deliveries to two different markets, but had not got out of the truck either time. He might be the recipient of small tips in exchange for silence. He might know nothing.

Draped in the usual bloodstained smock, Amato entered the office behind Lonano. He was much younger, shorter, a bit overweight, rosy cheeked, with jet-black hair. He looked sheepish, as if embarrassed to have been singled out for this questionnaire, or whatever it was.

Conte closed the door, again leaving Tinsley and Lonano in the hall. "Sit down, Anthony," he said, "make yourself comfortable."

So they sat opposite each other across the desk and to the young man Conte could not have sounded more friendly.

"How old are you, Anthony?"

"Twenty-two."

"Married, Anthony?"

"Yes."

"Kids?"

"My wife is pregnant right now."

"Well, good." Conte wrote each of the answers onto the clipboard before him. "And where do you live?"

Amato told him.

"And how long have you worked here now, Anthony?"

"A year ago next month."

"And you've been stealing meat all that time."

"What?"

Conte's smile had disappeared. The fake eyeglasses went down on the desk. "You're a thief, Amato. You've stolen meat. A lot of meat. And we've got you cold."

Amato's face had lost all color.

In addition to weight, guilt also had an odor, Conte believed. Some men, once accused, reeked of it, and Amato did now. It was not a fecal odor, but was more an emanation, like garlic on the breath. Amato's forehead looked bathed in it. It seemed to be caught in his clothes like cigar smoke.

It was an odor Conte had smelled many times in the past. It came perhaps from the sweat glands. Guilty men were betrayed by their bodies, and there was nothing they could do about it.

Conte's voice was hard. "This is the most important conversation you're going to have in your life, Amato. I'm a private investigator. We called you in here to give you the benefit of a private conversation. There are people in this plant stealing meat. We know you're part of it. My men have been watching you. I have a log here of what you've been doing." He brandished his clipboard. "On March 10 you're a helper on the truck with Ritinski. The two of you deliver a side of stolen beef to the King Supermarket. A few days later you go out with Roosevelt Kelley, same thing. You want to hear more?" Conte threw the clipboard down. "It's all here. We know all about you."

Amato seemed unable to speak.

"If you want to straighten this thing out, fine." Conte was watching carefully, judging which words to use. "If you don't, we'll handle it another way."

Amato licked his lips. His voice when he spoke could barely be heard. "What do I have to do?"

Outside in the hall Tinsley and Lonano had been staring at the door, which now opened. "Would you come in here please, Mr. Tinsley, Mr. Lonano."

The two men entered the office and closed the door.

"Anthony here is trying to level with us," Conte said. "It's just that he can't think of everything all at once. For the past ten months this thing has been going on as far as he knows. Is that right, Anthony? Right now

Anthony is trying to remember how they got the meat out of here. He'd like to tell us about it, if he can remember. Is that right, Anthony? Now Anthony can't remember if he's ever been out with Jack Ritinski, or Roosevelt Kelley, even though we saw those transactions, but he did go out with a driver by the name of Augie Tontillo, and they sold some stolen meat, and another time with a driver named Al Peters. Was all that beef put on the truck in the same way, Anthony?"

"All loaded the same way."

"Can you tell me for my own satisfaction, because I have never worked in a meat-packing plant—"

"You're not missing much."

"How do you think that merchandise gets on the trucks?"

"They are out there moving that pin."

"What pin? I don't know what a pin is."

"The hindquarters are hanging from hooks, and the hooks slide along a rail. When he brings five pieces up to the scale he's got the pin in the last piece and those five are weighed in full and are pushed onto the truck. How hard would it be to push six pieces up and move that pin? It's common sense."

"The times you went out with Tontillo and Peters, try to remember who was pushing the beef that day."

"Captain Midnight, Jack Johnson, and Duke."

"Who is Captain Midnight?"

"I don't know his real name."

"Is he a black man, Anthony?"

"Black."

"Roosevelt Kelley," said Lonano.

"And Duke?"

"I know him," said Lonano tightly. "Jack O'Hara."

"And who would be the main guy, Anthony?" said Conte. "The ring-leader. In your opinion?"

"I couldn't say positively."

"You mean you've never discussed it in the truck or talked about it?"

"They don't talk about it, and I don't ask. The driver gives me my cut. When the shift ends I punch out and go home."

"Every single driver is involved?" asked Tinsley in a stricken voice.

"I wouldn't say every driver. The stickmen know who they can trust."

"And Mel Winkler?" said Conte. "He's a scaler, I believe."

"If there is a truck out there being loaded, the scaler knows who is getting the truck, so the stickmen know from the scaler."

Conte put a check next to Winkler's name, and continued down his list: "Bo Ginger?" he said. "Dennis Parker?"

"You're trying to make me into the company fink. I had to go along because I was there. You think anybody is stupid enough to refuse $100, $200?"

"How much do you get paid?"

"Minimum wage."

"Do you work a forty-hour week?"

"Things are slow right now."

"Things are slow because you have been stealing meat."

"You are blaming me."

"Saul Goodman? Warren Burke?"

"Why should I have to be the fink?"

"If just one of you guys comes in here and fails to cooperate," said Conte, "we will have to go a different route. Goodman? Answer yes or no."

"Yes."

"Burke?"

"Yes."

When he had come to the end of his list, Conte said: "Now if you'll just step down the hall, my assistant will polygraph you. Then he will dictate a statement, and you will sign it."

They watched him go, shoulders slumped, eyes on the floor.

Turning to Lonano, Conte said: "I'll take the scaler, Winkler, next."

He worked all day. The big smile, the easy questions. Sometimes only a few, sometimes many, until the man was at ease, off guard. Then the violent accusation: You're a thief and we've got you. Do you want to work this out now, or do we go another route?

"I stole some meat. Everybody was doing it."

"This is the best job I ever had, and I'm loyal to the company and I don't want to lose my job. I did steal some meat."

At noon Tinsley went through into the cooler and came back with steaks which one of the secretaries cooked on a hot plate. Conte ate his between interrogations, washed down with a bottle of Coke.

"I worked at the last place and never got in no trouble. They trusted me with the keys to lock up at night. I come here and listen to these guys and…"

Always the detective pushed for details.

"When they steam the trucks out each day they take all the hooks out. That can be a couple of hundred pounds of hooks, and they make up that weight with extra meat…"

"Somebody's fooling with the gas. They must weigh the truck empty instead of full, or with just enough fuel to get where they have to go, and the rest of the weight is extra meat…"

The detective's focus was absolute. The rapture of total concentration. The rapture of triumph would come later. "And the ringleader was?"

Men answered with downcast eyes.

"Ritinski started it."

"Ritinski was the big hitter…"

"Ritinski said they worked it at his last job. Impossible to get caught, he said."

Conte interrogated 21 men in all, 20 of whom signed statements, and could now be fired. The union might lodge a protest, but it would be a weak one. Ritinski was arrested. Late in the afternoon the police came and took him out in handcuffs. Certain other men might be prosecuted too. A substantial claim could be made to the bonding company.

By the end of the day Tinsley was chortling and rubbing his hands. He was taking Conte and his team out to dinner, he announced. Make a night of it.

Exhausted, Conte started to refuse.

When he had joined Probe Consultations Conte had been offered only a job, not a partnership. Nobody said he was on probation, but it seemed to him that that's what he was, and because of the circumstances, he felt insecure. He could hear his new bosses at this minute at his shoulder saying what they always said: It was important to do what the client wants, and tonight the client wanted to take the successful detective out to dinner.

Though drained, Conte conceded.

The restaurant selected by Tinsley was possibly the most expensive in Chicago. Champagne was ordered, and flowed. The owner had a reporter there, notebook beside his plate. The happy client eulogized the detective as if he were dead, at one point likening him to an admiral who had sunk the entire enemy flotilla except one, twenty of twenty-one ships.

The reporter asked what he must have imagined were probing questions. He wrote down Conte's every answer. After the stresses of the day and two glasses of champagne the detective fell silent, and almost asleep. When dessert was served he declined it, stood up, said he had to catch an early plane, shook hands all around, and left.

At his hotel he sat on the bed staring at the rug. Snap out of it, he told himself. You have just had a big success. You ought to be feeling better than this.

He was a man who had recently lost most of what he treasured. He was trying to put his life back together, but some days it was hard.

He slept well, by morning felt better, and on the plane back to New York decided that what he wished for and needed was a really big case, one that would test him. As a cop he had broken a number of major cases, some had made headlines, but it was hard to believe that in this new job anything that big existed or could come his way.

FOUR THOUSAND MILES AWAY such a case was taking shape.

The café faced onto a square, one side of which was the cathedral, a great rectangular building with a tower on one corner and a steeple on the other, a peaked roof in the middle, dating in part from the 13th century. The steps that climbed to its principal entrance were steep, each one as high as a bench, and for most of each day, though not this early, there would be tourists sitting on them, usually young people in groups, some of them studying guidebooks, backpacks at their feet. A second side of the square was the Guild Hall, which was almost as old, almost as vast, and even more grandiose. It had arched doorways 15 or more feet high, and arched windows with columns in them.

The square's other two sides were more ordinary buildings with shops and cafés at ground level. But these buildings too were very old. The town reeked of age.

The casino was not visible from the square, and neither were most of the international banks — in the last ten or fifteen years dozens had been chartered here. Money and mountains, it was often said, made a sandwich of the city, which was the capital of the duchy — Grand Duchy, if you will. They dominated the hotels, restaurants, and shops, the tourist sites, the citizens themselves, and everything else caught in between. It was the two slabs of the sandwich that were responsible for the duchy's great wealth. They were what sucked in most of the tourists, most of the investors too. They sucked them out of the rest of the world, and then sucked the money out of their pockets.

It was the money alone that brought in the rogues of whom there also was no shortage.

On this particular morning Antonio Murano, 25 years old, sat in the early sunshine on a café terrace on the square. He sat on the front two inches of his chair, watching the two men across the table. Beside him, smiling, talking, sat his lawyer. Always smiling.

This was a breakfast meeting — it was not yet eight A.M. The four men sat under an awning, but the sun slanted in under it. Waiters in white coats bustled among the tables which were occupied mostly by people on their way to work. Traffic passed a few feet away, though not much this early, scooters and bicycles as well as cars.

Earlier, walking toward the café, the lawyer had told Murano: "You say to them, Hello, how are you, and I take it from there. You don't say anything else. Not a word."

So far the young man had obeyed.

He was tall, blue eyed, sandy haired. Until not very long ago he had been an athlete, a frequenter of weight rooms and Nautilus machines, and it showed. For a business meeting as important as he believed this one to be he wore a business suit with a big knot in his tie. But the suit did not fit well, his shoulders being a bit too broad. He was a young man not comfortable in his clothes.

In front of him on the café table half-empty cups stood on their saucers, and he looked across at the two men, Crespi and Balducci, who were possible investors in his scheme. Crespi was younger and did most of the talking. But it was Balducci, who rarely spoke, who seemed to have the money. For the past two days the two men had talked as if they wanted to invest — that is, Crespi had, and from time to time Balducci had nodded.

But there was no agreement so far. They had signed nothing.

This morning their faces seemed to have narrowed — possibly against the low sun. They listened to the smiling lawyer but were not smiling back.

Crespi was about 35. Balducci looked 50 at least. By Murano's standards both were old, and he could not read them. There was not much time left. The two men, who were Italians, were leaving in an hour — less than an hour now.

Called Tonio, or Tony, Murano had been a tennis pro and a lifeguard, and for a time down on the Mediterranean had worked on rich men's boats. He was married now, and about to become a father. This deal was to be his breakout as a businessman. And so he had sat silent. The lawyer and Crespi had talked only to each other, and Balducci had nodded only in the direction of the other two. If the deal fell through, Murano's investment would be lost, and it wasn't his money. The faces across from him were impassive. They showed nothing.

The architect's plans, together with the rendered drawings and the four-color brochures, were on the table amid the drying coffee cups and the basket of croissants no one had touched.

His own lawyer, in whom he had less and less faith, kept smiling. "So I trust you are close to making your decision," the lawyer said, still smiling. "You are, aren't you?"

The men from Italy looked at each other.

"Do you want to walk through the space again?" the lawyer asked.

The "space" was a building across the square, and for a moment all four men studied its facade. Murano's idea, the only one of this nature he had ever had, was to gut it, and install a luxurious spa that would cater to the international crowd that now frequented the duchy. There would be a pool, saunas, workout machines. A club with stiff dues.

"You have an option on the space," conceded Crespi. "Plus these projections here" — he gestured at the papers on the table — "which may be optimistic."

"This town is a luxury resort," said the lawyer. "The potential clientele here is enormous. Our projections are conservative."

"Have you counted the ski lifts?" burst out Murano. "The casino, the hotels, the banks. Count them, why don't you?"

"There are laws governing investment by foreigners like us," said Crespi, still speaking to the lawyer.

"That's been taken care of," said the lawyer.

Murano knew it hadn't been.

"So you say."

"Suppose we put up the rest of the money, what then?" asked Balducci.

Pretending to be perplexed, the lawyer said: "I don't follow you."

"You'll need variances, building permits. Getting them in this place is difficult, sometimes impossible." For Balducci this constituted a speech.

"Especially for foreigners," said Crespi.

"I'm not a foreigner," Murano said, "I can get them."

"It isn't enough to claim you can deliver. You also have to do it."

"I said it was no problem. How many times do I have to tell you?"

"Well, we have ways of checking."

The lawyer knew Murano to be hot-tempered. There had been "altercations." Usually these were brawls with paparazzi who swarmed around his wife. They had occurred in public places, unfortunately, and afterward people read about them in the papers.

Murano now was half out of his seat.

The lawyerly hand came down on the young man's arm.

After a momentary hesitation Murano subsided onto the same two inches of chair as before.

"All those legal problems have been taken care of," said the lawyer smoothly, and he gave an easy laugh. "Do you know who my client is? His father-in-law owns this place."

"Exactly," said Balducci.

"Augustin II—the duke—" said the lawyer.

But Crespi interrupted: "We heard they don't get along at all."

Although Murano and Maria Cristina, now his wife, had lived together more than two years, the duke had received the young man and permitted the marriage only when the girl was five months pregnant and beginning to show—a way of humiliating both of them perhaps. This was known to everyone in Europe who could read. The scandal sheets had reveled in the story. They had reveled in other stories about the young couple as well, most of them exaggerated, though not all. Some were even invented, though not all.

"Tony is part of the family now," said the lawyer, "the royal family," and the men from Italy nodded thoughtfully.

"Wait a minute," said Murano. "You're doing this deal with me, not the duke. Is that understood?"

The two men gazed at him while the lawyer studied his hands.

Finally Crespi nodded. Both men then got up from the table.

"I'll walk you to your hotel," said the lawyer, and he did so, and Murano watched their departing backs. As he watched he grabbed up a croissant, tore it to bits, then put it back in the basket. Finally the three men were out of sight.

Some minutes later the lawyer returned to the café table.

"Sorry I blew up like that," said Murano.

"The deal may still go through," said the lawyer grimly.

"I put it together and—"

"Correction. You put it half together. There is still much work to be done."

"Like what?" In an instant the young man's truculent tone had returned.

"You're going to have to provide approval in writing from your father-in-law."

"To have to ask him for something pisses me off."

"You're going to have to do it."

The waiter came over. Holding his tray at ear level, he took the lawyer's money and made a one-handed half tear of the check stubs with the other hand.

"Come back to the office and I'll draw up a paper you can get him to sign."

The two men stood up.

"What about your motorcycle?" the lawyer said. It was parked in front of the tables, and both men glanced at it.

"It's okay there," Murano said. "The cops all know who it belongs to."

The lawyer shrugged, and they left the café.

The troubled Murano moped about all day. It became afternoon, time to go home. He mounted his motorcycle and once at the edge of the town, opened it up. Amid thunderous noise, he ascended the mountain. As the big bike slid the turns, its tires spat back bits of gravel, bits of road, turned them into projectiles that machine-gunned walls, garage doors, and occasional parked cars, sometimes chipping paint.

There were walls to both sides of the road, with hidden villas behind them, so the noise was penned in. It climbed as he did. When he came to his own house he skidded to a stop, actuated the remote, and then waited, one foot on the ground, engine growling, while the big doors swung inward. The police car, he noted, was parked some distance up, snug against the wall, as always.

The cop behind the wheel threw him a salute through the windshield. He did not salute back.

As soon as the opening was wide enough he wobbled through, kicked the stand down, and got off.

Maria Cristina, who had been in the garden, came toward him. She was eight and a half months pregnant, perhaps a bit more, wearing a baggy dress whose hem rode too high in front, and she bumped him with her belly, and said: "Don't I get a kiss?"

The kiss lasted, becoming deeper, but with a laugh she broke it off. Although staying within his embrace, she put a finger to his lips and said: "Stop." Then: "You'll get all excited, and there's nothing much I can do for you, for the moment."

"It's still there," he said, meaning the police car.

"My father," she said.

"An heir is expected, and he's taking no chances."

"What do we care?" she said.

He shook his head.

She smiled. "Another week, two weeks, the car'll be gone." She patted her belly. "This will be gone too."

He squeezed her hand.

"I cut some flowers," she said, "if you'd like to pick them up. It's not something I can do myself, unfortunately."

He watched her cross the terrace and go through the open French doors, 23 years old but walking like a woman three times her age.

The house was Swiss chalet in style, with ochre stucco walls, on one of which the wisteria had climbed as high as the balcony outside their bedroom. Theirs was one of the smallest houses on the road, but for all of that had been expensive to buy and was expensive to maintain. The property was entirely walled in, which, for security reasons, was good. The garden contained two purple rhododendrons presently in bloom, and a mountain laurel about to bloom, plus a number of apple trees and ornamentals all crowded together. There were gravel paths among the trees, and flower beds here and there, but no swimming pool and no lawn, for there was no room. From the garden there was no view except the perimeter walls, but from the balcony above one looked out at mountains, and it was nice to sit out there on warm mornings having breakfast.

He gathered the flowers Maria Cristina had cut and carried them into the house.

In the kitchen she was filling vases with water. He laid the flowers on the countertop, and his wife turned, took his hands, and said: "My mother called. We're invited to the palace for dinner."

He said nothing.

"They're my parents."

He gave her a half smile. "It's all right. I have to speak to your father anyway."

She seemed to breathe a sigh of relief. "What about?"

"Nothing for you to worry about. I have a legal paper he has to sign."

"I'll speak to him about it."

"No, I'd rather speak to him myself."

He went upstairs with her and stood on the balcony looking at the view. When he went back inside he saw that she was studying clothes that she had laid out on the bed. Clothes to wear to the palace tonight. In bra and panties, she looked heavy breasted, and her navel was all punched out. Like almost every young husband, it was hard for him to believe she had ever been slim, or ever would be again.

She put on a skirt with the front cut out, and then a top that hung like a tent. Dressed, she came over and took his hands again. "I know you'll be nice to them," she said.

He nodded.

When it was time to go, he helped her into their small low car. They had only the one, Maria Cristina's Porsche, which predated their marriage, and which had been wrecked and repaired twice in the years before he knew her, for her father would not buy her a new car—he would indulge her only so much. She had been a wild girl in those days. Murano in his own way, in his very different world, had been wild as well, and it was hard to equate that girl with today's heavily pregnant young woman. He pushed the remote, and when the doors had opened he backed out of the carport into the road, and started down the mountain. In the mirror he saw the police car start up, pull away from the wall, and follow.

The palace faced onto an esplanade. It was a castle, really, parts of it dating from five or more centuries ago. Sometimes there were hundreds of tourists standing on the esplanade gawking up at its walls, or staring across at the guards in their medieval costumes as they marched up and down outside the main gate, but this evening Murano noted only a few. The outer side of the esplanade was a row of cafés and souvenir shops, plus the entrances to the narrow streets of the old town. The castle seemed to give itself a lot of space, which made it look elegant, opulent. Actually its other three sides were set on a crag that dropped down into a valley. Crags were ideal sites for castles in the days when this one was built. There would have been only the one side to defend against foreign armies or rioting peasants.

At the far end of the palace was a gate and a sentry box. The sentry saw them coming and opened the gate, saluting them as they went in past him.

The courtyard, Murano saw, already contained a number of parked cars. As they got out of the Porsche he said: "I guess we're not the only guests."

"Mother didn't say anything."

The private apartments were on the top floor, which was reached these days by an elevator installed before Maria Cristina was born because her father, a playboy himself at the time, had broken his leg skiing. In those days the man had thought of nothing except sports and women, apparently. Now, according to the articles written about him, he was considered a visionary and a builder. Something of a financial genius, as well. Every day, as Murano saw it, the ruler thought up new ways to cram more people and cars, more buildings into this small and insignificant European duchy.

The young couple stepped off into a hallway with brocaded walls, a marble floor, and a great hanging chandelier. The walls were hung with paintings, most of which were portraits of Maria Cristina's ancestors going back several hundred years. They could hear voices from the next room, and they went in, and Murano, despite himself, glanced self-consciously around, as if still awed to find himself here. Illumination was by three more chandeliers, bigger ones still, all blazing, spaced out the length of the room, which was twice as long as any other living room of Murano's experience. It was a place to intimidate a young man living in sin with the daughter of the house, and in fact had done so. About a month before the wedding he had finally been invited to the palace. With Maria Cristina holding his hand he had met his future in-laws for the first time, an hour's stiff conversation followed by dinner, which had been mostly silent. Even Maria Cristina, having finally brought her father and the father of her unborn child together in the same room, had been silent.

There had been a subsequent dinner here to which he had been invited, and at which he had met most of the cousins and aunts, 25 or 30 people, and then there had been the wedding reception which had been held in the public rooms downstairs, and in the courtyard. Also he had been in his father-in-law's office one time. Only on those few occasions had he set foot in the palace. Often enough, both before and after the wedding, Maria Cristina had invited her parents to dinner at the villa, but they had only come once.

Now Murano's mother-in-law, Lady Charlotte, came forward, her face thrust out to extort the ritual kisses, offering both cheeks, first to her daughter, then to him, after which she drew them forward into the room. Murano saw that they were going to be ten for dinner, for Maria Cristina's brother and sister-in-law were present, as were two other couples he did not know, or may have met at the wedding but did not remember. Her brother and his wife were much older, about 35, and so far they had not been able to conceive a child—which left it up to him and Maria Cristina, if the family dynasty was what you cared about.

Now Murano was being introduced to the prime minister, a man of about 45, and to the finance minister, who was older, and to their wives. Prime minister of what, Murano sometimes wanted to say, for, although technically an independent country, and even, as of two years previously, a member of the United Nations, this place was a collection of small mountain towns, neither more nor less. Anywhere else that was all it would have been considered, he believed. Here it had achieved glamour, and a grandeur out of all proportion to its size. The grandeur depended on people taking the independence and the royal titles seriously, and on making the rest of the world take them seriously too, which is what all the citizens tried to do, no one more so than Maria Cristina's parents.

Murano's father-in-law, the hereditary ruler known to his subjects as Augustin II, stood near a vast fireplace in which no fire burned, and seemed to be waiting to be approached, so the young man went over there and they shook hands. As always, the sovereign's grip was more or

less listless. Meeting him for the first time, some people imagined—
wrongly—that this weak handshake denoted a weak nature. The men
and women to whom he gave orders each day knew better, and sometimes joked that he was a man with a whim of steel.

The handshake was accompanied by a single word: "Son."

"Evening," Murano said, "—Sir." An effort, but he got it out. "I wonder if I might speak with you a moment."

"How are you?" said his father-in-law. "Everything all right?"

And without waiting for an answer he signaled the two servants in liv-
ery who stood at attention to either side of the entrance door.

"Open the champagne, please."

"Yes, my lord."

The servants went to a buffet table on which two bottles were leaning
in their coolers with, beside them, a tray of crystal flutes. Corks popped.

Murano withdrew the legal paper from his pocket. "What I wanted
to talk to you about—"

But the hand on his shoulder stopped him. "Why don't we let Tony
do the honors," his father-in-law said in a loud voice, gesturing toward the
champagne with his chin.

So the servants retreated to the doorway and watched Murano pour
and distribute the champagne.

When finished, the young man again approached the ruler.

"Sir—" he began.

"We're just having fun here, Son. We'll talk about whatever it is
later."

Dinner was announced.

The dining room chandeliers seemed especially brilliant. Murano
pushed his knees into the linen tablecloth, which reached nearly to the
floor. The silverware was heavy. From the head of the table Augustin II
presided. Into his glass one of the servants spilled a sampling of the wine,
which he swirled, sniffed, tasted, and pronounced excellent. As the servants circled the table pouring, Murano was able to read the label,

Château Margaux, and the year. He knew enough about wine to recognize this as a great name in a great vintage, but when his turn came to be served, he put his hand over his glass and said loudly: "Why don't you bring me a cold bottle of Heineken instead." From the corner of his eye he saw his father-in-law frown, and was pleased.

A rebellion, though only a small one.

At last it came time to leave, the sovereign accompanying his guests out to their cars — he was always an excellent host. One by one the cars drove out of the courtyard until only Murano and Maria Cristina were left. Augustin embraced his daughter, then gave his son-in-law the same listless handshake as before.

"Was there something you wanted to speak to me about?" he asked.

Murano started to withdraw the legal paper from his pocket.

"Why don't you come into the office. We'll talk there. Call my secretary and arrange an appointment. I'm afraid it won't be possible until sometime next week, though."

"Good night, Papa," said Maria Cristina, who was already seated in the car. Her father leaned through the window and kissed her.

Murano got in behind the wheel and drove out the gate into the night.

As promised he was granted an appointment, but on a date more than a week away, also as promised. Even so, the secretary told him, she would have to squeeze him in.

"Not good enough," his lawyer told the young man, when he reported back. "Your investors may not wait that long."

So Murano tried twice more on separate days, stressing the urgency of it. The second time the secretary snapped at him. Impossible, she said.

Seated now beside his lawyer in the outer office, he glared at his father-in-law's closed door, and the appointed hour came and went, and the message was clear. Though he had waited so long already, he was going to be made to wait longer.

Murano had been through that door only the one time previously, a memory he was not comfortable with, so he knew what the office would look like. It was a big, mostly bare place. Although part of a very old building, an American-style picture window had been cut into the old walls, giving a view down the sloping mountain toward more mountains that rose abruptly on the other side of the valley. The window was vast in extent, and the desk was oversized too, a great slab of glass two inches thick, resting on parts of Grecian pillars that had come out of an archaeological dig in one of the outlying hamlets some years previously. Augustin had demanded the pillars as the state's share of the dig, and after a long dispute they had been given to him. The office walls were white and on one of them hung a Picasso. The other walls were unadorned. There was a sideboard on which stood separate photos of Maria Cristina, her brother, and their mother. The only other decoration in the room was the national flag, furled, which stood behind the desk.

The purpose of the young man's only previous visit had been to sign the prenuptial agreement that his then future father-in-law had insisted on, a sobering document if there ever was one. It had taken him some time to read it, and some time longer to swallow it. Should the marriage be dissolved he would be allowed to take away only what he had brought to it; accordingly, he was obliged then and there to make a list of all his worldly goods of which there weren't many, and this list was made part of the agreement: his tennis rackets, his motorcycle, his clothes, his small bank account. Proof, if any was needed, that up until then he had been a man who traveled light.

The financial clauses had been sobering, but there were others. Among them was one whereby he contracted never to speak or write about or disclose anything he should see or hear or learn as a member of the ruling family, nor about any member of the family whether living or deceased, neither during the marriage nor, in the case of dissolution of the marriage, afterward. That he should conduct himself everywhere and always with dignity and restraint, failure to do so being grounds for divorce, as was conviction of any crime. That he should engage in no trade or profession that would tend to bring discredit on his new station.

The document stipulated how far from the palace he and his wife-to-be were allowed to live, and about how their eventual children were to be brought up, and to Murano it might have stood as an expression of the low degree of his father-in-law's opinion of him at that moment. Given its long-term clauses, it seemed to indicate also that nothing in the future was likely to cause that opinion to rise.

Today he and the lawyer waited ten minutes past the appointed hour, then fifteen, then twenty. Finally they were admitted to the sovereign's presence.

The light coming through the great expanse of glass was blinding. It hit him like a slap in the face.

His father-in-law was a meticulous man, and his office showed this. On the sovereign's desk reposed a telephone console and almost nothing else, apart from a single dossier, presumably the one they had waited for him to finish looking into, and which he now, as he came around the desk, scooped up and handed to the secretary. After that he stood with hand outstretched, greeting the lawyer first. "Maestro," he said, "good to see you again."

"My lord."

And then to Murano: "And you, Tony, everything all right?"

"Sir," said the young man.

Outwardly Augustin II was extremely cordial. He asked after the lawyer's wife and children, mentioned people they knew in common, even commented on the weather. There had been no rain in two months, it seemed.

But this conversation, which was virtually a monologue, took place in the center of the floor, for the hereditary ruler did not invite either of them to sit down.

When the lawyer decided he had waited long enough, he said: "Tony has something he has asked me to present to you."

"All right, I'm always happy to talk to Tony. But, say, why don't you step outside for a moment or two first, so as to let me talk with my son-in-law in private. We have things to discuss that wouldn't be of interest to you. You know, family stuff. Just for a few moments."

Even as he spoke he was escorting the lawyer to the door, the lawyer looking surprised, the sovereign adding as they crossed the threshold into the anteroom: "Better still, Maestro, no sense taking up your valuable time, making you wait. Why not go back to your office while Tony and I talk. Then, if there's anything you need to be consulted about, we can all meet again later in the week."

Having closed the door on the lawyer, Augustin II retreated toward the picture window, saying: "That's better, Tony, don't you think?"

The sovereign sat down behind his glass desk, and clasped his hands behind his head. The Greek columns supporting the glass looked 2,500 years old, which they were. The glass was really thick, Murano noted. It had beveled edges, and through it could be seen the royal trousers, the crossed royal ankles.

"What's on your mind, Son?"

His own son, Leon, he always called Leon. The only one he ever called "Son" was Tony.

Bereft of his lawyer, the young man walked over to the desk, and opened his briefcase, and as he spread out his rendered drawings and brochures, he wished he had brought his father-in-law into his plans much earlier on, that he had at least mentioned what he was up to. Springing the whole plan on the sovereign now in one sitting seemed to him now a mistake.

He wished also for support from his lawyer who was no longer there.

"What have we here, Son?" Outwardly Augustin II couldn't have seemed more affable.

"We feel there's a terrific market for it and—"

"Market for what, Son?"

"Which—this is the rendered drawing, these are the brochures."

"I can see that much."

"Affluent businessmen. That's who the clientele would be."

"What are you nervous about? Nothing to be nervous about."

The young man managed to slow down, to present his ideas almost slowly, almost in order, unveiling the saunas slowly, the pool —

"What's the address of this project?"

The young man told him, adding: "There have already been variances granted in that neighborhood."

"And you would need another."

"Yes, but considering the amount of business this would bring to the duchy —"

He watched his father-in-law's hand stir the drawings and brochures. "You've spent a good deal of money so far, I see," the ruler said. "Where did that come from?"

"We paid for it ourselves."

"We?"

Murano said nothing.

"I see. Used some of Maria Cristina's money, did you? And where would the rest come from?"

"I've found some investors."

"Well, they would need to see proof of variances from the board, cabinet approval, and so forth, before investing, wouldn't they?"

"There's a paper here for you to sign."

Murano produced it. The older man gave it a brief glance, then said: "And who are these investors?"

"Two gentlemen from Italy. Their names are on the paper."

"Yes, but who are they?"

"Signor Crespi is an investor in Bologna, and Signor Balducci is an important industrialist. He's from Rome."

"You're sure that's who they are."

"Yes, sir."

"Why do they want to invest with you?"

"They seemed to like the idea of a luxury spa. They said it couldn't miss. They're hoping to make a profit."

"I'm sure they are. How did you find them?"

"They contacted me."

"How did they happen to do that?"

"It was common knowledge that I was looking for investors."

"Was it indeed?"

"Do you know any reason why they should not be permitted to invest?"

"Me? No. I never heard of either of them." As he got up from behind the big glass desk, Murano understood that the interview was over.

"If you could sign this—" he said hurriedly, and he held out the paper that, if he could get it signed, would lock in his investors. But he was speaking overly fast.

His father-in-law took the paper from him, and put it down on the desk.

Hands fumbling, Murano began gathering his plans and brochures.

"Why don't you leave all that here?" his father-in-law said. "Give me a chance to study the project."

"How long will it take you to do that?"

"Shouldn't be long."

Murano's briefcase would stay empty, so he snapped it shut. "I hoped you might sign it today."

"Now stop worrying. Shouldn't be long at all."

"I really need the signature." To insist too much might make his father-in-law really angry. It was pushing his luck. "When do you think you might sign it?"

"I'll need time to consult with some of my ministers, perhaps one or two members of the privy council. People think I rule with an iron hand around here, but I don't."

This was a lie, and they both knew it.

"Put the noses of my advisors out of joint if I didn't consult them."

They had reached the door which the sovereign opened one-handed, his other, as if with affection, being draped over the shoulder of his son-in-law.

As the two men showed in the doorway Murano's lawyer, waiting in the anteroom, sprang to his feet. For the past ten minutes, having recognized the skill with which he had been separated from his client, the lawyer had been trying to decide whether to sit down and wait until the door opened again or leave.

He saw now that Murano looked glum, whereas Augustin II was smiling.

"You still here, Maestro?" the sovereign said. "Sorry to make you wait like that. Uselessly too, as it happens. Tony and I have talked everything out." He turned toward his son-in-law. "I'll be getting back to you on that matter as soon as I can, Son. Thanks to both of you for coming in." He shook hands with Murano and with the lawyer. "I enjoyed talking to you both."

And he went back into his office and the door closed.

CHAPTER

III

THE OFFICE WAS on the 35th floor of a tower off Maiden Lane in the financial district. The walls were mostly glass. Vince Conte, entering, stepped across flats of sunlight toward his friend, Carl Hallinan, who came out from behind his desk to shake hands.

The big windows framed the entire Narrows, the Statue of Liberty, and the open ocean beyond.

"Nice," Conte said.

"It impresses the clients," said Hallinan with a smirk.

"When I first knew you and Marge, you lived in a fourth-floor walk-up."

"And she worked at Macy's. Assistant DAs got paid practically nothing then. They don't get much now. The rent here is more in a month than I used to earn all year."

Near one of the huge windows stood a telescope on a tripod. Its barrel was a yard long. When Conte peered into the eyepiece he saw a ship heading out through the Narrows. Its decks filled the entire lens.

"Guy buys a telescope like that," he said, turning toward the lawyer, "usually it's to look across rooftops into bedroom windows."

"My motives are pure," said Hallinan. "You can see how wide the river is. The nearest bedroom is in Staten Island."

"So what do you usually see through that thing?"

"Once in a while you catch a couple making love in the torch of the Statue of Liberty."

"Really?"

"No." The lawyer went back behind his desk.

Conte smiled. "Ships only?"

"They can be interesting."

"The client pays $300 an hour while Carl watches ships going out to sea."

The lawyer smiled back. "I rarely bill telescope time."

They looked at each other and remembered how long ago they had met. Conte was a young detective working out of the two-eight precinct in Harlem, which had over a hundred murders that year. Carl Hallinan was a young ADA assigned to the complaint room, but hoping to get promoted into homicide, hoping to try big cases one day.

"You've been out of town a lot, I hear. Where have you come from this time?"

"I was in Kansas City, Chicago."

"Crime in Kansas City?"

"A Levi Strauss factory. You rich lawyers may never have heard of their product. They make blue jeans."

"I think I've heard of blue jeans, yes."

"Workers were dropping finished garments in the trash baskets. Stuff went out of the building as garbage. The secretaries were in on it, changing the numbers. The drivers delivered it wherever it was supposed to go."

"You broke up the ring."

"I got signed confessions from about thirty of them."

"And after that, Chicago?"

"A meat-packing plant. I got twenty signed statements there."

"Did you do all this by the book, tell them their rights, read them the Miranda warning? I sense not."

Conte laughed. "Don't you start."

"I know. In private practice you don't have to bother with all that."

"No, you don't."

"Your clients must have been pretty happy."

"They seemed happy. It'll start up again though. In three months, maybe less, the employees will begin stealing again in both places."

"Not too different from taking criminals off the street when you were a cop. Get rid of one scumbag and he's replaced by another."

"What's different," said Conte, "is I don't have to run it past anyone before I move in. District attorneys and judges. People like you were then."

But Conte frowned. There was more of a difference than that. That had been the big leagues, and this, to Conte, was not.

"People like me were obliged to work within the law. The law said—"

"I always knew what the law said."

"The law is a set of rules," said the lawyer. "You never liked obeying the rules."

"Most of the time I obeyed them."

"But it rubbed you the wrong way, didn't it? People like me were there to save you from yourself."

"You used to be on the side of the angels," retorted Conte. "Now you're one of those guys who defends scoundrels. I find it hard to put the two together."

"Somebody's got to defend them. The Constitution says—"

"Yes I know." After a pause the detective added: "And best of all, now that you're a defense attorney, the rules work to your advantage."

The lawyer nodded. "They can be useful."

"Don't get me wrong, Carl, I'm pleased by your success."

"Thank you." And then: "I think I know what's on your mind."

But Conte said: "Do you miss being a prosecutor?"

"Sometimes. I couldn't stay in the public sector forever. I miss it probably as much as you miss being a cop."

Conte did not answer.

"How long have you been out of the job, Vince?"

"A few months."

"You used to tell me that all you ever wanted to be was a cop."

Conte said nothing.

"And now you miss being part of something that big."

"Sometimes."

"All the time, I suspect."

Conte said nothing.

"The camaraderie."

Conte nodded.

"The danger too?"

"Maybe."

"Putting bad guys in jail."

The lawyer wore a starched white shirt with a wide silk necktie tied in a small tight knot. Conte wore a tweed sports coat over a turtleneck.

"You were a cop how long?" said the lawyer.

"Not quite fifteen years."

"Not long enough to qualify for the pension, as I remember."

"I'll get something."

The lawyer's eyebrows went up. "I thought fifteen was the minimum."

"Fifteen, yes."

"But in your case," the lawyer said, watching him closely, "they sweetened the pot if you'd go quietly."

Conte shrugged.

"You should have made a stink."

"There didn't seem much point."

Though it had never made the papers or the evening news, everyone in law enforcement knew about the fight, and for some days afterward had talked of little else.

"Both of you armed," the lawyer said, "it's a miracle you didn't kill each other."

"That was the night I learned the meaning of the words 'murderous rage.'"

"You tailed them to the hotel."

"I may have. I don't remember."

"You know something, Vince? Interrogating you is really hard."

Because this man was one of his closest friends, Conte laughed.

"You waited how long for them to come down?"

"A while."

"Couple of hours, wasn't it?"

These were memories Conte had been trying to repress. Now he was being forced to confront them, which was perhaps healthy. But hard.

Conte's wife's name was Anna Chiara Leone. Known professionally as Anne Fenton, she was co-anchor of *Eyewitness News at Six* on Channel Seven. She had got her start because of her looks, not her journalism skills, for she had had much of the one and none of the other. She was a dark-haired, dark-eyed beauty. Her face, better still, seemed also to show character. A face people would think they could trust, the station decided, and threw her in to see if she could swim. She was made the weather girl, and from there, jumping over people ahead of her, became a reporter, still knowing little or nothing about journalism, though she had since become competent enough. Her first beat was the police department. That was where she had met Conte, a sergeant at the time, who was acting commander of the 20th Precinct detective squad, a job that calls for a lieutenant. Conte had taken the lieutenant's test, but the results had not yet been posted. Anna was trying to do a story about a West Side serial rapist, and he had helped her. He had more than helped her. Determined to identify and arrest the rapist while she was there, he had concentrated his squad's every resource on this one case. He himself had worked around the clock, and had forced his men to work overtime too. At the end of three days, working almost without sleep, they brought the rapist in — he was later convicted at trial — and Conte had been able to hand her an exclusive.

Soon enough the detective sergeant and the rookie reporter got married. She did not want to be known as Mrs. Conte. She was trying to get away from that ethnic stuff, she said. She did want children, but not right away. Not until her career was in orbit, her name and face fixed in place as firmly as any newswoman's in television, her Q factor as high.

She did not stay a rookie long. As the marriage went on — it lasted
nine years — she became more and more recognizable to fellow New
Yorkers. People began coming up to her in stores. They would stop her
on the street. In restaurants they sometimes talked to her standing over
the Contes' table. When she became co-anchor this got even better, or
by another measurement worse. Inside the television world it was believed she would soon be promoted to network.

Conte had had promotions too — to lieutenant, to captain, nice pay
raises both, but in her latest job Anna was earning four times a captain's
salary, enough money, she told him, for them to move to the East Side,
to a bigger apartment, a better address. But what she was suggesting,
Conte insisted, he could not afford. He could not live off her money, he
had to pay his share and, besides, their present address was already elegant, their apartment more than big enough for the two of them, and it
was beautifully situated, half a block from the park in one direction, half
a block from the ABC studios in the other, and it was in the 20th Precinct
where he knew everybody, and everybody knew him. That they had this
apartment at all was pure luck, he reminded her. It belonged to a rich
and successful artist who had bought several apartments in the building
as investments, in one of which he was in the habit of storing completed
paintings until he had enough of them, 30 or so, for a new show. But one
night, when the otherwise unused apartment had collected nearly that
number, someone broke in and stole them all.

Conte had worked especially hard on that case too. Within a week he
had arrested the perpetrator and recovered all but one of the missing
paintings. In his gratitude the artist had offered the Contes one of his
apartments at a ridiculously low rent. They had been living out in
Queens at the time.

Of all this Conte reminded his wife, but still she wanted to move, she
no longer liked this apartment, she said. Which explained why, when
what happened later happened, it was she who moved out, leaving their
former apartment to him.

Promotion ceremonies in the NYPD are almost religious events. Held in the auditorium of the Police Academy on 20th Street, they begin with an invocation by one department chaplain, and end with benediction by another. Nearly all the official chaplains, and there are about a dozen, are seated onstage along with other dignitaries, including the mayor and the police commissioner who are there to make uplifting speeches to the officers being promoted. Both officials usually lean hard on the quasi-religious vocation that is the policeman's role. Cops, they intone, are men (and women) who devote their careers to helping others get through life in one piece; they are people who do good in the world. The hordes of promotees, who most times are of various ranks, wear dress uniforms that are as impeccable and in a way as improbable as cassocks, and on their hands, perhaps as a symbol of purity, they wear white gloves. They sit in solemn silence listening to the solemn speeches, then stand to renew their vows—that is, their oaths to the Constitution and to the laws of New York State—then mount one by one to the stage for the ritual handshakes. Their wives and children, meanwhile, have filled every seat in the auditorium, the children fidgeting and constantly being shushed, the wives beaming and proud, almost all of the women wearing for the occasion not only their best dresses and, like the men, white gloves, but also, like Catholic women at Mass in years gone by, hats.

For the ceremony at which Conte had been promoted to captain Anna was in attendance. Afterward in gloves and hat, her silk dress loose but clinging to her, the famous face half concealed by sunglasses, she stood with her husband in the well of the auditorium, other families swirling around them, and told him how happy she was for him. Just then a man in civilian clothes came up and Conte introduced them, one to the other, identifying the man as James McDermott, whose rank was First Deputy Police Commissioner.

McDermott was a big, well-built man, about 45 years old, meaning ten or twelve years older than Anna. There was beginning to be gray in his hair, and his suit was beautifully cut. He told Conte's wife that he watched her every night, that he thought her delivery excellent, and that her reports had a quality of truthfulness about them that was very rare.

Anna beamed. Of course she did.

Turning to Conte, McDermott asked the newly made captain to drop by his office at headquarters that afternoon. Say, about four o'clock.

Watching him go, Anna said: "He seems nice."

"He's the number two man in the department," Conte explained. "He's going to tell me my next assignment."

McDermott had once commanded the 20th Precinct. A deputy inspector at the time, worlds below his present rank, he had taken an interest in Conte. He said he always took an interest in bright young officers. They had several times stood in bars after work, McDermott offering headquarters gossip, and occasional advice on how to secure advancements in rank.

Promotions as far as captain are decided solely by civil service exams. From captain on, one serves at the pleasure of the commissioner. Meaning that future promotions, once a man had his captaincy, depended on who he knew, and how well. McDermott had said he expected to be transferred to headquarters soon, and might then be in a position to help push Conte's career.

Within three years he was an assistant chief, two stars on his shoulders, and then the administration changed and the new commissioner appointed him First Dep. To get anywhere in the job, every cop believed, a man needed a rabbi at headquarters, and now Conte had one.

But the meeting that afternoon did not go as Captain Conte had hoped. He had arrived thinking he would be given a choice of assignments, but he wasn't. Earlier Conte had told McDermott that what he wanted was Counterterrorism, a big new unit that was expanding at this time to meet the perceived global threat of Islamic extremists. It was new, vital, fascinating. Plenty to learn. Plenty of action as well. Counterterrorism was already perceived as possibly the most important work cops did. In addition it meant working out of headquarters, or close to headquarters, sometimes in conjunction with the FBI—close to the seat of power in any case. It was seen as a place where a cop who worked hard and had some brains would advance quickly in rank.

But First Deputy Commissioner McDermott had other ideas. What Conte's career needed now was experience in uniform on patrol, he told him, and he assigned him to one of the most violent of the ghetto precincts, the 77th in Bedford-Stuyvesant in deepest Brooklyn, as executive officer under the precinct commander, who was Deputy Inspector— the First Dep had to pause to look the name up—"Deputy Inspector Cole." As soon as some other precinct opened up it would go to Conte, and after a year or so in uniform in the field, said McDermott, "your future will know no bounds."

Well, rabbis don't grow on trees. Conte thanked him, and went home. Was it that day or later that McDermott phoned Anna at work, said he might have a story that would interest her, and invited her to lunch?

Meanwhile, with all his might, so to speak, Conte threw himself into his new job. He learned the names of most of the nearly 300 cops assigned to his precinct, he moved up and down the avenues introducing himself to shopkeepers, he showed up at crime scenes of which, in such a precinct, there were very many, watching carefully that every investigation got off to a proper start.

The police day is divided into three tours. Conte always stayed long enough to overlap two of them, and sometimes three. In his precinct as in all precincts, a number of neighborhood groups met regularly: block associations, merchants' associations, church groups. Conte attended all of these meetings, which were always at night, staying as late as necessary to do so, returning home long after Anna had finished with the six o'clock news. Nonetheless, she was often not there waiting for him, and when she came in she would describe the story she was working on that had kept her out so late, or else she had been delayed by a meeting with station executives.

From time to time First Deputy Commissioner McDermott telephoned Captain Conte at the stationhouse to ask how he was doing. And to make sure of his whereabouts, probably. Those were perhaps the nights of his trysts with Anna. "You're not forgotten," the First Dep would assure him. But the commanders of two other precincts moved out, moved on, their commands became vacant, and Conte did not get either of them.

Meanwhile, he was not seeing as much of his wife as he would have liked, and she seemed to have lost interest in sex. He bought tickets to a hit Broadway musical, and afterward they had dinner in a fine restaurant, and when they got home they made, as they called it, "whoopee." But that was the last time for a long time. In the mornings she would scamper out of his arms saying she would be late for work; or at night, having come home late, she was too tired. "We're both working too hard," she said. "Tomorrow," she would promise. But tomorrow she wasn't there, or he wasn't, or there was some other excuse. His marriage became the sound of her voice refusing.

When he asked her about this, she got annoyed, told him he was imagining things.

In her handbag he found a handkerchief that was not his. She had had a sneezing fit at the office and had borrowed it from one of the reporters, she said.

On a previous anniversary Conte had given her a pair of jade earrings which he had not seen her wear in a long time. They were around somewhere, she told him. But they did not seem to be. When she was in the tub soaking he went through her drawers, her various handbags. She could have left them at the office, but he did not think so. They could have fallen off her ears in the street and been lost. They could have been left behind somewhere. On a hotel pillow, perhaps.

Because he couldn't live with suspicions like this he decided to resolve them one way or the other. He began to take time off from work and to tail her wherever she went. He was a detective. There was no chance she would spot him. He had tailed innumerable felons in his day, and knew perfectly well how to tail people without being made.

He followed her away from her office and nothing happened. Sometimes she took cabs. Sometimes she walked. She never descended into the subways. He did not expect her to. She considered the air fetid down there, the platforms filthy, most of the passengers too. Following her, he used his own car, making whatever stops she made, putting his police plate in the window and following her on foot if necessary. One night she led him into Bloomingdale's, and the next night into Bergdorf Goodman. In both places she shopped for over an hour, him watching from two or three aisles away. When she came out she hailed cabs and went straight home. Another night she went into a bar on Columbus Avenue with colleagues from the station, some of whose faces he recognized from the screen. She was in there a long time too, him on the sidewalk opposite, pacing. Eventually she came out and walked home. She was fixing a potato omelet when he came in the door, and was surprised to see him. When he said he had come home early because he didn't feel well, she insisted on taking his temperature, and when it showed normal they shared the omelet. After which she prepared a second one, which they also shared.

Other times she walked home directly from the station, after which he remained on post outside their house as if on surveillance, in case she should come out again, but she did not.

Under such circumstances it was impossible for any man not to feel shamed by his own conduct — by his suspicions, by this sneaky surveillance. He was, after all, tailing — doubting — a well-loved wife.

Friday came. He sensed as soon as she came out onto the sidewalk that tonight was different. He was aware that she kept an almost complete wardrobe in her office closet; most of what she wore on screen she didn't even pay for. Couturiers donated it. After work she usually changed into more comfortable clothes before leaving the building. Pants, low shoes, a loose blouse or sweater. But now she came out wearing what looked like an expensive dress, one he had never seen before, and spike heels and much jewelry, looking very elegant indeed, and she hailed a cab, and he tailed her across the city to the Regent Carlton Hotel on 55th Street, a place where she had no business being or going.

He parked in a bus stop at the corner and rushed into the lobby after her. He was just in time to see her ask for a key at the desk. It was handed to her — not a key but an electronic card — and she continued on toward the elevators without looking back.

He went over to the newsstand, plucked a magazine out of the rack, and turned pages without seeing them, trying to think about it clearly — as clearly as he could. He did not know what to do. From where he riffled through the magazine he could see the entrance. Much of the lobby also. Some minutes passed. Suddenly the First Dep was crossing the lobby. Conte had not even seen him come in. He wore a dark suit that looked new. His shoes glowed. He looked like a man who had just had a haircut and been doused with an expensive scent, and Conte imagined he could smell him from where he stood.

The First Dep walked directly to the elevators, and went up.

Conte reached the elevator bank while the numbers were still winking above the door. They stopped at six, paused, then continued up, stopping next at eight where they stayed, as if glued there. After several minutes they moved again, starting down.

The First Dep could have got off on either floor, six or eight.

Conte went to the lobby phone, gave Anna's various names, Anna Leone, Anne Fenton, and her married name, Anna Conte, trying to make his voice sound different each time, and asked the operator to put him through to her room, but none of those names was registered. Disguising his voice still again he tried the First Dep's name. But no one of that name was registered either.

He boarded the elevator, got off at six, and skulked along the hall, listening at doors. He heard nothing. He tried the eighth floor. Same result.

He sat in the lobby waiting. He waited two hours.

Sexual jealousy is a terrible thing. If he hadn't known this already, he learned it now.

Finally they came down, both in the same elevator probably, but they crossed the lobby separately, Anna leading, and the First Dep several paces behind, as if they didn't know each other. Between them, jabbering back and forth, walked other patrons unknown to either of them, something they couldn't have planned, but a nice touch. So casual, so normal, proof that the lovers had come out of different elevators, or off different floors, that they had only happened to turn up at the same hotel at the same hour where neither had any business being. The purest of accidents. An utter coincidence.

Reaching the First Dep in three strides, Conte brought a punch up from the level of his knees. It carried with it every ounce of his shame, his dismay, his despair, plus other emotions he could not yet name. The punch landed with such force that he wondered if he might have broken his hand.

It caught First Deputy Commissioner McDermott, who had not noted Conte's approach and who never saw the punch coming, exactly under the right ear. He went down, and Anna, the significant witness, gave a yelp of surprise, of shock, and also, most likely, of fear, for no one could foretell how this scene would play out, or what would happen in the days to come, least of all her.

McDermott was up in an instant and coming hard, head down, head first. Conte landed two punches to the top of his head. They were completely ineffectual, and then the First Dep's carefully coifed skull rammed into his chest and both went down, Conte landing flat on his back on the carpet, all of the wind going out of him, so that for a moment he could not breathe. McDermott tried to get to his feet, a matter of dignity perhaps, both hands pushing up from the floor, momentarily freeing Conte who punched him in his unprotected face, hoping to smash his nose in, the offending nose immediately gushing blood. As McDermott fell forward half stunned, his shoulder hit Conte in the jaw, and he thought he felt all his teeth come loose on that side.

Conte was the younger man by eleven years, but McDermott was the taller, the heavier, a 200-pound six-footer who took as good care of his body as he did of his suits. He played squash regularly. He worked out with weights.

Wrestling, punching, they rolled off the rug and into some furniture, where Conte banged his nose against the leg of something, he didn't know what, didn't have the leisure to look, but feeling the blood. He banged his forehead too, opening a gash over his eye that would later require stitches, it bleeding as profusely as any nose. Conte was bleeding from two places, McDermott from only one. Within a minute both were covered in gore.

To THE LAWYER, Conte said: "I'd never experienced rage like that before." He shook his head because, looking back, such rage seemed to him impossible to understand. "I wanted to kill him. He's very lucky I didn't."

"So are you."

"Yes."

"At least he took her to a first-class hotel."

Conte did not smile.

"Sorry," said the lawyer. "Bad joke."

THE FIGHT WAS a saloon brawl, not a boxing match, complete with kneeing, gouging, hair pulling. Lamps and furniture went over. At some point Conte remembered Anna, and threw glances in all directions, searching for her, a momentary inattention that cost him new lumps on his forehead. She wasn't there, wasn't anywhere. They were fighting over a woman who had vanished.

THE LAWYER SAID: "Your wife left, you say."

"Wisely, I think. She's the one would have got headlines, not us."

THEY GRAPPLED, THEY PUNCHED, the two faces bloody, their clothing as well, their buttons, sleeves, and pockets half torn off. Their suits were in such disarray that the guns at their waists as they pummeled each other, as they rolled this way and that, came from time to time into view. Guns being a symbol of male virility, they were, as they rolled, like a pair of sexual deviates flashing their manhood in various directions for all to see.

Their guns were perceived by spectators who, perceiving them, shouted warnings or screamed.

"He's got a gun."

"Look out, they've got guns."

The lobby had been crowded enough: clerks and bellboys, patrons checking in or out or just moving through, others waiting in armchairs for someone to come down or come in. There even were several men standing close, Good Samaritans, looking for the chance to pull the brawlers apart.

"Guns!"

"Killers."

Words that resulted in the immediate evacuation of the lobby. The potential Good Samaritans were the first to run. From one second to the next the lobby was empty, except for a single terrified clerk at the reception desk who was on the phone with 911. The clerk reported a riot, men with guns, reported they were maybe terrorists or Mafia probably, and then, with the police operator still trying to question him, he dropped to the floor behind the counter, his hands over his ears, the telephone dangling, the police operator questioning the air.

The call went out over the police radio as a signal 10:30, armed robbery in progress, the operator evidently unable to make anything else out of what he had been told.

The 10:30 is a juicy call. Normally every car within earshot responds, every cop in every car wishing to get there first, to break up the robbery, save fellow citizens, win the shoot-out, apprehend the perpetrators single-handedly, get bathed in glory, and ever afterward be seen as a hero. There are a number of other calls as juicy as a 10:30, but none juicier, and never any shortage of aspirant heroes.

That is what happened this time too. Sirens could be heard coming from many streets away. When the first car reached the scene its doors were flung open and the two cops were out of it before it had stopped rolling. Having bailed out too soon, they went striding off in directions they had not chosen. The car itself rolled on, crashing into a lamppost from which it later had to be extricated by tow truck. The lamppost broke in two about halfway up, the top half hanging at a 45-degree angle like a swan with a broken neck. Behind that car was another, also coming too fast. Siren blaring, screeching and skidding, it rammed the first one, driving it farther into the lamppost, the top half of which toppled all the way down, smashing its face on the windshield, spraying glass. One of those two cops was hurt, his moans emerging from inside the half-collapsed car. His partner could be heard radioing for an ambulance. As an afterthought the partner said: "Send a tow truck too."

Still more sirens approached at speed.

The first two cops, once they had controlled their strides and come back, once they had observed with a certain stupefaction what had happened to their car, were surrounded by 20 people who, feeling that they had only narrowly escaped death in the hotel, were all talking at once. Many passersby had collected as well, and they listened to this babble, and demanded that the cops tell them what was happening, though the cops themselves didn't yet know.

Assailed by 20 descriptions of what they might find in the lobby, all coming at once and none of them the same, the two cops abandoned the effort and rushed inside, guns drawn, where they found the two brawlers rolling from one side of the rug to the other while locked in a seemingly unbreakable embrace. "On your feet," they shouted, and then: "Up against the wall."

Conte's suit was ruined, his career as well. Already he knew this. He did not have to be told. He understood also how quickly a scared cop's finger could tighten on the trigger, so he took the required position, First Deputy Commissioner McDermott doing likewise, even as more sirens squealed to a stop outside, and were abruptly cut off, and more cops poured into the lobby, followed, now that it seemed safe, by what seemed like a hundred people, patrons and bystanders both.

His hands on the wall, his Adam's apple feeling half caved in, Conte croaked: "I'm on the job." What any cop would have said. The phrase with which one New York cop identified himself to another. But a hand

reached around his waist and he felt his gun lifted out, his clip-on holster
with it. He sensed, or perhaps caught a glimpse of, his gun being passed
backward to the second cop.

"I'm on the job too," said the First Dep. But his gun was lifted also,
and passed back.

"Show me your shield," the first cop said to Conte. "Take it out
slowly, very slowly."

"Now you," the second cop said, waving his gun.

The cops' eyebrows went up when they saw Conte's captain's shield,
but when they looked down at McDermott's, one of them said: "Jesus!"

A sergeant in uniform came up bawling: "Whatdya got?"

When told, he too said: "Jesus."

The First Dep was at his elbow: "I want my gun back this instant. You
hear me? My gun and my shield. This instant."

For the moment the sergeant ignored him, for he had too many other
jobs to do. Cops were still flooding the lobby but he ordered them shooed
out again. "Back on patrol," he told them, "back on patrol."

"Arrest that man," demanded McDermott at his elbow. "Now. You
hear me? Now."

Keying his hand radio the sergeant raised Central: "On that ten-thirty
at the Regent Carlton, Central, no further necessary. No further at this
time."

McDermott was still beside him. "I'm ordering you to arrest that man
for assault."

The sergeant set his remaining cops to clearing civilians out of the
lobby. He had the radio in one hand, the two shields in the other. Someone else had their guns. He did not have to watch his two prisoners, who
were not exactly prisoners. He didn't know what they were exactly except
that they were cops. Without their shields they were like tourists separated
from their passports. They could go nowhere, and he walked off to a se-
cluded corner and radioed his command and asked what he was supposed to do next.

At that hour the precinct commander had already gone home. His exec was in charge. He too did not know what to do, and so ordered the two men brought into the 17th Precinct stationhouse in separate cars. While waiting he phoned the precinct commander who lived out on Long Island, who said that he himself would get there as soon as he could, 40 minutes, more or less. In the meantime the exec was to advise the police commissioner: "Call him at home. He lives on Staten Island, wake him up if necessary." Then he added: "When you send those cops back into the street, tell them not to say a word to anybody."

In their ruined clothes Conte and the First Dep reached the stationhouse, the First Dep still screaming that he wanted his gun and shield back, and he wanted Conte arrested for assault: "I want that man in handcuffs."

In the face of such rage, seeing his own career suddenly at stake, the exec spoke to him gently. "The PC is on the way in," he said. "Let's let him sort this thing out. He has ordered me to do nothing until he gets here."

The two brawlers were allowed — separately — into the bathroom to clean themselves up as best they could, and then placed in separate offices. The First Dep got the commander's office, Conte the exec's. Cops were placed at the doors to see they stayed there. Their shields and guns went into a drawer behind the muster desk.

THE LAWYER SAID: "I heard they wanted to arrest you on assault charges."

"Don't worry, I would have hired you to defend me."

"But cooler heads prevailed."

"Cooler heads, yes."

THE PC, HAVING BEEN ROUTED from in front of his television set, having been subjected to a long, wild ride, had gone into the office where they were holding his first deputy and had calmed him down. This thing had to be ended here and now, he said, or the publicity would ruin everybody. Had he seen the mess outside in the street? There was a badly injured cop and $50,000 worth of wrecked police cars out there. Not to mention the First Dep's affair with a subordinate's wife. McDermott should go home and get a good night's sleep. Don't worry about Conte. The PC would deal with Conte.

Or at least this is what Conte always assumed had happened.

Then the PC came into the office where Conte was being held.

Wasting no time on preliminaries, he said: "I want your shield on my desk in the morning."

The two men stared at each other for a moment. Then Conte said: "I don't see where I have to do that. The law says—"

The PC said: "If you stand on your so-called rights, you'll wish you hadn't."

Conte said: "What happens to the First Dep?"

"You assaulted him, he didn't assault you."

"Still, I'm curious."

The PC was a small, baldish man with, under normal circumstances, a voice so soft it was sometimes almost inaudible. He was a bookish man, an administrator, a man of ideas and theories. It was said that he had chosen McDermott as first deputy because he was big and bluff, a so-called cop's cop, the image of a police commander, the ideal image to put before the city and its 40,000 cops. A better image to put forth than his own.

The PC said: "The first deputy commissioner is not your affair."

"I see."

"You'll resign or else."

But Conte only shook his head. "I don't think so, no."

There was a big knot in the PC's tie, and Conte studied it while the small man sputtered.

Afterward it was seen that they couldn't easily fire him. The rank of captain being protected by civil service, a departmental trial would have been required first, and such trials were open to the public. To try Conte would make a terrific mess in the papers and on TV. It would have hurt them all, including Anna. Apparently McDermott cared enough about her to want to protect her if he could. What they decided to do was to allow much time to pass, during which they would make Conte's life a misery. If they made him miserable enough, he might quietly resign.

So they assigned him the role of fly captain. Day after day, month after month, he "flew," filled in wherever needed, almost always in precincts in Staten Island or the north Bronx or deepest Brooklyn or the far reaches of Queens, and almost always at night. His "friends" in the department, those with serious ambitions for higher rank, could not afford to be seen with him, and avoided him when they could. He realized this, and accepted it, which did not mean he liked it. There were no drinks after work, and not much camaraderie in the stationhouses.

The lonely months passed. He hung on, living alone in his elegant midtown flat, commuting two or more hours a day to whatever stationhouse he had been sent to. In November there would be an election. If the mayor should be defeated, then on January 1 a new mayor would move into city hall. Mayors always wanted their own PCs, so this new one almost certainly would appoint a new man, who in turn would want to name his own First Dep. With both of them gone, Conte might be given a chance to resurrect his career.

However, the elections came and went. The incumbent mayor having been reelected, the same PC sat ensconced on the 14th floor and, across the hall, sat the same First Dep.

The elections were November 3. Conte hung on through Thanksgiving, through Christmas, hoping something might happen. Perhaps the mayor would decide to make a change. But nothing happened. After the first of the year, as the police phrase has it, he put his papers in.

THE LAWYER SAID: "So you resigned."

"For the good of the department, as they say."

Conte shook his head, remembering. "I went looking for a job. Your wife does something like that, it doesn't look too good on your résumé, does it?"

"And nothing happens to the First Dep."

"No."

"Nor to your wife."

"I hope not. I hope it will work out for her."

"You got a raw deal all the way around, seems to me."

"Well, I brought it on myself, didn't I?"

"I remember your wedding," the lawyer said. "Her coming down the aisle in a long white dress, and when you lifted the veil off her face she was so beautiful. At the reception I danced with her, and she was more beautiful yet. I was so envious of you."

"She's still beautiful," said Conte.

"How long ago was the wedding, seven or eight years?"

"A bit more."

"So what went wrong?"

"My own fault, probably. She was a star. I guess I didn't give her enough attention."

Conte was at the window looking out toward the Statue of Liberty. "When we were first married I was a sergeant trying to make lieutenant. Then I was a lieutenant trying to make captain. When I made captain I was bucking for a precinct of my own. Crime goes on twenty-four hours a day. I felt I had to be there."

"And in your absence —"

"Yes. You almost can't blame her. She certainly didn't blame herself."

"How did you find out?"

Turning from the window, Conte was silent.

"Never mind," his friend said. "I'm behaving like a lawyer. I'm probing and I shouldn't be. You don't have to answer."

Conte laughed. "How did I wind up wrestling around on the floor of the lobby of the Regent Carlton with a man six or seven ranks higher and nearly fifty years old? She couldn't keep her explanations straight, for one thing. Once you get suspicious you imagine the rest. You get so you think you can smell the other man in her hair. That I started tailing her was shameful of me. There were other ways. I should have done something else."

Conte laughed again. "I can certainly see the comical aspects of all this."

"Tell me what brings you here, Vince, although I think I know."

"I've got a legal problem." Having said this much, Conte fell silent.

"I don't do divorces," said the lawyer.

"I figured you might do this one, as a favor to me."

They had known each other a very long time. Conte didn't mind leaning on friends when he needed something badly.

"I thought you might be able to do it quickly, and relatively cheaply. I thought you might keep the cost down." Conte gave a smile. "Despite that expensive telescope and the other heavy overhead you're carrying."

The lawyer was shaking his head. "I don't even know how to do divorces."

"I didn't know who to go to," said Conte. "Then I found myself remembering a certain case, the one that made your reputation. Made possible all of this—" He gestured around him. "I was the one arrested the killers, and then I brought in the key witness that got you your conviction."

The lawyer gazed at him across the desk.

"Even though you don't do divorces, I thought you might do this one because we've known each other so long. For old times' sake, so to speak."

His friend sighed.

"It should be pretty cut and dried," said Conte. "Just give her whatever she wants and get it done."

"Whatever she wants—are you crazy? You're the wronged party here. You could be paying through the nose till you die."

"I don't think alimony's a problem."

"It's always a problem."

"They want to get married, you see. Of course he has to get divorced first."

"All right," said the lawyer.

"Here's her lawyer's address," said Conte.

"This is a sad day for me," said the lawyer. "I always liked her."

"I always liked her myself," said Conte.

The lawyer gazed across the desk at him. "Marge and I haven't seen you lately."

"Tell her I haven't been seeing anybody lately." He shook hands with his friend. "I wouldn't have been very good company anyway." He started toward the door.

"Sit down, Vince, I'd really like to know how you are."

"I'm a little rushed for time."

At the door, Conte said: "I apologize for dumping my troubles on you, Carl."

"Come on, Vince."

Conte gave a wave and went out.

CHAPTER

IV

AT THE EDGE OF THE CITY, the villas climbed the mountain in rows like steps. In front of a house on the highest step the taxi stopped, and the two passengers got out.

There was a high surrounding wall. The young woman, standing with her suitcase in the sun while the man paid the driver, could see only part of the tile roof, plus the tops of trees in the garden. But as she went in through the gate, the size of the villa stopped her.

"It's big," she said. "Really big."

"Sumptuous, you might say," said the man, sounding smug. "You plan an operation like this, it's what you need."

For a moment the young woman studied him.

The wall was impenetrable: No one could see in or out. "The prison of wealth," she said.

"What?"

"Nothing." Most people lived inside a prison of some kind, she re-flected, sometimes a prison of their own making, and she saw herself as one of them. She was trying to break out, but it was hard. Some people lived within concentric prisons, several at once, so many they could never break out. Was she one of those too? She hoped not, that it was not too late.

The garden looked manicured. Brick paths. Flowers. The villa was painted a pale rose. The shutters and trim were green. Ivy climbed the walls.

She said: "How much does a place like this go for?"

"More than you'll ever be able to afford."

"Nor you either," she said, and followed him into the house. He did not offer to carry her bag, and she did not ask him to.

It had been hot outside; it was cool in here. She felt the coolness on her bare arms. She was a person keenly attuned to all things sensual.

She put the suitcase down, and peered around: marble floor, cut glass chandeliers, decorated ceilings.

Her name was Georgette Meyer, called Gigi. Her cheeks were smooth, her arms sleek and tanned. She wore a sleeveless dress cut low front and back, and rope sandals, and her dark hair was tied back in a ponytail. She had prominent cheekbones, a strong chin, and rather fleshy lips. Her teeth were big and white, her eyes a deep, deep blue, and there was an innocent look to her young face that sometimes puzzled people meeting her for the first time. In this day and age, earning her living the way she did, innocent she was not.

The man, a paparazzo named Georges Grizzard, had shut the front door. Grizzard's name was better known than Gigi's. Some of his photos were better known still. The mangled actress inside the wrecked car. The bishop and the choirboy. The judge nuzzling the senator's wife.

Advancing into the downstairs rooms, Gigi nodded her head in appreciation.

"This is your parents' summer place," said Grizzard behind her.

"I see," said Gigi, whose mother had died when she was a child.

"Your parents have a lot of money," said Grizzard, and he laughed. But it was a nervous laugh.

Gigi eyed him a moment. Her father was an attaché in the Dutch embassy in South Africa, the highest post he had yet attained, and she had not seen him in a number of years. But she said nothing, merely continued into the living room where the furniture was hidden under shrouds. It reminded her of coffins covered by flags. As she walked around lifting corners she provoked small clouds of dust.

"Your father's heavily invested," said Grizzard. "Oil, rubber. He's looking to move some of his money here." The one heavily invested was Grizzard, Gigi believed, and he sounded worried about it. Of course she herself would be invested soon enough.

Having let the last of the shrouds fall back, she said: "Get this place cleaned up, or your fairy story won't fool anybody."

"You know how to work a vacuum, don't you?"

"Oh," said Gigi, "you think I should do it? How amusing."

"While you're waiting."

Gigi looked at him.

"You'll be here a couple of days."

Gigi said: "Get someone."

"Only take you a few minutes."

"Get someone."

They were speaking English, Grizzard with a strong but indeterminate accent. Gigi sounded like an American college girl.

Grizzard took the cell phone out of his pocket and stretched it toward her. "How about making the call?"

Gigi glanced from the phone to the staircase, where her gaze lingered. "Do I get a bedroom?"

"There's seven up there," said Grizzard. "Take your pick." He held out the phone. "How about it?"

Gigi hefted her suitcase, and started for the stairs.

"Let me carry that," Grizzard said coming toward her, wearing a grin that was close to a leer. "I'll help you unpack."

She was three steps up by then. She dropped the suitcase, sat down on top of it, and gazed at him until his grin faded.

After a moment, still without speaking, she grasped the suitcase again, and continued up.

There were indeed many bedrooms, and she looked into several. The villa was as big as any of the embassies she had been in. She chose a corner room, whether it was the so-called master bedroom or not she did not know or care. Paintings hung from two of the walls. A seascape. A still life. There was an armoire several hundred years old, and end tables and commodes of about the same age.

Opening her suitcase on the bed, she carried her small trousse into the bathroom and stood it on a shelf. It was not a makeup kit. It contained only toothpaste and toothbrush, shampoo, Tampax, aspirin. She never used makeup and prided herself that she didn't need to.

The bathroom was all marble. A big deep tub. She used the toilet, then washed her face and hands. There was a cabinet that contained towels. She got one out and dried off, then left the bathroom and went over to the bed, a queen-sized four-poster with lace curtains. She bounced on it a bit. The mattress seemed firm.

There were two floor-to-ceiling windows. Both gave onto balconies. She went out onto the one that looked toward the mountains, and contemplated the view.

The other balcony looked down onto the garden. She saw where the pool must be, but it was behind hedges and not visible. She heard voices: Grizzard and someone else speaking Italian.

She hung the few clothes she had with her, skirt and jeans, blouses. She placed her underclothes into one of the top drawers.

A few minutes later she joined Grizzard at the pool where he introduced the other man as his assistant, giving his name as Renzo, one name only. An Italian apparently. Her slim brown hand shot out and she gave Renzo's a vigorous shake. "Hello, how are you," she said.

To which Renzo replied: "*Buon giorno.*"

Gigi spoke four languages, but Italian was not one of them.

"Only about a third of the pool is useful to us," Grizzard said to her. "This part here."

He said something to Renzo, who began dragging over the pool furniture, collecting it all at the one end.

"Everything has to happen here," said Grizzard.

"If you say so."

"The other end, anything goes on is no good to me."

"Draw a line in chalk," said Gigi. "Write: Don't cross this line."

"Nothing in the house. The house is useless."

"I heard you the first time." Gigi went into her sullen mode, and walked away.

"It's important," said Grizzard to her back.

Gigi at the end of the pool looked back at the house and at the mountains behind it.

"There's a lot at stake," Grizzard said.

She did not answer him. Finally he went to help Renzo arrange the furniture.

Gigi glanced over at what they were doing. "You put it all down at one end," she said, "and anybody but a moron would see it was fishy."

"Fishy?" said Grizzard. Not a word he knew perhaps, but he understood what she meant.

He said something to Renzo in Italian, and they began moving some of the furniture back.

"Make the call," Grizzard said. Having come up beside her, he again proffered his cell phone.

Gigi looked at it.

"Please make the call."

"At this point I'm supposed to be paid."

"Make the call first."

Gigi continued to study the view. "But I haven't been paid."

Grizzard took out a check and handed it to her.

After studying it for a moment, the young woman thrust it into the pocket of her dress then took the phone. "What's the number?"

The check represented to her an enormous amount of money. She was as aware of it as if it had weight. It weighed down her pocket.

"What are you going to say to him?"

"Whatever comes into my head."

"Your rich father's here, and may want to make an investment."

"Tell me the number."

"Invite him for tea tomorrow."

"The number."

Grizzard gave it.

"You stand over there," she told him. Holding the phone at her side, she waited until he had moved off several paces. Finally she tapped in the number.

Both waited to see who would answer. Grizzard, some distance off, looked nervous. Gigi, with the phone at her ear, looked bored.

"If his wife answers, hang up," joked Grizzard nervously.

"Is this his home number?" said Gigi, breaking the connection.

"His portable."

Gigi pushed redial.

A smile came onto her face as the phone was answered, and she turned away from Grizzard so that he could not hear her words, or see them either. Her manner had become voluble, vivacious.

After a time she looked down at the phone until she had found and punched the disconnect. She handed it back to him. "He's coming to tea day after tomorrow."

"I said tomorrow."

"Tomorrow you'll be busy."

"Busy?"

"Cleaning this place up."

"What name did you give him?"

"I told him to bring his wife."

"You didn't."

"I thought it sounded nice of me to invite his wife."

"Suppose he brings her?"

"Somehow I don't think he will."

"Does he suspect anything?"

Gigi gave this question a rather surly shrug. "That pool looks cool. What do you say we go swimming?"

"How do you know he'll react the way we want him to react?"

Another shrug from Gigi.

"You don't really know him."

"He'll remember me."

"He did like looking at you," conceded Grizzard, who seemed to be trying to encourage her and himself both. "I could see he liked looking at you." Grizzard liked looking at her himself. She was tall and slim, yet smooth and round where it counted. She was busty and hippy, but not too much of either.

"Everything rides on what happens," Grizzard said.

"The sun is very hot, isn't it?"

"A lot of money."

"This conversation bores me," Gigi said. "I'm going swimming."

Grizzard watched her hand search the back of her dress, watched her pull the zipper down all the way. It was a moment before he realized what she was doing. First the dress loosened and started down, showing that she wore no bra, then it fell to her rope sandals and pink painted toenails, and she stepped out of it.

The dress made a pile at her feet. She draped it over one of the pool chairs. She took off her wristwatch and laid it on the dress. She was practically naked already.

"You could read a newspaper through those panties," said Grizzard.

"Do you think so?"

The watching Grizzard wondered what she would do next. Use the panties as the bottom half of a bikini? Slough them off altogether?

She kept no one in suspense long. She was not trying to titillate anyone, it seemed.

It was as if she were alone. It was as if Grizzard and Renzo were eunuchs. It was as if they were not there, and Grizzard's face darkened. It was a way of showing contempt for them perhaps, for him in particular since she was supposed to be working for him. He watched her step out of the panties, then bend to retrieve them. For a moment she mooned the world.

She tossed the panties toward the dress on the chair, missing, then crossed the tiles to the edge of the pool, where she stepped out of the sandals. Wearing only a bracelet and her ponytail, she curled her toes and plunged in.

Renzo, who had come forward, stood gaping beside Grizzard. They watched Gigi swim one length, flip into a turn, and start back. She swam quite well, a strong crawl, gulping for air every other stroke, but with her head turning to the opposite side so that they could not see her face. Nor would she be able to see if they were watching her, though she must know they were, or judge her effect on them, though she must know what that effect was.

She swam four lengths like that, her butt muscles driving her legs, a portion of breast showing each time her stroke came out of the water. Flipping over, she backstroked four lengths more, the sun shining, the water sluicing off her.

"She's not bashful, is she?" said Grizzard.

"You get to bang that?" said Renzo.

Grizzard shrugged.

"Where'd you find her?"

Grizzard watched her swim.

"She's got the thickest pubic hair I've ever seen on a girl," said Renzo.

Grizzard said nothing.

"Hip to hip."

Grizzard still said nothing.

"It's jet-black."

Gigi, when she stopped swimming, sat on the bottom step at the shallow end of the pool, the water up to her shoulders. She called out: "I need a towel."

With a jerk of his chin, Grizzard sent Renzo into the house to find her one.

Gigi came up the steps and out of the pool, her body a wet mirror. Bouncing first on one foot, then the other, she cleared her ears. Still waiting for the towel, she went over and sprawled on one of the pool chairs.

Renzo returned with the towel. Holding it like a bullfighter's cape, Grizzard approached Gigi. Perhaps he hoped she would step into it, to be rubbed vigorously dry by him.

She sat with legs outstretched, ankles crossed, and she eyed him. When she judged he was close enough, she said: "Stop right there."

Grizzard did not stop immediately.

"One step more and the deal is off," she said.

Grizzard stopped.

She had been on her own, had not taken a cent from her father from the age of 16. There were many things in the world she was afraid of, herself most of all, but men were not one of them.

"Now throw it to me."

Grizzard did so.

She stood up, caught the towel, and wrapped herself up. "Thank you," she said. Walking over, she collected her dress, panties, wristwatch, and sandals, and carried them into the house.

The next morning, bare armed, ponytail swinging, wearing sandals and the same loose sundress as the day before, Gigi crossed the sidewalk and went into the bank where she handed over her certified check, not quite breathing during the moment it took the teller to study it. If he called it bogus, and handed it back, then what?

Instead, he nodded, smiled, and asked her where she wanted the money sent. Into a numbered account in Switzerland, she told him. This had been set up for her a week previously by a lawyer in Amsterdam. She handed over a paper with the numbers on it.

The money would be there within moments, the teller said.

Out in the street again Gigi moved along in crowds in the sun and felt immeasurably lighter. She window-shopped for an hour or more, which was a delight, for the duchy was one swanky shop after another. But she bought nothing. Such shops catered to the luxury trade only, and the luxury trade was not her. Though she walked as far as the *téléphérique* station where the shops petered out, she saw nothing she might want that seemed to her reasonably priced.

By then it was noon and she was hungry, so she decided to treat her-self to the one luxury she could afford, which was a nice lunch. She en-tered a restaurant.

It was already crowded, she saw, and she was shown to a small table near the window, where she ordered grilled fish and a salad, with a quar-ter liter of rosé wine. While she waited to be served, her hand opened and closed on the receipt in her pocket, and she was both happy and un-happy. Happy about the money which might enable her to change her life. Unhappy about what she now had to do to earn it.

At the next table sat two businessmen. Locals, perhaps. They were dressed like businessmen, and looked like businessmen to her. Both were about 35, maybe a bit older, and one said to her in English: "What are you smiling about?"

Immediately she ceased smiling, and she nodded at them without speaking, for she was a polite young woman, and minimum politeness seemed required, even at moments like this.

"Would you care to join us?" the other man said.

"Thank you, no," she said.

Because this kind of thing happened to her too often, she had come to dread eating alone in restaurants, had set a rule not to, and she won-dered now why she had broken her rule.

Her lunch was set down in front of her.

"Plenty of room over here," the first man said.

They went on with it, first one, then the other. She was not a person for confrontations, avoided them where she could, but she had now, it seemed to her, only two choices: She could get up and leave the restau-rant, her lunch uneaten, or she could make them stop pestering her — which meant saying something rude.

She said: "If I had wanted company, I could have picked up some jerk in the street."

They fell silent, and though the taste had gone out of it for her, she was able to finish her lunch in silence.

Later she shopped for a few groceries, then took a taxi back to the villa. The place had been cleaned in her absence, all the shrouds re-moved and stored somewhere, and she walked through the brilliant rooms and thought that this was as close to being rich as she would ever get.

She went out to the pool and had a solitary swim.

As the sun began to set she stood in her sundress on a balcony gaz-ing out at the view. Above her floated high clouds that had become tinged with pink. A little later, as it dropped below the mountains, the sun seemed to spew blood all over the sky. Below her the mountain fell away. Far below it was already dark. She watched the darkness climb. She watched the night throw a cloak over the houses one level at a time.

She became pensive, and after a moment took the receipt out of her pocket and in the bad light squinted at it. Her part in a scheme concocted by Georges Grizzard. She had not asked what the scheme was, did not want to know, and yet it wasn't hard to guess. She knew she shouldn't do it. But the money gave her hope for a future that for her was otherwise impossible. So she knew she would do it, but that the doing of it would not make her proud.

She was not going to do anything illegal, she encouraged herself. Her role as far as it went was not even, in these modern times, immoral. Stop the self-flogging, she told herself. She put the receipt back in her pocket, but continued to hold it.

As night swallowed even the mountains around her, she went back inside the house. She was not going to take an active part, she told her-self. She was just going to be there, letting happen whatever happened. Grizzard's scheme, through no fault of hers, could even fall apart. Sup-pose Murano simply said no. If he did, he was in the clear. But she did not consider this a real possibility. Men preyed on women. Give them a certain set of circumstances, and a certain reaction was inevitable. A fact of life. That men were programmed this way had nothing to do with her. It had always baffled her that they were. She had never admired them for it.

She would do what she would do because the money represented more security than she had ever had. It was like owning an insurance policy. She thought she could live a year on it if she were careful, perhaps longer, and this would give her time to get something going for herself. She had been on her own a long time without any safety net at all. Day after day she had counted her money. How much she had left. How far it had to stretch. There was no one else looking after her. She had had to look after herself. This too was a fact of life. She blamed no one. If she was in a hole, it was one she had dug herself.

Her reflections about herself were without self-pity. In a sense she was proud to have survived this long on her own.

With such thoughts, while pacing the living room carpet, her hand opening and closing on the receipt, she defended herself in advance.

AT THE LEVEL of the villa, Antonio Murano shut the engine down, fished his attaché case out of one of the saddlebags, and approached the gate. The attaché case would have some importance later, at least to him. He would offer it as proof of his intentions, for it contained the plans, brochures, rendered drawings, and cost estimates for his proposed spa. The two Italian investors had lost patience — the faxes from Italy had become importunate. If he couldn't produce the duke's signature, which he couldn't, they would move on to something else. Because he saw now that his father-in-law might never sign, his need had become to find backup investors. Which was why he approached this villa now. According to the woman on the phone, whom he knew only as Gigi, her father wanted to meet him. He gathered that her father was rich, had heard of the spa idea, was interested, and might invest.

Beside the gate hung a bell from which a chain dangled. He set the bell ringing and then, since the gate was not locked, stepped into the garden. He carried his attaché case in one hand, his helmet in the other. No one in the town knew he was there. He had not advised his pregnant wife, nor his lawyer, and certainly not the ruler.

There was some shrubbery which he rounded, and as he did so he nearly bumped into this Gigi, who was coming to meet him from the house. He was wearing loafers, khaki pants, and a sports shirt in a plaid pattern, blues and browns mostly, open necked, with a button-down collar. Gigi, who was barefoot, wore only a bikini, one of the briefest he had ever seen.

Murano had met her twice previously, once at an auto show in Amsterdam, and then in the hotel lobby later. Both times she was of course dressed, and confronting her now unexpectedly, so much flesh showing, threw him into momentary shock.

"Hi," said the young woman, putting her hand out, "I hope you remember me. I'm Gigi."

"Tony Murano."

"Gigi Saffran," she said, giving a last name that was not her own. They shook hands. "Your wife didn't come?"

"No."

The young man was trying hard not to stare.

"I'm sorry to have to tell you," Gigi said, "my father is not here, something came up. I'm alone."

Her father's check might have ended Murano's problems. He had not been counting on it, yet he had been.

"I called you on your portable to tell you."

"Yes," said Murano.

"My call didn't go through. You must have been in a tunnel, or out of range."

"Probably," said Murano.

They were speaking English, in which Murano was not entirely fluent.

"Well, you were right around the corner, weren't you. At least you didn't have to come far."

A silence fell between them. Gigi let this silence build, for she saw how uncomfortable he was, and it was her job to keep him that way.

"I would have enjoy meeting them," Murano said, his accent strong. "Your parents."

"Well, you're here now, and I'm glad to see you. Can I offer you a cup of tea?"

Murano started to refuse, but didn't. He glanced behind him at the gate through which he had entered, outside of which stood his motorcycle. He even took a half step in that direction, but when the girl took his hand, the one holding the helmet, he allowed her to lead him into the house.

In the kitchen they waited for the water to boil. Murano had watched her reach up for the cups, bringing them down from a high shelf, and for a moment the fragments of color that clothed so little of her clothed even less. She had put tea bags in the pot, and stood now with her smooth round rump against the sideboard. She had her arms crossed over her top, and she chattered away, asking him questions about himself, concentrating all her attention on him, rewarding certain of his answers with nods and smiles, completely at ease, practically naked but not aware of it, or so it seemed to Murano.

She gave the impression of being well educated, well mannered, and obviously rich, and she wasn't coming on to him at all, even though most of the other signals he was receiving read the opposite.

He was not surprised that she seemed interested in him. He had been featured in the scandal sheets dozens of times. Certainly he had resented many of those stories, especially the ones that treated him as an appendage to Maria Cristina. Nonetheless, in his own way he was famous. During all those months — in fact it had been years — when his father-in-law would not receive him or permit him to marry his now wife, he had had half of Europe rooting for him, or at least on his side, according to those same scandal sheets.

So people had known for a long time who he was.

About Gigi Saffran now he learned very little, apart from the fact that she loved to play tennis.

"Me too," said Murano. "In fact I play professional for one year, two year."

"You were good, I bet."

"Not good as players you see on television."

"You sound sad."

"Oh, I make some money at it. But I would have like to make more." After a moment he added: "Maybe together we can play this summer. You will be around?"

"I'd like to be. I don't know."

Feeling disloyal, Murano added: "My wife plays. Very well, too. Get a fourth and we play doubles."

"Tell me about your wife."

"She's pregnant right now."

"That's very hard on a young husband, isn't it. For the last few months of a pregnancy you can't, you know, do anything."

Not exactly a leading remark. Or was it? She hadn't even been looking at him as she said it, but had been searching through another of the high cabinets for cookies, which she found, brought down, and placed on a plate.

Murano would have been the first to admit, though not to her, how difficult for him the pregnancy had been. First Maria Cristina had been nauseous for three months, after which she had developed a rash between her legs, so that sex became painful for her. Then came the wedding preparations, during which she was made to live in the palace for a week and he did not see her. The night of their wedding she had had to be taken to the hospital with severe cramps. For three days the paparazzi had been camped out in the street below.

After that it was touch and go that she would be able to carry the baby to term.

Murano had been celibate for over four months.

"There are women who won't let their husbands near them when they're pregnant," Gigi said. "I hope I'm not going to be like that."

It was a remark that made him like her. "You plan to get pregnant?" he said with a smile.

"Not until I'm married," she said firmly.

This caused another silence, during which he searched for something to say, coming up with: "What else you like beside tennis?"

The watched pot never boils, watched by Murano, not her, but this one did, and the water spattered a bit as Gigi poured it into the pot over the tea bags.

"Well, I love to swim," she said, "don't you?" Having arranged everything on a tray, she suggested they go out and sit beside the pool. "In fact, we could go for a swim right now, if you brought your suit. Did you?" They were crossing the living room by then and she looked around somewhat distractedly. "If not, I could probably find something for you upstairs."

He had visualized himself talking business with her father beside the pool, and so had brought with him modest boxer trunks—more modest by far than what this young woman had on—exactly what a sober young businessman should wear to such a meeting. They were in his attaché case along with the brochures and rendered drawings which perhaps he should show to Gigi, who might intercede with her father later.

"I do have a swimsuit with me."

"Well, good. Go in there and change"—she pointed toward the downstairs lavatory—"while I pour."

The lavatory was tiny. He stripped naked then had to take several deep breaths in an effort to calm himself down. As he pulled the boxer trunks up his legs he was suffering not so much from excitement as from confusion—although he was excited too. Usually he was at ease with girls, but not with this one.

He came out, crossed the living room, and went out through the French doors.

At the far end of the pool in her flimsy bikini waited Gigi.

He stepped out onto tiles that were uncomfortably hot under his bare feet, and started toward her.

CHAPTER

V

THAT NIGHT MURANO'S WIFE went into labor. He phoned the palace as he had been instructed to do—he was in many ways an obedient young man—then got Maria Cristina and a small bag into the Porsche, opened the gate, and drove out onto the road. The guard car was still up there, parked against the wall, and the cop inside it was, he saw, asleep. It would have been easy enough for Murano to roll down the hill without waking him. Let him guard an empty villa while the heir was born down in the town. But if he did this, the man's career was over, and probably he would lose his job. Much as he had always resented the car's presence, Murano got out of the Porsche, walked up, reached in the window and shook him.

Half stupid with sleep, the cop grabbed his cap, clapped it on his head, and attempted to look fierce.

"We're on our way to the hospital."

"I'll put the siren on."

"No, just follow us down."

By the time they reached the hospital there was a ring of cops around it, orders from the palace, the object being to keep away any photographers who might have been tipped off by someone on the hospital staff, or perhaps by someone else—how could anyone know how they found out what they did. Augustin II hated photographers, and had once remarked, with reference to a certain actress, that they would shoot a photo up her legs as the baby came out, if they could, and then sell it all over Europe. The remark had application to his daughter as well, except that a picture of Maria Cristina giving birth would be worth far more than any actress.

For most of the next 42 hours Murano sat beside his wife. He bathed her forehead, held her hand, timed the contractions. At noon the next day Maria Cristina's mother came in and sat silently in the corner, and when nothing had happened by nightfall began badgering the doctors. The girl's father never came at all. In the chair beside the bed Murano fell from time to time briefly asleep. Each morning he hurried home to shave and change his clothes, moving in and out through journalists and photographers both times.

In the delivery room in a hospital gown, holding her hand, he saw his wife's face get redder than he had ever seen it, redder even than in the throes of sexual passion, his previous point of reference, until finally she squeezed the baby out. Murano had had no idea that babies were born facedown, nor that they came out in such a gout of blood and slime. To see Maria Cristina's stomach sag as if suddenly punctured was still another shock. He did not watch everything. At a certain point, he turned away quickly and faced the wall. There were six or seven people in the delivery room, enough to insure that if he fainted, the world would hear about it, and what this would do to the image of virility that was so important to him he hated to think.

What he most feared in life was that people might laugh at him.

The newborn was handed to him in a towel.

"Congratulations," a male voice said — in those gowns no one could tell man from woman. "You have a son."

The young man looked down at this tiny new creature, still all slimy and bloody.

He wanted him cleaned up, and he handed him back.

Maria Cristina was unconscious as he wheeled her back to her room, a nurse in a green gown walking alongside. He and the nurse lifted her onto the bed. Maria Cristina's gown was very short, it rode up, and he saw that she had a towel between her legs. The towel was wet and red, and the nurse pulled the sheet up over her.

Her mother came in, nodded to him, and pulled up a chair on the other side of the bed.

Finally Maria Cristina stirred. Her lips moved, and she muttered to him: "I've got an awfully sore pussy."

He looked quickly at his mother-in-law but the woman's face showed nothing.

Maria Cristina's tongue sounded dry and thick. She said: "I want to see my baby."

Murano went to the door and found a nurse. "Bring in my son, please," he told her.

He took the baby from the nurse, brought it to Maria Cristina, and placed it in her arms. Her face glowed.

A crushing fatigue came down on him, and his eyes began to close. From one minute to the next it required all his concentration to make them stay open.

Maria Cristina took his hand. "Go home and get some sleep. My mother will stay with me."

Murano went downstairs and out into the night.

That his mother-in-law did not like him had long been clear to him; the royal couple didn't do much to hide their feelings. The sovereign especially would give almost anything to get rid of him, he was sure, but it was too late, for he had now become the father of the heir, his place at last was secure. Outside it was early evening, warm, a bit muggy, and he did a little dance, and cried out exultantly: "You're stuck with me now, folks."

The air was balmy, and the new father stood beside the Porsche in the hospital lot and turned his portable phone back on, planning to call his lawyer, see if anything had happened with the investors.

Before he could do this, the phone rang in his hand.

It was Georges Grizzard, who did not give his name. "We have to meet," Grizzard said in his ear. The new father's future had just gone up in the air, but he did not know this yet. "It's a matter of grave concern to you," said Grizzard. "How soon can we meet?"

"Who are you? What's it about?"

"How soon?"

"I haven't been to bed in two days."

"It has to be tonight." The café Grizzard named was in the upper part of the city.

To Murano it had something to do with his proposed health club. It was on his way home, and at this hour there would be little traffic.

"How will I know you?" he asked.

"I'll know you. I've seen pictures of you. In fact I've been studying some of them."

Although this remark much pleased Grizzard, the double meaning went over Murano's head. The young man saw no menace in Grizzard's words, and instead found them gratifying, proof again that he was really quite famous.

So he drove over there, double-parking outside the café. The wicker chairs and tables were out, and since it was aperitif time most were occupied. People sipped their drinks in the night air and talked most likely about where to go for dinner.

The new father stood amid the tables peering around.

"Over here," the voice called.

Georges Grizzard sat at a table just beside the café entrance. Except for waiters hurrying past with their trays, that part of the terrace was empty. Grizzard had stood up to beckon Murano forward; now he sat down again waiting.

Murano stood over the table. "Do I know you?"

"You should."

"I don't know," said Murano, trying to appraise him.

"We've had business together in the past."

"You'll have to excuse me. I've just become a father. So I'm a bit giddy. I'm also in need of a night's sleep."

"So you don't remember me," commented Grizzard. He found this news offensive, and he had reasons. "But that doesn't matter now, does it. And you'll remember me a great deal better in the future."

Some months previously Grizzard had tailed Murano and the young duchess, his not yet wife, to a café. This was late at night. With a long lens, he had caught them kissing. He had followed them to a dark doorway where they had apparently intended to fuck standing up. When his flash attachment exposed them—not once but several times—her jeans and panties were down around one ankle, the other leg being bare, barefoot, and raised more or less to Murano's waist. What had amazed Grizzard was the speed with which the young man had reacted. Regained his balance and come running. He caught Grizzard within 20 strides, ripped the camera off his neck, and swung it with all his might over and over again against a column supporting the arcade overhead. Grizzard did not stay to watch his camera destroyed. He abandoned it and kept running. Young Murano had caught him again and was pummeling him when bystanders dragged him off.

A traumatic night for Grizzard that this young lout didn't even remember.

A costly night too. Grizzard was out an expensive camera, and the thousands of euros the lost photos would have brought. Not to mention his bruised face and bruised dignity.

But it would prove more costly still for Murano, he had promised himself. One day he would get even.

That day had come.

"I've got to get some sleep," said the young man. "We'll have to do this another time. Whatever it is."

"I have some photos of you with a certain person that you might like to see. A certain nude female person. Her name is Gigi, I believe."

This stopped Murano in his tracks.

"I think we should sit down and talk this over," Grizzard said.

On the table lay a thick manila envelope, and Grizzard pointed to it. "Sit down. Take a look."

Murano, who remained standing, stared at the envelope. The color had gone out of his face, and his jaw was rigid. Reaching, he tried to get the package open, but succeeded mostly in moving it around on the table.

Finally Grizzard's hands entered his field of vision. The proud photographer picked up the envelope, withdrew some photos, and fanned them out.

The young man glanced at three or four, himself with Gigi, then looked away, even as the other man laughed. "That's a nice handful of titties you've got in that one, wouldn't you say? How did they feel?"

Murano appeared to be trying to speak, but nothing came out.

"You should ask yourself how much these photos would be worth to your wife."

Finally Murano managed to speak—it was almost as a croak: "How much do you want?"

Grizzard carried a sap in his pocket, for he had feared violence. Now he realized there would be none. If you considered this café as a kind of battlefield, then Murano was like a soldier who has been hit. Even a minor wound—and Murano's was major—changes one's focus from the enemy to oneself. The trauma is such that a wounded soldier no longer constitutes a threat to anyone.

Grizzard appeared unable to stop grinning. "I wonder what would be the reaction of the palace, if these photos came to light? What would your future there be? How would your father-in-law react, do you think?"

Murano was trying to force the photos back into the envelope.

"I would give your tenure there about two days, heir or no heir."

The photos were bending, tearing the envelope.

"There are any number of magazines that would like to publish those pictures, don't you think?"

"How much do you want?"

"They would pay me, say, seventy or eighty thousand euros."

"I don't have that much money—"

"What's the matter with your voice?"

"But I can get it."

"Your voice has almost disappeared."

"I'll pay you—"

"Speak up, I can't hear you."

"—you more than that."

"Well, for a hundred thousand, I might be persuaded to sell them to you."

Murano moved away from the table but stumbled over some chairs.

"I have an extra set," said Grizzard, coming up behind him, and he shoved the envelope under Murano's arm. "You keep these. Take them out and look at them from time to time. You have three days. I'll call you and we'll meet."

Murano moved toward the street.

"And don't try anything funny," Grizzard called after him. "If you do, the pictures will be released everywhere."

Murano's next decision would have been anyone's. Gigi wouldn't want such pictures in magazines any more than he did. Or she might know what to do, could straighten this mess out. Or, since she was from a rich family, she might be able to lend him the vast sum needed. He drove directly to the villa where they had met.

But when he got there the windows were dark. He pulled the bell chain, but no one answered, and the gates remained locked, though he tugged at them over and over. Stepping across the road, he rang there. The woman who came to the door, because she recognized him as the ruler's son-in-law, let him in. She had never heard of Gigi Saffran, she told him, or of her supposedly rich parents, either. The villa was owned by an industrialist from Paris, who used to use it for vacations. She gave the man's name, which meant nothing to Murano. But the owner hadn't been around for, oh, probably two years. She had noted people inside it a few days ago, but they hadn't stayed. People looking to rent probably.

Murano crossed back toward what to him was still Gigi's villa, and several times more rattled the bars. Finally he got into his car, put his head on the steering wheel, and began to cry. Then he fell asleep. He was awakened when his body fell sideways and the gear lever jammed him in the ribs.

On his cell phone he phoned his lawyer, waking him, for it was by then past midnight.

"I hear you're a father," the lawyer said. "A son and heir. Congratulations."

"Yes."

"Smart idea naming him after your father-in-law too."

"Naming him?"

"Augustin III may be a heavy load for the little tyke, but he'll grow into it."

"Listen—"

"Your father-in-law has declared a national holiday a week from today. You know what that means?"

Murano shook his head, which could not be seen at the other end of the line.

"The royal family on the palace balcony presenting the heir to the populace," the lawyer said. "Followed by parades, dancing in the streets, fireworks. You'll be up there on that balcony too. You're in good shape now. Getting that girl pregnant is the smartest thing you ever did."

The lawyer then said: "You didn't wake me up to talk about that. What do you want?"

Murano's thoughts were fixed on the men from Italy. If they would sign the contract and make a down payment he could use the money to pay off the blackmailer.

"Have they called?" he asked the lawyer.

"Have who called?"

"The men from Italy."

"I told you, they won't go any further until your father-in-law signs that paper."

"Ask them for—for good faith money."

"Not a chance. So why hasn't he signed it?"

Murano began a somewhat garbled speech. Good faith money in cases like this was normal, he said, if the lawyer would only call and demand it, tell them the deal was in jeopardy, someone else was offering money, there must be some way to get money out of them...

"My advice to you is to get some sleep," the lawyer said. "You sound like you need it. Good night." And he hung up.

Murano dialed the palace and asked for Augustin II. He was put through—perhaps the operator thought that a call like this on a day like this was normal.

Apparently he woke Augustin II out of a sound sleep as well. "Congratulations on the birth of my grandson," the sovereign said, when he had figured out who was on the line. "He'll rule this place one day. We'll all see that he gets a good start in life, won't we. What's on your mind?"

Murano began to speak of the document to be signed. But his tongue was thick, and the words seemed to bump into each other on the way out of his mouth. He really needed the paper signed. How much longer would it be?

"These things take time," said the sovereign.

Murano began another blurred, impassioned speech. "If I come to your office in the morning—"

"No," said Augustin II. "That wouldn't work. Why don't we meet at the hospital. I'll be going to see my daughter at some point in the day. Why don't we talk then."

Sounding overly jovial he added: "This is a big day for you, isn't it. Congratulations again." And he rang off.

The telephone still clutched in his hand, Murano fell asleep. He was awakened when his fingers relaxed and he dropped it. He decided to start the car but nodded off before he could turn the key, and once asleep dreamed he was drowning.

At daylight Murano drove home, made himself a café au lait, and tried to eat something. Although he had had no dinner the night before, he wasn't hungry. The thick envelope was on the sideboard. Inside it were pictures of the half-naked Gigi in his arms. Finally he went and looked at them all.

He decided he must give the illusion to Maria Cristina, to her father, to everyone, that today was as normal as any other day. He was determined to do this for as long as he could, in the hope that a solution would present itself. He went to the hospital.

Only a few journalists and photographers waited outside this morning. He smiled into the lenses, said he was proud to be the father of the royal heir, then went past the guard and up to Maria Cristina's room.

He found her sitting up, wearing a white nightgown with lace across the bosom. Her hair was combed and she wore eye shadow and a little lip gloss. She smiled at him. The baby was asleep in a bassinet beside the bed.

Murano bent over and kissed his wife. When he tried to pull away she held the back of his head and said: "Give me a good one."

So he kissed her again briefly. "How do you feel?"

"A little sore down there, but otherwise fine."

"Did you sleep?"

"I fed him a few times. Otherwise I slept okay. How about you?"

"Like a log," he lied.

"Did you get any dinner?"

"Sure."

"I worried about you. If anything happened to me you'd starve to death."

He studied his sleeping son.

"It's time for him to eat," Maria Cristina said.

He watched her slide one of the straps down her arm, then reach for the baby. She put the baby on the nipple, and they both watched him suck.

"Did your father call?" Murano asked. "Did he say when he would come by?"

"This afternoon, if he can get away."

"What does that mean? Early? Late?"

"You know my father."

He stayed as long as he could, but the sovereign did not appear. Finally he fashioned a constricted smile and excused himself. "Business," he explained.

She pouted, but allowed him to depart. When he glanced back from the doorway she was gazing dreamy eyed into the face of her baby.

That day and the next he raised what money he could, knowing all along it would not be enough. He emptied out the joint bank account. He could not believe, did not want to believe, Gigi had done this to him. What had he ever done to her? He was 25 years old and she had ruined his life. He owned six expensive tennis rackets, once the tools of his trade. He went to the national tennis club and sold them to the pros there for less than half their value. He drove out of the duchy and across the border to the nearest city on the other side, walked into a jewelry store, and sold certain of his wedding gifts, the Rolex from Maria Cristina's parents, the solid gold cuff links from one of Augustin's ministers. Maria Cristina had jewelry which he refused to touch, but there was a gold and ruby ring he had given her the day after they made love for the first time. This ring had cost him his then life savings. Although she had been appreciative, had laughed delightedly, he had never seen her wear it. So he sold that too, hoping she might not miss it. This alone had cost more than the jeweler wanted to pay for everything.

He borrowed what he could from his father, proprietor of a butcher shop; from his sister, whose husband was a government functionary; from his grandmother who was living on a small pension; from young men he had played tennis with or against. He went into banks. To his surprise two of them were eager to do business with him, and he was accorded loans without collateral, on the basis of his signature alone.

It wasn't enough. To go to the police occurred to him. Have the extortionist arrested, and after him, Gigi. But the photos would then be published. Or he could kill him. Murano had a temper, he could wreck the cameras of paparazzi. But kill someone? Could he do it? If he got caught he would be worse off, and probably the photos would come to light anyway.

He had no rich friends from whom he might borrow money. Those he had come to know, those who acted so pleased to be seen in his presence, such people were members of Maria Cristina's crowd, not his, and if he went to them the news would get back to her—and to her father.

His only other possession of value was his motorcycle, a 500 cc Honda. He had loved this machine for its noise and power, and for sentimental reasons as well, for it had played an important role in his seduction of Maria Cristina—their mutual seduction of each other. They used to go on drives at the end of a night of partying, the roads empty, never slowing down, thundering under closed shutters, and then through and out among the cliffs again, the day beginning to brighten, the cliffs turning brown and then red, him driving at great speed, Maria Cristina clinging to his back, her hair sometimes whipping against his cheek or neck. And sometimes they would come to a bit of forest and push the bike in among the trees and lie down on the pine needles, and have their way with each other as the sun rose, and the early morning traffic began to go by in the road a few feet away.

He sold the motorcycle.

It still wasn't enough. With nothing left to sell or borrow, no possibility of raising more money, he went to the hospital, found Augustin II seated beside Maria Cristina's bed, and invited him out into the hall where, though he knew this was a wrong move, he asked for a loan.

"I don't think lending you money is a very good idea," the sovereign said. "Not a good idea at all."

Murano said nothing.

"Lend money and lose a friend, they always say," commented the sovereign. "I wouldn't want a sum of money to come between you and me, would you?"

An answer from Murano seemed required, and the sovereign waited for it. "No," the young man said, "of course not."

"What do you need so much money for, anyway?"

"I can't go forward on my project until you sign that paper, and I have creditors I must pay."

"Hmm," said Augustin II.

"If you would just sign the paper I wouldn't need to borrow—"

"One can't rush these things, Son. We have to find out who these people are who want to invest with you, are they on the up-and-up, and so forth. I have men looking into that. It shouldn't be much longer."

Murano imagined himself saying to him: Either sign the paper, you sonuva bitch, or give me the money. Instead, he remained silent.

"Tell you what, Son. Have those creditors of yours call my office. I'll have someone talk to them for you, ask them to wait a little longer. How's that?"

Murano nodded, and they both went back into Maria Cristina's room.

His portable phone rang in his pocket.

He stepped out into the hall to answer, and it was Grizzard, demanding an immediate meeting.

"I'm busy right now—"

"Do you have the money?"

"I have some of it."

"Bring what you have. Now."

The new father had been spending less and less time with his wife, who had grumbled. He had constantly apologized, and he did so again now as he rushed out—apologized to his father-in-law as well.

Tonight's meeting took place in the same busy café at which he had sat with his lawyer and the two investors, Balducci and the other one. In the center of the square a fountain threw a cascade of water up into the darkness.

The tables facing the cathedral and the Guild Hall were all taken. He went into the café and there, at a table in the back, sat Grizzard.

There were barmen behind the bar, and waiters moving in and out, their trays carried shoulder high, and he handed the photographer an envelope that contained euros and dollars in almost equal amounts. Grizzard looked into the envelope and without counting it said:

"Is that all?"

"It comes to the equivalent of over fifty thousand."

"The deal was a hundred."

"To get more I need more time."

"You failed to do your part, kid. Now you're going to have to face the consequences."

It put Murano in an obvious rage, the veins in his forehead standing out, so that Grizzard immediately became conciliatory. If attacked, it would be seconds or minutes before anyone could pull Murano off him. He had no wish to get his nose broken or lose teeth. "Calm down," he said hurriedly. "Give me time to think." He spoke partly from fear, and partly because of something else, for the situation here was not exactly what Murano supposed. And now Grizzard decided he had pushed this thing as far as it would go. Additional risk had become pointless.

"You seem like a nice kid," he said, getting up from the table, beginning to back out of the café. "Maybe you have done the best you could. What do you say we call it quits?"

"The negatives," Murano said.

Grizzard thought for a minute. "Come back tomorrow night at this time," he said. "There'll be an envelope here for you."

Grizzard was moving toward the door.

"Tomorrow night," Murano said.

"Right."

Murano stood by the table clenching and unclenching his fists, watching Grizzard thread through the outdoor tables until he turned and was gone.

Unsure that the nightmare was truly over, the young man went out and slid into the Porsche. When he got home he paced back and forth worrying, knowing he could be sure of nothing until he had the negatives. Nonetheless, he began to feel relieved. He fixed a sandwich and ate it. He phoned Maria Cristina and talked to her for thirty minutes. Then he went to bed and for the first time in days slept soundly.

The next night he returned to the café at the same hour. He looked, did not see Grizzard, and so spoke to one of the barmen.

"Guy left something here for you," the barman said, and he found and handed over a manila envelope.

The young man carried the envelope out to his double-parked car. It felt thin, but he told himself this was to be expected. Negatives would take up less room than prints. He settled himself behind the wheel, opened the envelope and looked into it, and the physical reaction was immediate. His body went hot, then cold, then hot again. And weak. He couldn't breathe. Pearls of sweat ran down his back, his face. His hands were wet, his heart thumped. He was being sucked down into nothingness, or perhaps only wished to be. The weakness was so great that he clutched the wheel. To die of a heart attack perhaps felt this way, a thought that would come to him only later.

Staring out through the glass, the envelope on his lap, he waited for the weakness to go away.

In the envelope were tear sheets from a Milan magazine called *Secrets*. The English word, being foreign, had no doubt been judged to have more scandalous connotations to Italian readers than the Italian equivalent. Page after page of him with Gigi. Big pictures, small pictures, grainy ones, sharp ones, all in living color. Sweating, trembling, he paged through them. The editors had thrown none away, it seemed.

Pool water scintillating around their heads, to set the scene.

Then a close-up of them kissing, followed by the bra removal scene, as if it had come after the kiss instead of before.

A bare breast in his hand. Well it had happened. And, after that, bare breasts in every shot. A double-page spread framing another kiss or perhaps the same one, but it looked more soulful, more endless by far on the two pages than it had seemed to him in real life.

He did not even notice at first that in some of the pictures his swim trunks had disappeared—airbrushed out of the shot—so that he looked nude himself.

These were proofs—the word *prova* was stamped all over them—but there was also a date. Publication would occur in three days' time.

In the morning he brought Maria Cristina and the baby home from the hospital. Or rather he brought them to the palace where clothes had been laid out. In the Blue Room under a massive chandelier the royal photographer waited to take mother and baby's official photos. In addition to gracing public buildings, they would be sold, mostly in the form of postcards, at all the curio stands. No one asked the father to be part of the picture. Murano stood out from under the chandelier watching.

The photo session took about two hours, after which the young husband and father drove his wife and infant son home. He found that a woman from the palace was already installed in the villa. She would do the cooking, cleaning, and laundry during the first few weeks while Maria Cristina got her strength back. She would even get up with the baby in the night, if necessary, she told them. Maria Cristina smiled and thanked her, but no, she'd rather have the baby in its bassinet beside her bed, she said.

But the woman's presence meant they were never alone until night.

At last husband and wife were in their bedroom, the door closed. Maria Cristina reclined against the headboard with the baby at her breast.

"There's a magazine coming out that's mostly about me."

Maria Cristina laughed. "Another one?"

Murano kept hoping his phone would ring, and it would be Grizzard giving him more time, telling him that the proofs were only a threat. That if he raised more money the pictures would not appear.

"Are you preparing me for it?"

Murano nodded.

"What are you so nervous about? What can they say they haven't said already. Are you having an affair with the queen of England now? Have you turned into a homosexual? Nobody believes those magazines."

"Well —"

"How was it with the queen, by the way?"

"People might believe what they say this time."

"Forget about it."

She was smiling down at the nuzzling baby.

A little later, leaning over, she placed the baby in the bassinet, then reached to turn out the light. In the dark she snuggled into the crook of her husband's arm and he judged by her breathing that she was soon asleep.

The next day she spoke to him several times of the national holiday. She was looking forward to it. She would stand on the balcony with her mother and father, with her husband and son, and she and the baby would be presented to the populace. She was a woman now, not a girl. She was somebody's mother, and she wanted everyone to see her in this new role.

A woman came from the palace with the dress Maria Cristina was to wear on the balcony. There were a number of fittings, and Murano watched some of them. The woman worked with a row of pins in her mouth. At times Maria Cristina pirouetted this way and that, patting her tummy and admiring herself in the full-length mirror. She had a good distance to go yet, she said over her shoulder, but look, she was already getting her figure back.

The presentation scene was to take place at noon the following day. The parades, the dancing in the streets, would have been under way for several hours by then.

The magazine would have been on the stands for several hours as well.

The next morning Murano woke early. Maria Cristina's dress hung in a plastic bag from the closet door and was visible in the first light. Even the baby was not yet awake.

Murano dressed and left the house.

There was a newspaper kiosk at the edge of the public gardens that sold papers and magazines from all over Europe, and he was standing beside it when the truck pulled up to drop that day's bundle onto the pavement.

The proprietor was just opening up. Murano broke open the bundle and rummaged through until he found and pulled loose what he was looking for. He thrust money at the proprietor, and ran back to the Porsche, the engine of which was still running. His tires squealed, and he was gone.

The proprietor had recognized him of course, and he went now to the bundle to see what had so attracted his illustrious customer. When he saw what it was he gazed in a bemused sort of way in the direction Murano's car had taken, and wished he had ordered many more copies of that week's *Secrets*.

Murano steered the Porsche up into the high mountains. The road wound through gorges along a river, climbing all the time, heading toward ski stations that would be empty at this time of year. He drove through several of them. Some of the hotels looked closed, most of the lifts stationary, but the village stores were open and there were people in the cafés under the trees. He found a logging road that climbed still higher, and followed it, and when it petered out he locked the car and started hiking. He met no one. He had nothing with him to eat but was not hungry. When he got thirsty he found a stream and drank from his cupped hand. The sun rose higher and he was hot, even under the trees. He tied his sweater around his waist.

By the time the sun began to descend he was above the tree line. There was nothing to protect him from the wind, and each time he stopped moving he was cold, sometimes very cold. He found a kind of cave and sat in it shivering, but out of the wind. Darkness came down on him there. He rolled his sweater into a ball, and put it under his head and slept. About four A.M. he awoke freezing and put the sweater on and sat up for the rest of the night.

In the morning he went over the shoulder of that mountain and down the other side. He picked berries off trees and ate them, and found mushrooms that did not look poisonous to him, and if they were he didn't care, and picked them and ate his fill. He tramped around all day, climbing, descending, and never saw a soul or heard a sound except for the wind, an occasional bird, and once a jet fighter plane swooping low. In late afternoon he came to a refuge belonging to the alpine club whose door was not locked. He went inside and found bunks and blankets.

He sat outside watching the sun go down. When it was dark he wrapped himself in a blanket in a bunk, and began to wonder if he could find his way out of these mountains, most of which were as indistinguish-able one from the other as were the waves of the sea. He was thoroughly lost, but that was the least of his worries, and he fell asleep.

The mountains could not hide him indefinitely. Sooner or later he would have to go down, face Maria Cristina and her parents and the world, and he knew this, so on the third morning he started back to civi-lization, if he could find it. The mountains looked more alike than he had ever imagined. Gazing around at them was like looking for landmarks in the sky. He tramped and tramped. At midday the sun disappeared, and he had nothing at all on which to orient himself.

Finally he came in sight of a line of stilled chairlifts. They hung over his head as he climbed the mountain under them, and when he came to the top he could see the village at the bottom of another line of chairlifts, and he started down.

The hardest part was finding the logging road where he had left his car.

He was unshaven, dirty, and every muscle ached, and he got behind the wheel and started back the way he had come, descending in switch-backs, following the river through the gorges. Once he stopped in a vil-lage where he ate a sandwich and drank a beer, which was all he had money to pay for.

It was night when he reached his villa. He wanted a shave, a shower, and a change of clothes, and then perhaps he and Maria Cristina could begin to talk it out. The mountains behind him had somehow given him hope. He did not want to lose this woman. He would fight to keep her. He would fight whatever his father-in-law would decree and he would keep her.

His remote control opened the big doors and he drove in through them but as he did so he noted that no lights burned inside the villa, and that all the shutters were closed. When he pulled under the carport he noted a neat stack of cartons and suitcases. The suitcases were his, he saw, and when he pulled open one of the cartons it proved to contain books and records belonging to him; others contained his clothes.

He ran to the front door but his key would not open it. Peering closely he saw that the lock had been changed. He went to the door that led from the garden into the kitchen. In the dim light that lock too shone brand new.

So he couldn't get into his own house. It wasn't his house anymore. Well, it had never been. He hadn't owned it, and neither had Maria Cristina. The palace owned the house, meaning his father-in-law owned it.

All this amounted to still more defeats piled on top of a week's worth, and at first his only reaction was humiliation. Then he began to get angry. Using the vines and the drainpipe for hand and footholds he scaled the wall to the balcony outside the bedroom he had shared with Maria Cristina, and there forced open the shutter. Once inside he opened every shutter in the house, and all the windows, and turned on all the lights.

He phoned the palace and asked for Maria Cristina, but the operator recognized his voice and refused to put him through.

He went out to the cartons and brought inside what he needed. After that he shaved, showered, put on clean clothes, closed up the house again, and drove to the palace. A gigantic national flag, illuminated by spotlights, flew above the battlements, the wind beating at it, and a gaggle of tourists stood staring at its walls.

Murano came across the esplanade at great speed and approached the family entrance, but the guard came out of the box and would not raise the barrier. Stepping around to Murano's window he was polite but firm. He couldn't let him in. He had been ordered not to. He would lose his job.

Murano considered standing in front of the palace and screaming Maria Cristina's name until she came out.

"I know what you're probably thinking," the guard said. "Better not. The police have been ordered to arrest you if you make any sort of demonstration."

This announcement defeated Murano for the moment, and he backed up, made a U-turn, and drove away.

He went to his parents' house where he rang the bell.

"Could I stay here for a few days?" he asked his mother when she came to the door.

"Come in," she said. "Of course you can."

His father stood in the hallway behind her. "Nice mess you got yourself into," he said. "You got a real zipper problem, don't you." He shook his head in disgust. "You had everything in the world going for you, and you threw it all away over some slut. I hope she was worth it."

CHAPTER
VI

VINCE CONTE LIVED at 1 West 67th Street, the building called Des Artistes, one of the classic New York addresses known as much by name as by number. Many of the apartments were two-story studios with northern light, formerly popular with artists, few of whom in the last 30 years could afford to live there. They had been succeeded by famous people — actors, politicians, Wall Street dealers. It was a landmark building, very expensive, and not the kind of place in which a New York cop was expected to reside. Nonetheless Conte was there, living alone now in a duplex apartment that was, by New York standards, princely. His entrance door gave onto a large foyer which also served as a dining room, with a kitchenette beside it. Ahead was a nice-sized living room whose ceiling was two stories high, one entire wall being windows that had become, after years and years of New York grime, more or less opaque. They overlooked, where one could see out, lower buildings in back. Upstairs was a bedroom, a large enough bathroom, and closets.

Since the day Anna moved out, Conte had not been doing much housework. Besides, he was often away on cases. At present, newspapers and magazines nearly covered his sofa, and on the coffee table stood an unwashed mug. A side table was obscured by folders in an unstable pile, a landslide waiting to happen. A pillowcase stuffed with sheets and soiled shirts had nestled itself into an armchair some days ago and was still awaiting transport to the laundry.

His flat, once ample for two people and considered both elegant and comfortable, seemed to have become cluttered and small.

He had spent the previous week shuttling between Little Rock and St. Louis, setting up one case, resolving another. The Little Rock case involved a furniture factory. About once a week in the middle of the night a truck would back up to the dock, and caseloads of merchandise would be loaded on board: bedroom sets, dinettes, whatever. Some of it would later turn up at auction houses throughout the state, selling at half price or less. How the rest was disposed of Conte did not yet know. He had looked over the factory on a Sunday, all the machines stilled, moving through the mechanical silence, through alternating odors of machine oil and wood shavings. Having called in the agents he wanted, he had explained the parameters of the case as he saw it, had assigned them various roles, and had gone on to St. Louis. Days later, on the way home, he had stopped in again, had met with agents and client again, making sure that the case was progressing as it should.

The St. Louis case was still another clothing factory being looted by its employees. The women were punching out with the latest fashions stuffed into the big handbags they all favored. The men would roll stolen trousers around their calves, pull their socks up over them, and then nonchalantly stroll out. Someone had told them not to wear or sell anything until they saw that particular model on sale in the shops, which they obeyed. Which also posited a mastermind among them. Conte had got confessions from more than 20 workers, including the supposed genius, a 23-year-old cutter, which did not mean he had found everybody. When the loudspeaker announced that all handbags would henceforth be searched, many of the women suddenly had to go to the bathroom, and shortly after that it was discovered that the toilets in the ladies' room had become stopped up.

For Conte it was another disquieting experience. The felons he had dealt with in his prior life had needed urgently to be taken off the street, and he had done it. Most had been violent men, and some were sociopaths. They were aberrations. But the men and women with whom he came in contact in this new job were not aberrations. They were ordinary Americans, most of them between 20 and 25 years old. And they were all stealing, whole factory workforces of them, which they justified by saying "well, everybody does it."

What has happened to America, Conte kept asking himself. But he had no answers.

In his kitchenette he went to his fridge, not remembering what its shelves might hold, bent over, and peered in. There was some sliced ham which smelled all right when he sniffed it, so he got bread out of the freezer, toasted it, and then fixed himself a ham and Swiss cheese sandwich, and popped a beer.

So that was lunch.

Afterward he took the subway down to the office, for he had reports to write, and the expense bills for his entire team to sort out.

Probe Consultations had most of a floor high up in a tower on Times Square. Conte's office was spare. Except for some framed newspaper clippings its walls were bare. The clippings showed him being congratulated by the mayor and various police commissioners after cases he had broken during his nearly 15 years as a cop. They were there to impress any prospective clients who might wander in, but mostly they served to remind him of what he no longer had and was.

He often thought he should spruce up this office. He thought he should clean up his apartment too, but so far hadn't done either.

He was dictating the first of his reports to his secretary when Prescott, the former prosecutor who was one of the partners, came in. He was much older than Conte, a big man in a white shirt, his sleeves rolled up over hairy forearms. When he moved his shoulders his tie swayed.

"You did a good job in Chicago," Prescott said, "St. Louis too. Congratulations."

"Well," said Conte warily, "it worked out."

It was Prescott who administered the firm, and Conte did not entirely trust him.

"In St. Louis, the client had all those young people arrested," Prescott said. "I talked to him this morning."

"Arrested?" said Conte.

"He seemed quite pleased."

"I don't think he should have had them arrested."

"Why not, they were thieves."

"He's the one should have been arrested. He put in no controls at all. He was practically asking them to steal. In law enforcement terms, the situation was practically entrapment. He made it so easy some of his people couldn't help themselves."

"I hope you didn't talk this way in front of him."

"No, of course not. But if he hadn't made it so easy they wouldn't steal. Most of them wouldn't."

"Yes," said Prescott. "In a perfect world—"

"These owners should be putting in controls, not having people arrested. You know as well as I do what jails are like."

"Sounds like you don't approve of what we do here."

After a moment Conte decided to say: "The clients are pleased. That's the main thing."

"Would you excuse us a moment, Mary?" Prescott said to the secretary.

And then, when the young woman had gone out: "What I came in here for was, we have a new case that sounds right up your alley."

"Good. What is it?"

"What do you know about the crowned heads of Europe, Vince?"

The notion of "crowned heads" was amusing to Prescott, for he grinned.

Conte too smiled, possibly realizing that he had come perilously close to an open confrontation with his boss. "The subject hasn't been one of my principal concerns," he said.

"There aren't many in circulation anymore," agreed Prescott. "And those that are left, with the possible exception of the queen of England, don't amount to much."

"Even she is a relic from a former time."

"Ever hear of a guy called Augustin II?"

"Sure. Everyone's heard of him."

"A tiny kingdom in the mountains. Second smallest throne in Europe."

"Which he rules with an iron hand, I hear." There were five or six of these miniature kingdoms in Europe.

"Socially," Conte added, "these people still have clout, I guess. Otherwise they're anachronisms, aren't they?"

"He called me yesterday. Or rather his wife did. They want an Italian-speaking detective. I suggested you. As soon as possible, by the way."

"Why Italian?"

"I don't know."

"What's the case about?"

"She wouldn't say. She's a duchess, I think. You address her as Lady Charlotte."

"Somebody steal the royal silver?"

"Secrecy is very important, apparently. They don't want to bring the police into it. She didn't want anyone to know she called me, either."

Conte said: "Another hush-hush case."

"Secret, yeah."

"They're all hush-hush."

"She sounded extremely agitated."

"Clients are always agitated too."

"Wanted you on the next plane. She's already wired money into our account."

Judging from Prescott's demeanor, it must have been a great deal of money. But the administrator did not say how much, and Conte did not ask. Instead he said: "Hmmm."

"If they're willing to pay fees in advance it's important to them," said Prescott.

"Do they have an airport? I don't think so."

"Too small."

"How do I get there?"

"Mary can set it up for you."

"What do you think it is?"

"If I had to guess?"

"Yes."

"Blackmail, maybe."

"Blackmail?"

"She didn't say anything overt. But behind her words I detected a whiff of something. A whiff of blackmail, maybe. That she didn't want to talk about. Perhaps I'm imagining things."

"You say Lady Charlotte called? Why didn't the husband call? He's the big cheese, isn't he?"

"I imagine you'll get your answer when you get there." He put his hand on Conte's shoulder. "I know you've been working hard, and I'm sorry to send you off again so soon."

"Not at all," said Conte. "I look forward to it, whatever it is."

"After what you've been through lately, the divorce and all, perhaps a case like this will be nice for you."

Conte was silent.

"You have no other cases about to break right now, do you?"

"Nothing about to break, no."

"If you can close this one off quickly, why don't you take a few days' vacation while you're over there?"

"We'll see."

"Picture yourself in a sailboat on the Mediterranean with some lovely young thing whose life you've just saved. Or climbing a mountain with an Italian girl on the other end of the rope, maybe a French girl. Not an American girl anyway, and—"

The idea made Conte smile.

"That's the kind of thing you need right now," Prescott said. "Crack this one, then take as much time off as you need."

Prescott was trying to give the impression that the emotional well-being of his employees was important to him. Despite himself, Conte was touched. "Well—" he said.

"No, I mean it." And then: "You'll go tonight, of course."

"No, I can't," said Conte.

"I promised that you'd be there tomorrow."

"The next day," Conte said. "Today is taken. Tonight too. I can't go until tomorrow."

"Why not?" Conte had felt Prescott stiffen. Like the First Dep, he was a man who did not like to be resisted by subordinates.

"Personal matters," the detective said.

"It's important," said Prescott.

So that's what the guy's praise and kindness were for, Conte thought. Soften me up the better to push me around. "Important" to Prescott meant money. How much had he asked them for, anyway?

But Conte was not in the mood to be pushed around by anybody. Like a formerly great player, he had been cut from the big team and had had to catch on wherever he could—meaning this job here. His focus had been shifted from the crimes and depravity of the greatest city in the world, to petty thievery in a pants factory in St. Louis. In his former life he had arrested rapists and killers, sometimes at the point of a gun, often enough at great risk to himself, and afterward had been obliged as best he could to console overwrought victims. Now he was being asked to fly 4,000 miles at the behest of some silly duchess. In his own eyes he had become a minor leaguer. Worse, he saw no way back.

In addition he did have personal matters to attend to this afternoon and tonight.

"Sorry," he told Prescott, "but I can't go until tomorrow."

Prescott's eyes narrowed. "What is it?"

"Stuff I can't put off. Sorry."

They argued a bit longer, before Prescott went out shaking his head.

From the office Conte went to Roosevelt Hospital, where his mother was recovering—or not recovering—from a hysterectomy. She looked a little better than a week ago, not much. His father sat beside the bed holding her hand. He looked worse than she did, knowing, as she presumably did not, that her cancer was incurable.

Conte pretended to be cheerful, which seemed to please his mother. For an hour he let her cluck over him. Was he getting enough sleep, was he eating properly, she wanted to know—even adding that she had never liked Anna who was not good enough for him, it was a marriage he was better off out of. And how was his new job?

"Great, Mom," he told her. What a fascinating job it was, he told her, he couldn't be happier. He was off to Europe tomorrow, great case, there was a duchess involved and—

His father sat silent and glum, but his mother brightened. His mother liked to hear about duchesses.

"Come by the restaurant tonight," his father said when he rose to go. "Have dinner. We can talk."

"I can't, Pop."

"Let your father give you a good meal," his mother said.

Conte, who had a dinner date that night with a woman he hardly knew, did not want to take her to the family restaurant where he would not be allowed to pay, and where his father would hover over the table asking if they wanted this or that.

"When I come back, Pop, I promise. I'll only be gone a few days." He had no idea how long he'd be gone. "By then Mom will be home." Would she be? He didn't know, and doubted anyone did. "We can all have dinner together."

His next stop was a nursing home in Long Island City where Salvatore Leone, his ex-father-in-law, was confined. Since Anna was paying the bills, it was a high-class nursing home, but it was a nursing home nonetheless, and Leone, he knew, felt a prisoner there.

Conte knew about prisons. Not a nice feeling.

The old man was sitting in a chair reading when Conte came in. "Did our welcoming committee greet you at the elevator?" Leone wanted to know. "The drooler in the wheelchair? He's a beauty, that one. Sit down, Vince, I'm glad to see you."

The old man had always been nice to him, had in fact treated him as a son.

"What's new in the world?" Leone wanted to know. "The conversation in here is usually about bowel movements. I'm hoping you can do better than that."

So they talked about the mess that was the war in Iraq, about an administration that bungled nearly everything it touched.

When Conte rose to go, Leone asked: "What do you hear from my daughter?"

"Not much," Conte admitted.

"She calls me once in a while. She sees to it that I get the best in here. But the best would be her, and they can't give me that."

"Well," said Conte lamely, "she's very busy."

"Me too, trying to keep out of the way of the wheelchairs."

A month ago Leone had fallen against the bathtub and knocked himself cold. He was not found until the tub overflowed and water seeped into the apartment below.

"I'd like to go home, Vince. You see any chance I can convince her I'm competent to live alone?"

"I'll talk to her," Conte promised, and shook hands with his ex-father-in-law, and went out. When he got back to his flat he dialed Anna's number, which was a difficult thing to make himself do. To his surprise she took the call. But when he asked how she was she said:

"What do you want?"

He spent ten minutes on the phone with her talking about her father, but did not think he reached her. "You should go see him once in a while," he said finally, and rang off.

That night he took a woman named Natalie Bernstein to dinner in a midtown restaurant. She was about 30 years old, divorced, an assistant district attorney who worked out of the Manhattan DA's homicide bureau. He had met her on a case some years previously, and then again at someone's house a few weeks ago. She was tall and thin, and wore a black dress. It had been more than nine years since he had gone out with a woman he didn't know, and he had forgotten, if he ever knew, what was expected of him. He certainly did not know what pose to strike. He rang her bell and handed over the bouquet of roses he had been carrying. The bouquet seemed to surprise her. She had opened the door with her hand-bag over her shoulder, her keys in her other hand, obviously ready to lock up and go, and now had to go back inside, her surprise still showing, and put the flowers in water. So Conte realized that the flowers had not been a great idea.

In the taxi, both were mostly silent, and in the restaurant it did not get much better. She must have been ill at ease too, for she began to de-scribe the cases she was working on, each one more lurid than the next. She talked and talked. A wooden smile on his face, Conte listened, ask-ing questions from time to time to keep her talking. There was certainly nothing about himself he wished to tell her, not that she asked.

When they came out after dinner they stood indecisively on the side-walk, then Conte asked if she would mind if he sent her home in a cab; he was going to Europe tomorrow as he had already told her, and had so much to do to get ready. But she cut him off, saying: "Sure."

He flagged down a cab and put her into it, promising to call her again as soon as he got back, then thrust a $20 bill in at the driver saying: "Keep the change."

Installed in the backseat, Natalie rolled the window down. "Thanks for the flowers," she said with a smile.

The taxi motored off, and that was that.

Conte went home and began to pack.

CHAPTER

VII

BEFORE GOING TO BED, Lady Charlotte padded in slippers along the hall to her daughter's room—the room Maria Cristina had inhabited as a teenager, and to which she had now returned.

Light still showed beneath the door, so Lady Charlotte knocked, and waited.

"Who is it?"

"It's your mother."

Still fully dressed, Maria Cristina was sitting on the bed with a wastebasket between her knees. The walls, Lady Charlotte saw, were bare. She had expected to see rows of dolls on shelves, rock stars staring down from the walls, for the room had never been redecorated. But the dolls were gone, she didn't know where. The rock posters had been torn down, furled, then jammed into the basket where they protruded like umbrellas from a stand. There were CDs in the basket as well, and more CDs piled beside the girl. She looked up as her mother entered, then read the cover of the CD in her hand before dropping it into the basket on top of the others.

Her daughter, Lady Charlotte speculated, was perhaps trying to jettison a former part of her life. Which signified what? The final end of her girlhood? That she carried a woman's burdens now? Lady Charlotte didn't know what it signified. One couldn't jettison parts of one's life. They were there forever.

The real change in the room was the presence of the baby, plus its paraphernalia: the layette, the crib, the boxes of diapers scattered about.

"You haven't been eating," she said to her daughter. "You have to eat or you'll get sick. You'll be no good to your baby if you get sick."

Maria Cristina nodded, picked up another CD, read the label, and dropped it into the basket.

"You haven't been sleeping either."

Maria Cristina looked at her.

"I hear you moving around. You're up half the night."

"I'll try to be quieter."

"A few good nights' sleep and things will look a lot brighter, believe me."

"When the baby wakes up I have to feed him."

"That's what you have Mrs. Gladstone for. So you can sleep nights."

Maria Cristina picked up another CD.

"I'll ask her to come upstairs," her mother said. "Let her take the baby tonight."

Maria Cristina gave a wry smile and shook her head.

"So you can sleep through. Let me call her."

"Please, Mama."

Maria Cristina had got to her feet. "It's time to feed him now."

There was a baby bottle on the dresser beside the crib. She picked it up, then lifted the sleeping baby from his crib, draping him over her shoulder. "I have to heat this," the girl said.

"I thought you were breast-feeding him."

"The last couple of days I haven't had much milk."

"Because you're not sleeping properly."

Without answering, the girl went past her. Lady Charlotte heard her go down the hall toward the small kitchen the family sometimes used. There were no servants on this floor at this hour, none on duty at all except for the telephone operator downstairs.

Seated on the bed, Lady Charlotte waited for her daughter and tried to think of what to say when she came back, what advice to offer.

Now 60 years old, Lady Charlotte was a small, quiet woman who had almost never raised her voice to her children, and had seldom made her opinions known to anyone. She was nonetheless the power behind her husband's rise to prominence. She was the daughter of a duke, a cousin of the queen of England, and she had been advised not to marry Augustin II, the then impecunious sovereign of a miniature realm that had been mismanaged for years by his father. The place was shabby, she had been warned. It was out of date, nearly bankrupt, and of course tiny. Augustin himself was renowned only as a playboy, and was not received in the other courts of Europe. He and his realm were considered worse than anachronisms. They were of no importance whatever.

Lady Charlotte, who was not a beauty, had found Augustin dashing; she had had few other suitors, and so she had ignored her family and peers, and had married him anyway, and as an authentic member of the British royal family she had brought with her into the marriage a different kind of dowry: respectability, prestige, and access to people with money. The young Augustin had had plans for renovating his realm even then, but it was Lady Charlotte who made implementing them possible. Over the years the realm had grown not only more and more famous, but as rich as any of the other miniature states of Europe, and richer than most.

Her daughter Maria Cristina, who had been born relatively late in Charlotte's life and marriage, had always been and still was her baby. The child had grown into the beauty her mother had never been, and although she sometimes made Lady Charlotte sick with worry, she had spirit, and this her mother admired. The girl regularly stood up to her father, something the boy Leon never dared do, something Lady Charlotte herself could manage only rarely.

Now, sitting on the bed, she realized Maria Cristina had been in the kitchen a long time, obviously wanting to avoid whatever her mother might choose to say to her, and so wasn't coming back soon. This would have been a disappointment to any mother, and was to Charlotte. She could have gone into the kitchen of course, but decided not to, and instead went back to the sitting room outside the bedroom she shared with Augustin. Her husband was already in bed; she could glimpse him through the partly open door. There was a pencil in his teeth and he was studying reports.

Charlotte sat down in an armchair opposite a blank television screen, and stared into space. In the last hour she had allowed herself to become extremely troubled. Her daughter, obsessed with the loss of Antonio Murano, had fallen, it seemed to her, into a state very like grief, as if a beloved had died. It had gone on much too long, Lady Charlotte thought. It wasn't normal, unless there had existed between them a level of trust—Lady Charlotte would never have called it love—higher than she had suspected. If so, then the girl's pain was not going to go away anytime soon, not by itself. Something had to be done before her health became seriously affected—the baby's health too, most likely.

Some ideas moved through Lady Charlotte's head, and she examined them. Suppose proof could be found that Tony had been carrying on a long-term love affair with the woman in the magazine. If judiciously obtained, and if exposed to her daughter with love and care, such proof could possibly effect a cure in a hurry.

But suppose Tony had been more or less innocent. This was a difficult notion for a mother—for any woman—to entertain. But suppose somebody had set out to ruin him, ruin his marriage, by throwing that woman in his lap. This posited an elaborate plot, and Tony wasn't a big enough target to merit one. So if he wasn't the target, who was? Her daughter?

But to her mother, Maria Cristina didn't seem big enough either.

These ideas led Lady Charlotte to other questions, all of which were without answers. Suppose the target was her husband, or the nation. Or even herself, as a means of further discrediting the British royal family; she could hear the malicious tongues wagging from here—can none of those royals manage their children? Herself as target was a bit far-fetched perhaps. More likely the target was Augustin and the nation, the two being virtually interchangeable. In addition, discrediting Augustin could be counted on to revive all those tales of his years as a playboy. It could cause real estate values to drop, their own holdings included. Investments could

fall off. There would be financial killings to be made that would not benefit themselves or the nation. Some of the banks would leave. The fragile
structure that Augustin had worked so hard to build up could collapse.

Where the realm was concerned, the sovereign was usually percep-
tive, and sometimes suspicious to the point of paranoia, but he seemed to
have asked himself none of the questions she was asking herself now. Augustin had been so glad to get rid of Tony that he had become blind.

Lady Charlotte got up from her armchair and began to pace.

There was one central fact. She needed to know—Augustin needed
to know—more about what had happened and why. For Maria Cristina's
sake certainly, but for their own sake too.

It was at this point in her brooding that she came to a certain decision. Some time ago in an English magazine she had read an article
about Probe Consultations of New York. Probe was not only international
in scope, but numbered multinational corporations, and even govern-
ments, among its clients. Its agents had had some famous successes.

Most important of all, it prided itself on its discretion.

After closing the door on Augustin in the bedroom, and turning the
TV on to mask whatever noise she was about to make, she lifted the telephone and got Probe's number from information. Since there was a six-
hour time difference, she thought she might catch somebody in New
York still at his desk.

Which she did. A man named Prescott came on the line, and they
had a discussion about sending a detective to investigate a matter that was
sensitive. How soon could the detective get here? As she spoke she could
picture the sovereign's wrath when he found out about this. But her
daughter's happiness was at stake, she believed. Her husband's well-being
also, whether he realized it or not. These notions gave her courage, but
not very much courage. She refused to answer Prescott's many questions.
She told him she would explain everything to the detective. When could
she expect him? They discussed terms. She agreed to them. She said she
would wire the money tomorrow as soon as the banks opened.

She did not tell Augustin what she had done, not that night, nor the next day either, postponing his rage as long as possible. She did tell her daughter. She went into her room and sat with her and promised her that the detective would do his work and all questions would be answered. The girl seemed to brighten immediately. A smile came on, the first in days, as if any thorough investigation would somehow prove the innocence of her husband, an outcome that Lady Charlotte considered unlikely. Nonetheless, it heartened her considerably to see the girl show some animation again.

"Now all I have to do is tell your father," said Lady Charlotte.

"Do you want me to tell him?"

Lady Charlotte patted her hand. "No, that's my job."

It took her two days to work up the nerve to face Augustin. Probably she would have put it off even longer, but the detective was due to arrive any minute.

She walked into his office.

He did not greet her, nor even look up from the dossier he was studying. He said: "What do you want?"

Bad start. So she stalled.

"Do you know where Tony is?" she asked.

"I'm too busy to talk about that now."

"But do you know?"

"Yes. Look, Charlotte—"

"Where?"

"Living with his parents. Please—"

"How do you know?"

"There isn't much goes on here I don't know. He never leaves the house. Ashamed to, I imagine."

Lady Charlotte said: "You might have informed me."

"Why?"

"I have a right to know such things."

"You have a right to know what I choose to tell you."

Lady Charlotte was silent, eyes on the floor.

In a milder tone Augustin said: "He sold his motorcycle, his watch, his cuff links, and a ring belonging to Maria Cristina. He also borrowed from banks."

"Why?"

"To get money to run off with that bimbo, what else."

"Then why hasn't he done it?"

"How should I know."

"Maybe it was to pay a blackmailer," suggested Lady Charlotte.

"Rubbish."

"Suppose he was being blackmailed," she said.

Augustin shrugged.

"Blackmail's a crime," she persisted. "The blackmailer should be arrested and prosecuted."

"I don't have time to go into this now. Charlotte—"

"This is your country. Don't you care?"

The sovereign gave a sigh of annoyance. "Difficult to prove. No witnesses, no evidence."

"There's"—she hesitated, then plunged forward—"something you need to know."

"There's nothing you could possibly tell me that I need to know, I'm busy, and I don't want you coming in here interrupting me. I've told you and told you."

"Please."

"How many times do you need to be told?"

She said: "I've done something."

This got his attention. "Done what?"

"—And you should know about it."

"What have you done?"

When she informed him that she had hired a New York detective agency to find out how those photos came to be made, and that a man named Vincent Conte—here her voice broke slightly—was due to arrive that morning—arrive perhaps any minute in fact—his face went as red as his tie.

"You did what?"

Lady Charlotte told him a second time.

He had jumped up from behind his glass slab of a desk. "Without informing me?"

"Please don't shout at me."

"Are you out of your mind?"

"I hired him and paid him. Paid his firm."

"With what?" demanded Augustin.

"Not your money. My money."

"You stupid woman."

"Somebody set those photos up."

"The photographer set them up. And it probably wasn't hard to do either."

Lady Charlotte's defiance did not last long. When she spoke, she could barely be heard. "But we don't know that for sure," she said.

"Put a girl in the way of that young man, any girl, and—"

"Please calm down."

"You're meddling in things that don't concern you."

"I'm not meddling."

"Meddle, meddle, meddle. That's all you do. You meddle. Every time my back is turned you meddle."

"There could have been a plot." She was pleading with him to listen to her. "Others could be involved. People we don't know about who put the photographer onto Tony. If so, for what reason?"

"For no reason, any reason—what does it matter. The marriage is over. Very soon we will no longer have a son-in-law, which I see as a good thing. Maria Cristina is suffering, sure, but she'll get over it, and her next husband might be someone we can be proud of."

After a momentary silence, Lady Charlotte said: "Was whoever set up those photos trying to embarrass Tony? Embarrass our daughter? I can't really believe that, can you? What would be the point?"

Augustin said: "A detective. That's all we need."

"Or was he trying to embarrass you, us, the nation? And if so, why?"

She was speaking fast to get it all in. "Or was something else being planned that hasn't happened yet, but will?"

Augustin had turned and was staring out the window.

She said: "A detective might be able to answer those questions."

"Unlikely."

"I could kill whoever did this to our daughter."

After a moment, Augustin said: "Yes, so could I."

"Maybe there's no plot, or threat, just some photos of Tony with a nude girl. Even so, we need to know exactly what happened and how and why. And Maria Cristina needs to know. Only then can she begin to get over what's been done to her." Lady Charlotte smothered a sigh of relief. She had been allowed to speak. She took a deep breath. She had been allowed to say everything that needed to be said.

"The press hears of your private detective," muttered Augustin, "we'll have the biggest scandal yet."

"This agency is very discreet. That's why I chose them."

"They'll sell the story to the press."

"I don't think so." Lady Charlotte gazed placatingly, appealingly, reassuringly at her husband.

"Do you understand the risks to my reputation?" Augustin said. "The nation's reputation? You don't or you wouldn't have pulled such a crazy stunt."

"The detective will be here any minute." She tried to project confidence in this fact—what she had done—but her chin quivered. "I've asked that he be brought directly to my office." She kept an office in another part of the palace.

"Negative," said Augustin. "He's to be brought here. No one speaks to him but me. I'll talk to him, and then send him right back to New York."

"Maria Cristina knows."

"Knows?"

"I told her. She's very pleased. You should have seen her come to life. I think we owe it to her, don't you? To ourselves too, but mostly to her."

VINCE CONTE, carrying his one small bag, came out through customs and found a liveried chauffeur holding up a placard with his name on it. He followed him out through the airport to a pastel blue Rolls-Royce. When the man held open the rear door, Conte tossed his bag onto the seat, but he got in up front.

The chauffeur looked surprised, but said nothing, and that's the way the trip was made.

Although he had never ridden in a Rolls before, chauffeurs were not new to Conte. In the NYPD, officers from sergeant on up were entitled to drivers when on duty, and their place when being driven was beside the driver, not in back. This was for two reasons: One could see better up front, and one was in reach of the radio. A commander whose view was limited, and who couldn't communicate quickly, was useless.

The front seat was the only place where ex-Captain Conte could feel comfortable.

The road was four lanes at first, and the divider was brilliant with flowers, out of which rose various types of trees, most of them evergreens. They passed through a city and out the other side, and then they were on a two-lane road that began to climb and then they were in the mountains. At the border into the duchy there were no controls, and they crossed without slowing down. They passed through hamlets where old, old houses huddled under chalet-type roofs, shutters closed against the midday sun. Sometimes Conte could gaze upward at villas, or peer below at trees standing guard over gardens full of flowers.

In all, the ride lasted almost two hours. It reminded Conte that he was in a new place on a new case. All was new to him here, and a strange sensation took hold of him: that his life was perhaps about to change. But he shrugged this off. Romantic nonsense brought on by a romantic part of the world. He was not a kid anymore. After what he had already seen these past 15 years, there was little out there that was likely to surprise him very much. He felt a bit jaded, and far older than he was. It was more probable that from here on his life was not going to change much at all. The police department was gone, his marriage was gone, and nothing was going to bring back either. There would be small changes in his life certainly, and he might someday marry again. Otherwise nothing important or severe was likely to occur, an idea he had best get used to.

The so-called palace was really a castle, he saw as they approached it. They entered the courtyard through walls thick enough to form a tunnel. As he got out of the car, Conte had the impression of being surrounded by great weight and age, and he peered up at crenellated walls. Then he was inside, following his driver through echoing halls. At length they reached the big office with the big window overlooking the big view, and Augustin came forward from behind the big glass desk. Conte, recognizing him from television, shook hands with him, and then was introduced to the other two people present, Lady Charlotte, who smiled at him, but said nothing, and a man in a dark business suit whose name was given as De Blondin, and who had only one arm, the superfluous sleeve being tucked into the pocket on that side.

The man's surviving hand shot out, the left one. As always in situations of this kind Conte did not know how to grasp it. With his own left hand or, awkwardly, with the usual right. Left to left, he thought, wondering (also as always) where the missing arm had got to. An important question. The loss of an arm was no doubt the central fact of any man's existence, and there was no way to understand who you were dealing with until you knew how and why.

Nonetheless, it was not a question he could ask immediately, and perhaps never.

"D.B. knows more about running this duchy than I do," said Augustin genially.

Other than this De Blondin's role and purpose at this meeting remained unspecified.

Conte was invited to take the chair in front of the desk, which he did.

Immediately, Augustin began a lecture about the duchy—he referred to it as the nation—what it was and what it stood for—and for the next ten minutes Conte was obliged to listen.

Lady Charlotte and the one-armed De Blondin had retreated to other chairs, her to one side of the room, him to the other, both of them behind Conte and out of his line of vision. As the minutes passed and neither spoke, it was almost possible to forget they were there.

"People think our prosperity comes from our banks, our casino, sales of our postage stamps, and from the tourists and sportsmen who spend money here," Augustin was saying. "Not so. Rather, our prosperity depends on something else entirely—on the honor of the royal family, and on the nation's never besmirched reputation."

In New York Conte had never had to deal with crowned heads, nor seen any up close, his usual clientele ranking much further down the social scale. So now, despite himself, he felt somewhat awed to find himself in this castle, this office, in what many people would consider the royal presence. It was a reaction he was not used to and did not like; it puzzled him, and in his head, as Augustin droned on, he turned it this way and that, but it only puzzled him more. At this stage of his life he thought he had seen enough of the human species not to be awed by anyone, especially not by this guy and his miniature kingdom.

The sovereign had begun to explain that the duchy's principal business was not so much gambling or tourism as what he termed "financial services." Crowded into these few streets, he said, one would find, probably, more lawyers, brokers, bankers, investors, insurance companies, all operating on an international scale, than in any other world city even ten times its size.

The sovereign was smaller than he had looked on television, he had gray hair, and he looked older than his age, which Conte knew to be 67.

Tax laws, Augustin continued, had been written that favored such people. Bank secrecy was virtually absolute.

Conte's awe, if that's what it was, was dissipating fast.

People sometimes described the nation as an offshore tax shelter, Augustin said. But this was not true. Strict legality was observed at all times.

The Picasso on the otherwise bare wall held Conte's gaze for a time, or else he studied the sovereign's knees through the inch-thick glass of the totally bare, totally uncluttered desk.

People, Augustin said, sometimes suggested that the Italian Mafia or other criminals had established dummy corporations through which they controlled the duchy so that they could hatch their schemes and launder their money—another accusation far from the truth. The truth was that he and his ministers worked night and day to assure that no criminal enterprise ever got a foothold here. Background checks were run on all foreigners attempting to make investments.

He must get those trousers pressed twice a day, Conte thought. There was no other way to assure such sharp creases.

Investors, Augustin said, all of them thoroughly checked out first, had brought in the money that had stoked the building boom—and it had been a boom. Tall buildings had gone up, 18 or 20 stories high, not skyscrapers by New York standards but immense by the standards of mountain cities such as this one.

In the silence that had been imposed upon him, Conte had begun asking himself multiple questions. He still didn't know why he was here. He didn't know who he was working for, either. Not the duchess, obviously. She was the one who had telephoned Probe in New York, but she must have done it secretly because here she wasn't allowed to open her mouth. No one was. There was only one boss in the room.

Then who was this one-armed guy?

Suddenly Augustin's tone changed and he remarked that he had need of an Italian-speaking detective. In fact, that's what his wife had asked for. "You speak Italian, I believe."

Conte said he did.

"How is it you speak Italian?"

Conte's credentials were being examined, and he was annoyed. But it couldn't be helped. He was no longer a policeman who could impose authority by flashing his shield.

"I grew up in an Italian restaurant."

"In New York?"

Conte said shortly: "Little Italy in lower Manhattan. Ever been there?"

Augustin II waited, apparently, for more details.

But Conte kept silent. His grandfather had emigrated to New York and after some years as someone else's waiter, had founded the restaurant. His son had worked in it before inheriting it, and in high school the son's son, young Vincent, had helped out too. To keep the atmosphere real the waiters were imported raw from Italy, new ones every time there was a vacancy. How was a small boy in that kind of an Italian family not to learn Italian? Later as an NYPD detective he had for a time been assigned almost exclusively to Mafia cases.

None of this, he judged, was any of Augustin's business.

The sovereign was talking volubly again, but this time in Italian, and the purpose, it seemed to Conte, was to decide how much Italian, if any, the detective actually spoke — to catch him in the lie. Italian was a useful language, the man was saying. And there used to be a local patois the common people spoke, containing a mixture of Italian, French, and some German as well, but that had pretty much died out now.

Augustin II stopped. "You understand what I said?" he asked in Italian.

Conte found the question demeaning, but he said in English, apparently amiably: "How many languages do you speak?"

"English, French, German, and Italian."

"It must be so easy."

"Easy?"

"To be rude when you speak so many."

And they smiled at each other as if both of them failed to grasp what might have been considered an insult.

This is getting off to a bad start, Conte thought.

He knew he was supposed to defer to clients, but there was too much New York cop left in him still. A detective was a man who dealt in dominance. Dominance of suspects, witnesses, complainants — whoever. One dominated them because it was the only way one could do the job. The situation here was slightly different, but not much. If he had read this man correctly, and Conte believed he had, then he had best put him on the defensive at once, or he would become impossible to deal with.

"You asked that an Italian-speaking detective be sent to you," Conte said in a slow, even voice. "You asked me if I spoke Italian, and I said I do."

Switching to Italian, Conte said: "If you believe it possible that my firm, or I myself, would amuse ourselves by lying to you, the client, about anything at all, much less about a prerequisite for whatever job you want me to do, then perhaps you should pick some other agency. There are a number of them out there."

This statement was followed by a long silence during which the two men studied each other, no expression showing on either face.

Finally Augustin II nodded.

Conte took this as the only apology of which a supreme ruler — and that's what he was, though on a small scale — was capable.

Conte decided to accept the unspoken apology. He said: "What is it you want me to do?"

"Speed and discretion," said Augustin. "That's what your firm is known for, and that's what I need."

"Why?"

Augustin pushed a magazine, opened to some poolside photos, across the desk.

Conte glanced at several pages, pushed it back, and waited.

Now Lady Charlotte said: "That magazine is published in Italy. In Milan, I believe."

Augustin said to her: "When we want your input we'll ask for it."

But Lady Charlotte, her voice on a halting, descending note, persisted. "Who made the photos? Who's behind them? Who is the girl?" Her voice trailed off. "And so forth."

Conte turned back to the duke, and waited.

Augustin said patronizingly: "My wife is sometimes subject to delusions, you'll find. She thinks the nation may be menaced in some way. I doubt it, but in this case I've decided to indulge her."

"I have the sense that there is some personal aspect that you haven't yet mentioned."

"The personal aspect is not important."

"I need to know the whole story."

This resulted in another staring contest.

"If I am to help you," Conte said, "if I am to get you the information you require, I need to know exactly what I am looking for and why."

At length Augustin II sighed. Although he began to speak, he did not at first mention his daughter's name, nor that of his son-in-law.

"Who is the young man in the photos?" Conte interrupted.

The sovereign studied his fingernails. "I'm sure you know about my son-in-law," he said finally.

"I never heard of your son-in-law, sorry to say."

The sovereign looked surprised. "He's quite well known in Europe."

"That may be."

"For all the wrong reasons, I might add." After a moment Augustin said: "He's the young man in the photos."

They looked at each other in silence.

Conte said: "And the bare breasts pressed into his chest are not your daughter's."

The sovereign had winced. His wife's reaction was unknown to Conte, who was studying Augustin closely, Lady Charlotte being out of his line of vision.

He said: "So tell me about your son-in-law."

"Name's Antonio Murano. He's a failed tennis pro who became a lifeguard."

"And then your son-in-law."

"Yes."

"You make him sound like a lout."

"He left school at sixteen. He's got no family behind him, no formation. Father's a butcher."

"And he runs after other women," said Conte. It was a question, but Augustin II let it pass without comment.

"Recently," said Lady Charlotte, "he came up with the idea for a luxury health spa. Did a great deal of work on it, which is all to his credit."

Conte had the impression she was trying in a minor way to defend her son-in-law.

Augustin said to her: "I thought I told you to stay out of this."

What kind of man, Conte asked himself, embarrasses his wife in front of strangers? What did this tell you about him?

The sovereign said: "Murano had some studies made, plans drawn up. The project had possibilities."

He turned his chair and gazed out the window for a time, then turned back. "For my daughter's sake I wanted to see the young man get a career going. I wanted to see him succeed."

Conte, who was receiving vibes he could not sort out, did not believe him.

"The spa idea is all moot now, of course. Unless I decide to go forward with it myself."

Sounding surprised, Lady Charlotte said: "I didn't know you were thinking in that direction."

Augustin stared at her until her gaze dropped, and she again fell silent.

"Out of nowhere two Italians turn up and tell Tony they want to invest with him. Does that seem suspicious to you?"

"I don't know. Does it?"

Conte waited. Underneath the thick glass desk the sovereign's right knee had begun to twitch.

"Do you think the fact that he was my son-in-law had anything to do with their interest in him?"

"Could be," said Conte.

"It would not have made sense to let the project go forward. Affairs of state take precedence over affairs of the heart, eh?"

He must use that line a lot, Conte thought. He said: "I'm not sure I understand."

"Two unknown men from Italy. If it were a setup, Tony would never see it. He was getting his legal and financial advice from a lawyer I've known for years. Fellow would sell out to the highest bidder. To two gentlemen from Italy, for instance. Wouldn't even hesitate."

"So you held up approval?"

"Tony was too young, too naive, to get involved in such a project. Perhaps I might have put in someone to run it for him. To get my approval he might have been willing to accept such a person. That was one of my ideas. I was too busy to devote much time to the project, however."

While your son-in-law twisted in the wind, Conte guessed.

After searching through the only dossier on his glass desk, the sovereign pushed across a sheet of paper, and Conte took it. "The men from Italy. Their names, addresses, and phone numbers."

Conte wondered why he was hearing so much about the two Italians. "Are you telling me they had something to do with your son-in-law and the nude broad?"

"You should check them out."

"We want to know about those magazine photos," said Lady Charlotte stubbornly. "Who is the young woman? What was going on between her and Tony?"

Conte was listening more to interior vibes than to the protestations of these two. He turned to Lady Charlotte. "Am I looking for something to save the marriage?" he asked.

"No," said the sovereign, before she could answer. "The marriage is over."

"Whatever you would find out about those photos we would want to know," Lady Charlotte said in a low voice.

"The divorce will go through on schedule," said Augustin.

This produced another long silence.

"The state may or may not be menaced in some way," the sovereign said finally. His face was expressionless. "That's what you should concentrate on."

Conte stood up. "All right. I'd best get to work."

"You'll stay in the palace, of course," said the sovereign. "I understand Lady Charlotte has prepared a suite for you."

Conte had no wish to be under the thumb of these two. "Thank you, but I'd prefer a hotel. I've reserved at the Crowne Plaza."

"As you wish," said Lady Charlotte.

"The magazine is published in Milan," stated the sovereign. "And those two investors, whoever they are, have business there supposedly. So Milan is where you'll want to start."

As yet there was no connection whatever between the damning photos and the Italian investors. Conte wondered if Augustin was trying to send him off on a false trail, and if so why? He picked up the magazine and studied the photos, noting no credit line. "I don't suppose you know the photographer's name?"

"No."

"The girl's name?" Although she appeared in every photo, her face behind all that hair was difficult to see.

"Every journalist in Europe has been trying to find out who she is."

"It would help to know her name and where to find her."

Augustin shrugged. "A bimbo. What difference does it make?"

Conte studied the photos a moment, then said: "I'll start with your son-in-law, I believe."

"That seems a waste of effort to me."

"I'll keep this, if I may." Conte thrust the magazine into the pocket of his bag. "On second thought, I think I should start with your daughter."

"My daughter?"

The sovereign could not be allowed to dictate the avenues of the investigation.

"My daughter knows nothing about any of this."

Conte said gently: "I think we should find out what she knows, don't you?"

They eyed each other.

"She may not be strong enough."

"She's not an invalid, is she?"

"No, but—"

"How old is she?" said Conte, who had been studying dossiers on the plane and knew much about Maria Cristina. "Twenty-two, twenty-three. They recover quickly at that age."

"But—"

"Is she here in the palace? Do you have an office in which we could meet? I suggest you call her up, tell her I'd like to see her."

This was followed by a long pause.

"Pick up the phone there, why don't you?"

"I'll go with you," said Lady Charlotte.

Conte appraised her. "Well, you can show me the way."

"She'll want me there."

Conte shook his head. "I'd best see her alone."

Another long silence fell. Conte stood motionless until Augustin, having picked up his phone, turned away and spoke for some time into the receiver.

The royal couple accompanied him to the door, where Augustin shook hands with him, wished him luck, and turned back.

He stood in the corridor with Lady Charlotte. "We're interested in whatever you can find out about those photos," she said urgently. "And as soon as possible. Now, if you'll follow me—"

She led him to one of the smaller downstairs offices. "In here," she said. "My daughter will be along in a few minutes."

He stood in the doorway and watched her go. Her head was down, eyes on the floor. She looked withdrawn into herself, focused on problems of her own that she was unable to resolve.

This is a dysfunctional family, Conte told himself.

What she had set in motion was now out of her control.

Conte shrugged. It was not his job to worry about Lady Charlotte's role in her own family.

In the sovereign's office, having come forward, the one-armed man sat down in the chair vacated by Conte.

Augustin was pacing. He said: "What did you think?"

"Probably exactly what you are thinking yourself." De Blondin knew better than to offer opinions until he knew which ones were wanted.

Standing behind his swivel chair, arms resting on its back, Augustin said, "A tough guy. Not too bright, probably."

A prudent man was careful not to step on the sovereign's lines. "He's been in some fights, judging from his face."

"Do you think he'll find out anything?"

"Nope."

"Nothing to worry about?"

De Blondin said: "Nothing we're not already taking care of."

"But it would be better if he weren't here."

"Well," said De Blondin.

"That's what you were thinking."

"I was surprised you didn't just send him back where he came from."

"You're not married. You don't have a daughter."

"No."

"Sometimes you do things you don't want to do just to keep peace in the family."

"I understand."

Augustin had turned and was gazing out his window. He said over his shoulder: "This thing is a bit more complicated than we originally thought."

MARIA CRISTINA came into the office where Conte waited. She was tall and, from the look of her, normally slim. If so, she had not yet fully regained her figure. Body still a little puffy, face too. A quiet girl with a small hand but a firm handshake. She had red-rimmed eyes.

The office in which they sat was not used much, apparently. Baroque desk and chairs. Plenty of gilt. On the wall in a heavy frame hung the official portrait of Augustin II in uniform. Was he smiling, or only half blinded by the photographer's lights ricocheting off all the medals — 20 pounds of them at least — on his chest?

"Could I offer you coffee?" said Maria Cristina. "Tea?" A servant in a white coat had come in behind her.

Fugitive thought by Conte: They have their own waiters here.

"Coffee, please," he said.

She wore black pants and a dark green blouse that looked to Conte to be silk, and she was more scared than wary, but trying to hide it.

When the waiter had gone out, the girl began to ask polite questions about Conte's flight — was this his first visit to the country? Her good manners impressed him. Somebody had drummed them into her early, it seemed to him.

He smiled at her, and she gave a kind of smile back.

Then: "Have you seen my husband?" Had her voice cracked slightly? He wasn't sure.

"Not yet, no."

"You will see him?"

"I'll ask him about the photos in the magazine, yes."

"What kind of questions?" Waiting for the answer, she seemed to become even more tense.

"The same kind I'm about to ask you."

Having reentered the room, the waiter set down his silver tray with its silver pot, silver sugar bowl, silver milk pitcher, silver spoons. Everything was silver except the tiny cups, which were wisps of china.

The waiter poured the coffee and passed it around.

"Thank you, Paolo," said Maria Cristina.

When the waiter had gone out she seemed to take a big breath, as if nerving herself up to face the interrogation that was coming.

Conte said: "There was a magazine came out not long ago."

She nodded.

"Did you happen to see it, by any chance?"

"I glanced at it."

"There were a number of pages of photos—"

"I didn't study them."

"But you did see them."

"I looked at the first couple."

"The first couple?"

She nodded and looked away.

"Were you able to recognize the woman?"

"All I could see was her—"

"Her hair," supplied Conte.

"That's right, her hair."

"Not someone you know, or your husband knows?"

"I really couldn't tell."

"You didn't recognize her face?"

The girl bit down on her lower lip, and shook her head.

There were fracture lines in this young woman, and they showed.

"An old girlfriend of your husband's perhaps?" Conte persisted. It was like dealing with a victim of rape, he saw. Her wounds were so raw that she scarcely heard his questions. Something had been done to her that she never saw coming, that she couldn't now fathom or explain.

"Someone you may have noticed him paying a little too much attention to?"

She reminded him of a child's toy repaired with glue. Press hard and the toy—the girl—would fly into pieces.

Yet pressure was what he was obliged to maintain. "An acquaintance of yours, or of his? Someone one of you may have gone to school with? Perhaps the wife of a friend?"

No answer.

"Not a woman you know? You're sure of that."

Again no answer.

"Was there any indication that your husband had"—Conte struggled to find neutral words—"other interests, and who—"

"He loved me."

"—who she might be? Was he away often? Business trips, whatever?"

"I was pregnant."

"Yes, I know."

"He was home every night."

Conte withdrew the magazine from the briefcase between his knees.

"I don't want to see it."

He was searching through pages. "It would really help if you could identify the woman."

"Please," said Maria Cristina.

"You only glanced at the first couple of pictures, you said." Having found the photo he was looking for, he folded the page so that only the girl's face showed—though not much of it, unfortunately—through her hair. Eliminated were her bare breasts and all of Tony. "Can I ask you to look at this?"

"No."

"Please help me."

"Ask my husband who she was."

"I will, but he may not want to tell me. That's why I want you to tell me, if you can. If you would just glance at this one picture—"

"No."

"Just a quick glance."

"No."

"Please."

She had turned surly. He had tried to be gentle, but had not been gentle enough, it seemed. He got nothing more out of her.

ON THE PHONE with Prescott in New York, Conte outlined the case. He said: "What it boils down to is I'm supposed to find a bimbo with nice tits who'll put me onto a paparazzo with nice cameras."

"Interesting," said Prescott.

"It's okay as a puzzle," conceded Conte, "but a case of world importance it is not."

"It is to the client, or they wouldn't have hired us."

Rebuked, Conte was silent.

"Try to remember that, Vince."

"Yes, of course."

"Your job is to serve the client's needs. That means you give them what they want."

"I don't even know who the client is. She's paying the bills, but he's the boss."

"Then give them both what they want," Prescott said.

"Their agendas may not be the same."

"Close enough, I'm sure."

"And there's something else going on in this case, some undercurrent, I don't know what."

"What are you talking about?"

"An impression I came away with, a feeling."

"Worry about your impressions when the job is done and you get home. The case sounds to me cut-and-dried. How long do you think it will take you?"

"No idea."

"They've paid us for about ten days of your time. Any more than that you better call me. Keep track of your expenses. Give the clients the results they're looking for and they'll probably pay whatever you spend. Give them something else, they may try to stiff us."

"Fine. I'll try to remember that."

"And I want to hear from you before you close the case."

Did he mean that Conte had to ask permission first? The detective was not sure. But he felt a doubt building that had not been there previously.

"We're trying to expand into Europe, Vince. You know that. So this case is important to us. It could be the making of us in Europe. The fall-out. The publicity. I can't overstress its potential importance."

"I don't understand," said Conte. "We never make our cases public. Discretion is our byword and—"

"And word gets around anyway. Break a case involving the royals, and you'll have every noble family in Europe looking to hire us."

"This guy, realistically speaking, is so small he's not royal at all."

"One of the least of the royals, maybe, but royal nonetheless. Think of him as the doorway to lots of lucrative business. Good luck."

Conte hung up thinking: That's what I needed, additional pressure. He said the words aloud: pressure, pressure, pressure. In fact they were just words, they didn't sound bad at all, and he laughed at them and at himself.

CHAPTER

IX

VINCENT CONTE CLIMBED THE STAIRS to the apartment over the butcher shop.

Breathing a bit hard by the time he got up to the fourth floor, he rang the bell. The building was in the old part of the city. Waiting, he inhaled cooking odors that went back 200 or more years.

Though he could hear no sound or movement, he became aware of being appraised through the spyhole. He rang again.

The door opened on a chain. A middle-aged woman peered at him in the gap. Gray hair. Heavyset. Wore an apron. Chewing on something.

"What do you want?"

"Antonio Murano."

"You a pressman?"

"No."

"You're a pressman. Haven't you done enough to him?"

Conte did not speak the language here, but he understood her words well enough. "I'm not a pressman."

"He doesn't want to see your kind."

"I've come from the palace." Conte was speaking a mixture of English, Italian, and some French remembered from school. He saw she understood him. "Tell him I've talked to his wife."

The door was pushed closed. He could hear muttering inside, and what sounded like the woman being muscled aside.

Then her voice: "He's a pressman."

A young man's voice. "I want to hear what he has to say."

"Don't do it, Tony."

"He's seen Maria Cristina."

The chain was removed, the door opened. The glowering Murano stood beside his mother. "You see my wife?"

"Yes."

"When?"

"Earlier this afternoon."

The young man's fists were clenched. "You better not to lie to me, Mister."

Conte studied the mother a moment. "Get your coat," he said to Murano. "I've got a rental downstairs. Let's go for a ride."

They went downstairs and outside. The fresh air smelled good to Conte after the odors of that building. The streets were narrow as a necktie. Overhanging eaves almost blocked out the sky, which still contained a good deal of light. The old town itself had an odor too, but not as strong.

"Tell me what she say, Maria Cristina."

"The car is this way," said Conte.

There were shops at ground level, apartments above. The shops were dark, iron shutters pulled down. The street was not much more than an alley. Their shoes rang on the cobbles.

"What about Maria Cristina?"

"Wait till we get to the car."

The cobbles were damp, somewhat slick, the stones smoothed by hundreds of years of shoes.

They came out onto a small square where the detective's car was nosed in among bicycles and scooters. Conte tossed Murano the car keys and said: "You drive."

They got into the car.

In a few streets they were out of the old town, and the sky opened up. There were mountains to the west with the sun behind them.

"Where do I go?" said Murano. He sounded angry.

"Take me to that villa."

"Villa?"

"The one with the swimming pool. Know the one I mean, by any chance?"

Murano jammed on the brakes. "Wait a minute, Mister."

"Look," said Conte, "I'm not a pressman, as your mother calls them." He was not afraid of Murano. Nonetheless, the young man was bigger and more heavily muscled than he had at first seemed. Six-two, Conte judged, 200 or more pounds.

"I have no cameras, no tape recorder. I'm not in this to hurt you. I'm a private detective."

Murano was silent.

"Your mother-in-law called me. She wants me to find out how this thing happened."

"What does she care how it happen?"

"That I can't tell you."

For a moment they rode in silence.

"So how do you think it happened?" said Conte.

"Set up, I think you call it. Somebody set me up, that is how it happened."

"Entrapment? Is that the grounds of your defense?"

"I did not even do anything."

Conte was nodding thoughtfully. "In a criminal trial an entrapment defense might win you an acquittal. A jury might believe it. Unfortunately, no crime was committed — not by you in any case. And there's no jury to appeal to, just a judge, who is either your father-in-law or your wife, maybe both, and your entrapment defense is not going to get you off."

After a time Murano said: "You do not really talk to Maria Cristina, do you?"

"As a matter of fact I did. We met in that little room downstairs with all the gilt furniture, and the big picture of your father-in-law on the wall."

"In the palace his picture is everywhere."

"I didn't know that."

"What did she say about me?"

"I tried to show her the photos in the magazine, see if she could identify the girl. She said to ask you to identify her. Other than that, she didn't say much."

"She must say something about me."

"No."

They had been climbing one of the hills behind the city, a rich area apparently, for there were walled-in villas to either side. After a time Murano stopped the car and pointed to a gate.

"That is it there."

Conte got out of the car, and studied as much of the villa as showed above the wall. He then approached the gate.

"You cannot go in," said Murano. "Gate is locked. House is locked."

"How do you know?"

"Afterward, I come up here looking for her."

"The babe with the boobs? Did you want to get your hands burned again, or what?"

"I wanted to kill her."

"Hmm," said Conte.

He noted the Realtor's sign on the gate. "Was that here?"

"No."

The detective got his notebook out, made a note of the name and phone number, then walked up the road above the villa, Murano trailing. Where the road petered out he walked out onto the steep, stony hillside. He had the magazine in his hand, and was trying to calculate the spot from which the photos must have been made. Repeatedly he stopped to glance from the magazine down to the villa and back again.

Presently he was high enough to see as much of the pool as showed in the photos. "Just about here," he muttered.

Looking up from the magazine he noted the blind that Georges Grizzard had constructed with branches from bushes, the leaves now withered and dry, and he walked over there and peered at the ground, which was littered with empty film packages.

Using his handkerchief, Conte picked up several of these packages and shoved them wrapped in the handkerchief into his pocket. Force of habit, probably. They might or might not hold any prints after so long out in the air, and this was not a criminal case anyway, at least not yet.

Murano began kicking at the remaining film packages, sending stones down the hill too, his kicks increasingly vicious, kicking the packages out of his life, out of existence.

"Pretty barren out here, isn't it," Conte said to him, when he stopped.

From up here, even in the failing light, the villa seemed like an oasis, pastel walls, dark shutters, tile roof, flowering bushes, trees poking up. And at the end of the garden the blue sheen of the pool.

Looking down at the magazine, Conte said to him: "You certainly are photogenic, aren't you."

It made Murano gaze stolidly at the ground.

"Her even more so."

Murano said nothing.

"I don't know what the hell you were thinking of."

"Is not my fault," said Murano in a small voice. "Is not my fault."

"No? Whose hand is that wrapped around her tit?"

This was called intimidating the witness, a tactic not allowed in court. But if Conte needed Antonio Murano docile, which he did, intimidation was essential.

In the same small voice, Murano said: "I was set up."

"Who set you up?"

"I don't know."

"And why would anyone bother?"

"I don't know."

After a moment Conte said: "So who's the girl?"

"I don't know."

"You must know her name."

"Gigi."

"Gigi what?"

"Saffran, she tell me. I only see her twice before."

"And the third time you got to play with all of her, starting with those boobs."

"I didn't."

"Is she a hooker, or what?"

"I did not think so. I still do not think so. I don't know what she is."

"Wonderful."

"I thought I know her, but I was wrong."

"All right," said Conte, "where'd you meet her?"

At an auto show in Amsterdam, it seemed—once he started talking about her, Murano couldn't stop. There had been motorcycles on display too. According to him she came up to him at the show, and asked his advice about one of the bikes. Said she wanted to buy one as a birthday present for her boyfriend. Said her name was Gigi. They talked 20 minutes or so. Exclusively about bikes, according to Murano.

"You said you met her twice."

"She staying in my hotel. At least I think so. That night I meet her crossing the lobby. She say she has ordered the bike I recommend, and thank me."

"By this time she knew your name and who you were."

"Yes."

"You told her you had a spa and were looking for investors."

"Why should I tell her that?"

"To make yourself sound important. Did you or didn't you?"

"No, I don't think so. Well maybe I did. I do not remember."

"What else did you talk about?"

"She tell me her parents have a villa here." Murano pointed to it. "She said maybe we run into each other in the street someday."

"That's all?"

"I never touch her, never proposition her. Nothing."

"Until you saw her again here."

"Despite how photos look, I never fuck her." His voice was low, and he said the same thing again: " — Never fuck her."

Into Conte's continuing silence he added: "You believe me, please?"

"No."

"I come up here to the villa with a briefcase of brochures and drawings. I think her father would be here and invest maybe. But he was not here. She was here, the only one. I go through the gate and bump into her almost. She was wearing a bikini only. It does not hide anything much. It was one of the most small I ever saw."

"Go on."

"She invite me in for tea. Then she say I must change into my swim trunks and go for a swim with her."

"Which you did."

"Yes."

"All right. Tell me exactly what happened."

Standing on the hillside as the light faded and the incriminating villa disappeared into the night, Murano told the following story, mangling the English language here and there, but speaking so vividly that Conte could picture exactly how it had been.

In the bathroom he had got his swim trunks on with some difficulty. Under the circumstances it was not an easy thing to do. When he had come out of the bathroom finally, as calm as he was likely to be for some time, he had gone out through the French doors barefoot, and crossed the garden, and found Gigi standing at the far end of the pool waiting for him. As he approached she gave him a welcoming smile. She in no sense looked him over. There was no salacious appraisal of his body or its sexual possibilities. He was proud of his body: straight legs, muscled shoulders, moderately hairy chest; but she had seemed to accept all this without any particular notice. She had made no comment, just accorded him the friendly smile, then moved toward the wicker table on which lay the tea tray.

They had sat at either side of the table, and the ritual of the tea began.

As she poured, Gigi said: "Who picked out the color of your swim trunks?"

"I myself. Why?"

"It exactly matches the color of your eyes. One sugar? Two?"

"One, please. Always you notice color of people's eyes?"

"Of course. Doesn't everybody?"

"Me, no. Usually. I notice color of your eyes, though."

In the silence that then fell between them he felt nervous, but she had seemed to him completely relaxed, and he watched her remove the ribbon that held her ponytail, and shake out her hair. Nice hair, thick as a horse's tail, and very long. Any young man would have wanted to rake his fingers through it, though of course Murano did nothing. Hanging straight down beside her eyes, it almost obscured her face.

"The tea's too hot," Gigi said. She stood up. "We'll go for a swim first, let it cool a bit." As she stepped to the edge of the pool, she said over her shoulder: "Do you mind if I take off my top?"

Topless sunbathing was common in all the European countries, even in once prissy Spain. The surprised Murano said: "No, not at all."

To Conte now, Murano said: "What else I could have say?"

"And those noble tits came into view," commented Conte.

Not right away, it seems. She couldn't make the clip let go, according to Murano. Elbows all pointed she worked behind her back for a time, then asked him to help. He came over and undid it for her.

"Thank you," she said, and she turned almost in his arms, so that her left breast slapped him in the hand.

"Sorry," he said, dropping the offending hand as if scalded.

"Girl put her tit in your hand, you take it, right?" said Murano to Conte, and he grinned. "It is instinctive. You would have do the same, right? Any man do it."

Conte said nothing.

"Last about two seconds. That is the first of those pictures," said

Murano. His voice turned bitter, and he pointed toward Conte's magazine. "Photograph man get five pictures out of it."

"Go on with your story," said Conte.

Gigi had smiled at him through her hair. "You're forgiven," she had told him. "My fault anyway, I turned too fast."

She then tossed the bra onto a deck chair, commenting: "When I put it back on after our swim, at least it won't be wet."

After giving him another smile, she plunged into the pool.

Though her flesh had felt sleek and cool, his hand felt too hot to touch, so he dove into the pool after her, hoping to cool it off, cool himself off.

They swam back and forth several times, Murano aware every second of where she was. Smiling, talking, they treaded water, heads close together which, because of the way the sunlight splashed up into their faces, made for a page and a half of artistic photos, calm photos, leading into the torrid ones that came next.

Now Gigi said to him: "The tea's probably ready."

She swam to the ladder and hauled herself out of the pool, Murano right behind her. As she climbed up, the weight of the water enveloped by her bikini bottom caused it to sag still lower, a certain amount of cleavage being suddenly disclosed, Murano's head just below it.

From the top of the ladder Gigi stepped onto the tiles, tugged the cloth up on both sides, and turned and the young man was there, and she fell against him. Either she slipped or did it deliberately, so that he caught a breast again, and then they were kissing.

Conte said: "A number of kisses, I gather." From this duck blind beside him each one had been photographed in living color through a long lens. A very long lens. And using film, not digital cameras, probably because the subjects were so distant. Film would give greater clarity.

Conte said: "How far up the mountain would you say we're standing, a hundred yards?"

The kissing photos differed one from the other only slightly — it could even have been a single kiss, though a prolonged one. The breast fondling appeared to have lasted throughout.

Judging by the intensity of the kissing, the young couple had forgotten completely about the tea.

How steadily, methodically, the photographer must have worked. Conte could picture the automatic camera whirring away — it must have been automatic to use up so many rolls. Judging from the photos, several cameras, several lengths of lenses. He tried to picture it. One camera on a tripod working by itself, or possibly two tripods, two cameras working by themselves, another zooming in and out for close-ups, one or two more waiting loaded on the ground. Except during the swimming there would not have been time to reload.

As soon as he had shot that bra removal business, the photographer would have realized that his plot was working to perfection. Probably he had got very excited. Those bra photos alone were enough to cause a scandal. Probably he was in a state of sexual arousal as well, Conte supposed, no doubt hoping to see Miss Tits peel those boxer shorts down Murano's legs. What would happen then? Would she fuck him out in the open on the pool deck in front of the cameras? How far would the couple go? Arousal enhanced by suspense. In a moment the person in this blind might see them rolling around on that pneumatic mat beside the pool. A pneumatic babe on a pneumatic mat, ha!

What about the girl? Conte asked himself. Was it possible that this Gigi did not know the cameras were there? Or had she known all along? Was she a hooker working for the photographer? Or perhaps not a hooker but an actress playing a role? Or was she just a girl caught as unaware as Murano? Who was she?

It was getting dark, a bit too dark already to study the photos further. For the moment Conte had no idea who she was, or what she was capable of — what her exact role may have been.

He said: "So what happened next?"

"Nothing happen next. The kiss end. Which of us stop it I cannot say. I admit that much."

Murano's hand had dropped from her breast. They talked a moment, earnestly it seemed from the photos, and then, hand in hand, they walked toward the house.

"All the while gazing soulfully at each other," said Conte, and he slapped the magazine with the back of his hand, "according to these photos here."

"We go in the house," said Murano.

"And then you fucked her," said Conte.

"I never do it."

"Where'd you fuck her? The house was empty, you said. In a bedroom? On the floor just inside the door? Where?"

"I go in the bathroom and put back my clothes, and then I leave."

"I can believe you didn't fuck her on the pool deck. If you had, there would probably be a photo of it."

"I swear it to you—"

"In the house then."

"Tell Maria Cristina I do not."

Conte was silent.

"You should believe me," said Murano. "Somebody should believe me."

"At this stage it makes no difference whether you did or not, Pal. We're not dealing with sex anymore, but with public humiliation."

This silenced Murano.

The final photos in the magazine's photo essay, if you could call it a photo essay, showed Murano, now dressed, attaché case in one hand, helmet in the other, coming out the front door, Gigi standing there also dressed, Murano crossing to the gate, and then, having tugged the helmet on, having straddled his big machine and kicked the engine on, waving to Gigi standing in the doorway.

As he rolled down the road the noise must have come up big, and then he was gone. The photo essay was over.

"The photo man, he blackmail me too. Tall skinny, about forty years. He say if I pay he give me the negatives. But he do not."

"You paid him?"

Murano nodded. "Over fifty thousand euros."

Conte wanted to whistle, but made no sign. A crime had been committed after all.

"I sell everything. I have nothing now. It not do any good."

"You don't know his name."

"No."

"But you'd recognize him if you saw him again."

The young man nodded.

"What about the girl? What language did you speak to her in?"

"English."

"She have an accent?"

"I speak English not enough to tell. Her accent like yours maybe."

"What nationality do you think she was?"

"Dutch, I think."

"You think?"

"She know Amsterdam."

"She speak to somebody in Dutch?"

"I think."

"You're a really big help," said Conte, "really big."

The detective asked a good many more questions, but the answers he
got were no more specific. It was full dark by this time. The lights of the
town could be seen below, the lighted canyons of the old town, the jew-
eled necklaces that were the boulevards. They returned to the car, Conte
drove, and they went down.

The detective had not learned much, did not have much to go on,
and was already worried about it.

CHAPTER

X

THE REAL ESTATE WOMAN, showing the villa, idled through rooms, Conte trailing. She extolled the elegant molding, the parquet floors. She was used to dealing with foreigners and spoke excellent English.

Conte said nothing, did not react, which ought to have told her something, but apparently did not.

She extolled the woodwork, all in walnut and —

He wasn't here for the woodwork.

— and the ceilings, four meters high.

Her skirt swished. Her heels went *tap tap* on the floor. "Upstairs there's —"

He examined every room, looking for — he did not know what he was looking for. Something that the photographer, or perhaps the girl, might have left behind. Something to give him a handle on them, a clue as to how to find them. But there was nothing.

He said: "The place is spotless, isn't it."

"We have it cleaned regularly."

"So when did you have it cleaned last?"

"A few days ago."

"Just after the last people moved out," said Conte.

"Oh no, the villa has been unoccupied for a long time."

"You're lying, Doll."

She looked at him.

"Since the owner's wife died last year," she said.

"I don't like to be lied to."

After a moment she said: "Who are you?"

"I'm investigating the man who rented this place last."

She took a long breath. "This was the villa?"

"Yes."

Another long breath. "I thought it might be."

"Who did you rent it to?"

At first she was silent.

"I don't want to bring your agency into it, but I will if I have to."

"I didn't know who he was. He came in here just like you, looking all around. I knew he wasn't your ordinary client. I knew you weren't either."

"Oh?" said Conte.

"He said his name was Georges Dural."

"His real name."

"I don't know."

"What did he look like?"

"He was tall, thin, thirty-five years old."

"I have information he was closer to forty."

"Maybe."

"Go on."

"Dark curly hair. Dark sunglasses too."

She had tried, she said, to read his eyes, though she couldn't see them, much less read them. He had worn jeans, tennis shoes, a crocodile shirt. Couldn't read any of that either. No one wore expensive clothes anymore, though she did. In the early years of the third millennium, fashion was dead, had been for some time.

"He never looked at me at all, just as you didn't."

"I'm listening," said Conte.

She considered herself a good-looking woman. Chic. Still in her prime. Therefore the man's reaction to her — his lack of reaction — had puzzled her at first, then began to annoy her. He annoyed her. Though he followed where she led he had appraised no details, neither hers nor the villa's. Finally she became angry. He was wasting her time.

"It's quite a sumptuous villa," she had said to him suddenly, coolly — or so she now told Conte. "Of course the price is sumptuous too."

Her profession had guidelines. Price was always delicate. Normally one didn't mention price until the client did. But she had glanced at him through half-closed eyes, had become certain he couldn't afford this villa, nor any of the others she had shown him.

"You said I could rent it for a month. See if I liked it."

"The price for that is sumptuous too, I'm afraid."

When she named it, "Dural" had nodded agreeably. "Cheap at twice that, I'd say."

This left her perplexed again. Sarcasm? She couldn't tell. "Some who have seen it thought it on the expensive side," she said tartly.

How long had she been showing this place. A year? Two years? People who owned villas like this could afford to wait. The owner of this one had waited a long time. No takers, rent or buy.

In her confusion she said: "If you'll just follow me upstairs — "

"The pool, Sweetie," said the man, "the pool."

She was not his "Sweetie." Her mouth had set into a line, which he seemed to see as so predictable it made him smile.

Using more energy than the job called for, she had flung open the French doors to the terrace, which, as Dural had seen, and as Conte saw now, was delineated by urns overflowing with gardenias. It was a garden of flowering bushes, and vines that climbed the villa's walls.

"I led him under this arbor," said the Realtor to the detective. Conte glanced up into massed wisteria. The sun, which was hot and bright on all the other flowers, could barely get through it. He inhaled the odors and thought the colors around him — the mauves, reds, and purples — dazzling.

"I might have extolled the garden," the Realtor said, "but as far as I was concerned, the sales pitch was over."

Below them Conte could see a portion of road, and the rooftops of other villas. From here he could not see the town. A hot wind blew—he was wearing a short-sleeved shirt and could feel it on his bare arms. It was the wind that made the air so clear today, he decided, that etched line after line of mountains against the sky.

"I did not mention the view either. I did not intend to address another word to him."

She realized now, she told Conte, that the view was part of the situation this Georges Dural was trying to frame in his mind's eye. Otherwise he seemed to accord it no interest, and he went through to the pool where he turned around and gazed farther up the mountain. At the time she did not know why—there was nothing else up there, the rest of the mountainside being too steep for construction. It was rocky and arid, in color almost gray. Some low isolated pine trees, a few bushes, and there were patches of a kind of gorse.

The woman had watched Georges Dural, having begun to wonder what he was inspecting and why. What was he looking at or for up there?

He had moved to another part of the pool, still surveying the mountain above him.

"This villa may be perfect," he called out.

Conte said to the woman: "Perfect maybe not. Maybe only the best he had seen. Maybe he couldn't afford any more time searching." If so, Conte asked himself, in what way was this significant?

"All he said was, 'Let me think about it.'"

She had locked the villa, then the gate. In the road outside she and "Dural" had engaged in the obligatory handshake. Dural even smiled at her, but she did not smile back. Then she had got into her car, slammed the door, and started down the mountain.

"You left him here?" inquired Conte.

"He had a rental of his own."

Dural must have watched her go. As soon as her car turned the corner he would have walked up the road till it petered out, and then out onto the flank of the mountain where two trees stood in a fold in the terrain. Either then or later he had begun to construct his duck blind. The two trees didn't conceal much. They were scraggly, thin, and not very tall, but he had cut down some bushes and piled them in front, until satisfied that he was invisible from the road, and all but invisible from the pool area of the villa.

From the blind, Conte knew, he had been able to see and photograph only about half the pool area, maybe less than half, but he would have decided that might be enough, and in the end it had proven to be.

Then what, Conte asked himself.

"Did he have a cellular phone with him?" he asked the Realtor.

"Yes."

So he would have made some calls. He was about to pay out a month's rent, and a month's caution money. He would have checked with his employers first. *Secrets* magazine. Anyone else he was working for as well. Did they guarantee his expenses? A man like that would have inflated the cost of the villa by a few thousand. Did he still have a deal, he would have asked—Conte could almost hear the conversation. If the woman, Gigi, was in this with him, he would have called her too, wherever she was in the world, checked with her still again, and told her to get on down here.

Conte was going to have to find this man, about whom he knew almost nothing, and the woman too, about whom he knew even less. "What language did he speak?"

"French."

"Did he sound French?"

"No. He sounded Germanic. Said he was from Rome but sounded Germanic."

And Murano had met the woman in Amsterdam. "Dutch, maybe?" he suggested.

"Maybe."

"He must have filled out some forms for you."

"The usual forms, yes."

"I want to see them."

Back in her office the real estate woman got out the forms, and handed them across to Conte, who began glancing through them.

"I remember studying them after I left him that day," she said. "Just like you're doing." She shook her head. "I remember asking my associate at the next desk if the name Georges Dural meant anything to him."

"It didn't," said Conte.

"How did you guess?"

"Hmm," said Conte.

"I said to my associate: 'He's got the manners of a garbage collector, and he picks his nose. He doesn't have the money for the villas he's been making me show him. Nor the manners either.'"

She had crumpled the forms and thrown them in the basket, convinced the man had been wasting her time. As far as she was concerned that was the end of Georges Dural, but an hour later her phone rang, and it was him. He said he was taking the villa and was coming by to put money down.

"And he did."

"Yes."

"He must have shown you an ID?"

"No."

"Something? Anything?"

"He said he didn't have it with him. Said he'd bring it in the next day."

"So you put his money in the drawer and gave him the key."

She did not answer.

"And you never saw him again."

"About a week later I received the key in the mail. He gave no explanation. There was an address to which I was to send back his caution money."

"Ah," said Conte.

"I think I have it here somewhere."

Conte stared down at the address. Milan. A post office box, unfortunately.

"People think these post office boxes can't be traced," the detective muttered. "But they can be, sometimes." Not always, though. And by the time he got to Milan, found the correct post office, and got somebody to tell him who had rented the box he might find, probably would find, that it had been abandoned. Probably rented in a false name as well.

Outside in the street in his car he studied the magazine photos, and the first conclusion he came to was that the woman was no innocent. In nearly every photo she managed to keep her face averted while giving full play to the line of her boobs. Nice bare breasts, but never her face. Either it was pressed against Murano's chest or shoulder, or was obscured by her hair, or by the kissing itself. So she had known exactly where the cameras were, and had stage-managed every shot. She was in this thing as deeply as Dural himself.

At length he started the engine and drove back to the villa, where he climbed up to Dural's duck blind. The mountains still rose above him on three sides, but he ignored them, focusing instead on the ground still littered with empty film packages. More of them than there should be, he decided. Too many and too widely spread out for a single photographer. Such stony ground showed no footprints, but would a single pair of shoes have scuffed it up that much? So there had been a second man. But who?

This was no ordinary paparazzo job, Conte was convinced. It was a full-scale plot. It may have been hatched elsewhere, but it took root in Amsterdam. This posited travel expenses. Air tickets to and from Amsterdam, to and from Milan. To and from here. Hotels too. The second man had to be paid, not to mention Dural and the woman. And the month's rent on the villa had been enormous.

In sum, too elaborate and expensive an intrigue for Dural, or whatever his name was, to have financed by himself. So who was behind him, and why? The magazine alone? Conte doubted it. Magazines of that type, he believed, were willing to pay money for sensational photos, but they were no good for front money. Someone else, then. Who?

The detective had new respect for Lady Charlotte. A woman with good instincts. She had been right to be suspicious. He started down.

Tomorrow he would leave this place. The trail led from here to Amsterdam, to Milan, and perhaps crisscrossed back and forth. Milan was a city of over a million and a half people, Amsterdam a bit less, not much. He would have to search both major cities for a man and a woman for whom he did not even have reliable names.

CHAPTER

XI

In Amsterdam Gigi lived beside a canal on the fourth floor of a narrow house in a row of narrow houses, all of them noble in appearance and very old. Below her apartment was a narrow sidewalk, then a narrow street, and then the canal lined with trees with cars parked under them. Across the canal were more trees, more houses, more parked cars. In places the branches came together over the water. Under them boats, barges, sometimes moved.

Gigi's windows were narrow and high, almost floor length, and sunlight flooded in. On this particular day she got up about ten, which was normal for her. She put on some music and then, wearing only a bra, got down on the floor and began her exercise regime, yoga first, then moving to the machines for the harder stuff. The house being several centuries old, the floor creaked under her.

Before long she was grunting and sweating. She rowed, she dragged weights up and down rods. For more than an hour she worked. Her body was soaked and sticky when she finished. Her hair was soaked and now needed to be washed. While cooling down she turned the music off and ate the same breakfast as every day: herb tea, a diet yogurt, an apple. She had the body of a 20-year-old — 20 she was not — and was determined to keep it that way as long as possible.

Later, carrying a pillowcase of laundry, she went down the four flights to the street, and got her bicycle out. She was wearing flat heels, jeans, and a loose cashmere sweater, with a ring of discreet pearls around her neck. She also wore a cloche hat and wraparound sunglasses — what she thought of as her disguise.

Pedaling along the canal under the trees she reassessed her life, something she did too often these days, she believed. Because of its canals, which were mostly silent, and which seemed to deaden sound, Amsterdam was a quieter city than most, and Gigi's was an especially quiet street. It was also a rich one, and her apartment cost more than she could really afford. As she gripped her handlebars and pedaled along, as she gazed down on the plump pillowcase in the basket over the wheel, she considered her extravagant apartment still again. But because of her work she needed the good address, she believed. A place to which she could come home late, as she did each night, without worrying about being mugged or raped. Also, she was more anonymous on such a street, and this was important too.

The laundry having been dropped off, the bike's empty basket now leading her along, she pedaled until she came to the market, where she chained the front wheel to a rack, then went inside and did her food shopping, stocking up because, starting tonight, she would be sharing her apartment with a man. Not a boyfriend, but her father. For how long she could not say. Nor could she have said how she felt about the prospect.

In late afternoon, again wearing the cloche hat and sunglasses, she drove a borrowed Volkswagen out to Schiphol to meet him. The airport parking lots were mostly full, expanses of cars shining in all directions, but she found a spot in the far reaches. Once inside the vast shed that was the terminal, she headed toward the exit from customs, walking past rows of shops, past numerous sterile concourses, heels tapping.

But when she got there she saw from the overhead TV screens that the plane from Johannesburg would be very late. Backtracking, she entered one of the newspaper shops, thumbed through magazines, and watched the time pass. It passed slowly.

At last the plane landed. Standing outside the customs area she watched the opaque doors open and swing shut as passengers trickled

out, mostly couples or groups who walked grinning into the arms of families or friends. Gigi was watching for a man of 60 who would be alone.
She watched carefully. Several such men exited and she studied and discarded each of them. Not her father, not yet, although one candidate she
wasn't sure about, and she studied him again. He was standing beside
a suitcase glancing around, looking confused. Finally she went over to
him.

"*Vader?*" she asked.

"*Dochter,*" the man said. But in his voice too there had been a question mark.

He was shorter than she remembered, and had gone bald. His belly
now overhung his belt. No wonder I didn't recognize him, Gigi thought.

Having peeled the sunglasses off her, her father eyed her up and
down. "Yes, that's better." He was still speaking Dutch. "You're not a little
girl anymore, are you?" And he gave her a smile.

In response Gigi fashioned a smile of her own. A kind of a smile.

Retrieving her sunglasses, replacing them where they belonged,
she said in English: "Is that one bag all you have? Let's go out to the car,
shall we?"

And she grasped his suitcase, and started out of the terminal.

In the car she said conversationally: "What brings you back to
Amsterdam?"

"New posting coming up. Promotion too, I think. I have an appointment at the foreign office in The Hague tomorrow. I have appointments
all next week, as a matter of fact."

Presently they entered the city and drove along a canal on which a
full moon floated. The moon slid ahead of them as they advanced, and
they trailed it all the way to Gigi's house.

"And of course I wanted to see you, too," her father said.

"You didn't even know I was here."

"Yes I did. Your aunt told me. You ran into her in the street,
apparently."

That had been two months previously. Her father had not phoned her until last night.

"Here we are," said Gigi. She backed into a parking space under the trees, lifted the suitcase out of the trunk, and crossed to the sidewalk, her father following. At her building she carried the suitcase up the four flights and he let her do it. She heard him wheezing behind her.

Having unlocked the apartment door, she put the suitcase down inside.

Her father glanced all around, then patted an antique sideboard. "This stuff yours?"

"No."

"You rented the apartment furnished?"

"Yes." There was little of her in it, and once again Gigi realized this.

"Only the exercise machines are yours."

"They're rented too."

"In other words, you don't expect to stay long."

"Amsterdam is a way station."

"Like every place you've lived in so far."

Gigi shrugged.

"En route to where?" her father said.

"I don't know yet."

"You're thirty years old."

"I know how old I am."

"No need to get irritated."

"I'm not irritated."

"It's time you decided what you want to do with your life. A career, marriage, whatever."

"I'm trying to decide."

"Don't you want children?"

"Of course I do."

"Well then—"

"I think I should get married first, don't you? Before bringing babies into the world."

"So why don't you?"

"Nobody's ever asked me, if you want to know the truth. Guys are happy enough to sleep with me, even live with me. Marriage is another thing, it seems."

"Now you are irritated."

"The kitchen is here," Gigi said, pointing. "The bathroom is through there."

"How many bedrooms?"

"One." She walked over to the couch and patted it. "This is your bed. It pulls out. I made it up earlier today."

"I thought you might offer the bedroom to dear old Dad."

Gigi looked at him. "I don't think so, no."

"And that you'd take the pullout."

"I carried your bag up the stairs for you. That's as far as I'll go."

"I could have carried it."

He looked like an old man to her, and not particularly healthy, so she said: "All right, you can have the bedroom. Have you had dinner?"

"On the plane."

"If you get hungry there's bread, and some cold cuts in the fridge. Make yourself a sandwich. I have to go out."

"At this hour?"

"I have to go to work." She picked up the small suitcase that stood beside the door.

"Your work clothes?"

"Sort of."

"What kind of work?"

"Just work."

They looked at each other. "Who works this late besides whores?" he asked.

"There are all kinds of whores."

"I can see you're not one of them. A whore, I mean."

"How can you be sure?"

"You wouldn't go out dressed that way."

Gigi, still wearing flat shoes, jeans, and her cashmere sweater, shrugged.

"I was always a bit afraid you'd end up on the streets."

"Were you now?"

"Yes." He studied her speculatively.

"Your own daughter. How nice."

"There wasn't anything I could do about it, one way or another, was there?"

Gigi grasped the door handle. "You staying in, or going out?"

"I'm going to bed. I've been thirteen hours on an airplane. It's been a long day."

"I have to go now."

To her surprise he came over and embraced her. It felt like being enclosed by a total stranger.

He said: "I am glad to see you again. Really I am."

"I'll be home late."

"How late?"

"Late. Please don't wake me in the morning. If you want to go out, the keys are on the shelf there."

"Tomorrow, if things go as I hope, I may have a proposition for you. Want to hear what it is?"

"In the morning," she said.

When she was partway down the stairs she heard him lock the door behind her.

She got her bicycle out and pedaled to work, her small suitcase on the rack behind her, parking in the alley behind the building so that afterward she could get away quickly. She went in past the porter and began to get herself ready.

When she got home it was past two A.M. Her father behind the bedroom door was snoring, and she looked in on him for a moment, before gazing toward the kitchen. She was hungry but she stifled the hunger pangs, as she so often did at night, pulled out the sofa, and went to bed.

When she woke up on the pullout the apartment was empty, her father gone somewhere. But he might come back at any time, so she couldn't do exercises in her usual costume, but had to tug leotards up her legs, and over her body. She started in. She was half through her routine when she heard her father's key in the lock. He came in wearing a tan double-breasted suit, silk it looked like, with a vest and a paisley tie.

"I got the promotion," her father said, beaming.

Down the back and between her breasts, Gigi's leotards were wet with sweat. She was breathing so hard it was difficult to smile, but she forced one onto her face, for she wanted him to know she was happy for him. "Congratulations," she said. "That's terrific."

"I'm the new consul general in Philadelphia."

"That's really great, Dad."

"Do you know Philadelphia?"

"I've been there."

"And here's the proposition I spoke to you about last night. How would you like to come with me there, act as my official hostess?"

"What happened to your wife?"

"Divorce."

"Divorce number three."

"Your mother died," her father reminded her. "Only two wives after that."

"Neither of whom wanted anything to do with me. Or else you didn't."

"I haven't been a very good father, I'll grant you that. But maybe it's not too late."

Gigi tried to remember what little she knew about Philadelphia.

"I could give you a job. The government could. Employ you, say, in the visa section."

"Stamping passports. How interesting. Until you found another bimbo."

"I'm finished with that sort of thing."

"Are you now."

"I could pay you American wages."

"And I could become a fat government functionary."

"Will you consider it?"

"Okay, but I'm not sure it's the type career I've been looking for."

"Well, what are you looking for?"

Gigi was silent.

"I really want to know."

"Do you? How long has it been since we've seen each other?"

"Philadelphia would be a better life for you than what you have here."

"You think so?"

"It would get you out of that nightclub."

Gigi had got to her feet, had found a towel and was wiping her sweaty face. "What do you know about any nightclub?"

"Your aunt told me."

Gigi folded and put down the towel. Without taking her eyes off it, she said to her father: "Thanks for the offer, but it's not one I can accept."

"Don't say no right away."

"How long do you expect to be in Holland?"

"About a month, I would say."

"Are you thinking of staying with me for a month?"

Her father looked surprised, but after a moment he said: "I'll be at The Hague most of the time. If I come back to Amsterdam I'll find someplace else."

IT WAS THE NEXT DAY that Gigi first saw the pictures. She had been pedaling past a kiosk, in front of which stood a poster. The poster, blown up almost life size, was the cover of a Dutch magazine. The cover was her. Her bare-breasted self, face averted, being embraced by Murano.

She stopped, bought the magazine, then noted others in various languages with the same or similar covers: French, German, Italian, English. She bought them all, carried them home in a plastic bag, and then couldn't immediately read them because her father was there.

"Have you decided about my proposition?" he asked.

"I'm giving it a lot of thought. I have to change my clothes."

She went into her bedroom, closed and locked the door, and then, very frightened, paged through the magazines. Grizzard had told her the photos were only to "influence" somebody. He had given the impression they would never be published.

Had he? What exactly had he told her?

She was not stupid. She had known there was a chance the photos might appear somewhere, but had had no idea that the story would be played this big—that so many magazines would be this avid. The photos went on for page after page. In various languages so did the text. Apparently somebody had syndicated the photos—Grizzard probably. She read the text in those languages she spoke—English, German, Dutch, and French—and she did not have to read very far down to realize this was being treated as an international incident, and that she was at the heart of it. Criminal investigations had been opened, supposedly.

Frightening stories. The signal sexual betrayal of all time, it seemed. Horrendous stories. Her own name was not given, but Murano's was. Poor Murano. Her heart went out to him. In every photo her hair covered at least half her face, but Murano's was visible for all to see. She did not think she could be recognized. She was almost sure of it. No one could know who she was. Grizzard, though a sleaze, had protected her so far.

These were the first of her thoughts, and however sorry she felt for Murano, she was for about 20 seconds relieved, for it seemed that he would take the rap. She herself was in the clear.

But there were other realizations to come, and they began tumbling through her head. The stories were much, much too big. They were not going to end with the one issue lying in multiple languages on her bed. The newspapers and magazines would keep the story alive for weeks. They would spare no expense to locate her, identify her. How many journalists were already looking for her? Dozens? Hundreds? Who was the girl? They would lead the police to her door. Or perhaps it would be the other way around. Was she even safe for the moment? If so, for how much longer? She was about to become famous. She was about to be made to pay.

She remembered the last time she had seen Grizzard. By then she was no longer half nude. She had been dressed in pants and a short-sleeved shirt, exposing to the world not much more than her bare arms and painted toenails. Her wet hair was again tied back in a ponytail. Murano on his motorcycle had just left the villa.

Grizzard had come down from the hillside and in through the gate. "It took you long enough to get down to business," he said.

"I had to go slowly at first or he might have run right out the door."

"Did you fuck him?"

So immediately she had been on the defensive, and had felt ashamed. The question was not part of the contract between them. It was one he had no right to ask, except that by her conduct she had given him the right to ask any question he chose. Her reaction now arose from her contempt for him, which was total, her contempt for herself as well, so that she had answered: "Of course."

From the expression on his face, it was clear he did not know whether to believe her or not.

"Where?"

"Where what?"

"Where did you fuck him?"

This question had made her, if possible, even surlier. "On the kitchen floor, where else?"

"Why didn't you fuck him beside the pool so I could have got something?"

"A nice free show for you? I'm not that far gone as yet, thank you."

"It was part of the deal."

"Was it? You got plenty."

Even at that moment she had not realized that the photos he did have were so incendiary. She had been refusing to think about it one way or the other, telling herself that errant husbands were nothing new, and that if they wanted to stray, nobody (meaning principally herself) owed them any consideration whatever. Why should a man like Murano be allowed to get away with anything?

Grizzard asked: "Where are you going?"

Gigi had been standing beside her suitcase. "To the airport. When the next plane takes off I expect to be on it."

"The villa's rented for a month."

"The assignment's over."

"He'll be back tomorrow, you can count on it."

"And let me remind you of something else."

"Probably try to call you tonight."

"We have a contract." In Amsterdam two weeks previously she had dragged him before her lawyer who had prepared, he said, an unbreakable contract. Grizzard had blustered, but finally had signed.

She had said: "I don't know what you intend to do with those photos, and I don't want to know." A lie of course, although at the time she was still trying to convince herself that she didn't know, and that it wasn't any of her business. "But according to our contract my face doesn't appear, and my name doesn't appear. Is that clear?"

"I know what the contract says."

"See that you live up to it, or the penalties will be, shall we say, severe."

"Meaning what?"

"The contract's unbreakable. I'll sue you. I'll take your apartment, your cameras. I'll take every cent you've got."

Nodding to him, she had gone out the gate, had waited for the cab she had called, had got into it when it came, and had ordered the driver to take her to where the bus left for the airport. In the mirror she had seen Grizzard standing outside watching her disappear down the mountain.

Now, days later, carrying the magazines in a plastic bag, Gigi came out of the bedroom.

Turning from the window her father looked her over. "I thought you were going to change your clothes."

"I decided not to."

"What's in the bag?"

"The bag?" she said. "Nothing. Old magazines to throw out." Gigi went into the kitchen and thrust them into the garbage can. She was having trouble catching her breath. I've got to get out of Europe, she told herself. Standing at the sink she splashed cold water in her face.

"I think I'll take you up on your offer," she said to her father when she came back into the main room.

"Good girl," he said, and for the second time embraced her.

This was still a man she hardly knew. He was still short, bald, and 60 years old, but to stand in the circle of his arms was comforting. It was more comforting than she was ready for, and she felt herself begin to tremble.

"What's the matter?" her father said. "Is the idea of living with me that awful to you?"

Breaking the embrace, Gigi gave him a wan smile. "For me it's a big step, is all. When would we go?"

"Beginning of next month, maybe."

"What about if I go over ahead of you? Get things ready."

"Not a bad idea. I'll be in meetings at The Hague from tomorrow on. I'll talk to them, see what they say."

In America no one would find her, Gigi told herself. It was the only idea in her head, all she could think of. A few more days and she would be gone. Once in America she would be safe.

CHAPTER
XII

VINCE CONTE SAT at a café on the Piazza del Duomo. This is Milan's central piazza and it is huge. Also crowded, people crossing it at all angles. It is a vast esplanade that ends at the cathedral, which is also huge, the most colossal Gothic structure in Italy and perhaps the world, all in white marble. In all of Christendom no other cathedral is as gigantic as this or as white.

Conte, who sat alone, was worried. The time was late afternoon. The sky was low, most of it blue-black, a storm coming. The sun came in under the storm, and it looked pasted on, illuminating the cathedral's hundreds of belfries and gables, its barbed spires, raking them with light. It turned them into cake icing, at the same time creating halos around the 2,000 marble saints that stood like sentries around the perimeter of the roof.

There was so much curved and counter-curved tracery, Conte thought, most of it pointed skyward, that the cathedral bristled the way yacht marinas bristled. Instead of masts and spars, pinnacles in stone.

The detective sat over an empty cup of espresso. There was a guide-book on his lap. This and the espresso cup made him look like a tourist, which he was not. It was his fourth day in Milan, but so far he had not advanced his investigation, had been frustrated at every turn. The guide-book was closed. The cathedral did not hold his interest. Dozens of pigeons begging for crumbs bobbed and clucked close to his table—to all the tables. The espresso cup stared back at him with its one black eye.

He was waiting for a Milanese cop named Luigi Piccolo who was late, and his fingers drummed on his knee. In a city of one and a half million, Piccolo was his only contact, the only man he actually knew. Four days of dead ends. Nonetheless, he had not wanted to call on Piccolo, and there were reasons. But finally he had forced himself to dial the number.

Piccolo worked out of the *Questura*, police headquarters, which was on Via Fatebenefratelli, 11, a big yellow building whose narrow entrance was flanked by marble columns two stories high. Conte had gone to look at it, thinking that for him it would be safer if their meeting took place in a police facility, and he had telephoned from the street. When Piccolo came on the line Conte told him he was in Milan for a few days, and wanted to come up and say hello. They could chat about old times, go out to dinner later, it would be great to see him again.

A long, rather nervous speech.

"Don't come over," Piccolo had said, sounding immediately wary. "Wait for me on the Piazza del Duomo." He named the café. "I'll be right there." And he rang off.

Piccolo was a predator, Conte reminded himself. Without even knowing why I am here, he senses a profit to be made. He has an instinct for the deal. Money. But he is too careful to invite me to the *Questura*. The *Questura* is not the place for a deal to go down.

Why am I surprised, Conte asked himself. What reaction did I expect from this man?

Now, sitting in the Caffe Gennaro as directed, Conte watched the shadows creep up the cathedral walls, until only the statues on the roof were still lit. Finally he decided he had waited long enough for this meeting he had never wanted in the first place, and he called over the waiter, paid his check, and got to his feet. He was looking at the clouds, was anxious to beat the rain, and he was relieved that Piccolo had not come, but disappointed too. Conte had never intended to tell the Italian much, just a little, before asking for his help. Piccolo had contacts where he had none, and might also have come up with an idea for moving the investigation forward. Conte had thought that, if he were careful, he could use Piccolo at no risk to himself.

Just then Piccolo came toward him through tables, a huge man sidling, bumping a few shoulders, so big he couldn't help himself. Conte fashioned the welcoming grin he did not feel but thought necessary, and thrust out his hand, which Piccolo however ignored.

Instead, enfolding Conte in a meaty embrace, the Italian kissed him on both cheeks.

Despite his Italian roots, the American had never before been kissed in public by another man, and he glanced hurriedly around.

Piccolo was about ten years older than Conte, and stood six feet five, 250 pounds or more, with thick black hair. He sat down at the table that Conte had been about to vacate.

They had met at the FBI Academy in Quantico, Virginia, and they talked of this experience for a few minutes. The FBI's spotless crime labs. The museum filled with tommy guns from the 1930s. A conversation of this kind represented to Conte still more wasted time, but it had to be done.

With this man he must not sound eager, or in a hurry.

The FBI had regularly offered three-month courses in advanced criminology, inviting major U.S. police departments, as well as foreign ones, to send representatives. The NYPD that year had sent several cops, one of them Conte, who was already on the list for captain and from whom great things were expected; and Italy's Polizia Nationale had sent Piccolo from Milan and two other men from other cities. All three Italians were of the same rank, *commissario*, the equivalent perhaps of captain, and because Conte spoke Italian they had turned to him for help and information.

"You speak with a Sicilian accent," Piccolo had told him that first day.

"So do you," retorted Conte.

"It's true," said Piccolo. "Originally I'm from Palermo." Then he added, "With our accents you and I should not be *ghisa*, we should be Mafiosi."

And he laughed.

Was he joking, or was he identifying himself by code, in case Conte was a like-minded individual, for the possible future profit of both? Conte didn't know, but it made him uneasy. Police corruption was not a subject cops joked about.

Piccolo, meanwhile, seemed to be watching closely for whatever the American's reaction might be.

At the end of the three months, both knew, the FBI would give them a diploma to hang on their walls. "With an accent like mine," Piccolo joked, "when I get back to Milano that diploma will open new doors." And he laughed again. He had, thought Conte, a raucous, scary laugh.

The other two Italians, he soon became aware, steered clear of Piccolo.

"There have been rumors," said one of them when pressed. His name was Franco Cortile, and he was from Modena.

"What kind of rumors?"

"Some of them weren't rumors," said Dante Marino, who was from Rome.

Aggressive cops worked harder than other cops, Conte knew. But they paid for their success by acquiring allegations of corruption and brutality that were sometimes undeserved. Perhaps Piccolo was only an aggressive cop. Perhaps that's all this was.

"He's got protection," said Cortile. "In Italy the police come under the Interior Ministry. Guess who's minister of the Interior."

"His uncle," said Marino.

"In Sicily a lot of people are connected to the Mafia one way or another," said Cortile. "Especially certain cops. Piccolo's off-duty job when he was there was to go around collecting the Mafia's bad debts. Look how big he is. And he was a cop. His nickname is 'Horse,' and he had a gun. People paid what they owed."

"Promptly," said Marino.

Bad, Conte thought. If true. But he was trying to keep an open mind. He said: "Maybe these are just stories."

"I don't think so," said Marino.

Cortile said: "The people he collected from walked around with their faces swollen and lumps on their heads. Finally some guy filed a civilian complaint. He was warned. He was advised to withdraw it, but he didn't. As a result he fell off a roof."

"Nothing was ever proved," suggested the American.

"I know a lot of cops from down there," Cortile said. "It's not something one cop says about another if he's not sure."

Marino said: "The second time it happened, Horse got transferred to Milan. His uncle figured that would keep him out of trouble. There's much less Mafia penetration in Milan."

Cortile said: "Apparently that didn't work too well either, so his uncle arranged to send him to Virginia with us. The boy can't get into trouble here."

"Boy?" said Conte. "He's about forty."

"To his uncle he's his sister's kid. Family comes first."

They all laughed.

In ensuing days Piccolo asked many questions about money. When he learned what Conte's paycheck came to he only laughed. The American's salary was two and a half times what Italian cops of equivalent rank were paid, he commented. "But we probably pick up more on the side than you do."

So Conte too began to avoid him. This was not so much on moral grounds as on practical ones. As any cop would tell you, you don't want to stand close to such people. When eventually an outside agency comes in to scoop them up, you could get scooped up too.

Becoming aware of Conte's coolness to him, Piccolo seemed only to shrug it off. He went through the rest of the course alone.

Now here he was in a café on the Piazza del Duomo, hearty and smiling, even as the sky got lower, heavier, and the sun under it scaled the cathedral spires. But a silence had fallen between the two men.

"How can I help you?" said Piccolo. "Why did you call me?"

Conte showed his copy of *Secrets*, opening to the photos of Antonio Murano locked in a passionate embrace with the unknown girl, both of them naked.

"I've already seen this thing," Piccolo said. "The photos are in a lot of other magazines too."

"It's a bigger story in Europe than I would have thought," agreed Conte.

"Nice pair of *zizze*," said Piccolo leafing through pages. "Very nice *zizze*. That's a Neapolitan word, it means—"

"I know what it means. I need to find the guy who took these pictures."

"Find him for whom? You've left the police, you say. So who's your client?"

Conte said: "I'd rather not say."

The big man looked at him. "The palace," he said decisively. "The duke hired you, who else?" He tapped the pages. "This photographer upset their applecart. You find out who he is for them so they can have him killed."

"Oh, I don't think so," said Conte. And he hadn't until this moment.

"I hate these paparazzi," Piccolo said, turning pages. "String him up with the straps of his camera bag is my vote. That would be fitting, don't you think?" The Italian laughed. "Good thing, too. One less piece of shit in the world." Then: "The palace'd pay plenty, I think, to have him rubbed out. How much do you think they'd pay?"

He was smiling, pretending not to be serious. But to Conte he looked like a man who, for a fee, would be willing to take on the job. More than willing.

"My job is to find him," said Conte evenly. "What they do with the information is up to them." Then he added: "But I don't think they plan on killing anybody."

"She's got a really nice pair of *zizze*," said Piccolo, handing back the magazine. "In your place she's the one I'd like to find." He laughed. "Interrogate her for a few days. Maybe she'll let you stroke them for her. How about that."

"I'll need to find her too," said Conte. "But first him."

"What's her name?"

"I don't know yet."

"What's the photographer's name?"

"I don't know his name either."

"Go to *Secrets* and ask them. It's just down the street."

"I did ask them. They wouldn't tell me."

"Make them an offer they can't refuse." Piccolo rubbed thumb and forefinger together, the universal symbol of money.

Conte had met with the magazine's publisher and also its editor in chief, two well-dressed middle-aged men who were polite to him, but so firm in their refusal that it had not occurred to him to attempt to bribe them. He was not used to bribing people anyway, and was not sure he knew how to do it properly.

Piccolo said: "What's it like not being a cop anymore? You feel powerless, don't you? No way, as they say, to put people in a mood to cooperate."

Conte said nothing.

Piccolo laughed. "From one day to the next you're weak as a woman."

Conte still said nothing.

"Maybe I can find the photographer for you," Piccolo said. "Maybe her too. Unfortunately, there will be expenses. That shouldn't bother you. Your employers have plenty of money."

"What kind of expenses?" said Conte.

"A case like this, expenses can run high. But for you I can probably keep them down to, say, a thousand euros." He laughed again. "You put two thousand on your expense account, and we both make out."

"How long will it take you?"

"Depends how soon I can put that expense money to work."

They eyed each other.

You can't give this guy money, Conte told himself. Sooner or later they're going to catch him. There could be people watching him right now.

But it had to be done.

He said, looking around: "I need to take a leak. Where's the men's room?"

As Conte got to his feet, so did Piccolo. Conte stopped him. "Stay here," he ordered curtly. "Or we'll lose our table." He had no intention of letting the Italian follow him into the toilet, eyeing his roll as he peeled bills off it.

Piccolo nodded, and sat back down.

In the bar Conte asked directions to the men's room. He found the door marked UOMINI. After closing himself in a stall he got out his money, and began folding hundred-euro notes into the pages of his guidebook. The place had not been aired out recently, he noted as he worked. He was trying to hold his breath.

Outside again, he placed the guidebook on the table. "I have to go now," he told Piccolo. "When will I see you again?"

They made a date for the next day. He saw the Italian eyeing the guidebook. "Same time, same place," Piccolo said.

"Don't be late," said Conte.

"What about the dinner you promised me?"

They had become co-conspirators. Conspirators were not expected to dine together.

"Another time. Don't forget your guidebook."

Conte went off through the crowd. This case, for all the noble names involved, had a stink attached, and in the last few minutes the stink had got worse. By subverting Piccolo he had subverted himself too. But he was in too deep to get out now.

The next afternoon at the appointed hour he sat down at almost the same table, and ordered first one espresso, then another. Again Piccolo was making him wait. Fifteen minutes passed, 20, 35. He wanted to walk away but couldn't.

In time his guidebook landed with a thump beside his cup, which caused it to wobble in its saucer. He looked up, and standing above him was Piccolo.

No kisses this time, a heavy handshake instead, plus the same broad grin. "Pay the man for your coffee," the Italian said. "We'll go look over the cathedral. All the tourists do it. It's the thing to see in Milano."

Angry at being made to wait, but trying to hide it, Conte put money down and together they started across the esplanade, wading through a community of pigeons that burst above their heads. They pushed through the heavy door. Inside the cathedral Conte marveled at its size. It was huge enough, the guidebook said, to hold 40,000 people at one time even though, during the centuries it took to build, the population of the city had been half that number, or less. The ceiling was so high he could hardly see it. A gigantic, empty cavern, and as silent as—Conte smiled to himself as the cliché came into his head—as a church.

They stood in gloom. The cathedral seemed darker than any Conte remembered. Colder too.

"The four aisles are separated by fifty-two pillars of tremendous height," said Piccolo beside him. He was reading from the guidebook, then glancing upward. "One hundred forty-eight meters."

"So I've read."

"Dates from 1386," he said. "Did you know that?"

"Yes."

"The width across the transept is ninety-one meters." Piccolo spread his arms wide.

"What, if anything, did you find out for me?"

"What I like best about this place," said Piccolo, closing the guidebook and glancing around, "is you don't have to worry about listening devices."

So he was a careful man. Or else was under surveillance, and knew it. And if some agency was watching Piccolo, Conte was now being watched as well, an idea not pleasant to contemplate.

"Get on with it, please, what did you find out?"

They stood in the center of the nave, no one within 50 yards.

"His name is Georges Grizzard."

"Where do I find him?"

"He's not Italian. Lives in France."

"Where?"

"The Riviera. Nice, maybe. Cannes."

"Wonderful."

Piccolo said: "You should be able to find him there."

Conte was furious. "His magazine has to be able to contact him. How do they do it?"

"They call him on his cell phone. Here's the number."

Conte stared down at a square of paper with numbers on it. Now he could talk to Grizzard any time he wanted, his words dropping down out of the sky and into the guy's head wherever he happened to be standing. But this didn't localize him, or help Conte find him. Didn't even reveal what country he might be in.

And if you called him, then he knew you were looking for him, and he would have plenty of time to disappear.

It seemed to Conte that he had learned nothing of value for his thousand euros, a sum that was going to be difficult to justify. "The phone company must have an address for him," he said evenly, "a place to send the bill."

"That's not the system here. He buys a card each month. Gives him the right to so many calls. When the card runs out he buys another. Even if the company had an address, they wouldn't give it to you without a warrant, which you couldn't get because he hasn't committed any crime. Not here, not in France."

"The magazine must pay him. Where do they send the money?"

"Switzerland."

"A name and a cell phone number. What else?" Suddenly Conte realized there must be more, for the big Italian was grinning at him. "You've got something else. What?"

"The address he uses here."

"Is he there now?"

"Let's find out, shall we. We'll go over there."

"We?"

"Both of us. In the event something comes up and you would need me."

"That won't be necessary."

"In Italy we give value for our money."

"You've already given value."

"You're not a cop anymore, whereas I am. People may not cooperate with you the way they would with me. I may be able to make them answer questions by showing that it's in their own best interest."

"I don't need that kind of cooperation."

"You very well might."

"Why should you want to get involved?"

"Let's say I've taken an interest in the case."

Conte did not like the sound of this. "An interest in the case?"

Piccolo nodded. "An interest in the case."

Grizzard's address was an apartment house on the Via Sismondi. Middle-class neighborhood. A building in no way distinguished from any other on the block. Five stories. Brick. Posted outside was a row of names, each with its own bell. Conte was still studying the names when Piccolo reached over his shoulder and pushed the button marked PORTIERE.

Again the big heavy grin. "No sense wasting time."

Through the glass they watched a man crossing the lobby toward them. He was small, bald, about 50.

"*Signori?*" he said, opening the glass door.

When he saw Piccolo's police card his posture went stiff, and after that he looked scared. Piccolo was such a big man, and his questions now were so abrupt, so threatening, that the *portiere* began to stutter. There was no one here named Georges Grizzard, he managed to say. All the tenants in the building were law-abiding. He himself also. He had never done anything wrong. A photographer? *Sì, Signore*, there was a photographer who had a flat here, who came and went, but, but—

People feared the police. Most times this fear was unreasonable, in Conte's opinion, but it was always there. In the past he had seen such reactions as this man's many times. A detective's first job, as Conte saw it, was to calm the subject down. He was no good to you until he could give coherent answers. Calm him down also so he would be less likely to file a civilian complaint on you.

But Piccolo played by different rules. He was shouting at the little man, poking him in the chest, pushing him backward.

Finally: "Which is the photographer's apartment? Show me."

The *portiere* led them up a flight of stairs and along a dark hallway.

"That his door?" said Piccolo.

"Sì, *Signore*, but—but—" But he wasn't home, hadn't been in weeks, was rarely there, it was a law-abiding building and—

"Open it."

He couldn't, the *portiere* stuttered, it was not permitted, he would lose his post, please, *Signore*—

Piccolo was sniffing the air. "Smell that? What's that terrible odor?"

Conte could smell nothing.

"Smells like a dead body," said Piccolo. "Smells like a corpse in there been dead a week. Open the door."

Conte knew very well what ripe corpses smelled like. They could be smelled all over the building, and cops knew what they were in for before they broke down the door. There was no such odor here.

"Open it," Piccolo ordered. "Or somebody's going to get arrested."

Still the *portiere* hesitated.

"Hands behind your back." Piccolo had his handcuffs out and rattling.

The *portiere* produced a passkey and aimed it at the lock, but couldn't insert it. He kept missing.

Piccolo snatched away the key. "Give it here."

"My key," the *portiere* said.

After opening the door, holding it ajar, Piccolo turned toward the *portiere*. "Ever see a corpse been dead a week? It's not something you want to see. Wait downstairs."

They listened to the descending footsteps, then went in.

A studio apartment sparsely furnished. A single bed, unmade. A chair. A table with papers on it, some of them crumpled. An overflowing wastebasket. Phone numbers penciled on the wall. A small kitchen. Very few utensils. Clotted dishes, some in the sink, some on a sideboard. A closet. A toilet. A fax, a scanner on a table, some other gear too. A bathroom that had been fitted out as a darkroom and lab. Its window had been blacked out, and the door had been insulated to keep out light. When Conte moved the door back and forth it made an audible brushing noise. A strip of negatives hung from a string. He must use both film and digital, Conte thought. Sink and bathtub were stained purple. On one wall hung a corkboard, some enlargements tacked to it. The artist's favorites, perhaps. The queen of England, caught unawares, grinning like a fool. The one next to it made Conte catch his breath, though he gave no sign.

They stepped back into the main room.

"Entering a domicile without a warrant," murmured Conte to Piccolo. "In New York we have laws against that."

"This is Italy."

"In New York it's a felony. Get caught and you go to jail. You must have the same laws here."

"The guy's a foreigner. Foreigners' rights are sometimes overlooked. For the good of the *Repubblica*, you might say. What's he going to do? And who cares?"

Conte had his notebook out and was taking down the phone numbers off the wall. To his surprise Piccolo was doing the same.

Conte said: "This is not your case."

"But I've taken an interest in it."

"It's not your case."

"You never know."

Conte began going through the wastebasket.

"I draw the line on other people's garbage," the big man said.

"Garbage is good," said Conte. "You sometimes find interesting items in garbage, though not this time." He was studying the back of an envelope on which was written *Gigi Amsterdam,* and a phone number — one of the same numbers as on the wall — he glanced up to make sure. Without calling attention to the envelope he left it there and turned away. "I'm finished," he said. "Let's go before somebody catches us here."

But at the door, instead of stepping out into the hall, he said: "Wait a second. Just let me take a final look at that darkroom."

He went in there and at the corkboard snatched off the photo that had caught his attention, folded it quickly, and thrust it into his pocket.

"Okay," he said when he came out, "let's go." As they went down the steps, they could hear the *portiere* nervously pacing the lobby, and Conte said: "And I think you should tell that little man about the dead body we didn't find. Ease his mind. Put the poor bastard out of his misery."

Piccolo's car was parked in front of the building. It was a dark green Jaguar. Conte knew very well how much such cars cost in Italy. "This is not a cop-type car," he commented as he got into it.

Piccolo laughed. "Depends on the cop."

"You're calling attention to yourself."

"Let them look." Piccolo had slid under the wheel. The driver's door slammed shut.

Conte said: "They may decide that no cop has the money to be driving a Jaguar."

"My wife is very frugal," Piccolo said.

"They start looking, who knows what else they'll find."

Piccolo seemed highly amused at the American's reasoning. "I'll take you back to your hotel," he said.

He's amazing, thought Conte. He is what he is. Doesn't try to hide anything.

Having parked in front of the hotel, Piccolo said: "I'm still waiting for that dinner you promised." His big grin came on, and he named what Conte knew to be the most expensive restaurant in Milan. "Successful day today," he said. "The palace will be glad to foot the bill."

"The palace?"

"Your employer."

"I don't know where you got that idea from. Anyway, I can't take you to dinner. I've got to fly out of here tonight."

"Where to? The Riviera?"

"Of course," lied Conte.

"Shouldn't be too hard finding Grizzard there."

"No."

"You'll keep me informed of your progress."

"Sure," lied Conte, "no problem."

Piccolo's car pulled away from the curb. Conte watched it go.

His flight that night was not to the Riviera but to Amsterdam.

In the air the American withdrew the photo he had ripped off Grizzard's corkboard and unfolded it. The young woman naked. Same breasts as in the magazine, but this time with a face attached. He was reasonably certain it was the same woman. In the magazine her face was always hidden by her hair, or buried in the neck of the young man. But here she was staring straight at the camera. Nothing to hide. Nothing hidden. At all.

Nice-looking girl, he observed, though why should he care? She was surely a prostitute. She had to be, what else could she be? He was surprised therefore at how young and innocent the photo made her look.

He studied the photo so long as to receive odd looks from the passengers strapped in between him and the aisle. Embarrassed, he refolded it and put it away.

He peered out the porthole at the immensity of the darkness outside, and at the dim clusters of lights far below. Since when am I interested in prostitutes, he asked himself.

He was flying to Amsterdam first because he believed the woman would be easier to find than the photographer. Not only is the Riviera a big place with many cities, but most likely the photographer was constantly on the move. He would be difficult to find at the best of times.

Whereas she was most likely stationary, because most women were, and if he could find her, she could lead him straight to him.

He thought he could count on the Dutch police to give him her name and address. He knew something about prostitution in Holland, because it was often spoken of in awe in the New York law enforcement world. Unlike New York, where the mayor regularly ordered massage parlors raided and girls scooped up off the streets, prostitution in Holland was both legal and out in the open. The police knew who the girls were. They were licensed, registered, fingerprinted, photographed too, he believed, identified by name, and regularly medically examined. Finding a specific girl should not be difficult.

Legalize prostitution in New York, Conte mused, and the mayor would be voted out. The police commissioner would be indicted.

He was feeling confident. This Gigi could be frightened into giving him Grizzard's address. He had part of her probable name. He had her probable phone number. Best of all he knew now what she looked like. She was certainly a beautiful girl and she should be easy to find.

It was almost as if he was looking forward to meeting her. Stop being a romantic, he berated himself. She's a whore, and for seducing Murano on camera she should be in jail.

CHAPTER

XIII

AMSTERDAM'S POLICE HEADQUARTERS is at Elandsgracht 117, a big, square building, high, imposing. It imposes itself on the street. A building with weight. A place of powerful men. A place of secrets. Looking up at it, Conte acknowledged all this but was not troubled by it. Every police building he had ever been in was similar, as if designed to overawe all who entered, not only criminals in handcuffs, but also any honest civilian who might imagine he had business inside. Civilians could expect to get short shrift within such buildings, and usually did. Conte's own reaction today was nothing of the kind. These were his people in there. Cops. Different nationality, different language, but otherwise cops. Men he knew well.

There was a street out front, the inevitable canal running alongside it, sometimes with boats going by. This Conte saw as he got out of the cab. He went inside, identified himself at the front desk, was made to wait a very short time, then was led to the office of a man named Van Meulen. The American ex-cop, wanting something from this man whom he did not know, was trying to read quickly whatever clues he could perceive. An institutional desk bare of papers. A Dutch flag, furled, in one corner. On one wall a portrait of Queen Beatrix. On another, a row of framed photos of Van Meulen with what Conte assumed to be Dutch celebrities, people unknown to him.

Not much different, then, from any police office anywhere. Not many clues to read.

Van Meulen had not risen to greet him. Nor did he invite Conte to sit down.

"Yes?" he said, looking up.

He was about 50. Supposedly he commanded the unit which, in New York, was called the Public Morals Division. His uniform bore insignia that meant nothing to Conte. What his rank might correspond to, Conte did not know either but, judging from Van Meulen's manner, which was distant, almost bored, it must be high up.

The Dutchman observed Conte as if from some superior station. He said: "And you are?"

The man outside must have given Conte's name. Nonetheless, he gave it again.

"I see. First trip to Holland, is it?"

Conte admitted this, then added: "I'm sure you know New York better than I know your country."

"We've had New York policemen here before. Most of them treat us as country bumpkins. Not one of those, are you?"

"No, I hope not."

The man spoke with an upper-class English accent, and his attitude was that of an English lord talking to his driver. It was an attitude Conte had encountered many times in many such offices in the past. Put stars and bars on a man's shoulder, he reflected, and that's often what you get.

"What's the size of the force in New York these days?"

"About forty thousand cops."

"More than we have in all of Holland," said Van Meulen. "Or need. Waste of manpower, as I see it."

A uniformed man came in and put papers down. Van Meulen gave them a glance, scrawled his initials, handed them back, and the man went out.

"I've been to New York several times on police matters," Van Meulen said. Watching Conte closely, he named the high-level commanders he had dealt with.

It was a form of name-dropping, and Conte saw this. He was meant to be impressed, which he wasn't. It was also a test. What circles did Conte himself move in?

The names mentioned were unknown to him, and in his annoyance he said so, realizing too late that this was a mistake.

"The reason I don't know those men," the American explained hurriedly, "is that I've never worked in headquarters."

Most cops who reached headquarters never left it. Including this man probably. They spent their time, as Conte saw it, kissing ass and bucking for promotion. He had little respect for such men. To Conte a cop's place was on the street.

The Dutchman's voice had become even more distant. "How can I help you, Mr. — I'm afraid I don't know how to address you. Captain Conte, is it?"

"Mr. Conte, or Vince — I'm not a captain here, Superintendent."

From his briefcase Conte withdrew the nude photo of Gigi. "I'm trying to find this woman. I'm pretty sure she's a prostitute, and since you have all these girls registered, I wonder if I could go through your photo files looking for her."

"We don't have photos of them, I'm afraid. The turnover among them is too great to make it worthwhile. Too expensive too."

"I assume your files are computerized."

This comment was enough to make Van Meulen bristle. "We don't live entirely in the Dark Ages in Holland."

"She's known as Gigi, I believe. Do you have the girls listed by nickname?"

"What's this all about?"

"It's a case I'm working on."

"What is it, a divorce case?" said Van Meulen distastefully.

It was closer to a divorce case than Conte cared to admit.

Van Meulen waited for an explanation.

"I'm sorry," said Conte. "It's rather sensitive. I can't talk about it."

"I see." And then: "Show me your credentials please."

The surprised Conte showed his captain's shield which he carried with him always, even though it was only a replica. When he resigned from the department he had been obliged to turn in his shield, so he had bought the replica on Hester Street, which runs behind the old police headquarters, in one of the row of shops that sold cop paraphernalia to cops. Fancy pistols, ankle holsters. A cop who lost his shield could get another one made, and no one need ever know. When promoted, some cops liked to get their old shields, or a replica, embedded in paperweights in one or another of these shops, or welded to lamps or desk calendars. Conte had bought the replica and carried it always because at first he had kept slapping his back pocket looking for his shield. Without it he had felt naked.

"You're a New York City policeman?"

"Ex. I'm in the private sector now."

"I was led to believe you were here on official business."

"That wasn't what I told your man outside."

"You're not a police officer at all."

"I was. I'm retired."

"They give you a card when you retire. May I see it please?"

"I have no such card." Conte was becoming very annoyed very fast.

"And what's this badge?"

"It's my captain's shield. When I left the job I kept it."

"You're not a policeman at all," said Van Meulen. "If I had known I would not have agreed to see you. How old are you?"

Conte gave his age.

"Let's say you really were a policeman once. Nobody retires at thirty-five. Why did you?"

Conte had no intention of explaining himself to this man.

"Had some trouble, did you?" suggested Van Meulen.

Conte knew what was being insinuated. "Not at all."

Needing to find Gigi, he had come into this building looking for help. He had been counting on the equivalent of the old boy network. Cops had the biggest old boy network in the world. If a cop needed something he could count on other cops. Every cop in the world believed this. It was like an insurance policy that cops carried around with them. A form of faith. A ticket to salvation.

The only trouble was, he was no longer a cop.

"What are you really? A pressman? Planning another article on the wicked ways of the immoral Dutch? Is that what you're here for?"

"No," said Conte evenly, "I came in here because I thought you might be able to help me, one cop to another. If that concept is too deep for you, then I won't take up any more of your valuable time."

Conte found himself in the street. And on his own.

The red-light district, then.

It was night. The girls sat on straight chairs in lighted windows that were at street level, or half a flight up, meaning eye level. Picture windows in which the girls sat eight feet away. They wore fetching smiles and eye-popping lingerie. One or two wore see-through housecoats over their see-through underwear — these were the more elegant ones, perhaps. The more modest. The occasional girl wore jewelry: an ankle bracelet, a necklace. When they crossed their legs one could see the soles of their sometimes dirty feet.

The district was crowded. Whole tour groups passed through as Conte watched. Men, women, and children ogling the girls. Groups of all nationalities, even Japanese. Groups led by guides reciting spiels. The guides were Dutch, the tourists were Italian, English, Asian, whatever, judging from the languages. Some individual tourists as well.

There were doors beside each window, each with a red light burning over it. Look down the street and above the heads of the crowds — dozens of red lights in a row. Sometimes a customer would detach himself from the crowd and go through a door. The girl would get up to let him into her room, then pull down the shade. Sometimes an entire group stayed in place and stared at the shade.

Moving from street to street, crossing the canals on pedestrian bridges with iron railings, Conte studied the windows looking for Gigi, but did not find her.

The district was hundreds of years old, one of the oldest in the city. Brick houses wedged in one against the other. Tall, narrow buildings, some dating from Rembrandt's time. The streets were brick, and ran beside canals. Many canals, many bridges. Trees along the canals, sometimes weeping willows. Cars parked under them.

The girls were young, some were quite pretty, and some looked virginal. Most were posing for the few customers and the many tourists. This was their stage. The spotlight was on them. They played at being actresses upon it. Some poses were prim, some wanton. Some girls were primping, some smoking. Some talked animatedly into cell phones.

On Stoofsteeg an especially pretty one. As Conte watched, she opened her window to chat with the people in the street.

Also there were individuals who moved through the district briskly, head down, ignoring the girls. People from the neighborhood, perhaps.

On one of the bridges two cops, one with his hat off, lounged against the railing, their bicycles close by. This was the only police presence Conte saw. As he scouted the windows he was also having cop thoughts he was powerless to stop. They had been hammered into his head long ago, had been driven in like nails. In New York, his instincts told him, this red-light district would be a place of assaults, robberies, murders. A hotbed of crime. Thugs on all sides. How could it be any different here? There should not be Japanese tour groups wending through, it wasn't safe. In New York the cops would be stationed in here from wall to wall. Unlike those two cops on the bridge, they would be looking in all directions at once, their hands on their guns.

He had other questions he wanted answered, the same ones any New York cop would ask. Who were these girls? Were they Dutch, or what? If not, where did they come from, how did they get to be in those windows? Were they controlled by pimps? By organized crime? How much did a seat in a window cost?

He walked on under the trees. On some streets were stores of a special type. In their windows were displayed pornographic posters and photos, pornographic books and videos, not to mention the vibrators and marital aids—erotic paraphernalia of all kinds. The stores were illuminated inside and out by neon signs that flared, died, flared, died, a symphony without sound, a tumult of silence. Farther on came neons more garish still, these announcing live sex shows, gay sex shows. The words splashed on and off. They lit up the street for ten yards to either side, and the canal out front as well.

Oudekennissteeg, the final street. Girls in every window. Rooms that could only be called cribs. In them cheap cots sometimes. Sometimes many chairs with only one girl. Or two girls.

For two hours Conte patrolled the district, but he did not find Gigi.

He went back the next morning. Perhaps she worked by day. But at this early hour most windows were vacant, the rooms behind them vacant. The exertions of the night before had emptied them out. Other windows were closed off by curtains, and he could not see in. Some did have girls in them. Older, uglier girls mostly.

Along the streets, meanwhile, normal commerce continued. Delivery trucks pulled up. People moved about who lived or worked in the neighborhood. Excursion boats went by under the bridges. The canals had brick walls, he noted now. Guides' voices came to him off the water, then were gone.

Architecturally speaking, the red-light district was handsome. There were stoops with wrought iron railings. Many of the doors were heavy and old, the wood carved and polished, with heavy brass knockers.

Who lived above the picture windows, he asked himself. But he had no answer.

The shops and bars of the night before were still there, their neons shut down but most of them open for business. He passed the Naughty Picture Studio. The store next to it called itself the Condomerie—its window displayed special condoms of all sorts, plus other sexual goods. Outside the Theatre Casa Rossa burbled a fountain in the shape of an erect penis. It stood as high as a man. Water spurted upward from its rosy nose. He passed the Cannabis Connoisseurs Club, and then Cannabis College, where marijuana grew in planters outside the front door. Next came the Hash Marijuana Hemp Museum, admission four euros.

It all seemed so normal. The water in the canals, the boats going by under the bridges, the leaves on the trees with the sun on them—all was normal in every way. The air smelled normal. He could feel his clothes on his body, his brown suit, his wingtip shoes. He could feel the air filling his chest. All was normal, except for everything else around him. In one of the houses there was a play school for children. Through the window he watched tots playing on the floor.

At night he tried again, studied all the same windows, all the same girls. If he passed a window with its shades drawn he remembered it and returned later when that particular window was again illuminated, that particular girl back on sale.

At length he approached the two cops on the bridge, and identified himself. Same two cops, different bridge. A brick bridge this one, dated 1728, handsome, two pedestrians wide and barely room for the excursion boat that, as he watched, passed underneath. The passengers had to duck their heads. If the water level were to rise even three inches, the boat could not pass, would be stuck under there. The company would be out of business. The tourists would have to go sightseeing somewhere else.

The two officers greeted him. They were beat cops, and this was their beat, had been for years, they told him. One spoke excellent English, the other not so good. It was easy duty for the most part, they said. The red-light district was the number one attraction in Holland, did Conte know that? Five million tourists a year go through here. Guess how many go to see the Rembrandts in the museum, said the other. And they all laughed. So much for culture.

Lots of drug dealing in here, the cops admitted, but little violence. As long as the girls stayed within the district they were not molested by the police. The vice squad controlled them regularly—men went along asking for papers. Van Meulen's men, Conte thought. Sometimes drunks beat up a girl. There were alarm bells in every crib, and when one went off these two cops, or two others, would mount their bicycles and pedal to the rescue. Or a drunk would strip himself naked and dive into the canal, and have to be fished out. But this was rare.

Of course on weekends there were always additional cops on duty in here.

They asked Conte about a cop's life in New York, and he answered. Soon the three men were telling each other stories, their own experiences, or colleagues'. This was cop talk, ribald, sometimes grotesque. They made each other laugh. They were all cops together talking shop. Conte enjoyed it, but it caused a pang as well. It made him miss New York, miss the NYPD, miss more than ever what he once had had.

He showed Gigi's picture, and talked of her, but they didn't recognize her, neither her photo nor her name. "She's gorgeous," one said, staring at the photo.

"Yes," said Conte.

"I think I'd recognize her if she was in here," said the cop.

"Maybe she's a call girl," said the other. "You wouldn't find her unless you had her phone number."

"I do have her phone number," said Conte.

"And?"

"No answer."

In a certain sense Conte was glad he hadn't found her in a window. Perhaps he hoped she wasn't a call girl either. What did he hope?

What's the matter with me, he asked himself.

"She looks expensive," said the first cop.

The other said: "Have you tried the nightclubs?"

"Maybe she does these live sex shows. There are a number of them along here."

Conte gazed at her picture. "She doesn't look to me like a live sex kind of girl."

"What can you tell from a photo?" scoffed the first cop.

"Photos lie," said the second.

Conte recognized police cynicism when he heard it. "What kind of nightclubs?" he said.

"Maybe she's a stripper. They're a little better."

"Not much," said the second cop.

"Oh yes. They're on a higher moral plane," said the first cop.

"Try the casino," suggested the second cop. "Great shows there, I hear. It's expensive, though. I know I can't afford it."

"The Lido Casino on the Max Euweplein," said the other. "They're supposed to have the best shows."

He said good-bye to them — this caused a slight pang too, for in just a few minutes these other cops had become his brothers.

He took a taxi. It pulled up in a broad street, the casino on one side of the street, a canal on the other. Crowded sidewalk. Everybody well dressed. A big building brilliantly lit up. A line of taxis in front, waiting to take away winners and losers afterward. Winners few, losers many, reflected Conte, who hated gambling. The house and the taxi drivers were guaranteed a night's profit no matter what, no one else. To the New York cop gambling was organized stealing. If you won anything it was a miracle.

He stood in front of what seemed to be the only entrance. It was two stories high and wide as a house. There were posters, and he read them. The games of chance to be found inside were extolled, the different restaurants as well. The poster for the nightclub was just as big. The show began at midnight. The performers were listed, their acts described in giant letters. Conte recognized none of the names and the descriptions were in Dutch.

There was no Gigi.

A number of names were women obviously, but for the most part they sounded French. Gigi, according to Antonio Murano, was not French.

Conte refused to let himself be discouraged.

The casino complex proved bigger than it looked, occupying most of two city blocks. Conte walked completely around it, for he was a careful man. Canals front and back. Parking lot to one side. In the rear a loading dock. To serve the restaurants, presumably. Truckloads of produce going in each day, truckloads of garbage going out the next morning. Here too the armored cars would pull up to take away the loot.

Conte was like a robber casing a job. What were the getaway routes? If he found her he did not want to lose her.

He located a number of fire exits rigged to set off alarms if used. Apart from these there was only one other door, which must be where the employees came and went, busboys and croupiers as well as *artistes*. The stage door for everybody. This door was steel, probably impregnable, and there would be a guard inside. Across from the stage door was a long rack stuffed with bicycles, and a small parking lot closed off by a barrier that lifted, but only if you had the correct card.

Having circumnavigated the complex, he entered the casino via the brilliantly lighted front doors. Once inside, all was gloom. Like a sinner he had stepped from light into darkness. There were tables for roulette, blackjack, craps, baccarat. The place was crowded, dark, and lit principally by the 200 or more slot machines that lined the walls. The cascade of raining coins was constant. He looked up at the ceiling, and saw a great stained glass dome. He felt like he was standing under an enormous Tiffany lampshade.

To reach the nightclub he had to cross the gambling hall, obviously. The nightclub was part of the attraction that brought people here, but it did not exist alone. Patrons were expected to drop a bundle getting to it, and another bundle on the way out.

The nightclub was a little smaller but even darker, more crowded, Conte saw. People sat elbow to elbow at tiny tables and were served. In front was the stage, at the rear the bar where Conte, pressed himself between two other men, sipped a glass of too expensive champagne, and waited to see whatever he would see.

Presently the show started. The emcee came out through the curtain and, employing many superlatives, introduced the first act in four languages, Dutch, German, English, French. The Japanese, who filled at least half the tables, were left to flounder. The curtain parted. Small stage. Small band playing. Carrying a cordless microphone a girl began to sing. Young. Bright red, bouffant hair. Nice gown. She sang ballads, but with a rock beat. A nice voice. Nice songs too. She was supposed to be the new sensation from New York. She had an American name and the songs sounded American but her accent was atrocious. What was she, German? Middle European?

She was followed by a trained dog act. Conte had the impression he had seen the same act on television when he was a boy. There followed a trio of girl tap dancers, another singer, then a magician with patter in English and French only. He got a few laughs, not many. All this lasted nearly an hour, and Conte was not interested in any of it. He was there to find Gigi, and was becoming less and less hopeful.

And lastly came the act, according to the emcee in his four languages, that everyone had been waiting for. And perhaps there was some truth in this claim for in the last few minutes more and more people had crowded in from the gambling rooms until they were packed around all the walls. The rows of standees at the bar had thickened, had doubled or tripled in size.

"Straight from Caesars Palace in Las Vegas and the Folies Bergère in Paris," the emcee's voice rang out, "I give you the beautiful, the voluptuous"—He spoke her name almost in a shout—"MARIE-THERESE DE FRANCE." And the curtain parted.

What followed was an act upon a stage that one could scoff at, but not for long. One watched it anchored solidly in present tense, for like a painting it seemed to stop time.

Soft music. Upstage, a bathtub in which Marie-Therese de France reposes, her arms and face visible, not much else, for there is too little light. She soaps and rinses her face with what proves to be real water, for one can hear the spill and splash of it. She shifts position. Water sluices off her. Now she kneels, sits on her heels, and reaches into the soap dish. She has a washcloth, she works on her upper body, more of which can now be seen though not all, for the spotlight, which had circled her face, is now behind her.

Men in the audience stir, strain to make out more of her than she has shown them, their needs far out in front of what she has so far given. Wait, she seems to be saying, it is not yet time. Already she seems to have captured time, made it obey her, slowed it way down.

For the moment Conte is immune, he strains only to decide on her face. Could this be Gigi? But there is too little light, the lights have been too artfully placed and he soon realizes that this is deliberate. Nearby is a sink with a cabinet and mirror over it. The mirror is illuminated, and most of the available light comes from there. But it is some distance off. Downstage is a vanity table, and its mirror too is lit. There seem to be floor lights here and there also, but none focused on the girl's portion of the stage — her present portion. Conte wonders if she designed the lighting herself to show exactly as much of herself as she wishes shown, in the order in which she chooses to show it. Will she ever move into the light?

She rises, steps from the tub. Her movements, all her movements, are languorous, or vigorous, or languorous again, always in time to the music. She titillates no one. She pays no attention to whoever might be watching. It is as if she does not know the audience is there.

As she reaches for a towel she is sopping, but because she is facing the back of the stage the audience views only rounded hips, rounded buttocks. Her body is well formed, and it is wet. The light, such as it is, snags in the drops that cling to her back, her arms. She blots herself dry, wraps herself in the towel. By the time she turns toward the audience the towel covers her, one corner tucked in over her breasts, as in a 1950s movie. All is chaste. One can see nothing.

She stands before the sink where she examines her teeth, her smile. In the mirror she grimaces, tries out other smiles. Her face then goes sad, as if she is disappointed in what she sees, and she turns away. For a time her face has been framed by light, causing Conte at the bar to give a start. This may indeed be Gigi. He can't be sure. She is too far away, is glimpsed only in reflection, and he has only a photo to go by. The photo has never changed expression, whereas her face does and has. To match the photo to this girl is not as easy as he would like.

Very soon the photo goes from his mind. He forgets that this is an actress performing on a stage. As he is drawn further and further into her world it comes to seem more real to him than his own. Emotions take hold that he is not ready for, and he is almost overcome by them. It is as if, by allowing him to witness her most private and intimate moments, this young woman has shown him his deepest loneliness, his deepest needs, and hers too.

There are other emotions as well, and they are equally unexpected. The apparent perfection of her face and body has left him dazzled. He feels privileged to see what he has seen.

He tries to come to grips with himself and with her, to focus on details. At her vanity table, seated, she drags a comb through her hair. She has an elastic between her teeth with which she means to tie up a ponytail. Having pulled her hair tight behind her head, she attempts to loop it into the elastic, but while doing so her towel slips. Her hands being occupied, she can't catch it in time. Instead her breasts come into view, one jiggles, then the other, each one glowing in turn in the light from the vanity mirror. Still sitting, she manages to fasten her ponytail. Standing up, she refastens her towel.

Realizing he has forgotten his champagne, Conte takes a gulp of it.

There is a full-length mirror on a stand. She adjusts its tilt. In front of it she holds dresses against herself. She is trying to decide what to wear. Each time she reaches for a new dress the towel comes partly undone. Quickly before it falls she refastens it. Finally she shakes her head in annoyance, gives up and lets it fall. It makes a puddle at her feet in which she stands. The mirror reflects her holding dresses against herself—reflects, between dresses, all of her, but only for a moment each time, after which the new dress again blocks the view. The audience can study her shoulders if it wishes, her bare back, her bottom, her fine long legs but once again the view is less than satisfying, for most of the light is elsewhere.

Conte leans intently forward, as intently as anyone. He has become starved for glimpses.

Having selected a red dress, which she carries over her arm, she turns and, walking directly toward him, tosses the dress over the back of a chair. Such is the state of suspense she has created that he almost gasps.

There seems nothing deliberately erotic about any of this. She is naked because she is alone in her room getting dressed. She gets a bra out of a drawer, bends to fill it, and straightens up. Hands and arms work behind her back. But there is a problem of some kind; she goes on working as the seconds pass. Despite the lines of concentration in her forehead, and the tossing of her head, she cannot attach the catch. Finally she takes the bra off, examines its catch, tosses it aside, and gets out another.

The homeliest of gestures, the most intimate.

All this has evoked, in Conte and presumably in others, a reaction that is too strong and that is not so easily described or explained. The reaction may be principally erotic, but the young woman cannot be blamed for it, for she does not know, according to the illusion she has created, that anyone is watching, or that any such reaction has occurred.

In the background the music has continued to play softly, her movements synchronized to it, as if she is dancing. She isn't dancing exactly, but she never makes an abrupt or discordant movement, and she never takes any note of the audience. It is not a striptease. There is no teasing, no bumps and grinds, nothing coy or suggestive at all. The result is the most intimate and erotic scene imaginable. It is as if, unknown to her, all these strangers are observing her through a keyhole. Peeping Toms, everybody. Every adolescent's daydream, realized at last.

Apart from the music there is no sound in the room. Nor is there movement. The room seems overcome by stillness. She has mesmerized everyone in it, every man certainly. Conte is aware of this. Without any apparent effort she commands the stage. No coughing, no fidgeting, no other movement anywhere in the hall. Even the women patrons are still.

It is a scene of great power. She is naked in what she imagines to be the privacy of her room, but it isn't private at all. The entire audience is peering in at her.

Once her bra is satisfactorily attached, once she has tugged on it in several places, arranging herself comfortably inside it, her hand digs into the same drawer as before, coming out this time with several pairs of panties. There is no sign of modesty, real or otherwise, no shame at her nakedness, she never tries to cover herself. The illusion that she thinks she is alone will be maintained to the end.

She selects the panty she wants, a rather scant piece of material from the look of it, steps into it, and pulls it up her legs. There are spike heel shoes beside her chair. She sits down and pulls them on, crossing first one leg then the other to tie the straps. When she stands again in her spike heels and her lacy underwear she seems more naked than any time yet, and once again she holds the red dress against herself, hesitating, looking across at the other hanging dresses, as if considering changing her selection. Perhaps one of the other dresses would look better. It depends on where she is going, obviously. To a dinner party, to a dance, to a job interview? To the audience the answer is not clear.

She shrugs, pulls the red dress over her head, and smoothes it into place. Another glance into her mirror: She smoothes her hair. Bending, she applies a bit of lip gloss. She picks up her handbag, looks into it as if checking that she has her keys, then turns, and, to a crescendo from the band, walks off the stage.

The show is over.

Behind her there is heavy silence, followed by a kind of collective sigh, and then by tumultuous applause. This goes on for some time, the crowd trying to summon her back. Finally the curtains part once more, the houselights come up, and the girl in the red dress walks to stage front

where she stands beaming into the applause. People are on their feet ap-
plauding. There are a few raucous whistles, some banging on tables. For
a minute or more she drinks in the noise, the approval. She waves this
way and that. Then the curtains close. She is gone.

The applause continues, but she does not reappear.

It was Gigi all right, by now Conte was sure of it. How long had she
been onstage? He had lost track of time. Twenty minutes. Perhaps a bit
longer. The length of time it takes to play a concerto. Like a pianist, one
concerto and you are finished for the night.

Conte was feeling a bit stunned and so did not immediately react to
a situation that was changing fast.

He then realized a number of facts, one of them being that the actress had no costume or makeup to remove, was already dressed in street
clothes and so was not going to linger in any dressing room backstage.
Probably she would leave instantly, because if she hung around she was
likely to get accosted by the amorous and the drunks.

If he wanted to confront her, he had best hurry.

But he was pinned in at the bar, which was buzzing with conversation about this Marie-Therese de France, and had to push his way free.
There was another jam-up at the entrance to the gambling rooms, followed by its crowded aisles. It took him some minutes to reach the street,
and he got there just in time to see the red dress go by astride a bicycle.
He called out to her but she was pedaling fast, and did not stop.

He ran to the head of the cab line, yanked open the door, and
jumped in. "Follow that bicycle," he ordered the driver.

The driver seemed to take his time starting the motor. Traffic and red
lights slowed the cab, but not the bicycle. Finally they were gaining, but
as they got close Conte saw that the girl had become aware of them. She
kept glancing over her shoulder, and she seemed to be pedaling harder.
Perhaps she had been pursued other nights. Perhaps it happened often.
Perhaps she knew how to spot pursuers. Suddenly she veered left, lifted
her bike up the steps onto a footbridge, and ran it across the canal to the

other side where she calmly remounted and pedaled away. She did not look back. The chase was over.

"Can we go around, intercept her someplace?" asked Conte.

The driver said he would try.

Farther along they crossed on a bigger bridge, and on the other side moved up and down streets. But there were too many canals. After a time, even Conte could see that it was hopeless.

"Take me back to my hotel," he said, and gave the name.

In bed in the dark he could not sleep, tossed for hours and was tormented more by erotic images than by worry about his investigation. It had been his job to find this Gigi, interrogate her and get answers, an imperative that had somehow changed into something else that was either simpler, or much more complex. His need had become to meet her, spend time with her, find out who she was. But this is crazy, he told himself. He was here to do an investigation, which was progressing nicely. He should stick to the investigation only. What kind of girl she might be was of no importance.

But as he lay in the dark she would not let him be. Through his head floated visions of her that he knew to be fantastic but could not chase away. He could not even close his eyes, for when he did the visions only sharpened, imprinted themselves ever more deeply.

The next day, hungover from lack of sleep, he did what tourists do in Amsterdam: went to look at the Rembrandts and Vermeers in one museum, the Van Goghs in another. After that, with 30 or 40 others he boarded a long, exceedingly low excursion boat for a trip through some of the canals. He stared upward at buildings 400 years old, and ducked his head at bridges the boat could barely get under.

He was waiting for night.

He went late to the casino, missing more than half the acts, and stood at the bar and left his champagne untouched. When Gigi came on he tried not to look at her, for this only distracted him more than he was distracted already. Instead, he looked along the bar which was two or three deep in patrons, as many as last night and mostly men, and wondered vaguely who they were and what they imagined they were here for, and in this way his eye was caught by the one man in the world that he least expected to see here.

Or had expected to see all along. Had expected to see any day. Perhaps even feared to see any day.

At the outer rim of the bar patrons, nursing his champagne, eyes fixed on Gigi onstage, stood Luigi Piccolo, and on his face was an expression of almost fevered intensity.

Conte muscled his way toward him.

The big man, who saw him coming, gave a wolfish grin, and his usual huge handshake, and before being addressed explained himself: "The case led to Amsterdam."

"It's my case."

"I was afraid you wouldn't get here in time, so here I am."

"Stay out of my case." Conte's voice had risen.

"I've taken an interest in it. I can't help myself."

"What hotel are you at?" Conte was shouting in whispers in Italian. "We'll settle this in the morning."

"I've already checked out," Piccolo told him. "Going back to Milan tonight."

Among the emotions besetting the American was an absurd feeling of possessiveness. He couldn't bear for any man, particularly this one, to watch Gigi nude.

You're becoming obsessed, he told himself. What the hell has happened to you?

Piccolo gestured in the direction of Gigi. "Lovely piece of ass, wouldn't you say."

Conte was fuming. To Piccolo he said: "Just stay the hell out of my case."

At the nearby tables heads had turned. Bar patrons were trying to shush them.

"I'm leaving right now," said Piccolo, and he handed Conte his champagne glass and worked his way out of the hall. Clutching the two glasses, the American watched him go.

Gigi's act had about five minutes left. It was time for Conte to go too. He pushed through people who were focused totally on Gigi onstage. As he crossed the gambling room, he looked for Piccolo. He looked for him all the way out to the street, but did not see him.

Outside the night was clear, a big moon hanging over the houses. He put ankle clips around his pants legs, unchained his rented bike, and hid it and himself among the cars in the employee parking lot.

His eyes were fixed on the stage door, and he did not have long to wait before Gigi, wearing a yellow dress tonight, came out, and hurried to her own bike, which she unchained. Glancing nervously in every direction, she mounted it and pedaled out into the street.

It was past two o'clock in the morning. After giving her a few seconds' head start, Conte followed, pedaling along in front of the casino, and the rows of parked taxis waiting. Then the casino was behind him, and the street was darker. Gigi was a good distance ahead, but in sight. Apart from the two widely separated bikes, the street was empty.

He had considered carefully how to approach this young woman, and had decided it must be done as far as possible from the casino, where most probably she had often been accosted by strange men who, having seen her show, imagined she would find them as irresistible as they had found her. She was no doubt an expert at the quick, rude brush-off. As an investigator he could not afford to be brushed off, for he needed answers from her first, and as a smitten male, if that's what he was, he wanted to get close enough to her at least to find out who she was. His approach, when he made it, had to be circumspect.

And so he had determined to follow her home, find out where she lived, but not approach her tonight. He would work out later what to do next — perhaps he would try to meet her tomorrow in her supermarket, or some such place.

At present he was giving her plenty of room. For a time no cars passed them in either direction, and the city seemed as silent as the moon lying in its spotlight on the surface of the canal. If he was not to alarm her he had to keep well back. She was pedaling briskly, too briskly perhaps, for very soon he began to have trouble keeping up with her. He was two blocks back, then two and a half. He had not ridden a bike since he was a child, his thighs were tightening up, he was steadily losing ground, and he began to worry that she would go up onto a bridge, cross a canal, and he would lose her. By the time he got across himself she would have disappeared into the narrow streets on the other side.

And then she did pedal up onto a bridge. It made Conte stand on his pedals trying to sprint and a car burst by him, lights off, traveling fast, turned up onto the same bridge and he heard a screech of tires or brakes or both, and then the crash of rending metal, and he saw Gigi, or her body, propelled onto the parapet, where it hung for a moment before plummeting down into the water below. The drop must have been 20 feet, higher than any diving board. She made a heavy splash, the sound of which was followed by the noise the car made speeding down off the bridge and into the night.

Conte got there as fast as he could, jumped off his bike which clattered to the sidewalk behind him, and ran to the edge of the canal. He saw that Gigi had surfaced, and that there was movement, so at least she was alive. There was enough light from the moon and from distant streetlights to see that much. He had his shoes off, his jacket too, before he realized that the canal's brick walls were both straight and slick. If he went into the water after her, neither one of them would be able to get out. He looked all around but there was no one to help, no cars going by, nothing.

Gigi, he saw, had begun to swim, feebly at first, then more strongly.

"This way," cried Conte. And then: "Are you all right, are you hurt?" These words seemed idiotic to him even as he spoke them, exactly the type of idiocies, he would remember later with embarrassment, that one utters at such a time.

She reached the wall of the canal where there was nothing she could even grip. She seemed to be both gasping and crying. She was about six feet below him. Conte looked frantically about for a branch, a pole, something he could extend to her, found nothing, then saw his bike which he grabbed up and dangled over the edge to where she could reach it, front wheel first. He would haul her out with the bike.

"Put your toes between the spokes," he told her. "Hold on to the frame."

But she clung to the wheel, only her head and shoulders above water, and he had to repeat his instructions several times before she obeyed him and he was able to drag the bike and her raspingly up the wall and out of the canal.

Once on dry land she came into his arms, her face in his neck, weeping, and he held her.

"Are you all right?" he asked. "Are you all right?" He broke the embrace and began to examine her, first her arms, then her legs, her face. "Where do you hurt?" Her right shin was skinned, a nail on her right hand half torn off. There was a bruise under her right eye. "What about your ribs?" he said. "Can you breathe okay?"

She was of course sopping, her yellow dress now painted on, the paint sticky. Her ponytail had come apart and her hair hung in ropes. The yellow dress was spattered with mud and looked ruined. One shoe was missing.

"He hit me on purpose," she sobbed. "He drove straight toward me. I was way to the side. He tried to kill me. Why? Who was he?"

"You're imagining things," he told her. "It was an accident."

But he did not think it was an accident at all. Stop jumping to conclusions, he told himself. You have no evidence of any kind to back up what you are thinking.

He looked around for help, a police car, a taxi. The street was as empty as the canal that ran beside it.

"My handbag," she sobbed.

He understood that it was in the basket attached to her handlebars. Or at least it had been. She wanted her handbag. So he stepped back into his shoes, righted his own bike, and wheeled it toward the bridge.

"Don't leave me," she sobbed.

"I'm just going to get your handbag."

"You're going to leave me."

"No. I'm right here."

He didn't say so, but his police instincts had taken over. Her bike was evidence in a hit-and-run case, or perhaps the crime was attempted murder. He wanted to see the bike and after that he wanted to voucher it to preserve the chain of evidence.

He found it mashed into the wrought iron parapet.

She had followed him onto the bridge and stood close, staring at her ruined bike and trembling.

She's in as bad shape as the bike, he told himself, turning to look at her. He saw he would have to take care of her first, and come back for the bike later.

He handed her the handbag. "Can you sit on my bike?" he asked her. "We'll ride till we find a bar and can call a taxi."

She sat on the rack behind him, legs dangling, wet arms embracing him, wet face pressed against his back.

There weren't many bars open at this hour, but he found one that was, where he sat her down and ordered cognac. "And a Band-Aid," he called out to the barman.

The barman brought the cognac, and a box of Band-Aids on a tray. He could not take his eyes off Gigi. "We were horsing around and she fell in the canal," explained Conte.

"Cold, this time of night," the barman said.

"Can you call us a cab?"

The barman went back behind the bar and they saw him on the telephone. Conte handed her the snifter. "It will steady you. Drink it."

Drinking it, she made a grimace and said: "Ugh."

He bandaged her torn fingernail, while calling for another cognac, and when it came said: "Drink that one too."

Soon she seemed calmer, trembling as much from the wet and cold as from trauma, so he took off his suit coat and draped it over her shoulders and was rewarded by a grateful smile.

"A woman alone shouldn't be out as late as this. No woman alone. It isn't safe."

"It's my job," she mumbled, "I work nights."

Conte was trying to take the measure of her. "Where do you work?"

"The casino."

"As what?"

He waited to hear whatever her answer would be, but she only said again: "The casino."

"Don't you have someone who could see you home safely?"

"No." She seemed to have trouble talking, trouble breathing.

"No husband? No boyfriend?"

"No."

"What's your name?"

Another hesitation. "Georgette Meyer."

"Are you called Georgy?"

"Gigi."

"You're an American."

She said haltingly: "Dutch."

"You sound American."

The rest came out in broken phrases, first one, then the next, long hesitations in between as she tried to catch her breath. Her father, a diplomat, had been posted to Los Angeles, then Washington. She had graduated from UCLA.

To Conte it did not add up. How could a girl from such a background allow herself to get mixed up in the extortion that those photos represented? In the mess they had caused?

But he had another reaction that was even stronger, an old-fashioned one: prudery. How could a girl as splendid as this one take off her clothes for a paparazzo, or strip naked in a nightclub?

"Did you get a look at the driver? Could you identify him in court?"

"Big, I think. Dark. I don't know." Now it all poured out, a narrative interspersed with sobs or deep breaths, he wasn't sure which. "I'm riding on the hood of his car staring straight at him. He had big teeth and he was grinning." Again tears filled her eyes. "Tried to kill me. I'm pedaling along. A second later my bike is crushed and I'm riding on the front of his car. Then I'm in the water."

"You're going to have a shiner there," Conte said. Reaching across the table he stroked her bruised cheek. He had been wanting to do this since they had sat down, and it was a relief to do so finally. She winced from the pressure of his hand, then fashioned a weak smile.

"And you're going to be pretty stiff in the morning."

"I ache all over right now."

"You should see your eye. Your shin is all banged up too. You're not going to be able to work for a few days." Looking for a reaction he added: "If your appearance is important to your job, that is."

She nodded, but did not meet his eyes.

The barman called over that the cab was on its way.

Her dress was torn across the bodice exposing part of her bra, and as she grew calmer she kept trying to pull the pieces together.

"When the taxi comes I'm taking you to the police."

"No. Please."

"You were the victim of a hit and run. It should be reported. The police should be looking for the guy."

"It would get into the papers." She became agitated. "It would ruin me. I'd lose my job."

Police instincts again controlled him. The crime had to be reported, whatever her wishes might be. But for the moment he did not say so. "Okay," he said, "calm down."

"I've ruined your suit, your shirt." She shrugged out of his suit coat and tried to hand it back to him.

"You're cold. You keep it. At least until the taxi comes."

"I'm getting it all wet."

"It will dry."

"I'm sorry I hung on to you like that. We don't even know each other."

He smiled at her. "If you want to know the truth, I enjoyed having your arms around my neck."

She said: "I can't go on thinking of you as that nice man who fished me out of the canal. What's your name?"

Conte told her.

"Your poor tie." She reached out and touched it. "I wish I could at least buy you a new tie, Mr. Conte."

"It was a tie I never liked anyway." For the first time she smiled at him, a good, big smile. So he added: "How can I see you again?"

"You can't." The smile was already gone, replaced by an expression of — of he didn't know what.

"Why not?"

She bit her lip. "Don't think I'm not grateful to you. I'm very grateful. For pulling me out of the canal. For this cognac. For letting me cling to you when I needed to. But no."

Just then the cab pulled up outside. Seeing it she became agitated again, and in a moment was visibly trembling. She stood up, said: "Good night, Mr. Conte," and tried to shake hands with him.

"Finish your cognac."

"I can't."

By now she was shaking.

"You're afraid of something, aren't you? Deathly afraid."

"No, I'm not."

"You think somebody is trying to kill you."

"No."

"What have you done?"

"Nothing."

"You've done something. What?"

"I don't know."

They were both standing. He said: "I'll take you home."

"No."

"But—"

"I can go home by myself."

He took her arm and led her out onto the sidewalk. The cab was parked under a streetlight.

"Get in, I'm taking you home."

She is a nightclub stripper, he told himself. She is a hard piece of work. She must be. He had to keep reminding himself because at this particular moment she was none of these things.

"All right," she said in a voice he could hardly hear, a frightened voice, almost a little girl's voice.

The cab crossed some canals, turned, and drove alongside another on a dark street under trees. She was silent. He was too, and he watched her. The cab stopped and they got out.

A row of the very narrow 17th-century buildings of Amsterdam.

"This is where I live." But she did not move away from him.

"And you're afraid to go up there."

"No."

"What floor?"

"Top floor."

Conte looked up at it. The windows up there were dark, which didn't necessarily prove anything.

"Would you like me to check it out for you?"

"I don't know."

"Give me your keys."

But she had begun to resist him, and he could feel it. She said: "Wait a minute—"

"Stay with the cab driver, if you prefer."

The cabbie gave them a knowing look as she followed him into the building. They went up the four flights, Conte leading. She waited on the landing as he went through the rooms. He put on all the lights. He saw the bed she slept in, which was unmade. He saw some of her clothing lying about, her toothbrush on the sink, and a box of cereal on the sideboard in the kitchen. In some ways this experience was more intimate than watching her naked on a stage.

"There's no one in there," he told her when he came out on the landing again. He handed back her keys. "If you lock the door you should be safe enough. Take some aspirin, go to bed, and get a good night's sleep."

"Are you a cop?"

"Why would you ask that?"

"I've been thinking that you act like one."

"I was a New York cop until a few months ago. I'm not a cop now."

"Why are you being so nice to me?"

Conte smiled. "Am I the first man who's ever been nice to you?"

They were still on the landing. She came forward as if she meant to kiss him on the cheek, but instead only shook hands. She said: "Thank you for being nice to me."

"If you don't mind, I'll come back in the morning to make sure you're all right."

"You don't have to do that."

"I wanted to see you again anyway."

She nodded, and looked away.

"Perhaps we can go out and have breakfast together," he said to her back.

He heard her lock the door, then a second lock, then a third. He went down the stairs smiling, and the cab driver said to him: "That didn't take long."

Conte said: "I'm very fast."

He had himself driven first to the bridge where he lifted her ruined bike into the trunk of the cab, and then to police headquarters where he leaned it against the desk of a surprised desk officer, demanding that it be vouchered as evidence in a hit-and-run case, perhaps an attempted murder case. He gave his name and his hotel's name, forms were filled out, and he came away with a voucher number and the promise that detectives would contact him in the morning.

The same cab driver waited outside. This time he had himself driven to the bar where he had left his own bike. There he paid off the driver, tipping him well, then mounted the bike and pedaled slowly along through the night in a city that seemed absolutely silent. As he rode he was trying to work out a plan, but it came into existence in stages, not all of which were clear to him. He did not know what further surprises Gigi had in store for him, but he knew there would be some, and he had to plan for them. At his hotel he turned in the hotel's bike and went upstairs where he lay in bed and worked on his plan until it was as strong as he could make it. Only then did he permit himself to fall asleep.

In her vestibule he rang the bell, and she came downstairs, an unsmiling young woman, very pretty despite her swollen cheek and black eye. Her upper lip was somewhat puffy as well, and she nodded at him without speaking or looking into his face, then led him down the street toward a café whose terrace, as he could see from a distance, gave onto the canal. It was a warm morning, and they moved along under trees through arrows of sunlight. She wore dark glasses that only partially concealed the damage to her face. She was dressed in jeans, a sweater, and open-toed sandals, and she walked with a slight limp, but when he asked if she was in pain she did not answer.

On the café terrace they took a table and when the waiter came ordered coffee and croissants. She was responsive enough to the waiter, but not to him, for whenever he tried to talk to her she answered in monosyllables or not at all, and in between these attempts she studied the tabletop or her hands. Had she been able to sleep? he asked her. Did she want to go to the hospital and have x-rays made? No, and no. Was she still as frightened as she had been last night?

She had got over that for the time being, she said curtly, looking at him, really looking at him, for the first time. Otherwise she wouldn't be here, she would have locked herself in her apartment and not come out.

Her mood, whatever it was, put him on the defensive.

"In the night, since I couldn't sleep, I went over and over what had happened," she said, and he looked across the table into what had become a hard, unsmiling face. "The more I thought about it, the more certain things became clear to me."

"That's a beautiful shiner you have there."

"Who are you?"

"Don't worry, it will go away in a few days."

"We're not talking about me. We're talking about you. Who are you and why were you following me?"

"Who said I was following you?"

"You didn't just happen by. You saw my show, you had a bicycle stashed outside, and you were following me. Why?"

Conte decided to say: "I did see your show. It was beautifully choreographed."

"An interesting way to put it."

"You know how to command a stage. The audience was hardly even breathing."

"That's just sex. It's a reaction that's absolutely mindless."

"I don't think so."

She ripped her croissant in two. "You took the trouble to rent a bicycle somewhere. You saw my show and you were following me home. Trying to."

"I did have a bicycle. But you knew that. I hauled you out of the canal with it."

"Lots of creepy guys see my show and try to meet me, or follow me. Are you one of them? Just another creep?"

"I hope not."

"All right, then who are you?"

Conte's plan, that she would lead him to Grizzard, depended on her liking him, and feeling a debt to him, but already it seemed to be in tatters. She was behaving as if they were adversaries, which he hadn't wanted. But then they had always been adversaries, from the moment he had first seen her photos in the magazine.

"I told you who I was."

"You gave me a name, which for all I know is fake."

"No, it's my real name." Conte, who was busy rearranging his plan, needed a bit more time and so stalled. "What more can I tell you?"

"Either you're a creep, which I don't think is the case—"

"Thank you. That's one nice thing, anyway."

"Please don't trifle with me. Or there's something else going on here, and I have a right to know what it is."

Whether she realized it or not a pleading tone had come into her voice. It made her seem, for the moment, vulnerable and young. He could imagine her trying to sleep, imagine the dark hours passing one by one, while she lay trapped in her residual terror, and her pain, imagine her fretting, worrying, hurting. Who was the man who had tried to kill her, and why? Where did Conte fit in? How much did he know and what did he intend to do with it?

"So who are you? What do you want with me? Why are you here?"

Conte decided to say: "I'm looking for a man named Georges Grizzard."

This stopped her. Then she said: "I thought you might be."

"It occurred to me that you would know where I can find him."

She turned immediately surly. "He's a photographer. I know nothing about him. Why should I? He's not a friend. I've seen him only two or three times in my life."

"He takes very good pictures, I believe," Conte said, watching her closely.

She seemed to flinch. Conte said: "Drink your coffee, it's getting cold."

"Who are you?"

"I already told you. I'm an ex–New York cop, now in the private sector, and I have a client who's interested in Georges Grizzard."

"What client? Who?"

"That shouldn't concern you."

After a moment, sounding surly again, she said: "I don't know anything about Georges Grizzard."

"I think you do."

"And I don't intend to get involved in this thing, whatever it is."

"Honey, you're already involved."

"And don't call me Honey."

"Where does he live?"

Instead of answering, she said: "The car last night that hit me — it wasn't an accident, was it?"

"Probably not."

"Somebody really did try to kill me."

"I think so."

"Do you know who it was?"

"I think so."

"Am I in danger now?"

"Most likely the guy is somewhere else by now. But in your place I'd be careful."

"Somewhere else? Where?"

"Looking for Grizzard, just like me. Wherever Grizzard may happen to be."

She seemed to shiver.

"But why does anyone want to kill me? What did I do?"

"In some quarters you're extremely unpopular. And also—"

"Also what?"

"You have information those quarters don't want divulged."

"What information?"

"That's for you to tell me."

"I have nothing to tell you. I don't know anything."

"We'll see."

"No, we won't see."

"How can I find Grizzard?"

"I have no idea."

"I'm told he lives on the Riviera. Cannes or Nice."

Her mouth had gone hard. She said nothing. But he thought he saw something in her eyes.

"I think you know where he lives. I think we should take a trip down there together. You can help me find him. All expenses paid, of course. How's that for an offer?"

"No thank you."

"It's an offer you can't refuse."

"I just refused it."

"You stay here, Honey, and you're a target."

"I told you not to call me Honey."

"You're really beautiful when you're angry."

"They won't find me."

"I found you, didn't I?"

"I won't be here. I'm going away."

"These people will know how to find you. Wherever you go."

"You're just trying to scare me."

"Me, no. I don't scare you. They're the ones who scare you."

Conte, who had two suits with him, was wearing the blue one today, with a red tie, and out of his breast pocket he took two airline tickets he had bought that morning and laid them down between the saucers. As she examined them—somewhat frantically, he thought—he gazed off down the canal watching an excursion boat approach, then glide past in front, then disappear under the bridge farther on. It was an open launch with a number of passengers standing. Row by row they had to duck for the bridge.

"The KLM flight, Amsterdam–Nice," Conte said, coming back to her. "Today."

She was still fixed on the tickets.

"You're coming with me because you don't have any choice. And you're going to remember everything you ever knew about that guy, also because you don't have any choice. Understood?"

"And if I refuse?"

"Judging from all the magazines I've seen, you're famous. Or rather," he said harshly, "your tits are famous."

"That's not a nice thing to say."

"A lot of people would like to know who you are, and where you are. Reporters. The police."

"And you will tell them."

"I don't have to tell them. They'll find out by themselves. They're only a step or two behind me."

"The girl in those magazines is not me. You can't even see her face. No one can prove it's me."

"You don't think so?"

"There are no pictures of me, none."

From his briefcase Conte produced the photo from the corkboard in Grizzard's darkroom, half scaled it onto the table, and watched her unfold it. "Is that you?"

"Where did you get that?"

"What difference? If I found this one there must be copies others will find."

She was silent.

"Let me explain something, Gigi — may I call you Gigi? Grizzard used pictures of you to extort money from someone. Extortion is a crime, and legally, you are in it up to those beautiful tits of yours."

This time the word made her flinch. He saw this, and it caused him regret, or perhaps pain, because he had rarely seen a woman who looked so vulnerable and lost, and what he really wanted to do was comfort her in some way, perhaps hold her in his arms and stroke her hair.

"You're no better than the man who drives the getaway car at a robbery," he said, his voice hard. "You're as guilty as he is." Was she? Conte knew nothing about European law, and a prosecutor, he supposed, would have a tough job proving a case against her. But if she refused to cooperate he was willing to use every argument to force her. "For extortion, people do time. They go to jail. Is that what you want?"

"I don't believe you."

Conte said: "I think you do."

She was tearing her croissant to shreds.

"I think you've been expecting me. Expecting someone. You've seen all those magazines, the splash this has made. I think you've been looking over your shoulder for days. That's not fun, is it?"

"No." Her voice had got small.

"You help me and I'll help you. That's how it works."

"I have no way of helping you. How am I supposed to help you?"

"I need to find Grizzard. Where does he live, Nice or Cannes?"

"Try Monte Carlo."

"Where in Monte Carlo? Villa or apartment? Do you have an address? Have you ever been there?"

"Monte Carlo. That's all I know, and I'm not getting on a plane today or any other day, not with you or anybody else."

Though he kept trying to question her she would say nothing more. Her mouth set into a thin crease that made her look almost ugly.

He paid for the two coffees and her shattered croissant, and stood up. They both did. "Come," he said. He took her arm.

"Where are you taking me?" This question, and the fact that she allowed him to lead her out of the café and up onto the street, meant, he believed, that she felt herself in his power, was no longer able, at least for the moment, to disobey him.

As they crossed the street she was looking all around, as if for help.

He almost pushed her into her building.

"Get your things. Enough for two or three days."

"Wait for me downstairs," she ordered. But it seemed more of a wish, a final effort not to be dominated, to assert her independence.

Left alone she might get her nerve back, her strength, and simply lock the door on him. If she did that, what was he going to do, sit on the floor of her landing for the rest of the day?

"No," he said, "I want to make sure it doesn't take you too long."

"I don't need your help to pack a bag."

Conte was following her up the stairs.

"Are you going to tell me what to put in it too?"

"Two or three days on the Riviera. You don't need an evening dress. We're not going to any nightclubs."

She put her key into the lock, opened the door, and stepped inside, Conte following, though she tried to stop him.

"You have no right to come into my house."

"We're playing by different rules now, Gigi."

They stood looking at each other, before Conte crossed the living room to the telephone.

"You need to call in and cancel your show for the next week or so," Conte said. "I'll do that for you. What's the number?"

"I'll call myself."

"No, better if I do it. What's the number?"

"I don't know."

"What's the number, I said."

She looked ready to cry, but she gave him the number.

"I'm calling for Marie-Therese de France," he said when the connection was made. "This is her brother calling. She's been in a car crash. She's in a bad way. They're doing tests on her now. She won't be back to work for a week, maybe longer. Unless she dies we won't know anything immediately. I'll keep you apprised." He hung up.

"How dare you? I mean, how dare you?"

"The man who ran you down wants to know that you're dead or dying. Tonight he'll check with the casino. When he's told your act has been cancelled, he'll imagine he's succeeded. Now pack that bag."

He sat down on the sofa and put his feet up on the coffee table.

"Get comfortable," she said. "Make yourself at home."

"Thank you. I already have."

"Get your feet off my table."

When he did not move, but only looked at her, she spun on her heel and went into the bedroom. The door slammed. Inside he heard her banging drawers.

"The flight doesn't even leave until tonight," she said when she came out, small suitcase in hand.

"All the better. We can have a nice lunch, spend the day together. Maybe we'll even get to like each other. I hope we will." He liked her face, her figure, her voice, her spirit. There was a piercing intelligence about her too. Though how could there be, he asked himself, when she was a whore? This was what puzzled him so. Fascinated him as well.

He took his feet off the table. "Extortion is such an ugly crime," he said. "In addition you broke up Murano's marriage, probably ruined his life — his wife's life too. How did a girl with your education and upbringing get herself into such a mess?"

"I'm not a girl."

He corrected himself. "A woman, then. How did a woman like you get into such a mess?"

She put her suitcase down on the coffee table. "I didn't know anything about any extortion," she said in a low voice.

"But the rest of it was okay with you, wasn't it?"

She said nothing. She looked at the floor.

"How much did Grizzard pay you?"

To his surprise she told him and he was impressed.

"It's more money than I've ever had at one time," she said, as if begging him to understand her. "It's more than I can earn in six months." Such a large sum, to Conte, seemed proof that Grizzard did not finance this thing by himself. There were others involved, and they were people with money.

"You don't know what it's like to be a woman alone, to have no money, or very little money, and men trying to get you into bed, men leering at you everywhere you go. I didn't have the upbringing you seem to think. My mother died when I was ten. My father was always getting posted somewhere else. I've been on my own since I was sixteen, most of it in somebody else's country. America is your country, not mine. I brought myself up. I put myself through college by myself."

"And you fucked Murano and got paid for it."

"I'm a whore, right? That's what you think I am, isn't it?"

"I haven't made up my mind what I think about you."

"So I'm a whore. Sure I fucked him. Now you know. Now you can stop worrying about it."

"—And ruined his marriage."

"All he had to do was walk away. If he cared no more about his marriage than that, then he deserved whatever happened to him."

"Now that I know you," he said, looking up at her, "I find it hard to believe it was entirely his fault."

"What's that supposed to mean?"

"I imagine if a package as appetizing as you came on to a man, if you smiled and touched his arm a few times—"

"Of course it was his fault."

"—very few men would be able to say no."

"Men are led around by their cocks."

"Murano claims he never fucked you."

He watched her. She said nothing and did not look at him.

"Well?"

"This conversation bores me." She hefted her suitcase. "I thought we were going out."

They went downstairs where he stopped a taxi. Leaning in through the window he talked to the driver, then got in the back beside Gigi, her suitcase between them.

As the taxi moved off, in order to unnerve her further, Conte ignored her and instead watched the scenery pass. The stepped gables of the narrow houses. The tall thin windows. The hordes of parked bicycles outside. Some canals very wide, with houseboats moored against the embankments. Along the major streets, scraping and clanging, moved triple articulated trams.

Ten minutes passed without a word spoken between them before Gigi started looking around. "Where are you taking me?"

"To my hotel, I'm afraid. We can't afford to have you seen by someone from the casino."

"I'm not going to a hotel with you."

"We'll have to eat at the hotel too, for the same reason. We'll order from room service."

"No."

"Sorry, that's the way it will have to be."

"Room service," she said. "Delicious. Yum, yum."

More bridges passed, more canals. Bicycle racks outside office buildings, outside banks. An entire square ringed by parked bicycles; they surrounded it like a picket fence. To cross it one would have to move a bike to get into the square and move another to get out. In the middle one would have to slalom through scores of young tourists, many smoking pot, others playing instruments, most of them sitting on their backpacks, waiting for who knew what.

He said: "I'm at the Amstel. It's a good hotel. The food won't be that bad, I hope."

She said: "And then we hang around the hotel all afternoon."

She was angry, and getting angrier. He said: "You can watch television."

The taxi stopped, and they got out. Since Conte was carrying Gigi's suitcase he was obliged, as he paid the driver, to manipulate his billfold one-handed. Gigi was looking up at the hotel. "You're going to babysit me until it's time to go to the airport?"

"If that's the way you want to put it." Getting information from this young woman, he judged, would take time. Some interrogations went fast, some took forever. He believed she knew where Grizzard lived and would lead him there. Everything about her demeanor suggested this, including the way she followed him now into the hotel.

She followed him into the elevator too — whether she was following him or her suitcase, which he controlled like a hostage, he could not be sure. She followed him down the corridor to his room. The door closed on them.

That was the start of a long edgy day.

She reclined on the bed watching television, her shoes on the floor. The room wasn't very big and unless he reclined on the bed beside her, which he couldn't do — or could he? — there was no way to see the screen. In any case, she was watching a program in Dutch.

He didn't know where to put himself. He had nothing to read. He considered going down to the lobby and buying a paperback or some magazines, but couldn't, for fear that in his absence she might bolt. Maybe when he came back she would still be there, but he couldn't be sure. She was a difficult young woman to read, and he had no confidence in the signals he thought he was receiving. He found the hotel menu next to the TV, but when he offered to order lunch for her she would not answer. She had gone into her silent mode, it seemed. He began reading aloud down the list of dishes, with appropriate pauses so she could decide on something, but she ignored the menu and him. He must have read out 25 soups, sandwiches, dishes before she interrupted him sharply from the bed:

"You decide. You've decided everything else."

Lifting the phone, he ordered roast chicken, French fries, salad, and ice cream, two orders of each, and coffee in a thermos.

She heard him say into the phone: "To drink? Bring me up a bottle of champagne."

This caught her attention and she looked at him.

"Why not?" he said. "We'll pretend we just got married. We're celebrating our wedding. Today is the start of fifty years together."

She neither laughed nor smiled. Instead her gaze returned to the screen, and the program she was watching that was in Dutch.

After a long time the waiter knocked at the door, came in with a rolling table, took the silver covers off the dishes, pulled up two straight chairs, pocketed his tip, and left.

Conte sat down at the table, but Gigi on the bed did not move to join him.

"Your lunch is getting cold."

She got up, came toward him in stocking feet, picked up her dish, her cutlery, and her napkin, and returned to the bed where she balanced the plate on her lap and commenced eating while remaining as glued as before to whatever was transpiring on the screen.

She unnerved him.

Conte poured champagne into her glass and brought it to her, his own glass in one hand, hers in the other, meaning to force her to touch glasses with him, forcing this gesture out of her at least, the facsimile of a friendly toast, but she, ignoring his presence beside the bed, placed the champagne flute, untouched, on the bedside table.

Conte sighed.

This too caught her attention. She glanced at him briefly, then returned her attention to the screen.

Eventually she did drink some of the champagne, not much. It was the supposedly hard-bitten New York detective who drank most of it.

When luncheon was over he covered the remnants with the flaps of the tablecloth, pushed the table out into the hall, and closed the door on it. By this time his mood had changed to exasperation.

"What are you watching?" he said, dropping onto the other half of the bed.

Immediately she jumped up and moved to the armchair in the opposite corner where she sat looking straight ahead. Conte lifted the remote, clicked it, and the screen went blank.

"There," he said with satisfaction. "Let's talk."

"You kidnapped me. What is there to talk about?"

"I didn't kidnap you. You're here because it seems to you the safest and wisest place to be. How do I find Grizzard?"

Her mouth set into the thin line he was used to, and she did not answer.

"In Monte Carlo, you said. Do you know his address?"

Again she did not answer.

"All right, let's talk about something else."

She looked at him.

He said: "I know a girl at home who's just dying to get into your line of work. It's all she talks about. Wants to do the same act. But she needs help from a choreographer. It would be great if I could give her the name of yours. So what's his name?" And he grinned at her, but she did not react.

"You did the choreography yourself, didn't you?"

"Yes."

"And arranged the lighting and the music as well."

"Yes."

"I'm impressed. Because the result from beginning to end was first-rate theater. Proof of a great deal of talent, I thought."

"Hard work, mostly."

"I'm not putting you on." From the bed he applauded her. "I'm extremely impressed."

"Don't be. If you have to survive you learn to do all kinds of things."

"Why didn't you just get married?"

"And live off some guy? I never met one I wanted to marry. Or who wanted to marry me."

"You're not too bad looking," Conte said. "You must have had a big enough choice."

"Wanting to go to bed with me is not the same thing. And besides that I wanted to make good on my own."

And wound up alone in the world, he thought. Alone on a stage, naked.

"Have you ever been married?" he asked her.

"No." And then, after a pause: "Have you?"

"I was married, yes." Despite himself his voice had got somber, and he shook his head briefly, almost instinctively, as if to shake off both the memory and the marriage.

"I see," said Gigi. "A messy divorce. An unhappy experience all around, like ninety percent of the marriages I've seen."

"The percentage is not that high."

"You're a romantic. Count again."

It seemed to him she was rebuffing him and reaching out to him at the same time. But he cautioned himself to remain skeptical. Don't imagine things that aren't there, he told himself.

He did not know how to phrase what he wanted to ask next, and so said it awkwardly: "How does one get into your present line of work?"

"I had college bills to pay. If I ever hoped to graduate I had to figure out a way to pay them."

He waited.

"After sophomore year my father never sent me a cent. And not too much before that, either. If I wanted to stay in school what were my choices? I could work at Wal-Mart at minimum wage. But that wouldn't do it. I tried waitressing. You don't earn enough at that either. So I went to Las Vegas and auditioned for a job as a showgirl at the Strand Palace."

"Did it bother you, taking your clothes off?"

"At the audition it did. The audition was horrible. I was in this office facing five middle-aged men in business suits who asked me to strip to the waist so they could check out my breasts. That wasn't the way they put it, but that was the gist of it. They watched me getting undressed, none of them smiling, all of them nodding politely to each other and pretending they weren't getting off on it. I'm standing there half naked facing them. I'm horribly embarrassed. They're all still nodding. Then one of them gives the thumbs-up and then they all did. I put my clothes back on as fast as I could. They wanted me to stay and talk to them, but I couldn't get out of there fast enough. After that I worked as a showgirl four nights a week, commuting from school. I arranged my classes to fit. I had a secondhand Volkswagen. It took about four hours each way to get there. Every night I was one of about thirty bare-breasted girls on a runway. It was so anonymous I didn't even feel naked. The casino provided a kind of dormitory for the girls who wanted it, and that's where I slept. The pay was pretty good. I didn't get rich, but it was enough to pay tuition, and with what was left I could live, barely.

"After graduation I moved to Las Vegas. Now I was a showgirl six nights a week and no commuting. I was going to save my money and when I had enough I was going to New York and try to find a real job. Maybe work at the UN. I had all these languages. My degree, which was in English Literature, wasn't going to help me. Not much you can do with a degree in English Literature, something they never told us at UCLA. In Las Vegas with my days free I decided to go for a master's in computer science at the local branch of the University of Nevada. The casino paid for it."

"Why would they do that?"

"All the casinos do it. It's good publicity. Proves Las Vegas is not Sin City. Proves the casinos actually further the education of all these naked girls, the same girls they're so busy debauching in other ways.

"To keep expenses to a minimum I moved in with a boy I had known in college. I really liked him. Sometimes we talked of getting married. He was in a program the casinos ran, learning to become a croupier. The program included some on-the-job training, and my boyfriend got arrested for palming chips. A trainee stealing from the casino. What an idiot. They must have fifty guys in the ceiling of those casinos watching the croupiers and dealers like hawks. When they took him away in handcuffs I was desolate. At that time I had no bank account. I had kept my savings locked in a suitcase, and when I got back to our room I found the suitcase empty. He had stolen all my money too.

"So I wasn't going to New York for a while. I was starting from scratch. That was when I decided to put together an act of my own. Why not, I was already parading around naked and with an act I would get paid more. I worked on that act for months. It was similar to what you saw last night. Not as good, but similar. When I thought it was ready I took it to various casinos out on the Strip and auditioned for those guys in suits. Not the same guys, but they might just as well have been. One of them gave me a week's tryout in one of the smaller clubrooms. I was a hit, and pretty soon I moved into the main room. I kept trying to perfect my act. I also worked up a second act, because sooner or later the bosses would get tired of the first one, or me, or both.

"Because basically girls' bodies are all the same. Once men have seen yours they want to see a new one. I have no illusions about men."

She stopped talking and looked at him a moment.

"So I moved around a lot. From the Strip into the city, back out to the Strip. And then to everyplace else in Nevada where there were casinos. I was moving so much I could no longer attend classes or study, so I dropped my courses, dropped out of school. I worked in Reno, in Tahoe, then back to Vegas. Back to the Strand Palace, where I started. There one of the suits took a shine to me. I mean, in the worst way.

"He was about fifty, a big, powerful man beginning to go bald. He was one of the owners. He wore silk suits that must have cost thousands of dollars each, and an eau de cologne you could smell across the room. He wore pinky rings on both hands and a gold watch thin as a quarter."

"I get the picture," said Conte.

"He wasn't bad looking. He could be funny. He could be charming when he wanted to be. When he asked me to have dinner with him I was flattered. I went home and told my girlfriend: guess who asked me to dinner. You know what she said?"

"She said: Look out," said Conte.

Gigi looked amazed. "How did you know?"

"Well," said Conte, "I've been a detective for a while."

"He didn't offer to come and get me. I was to meet him at the restaurant. I got there on time and was bowed to a table, and there I sat by myself for thirty minutes before he showed up. Every time he invited me to dinner I sat there thirty minutes or more fending off guys, waiting for him. When I complained he apologized, then did the same thing the next time. Finally one night I said screw this, and I didn't show up. Made him furious. He was waiting in the wings after my next show. I thought he was going to hit me.

"These dinners were often in other casino restaurants. He needed to know what the competition was doing, he said. Afterward we would see the show there. This was fine with me. I wanted to look over the competition also, perhaps get some new ideas for my act. Obviously he liked to be seen with me. There were always flunkies around him. Maybe they were bodyguards. Or some of them were. Even in the restaurants, sitting at a nearby table, or standing against the wall. Sometimes he would call one over and tell him to do something. He liked to be seen giving orders to people. He lived in a penthouse apartment at the hotel. I was never up there but it was supposed to be sumptuous.

"Looking back it is clear to me that I should have cut him off at the beginning. But I was fascinated by this aura of power that came off him, along with the cologne. I was fascinated also by all the things he told me about the casino business, and the hotel business, some of it gossip, some of it facts and techniques. He was certainly never dull. He was in a business far more complicated than outsiders ever imagine, and he was making it work."

She looked at Conte reclining against the headboard. Her gaze moved from his socks, up to his face. "I suppose you think it was naive of me not to expect what happened next."

"You learn in life by getting knocked around. Life knocks people around."

"Not everybody."

"Yes, everybody."

She said: "One night he invites me to move in with him. Told me how much he would pay me. He'd find a replacement for my act. If I liked I could have a contract for, say, a year. After that, we'd see. He had never courted me, never tried to win me over. If he had, who knows how I would have reacted. He'd never even tried to kiss me. Now he wants to buy me. It gives that type of man a sense of power, I guess. He's too powerful and too busy to court a woman. The way for him to feel big, to feel really important, is just to buy her. It's disgusting.

"I had to be very careful. This man was my employer, and could fire me. Probably he was powerful enough to blackball me with every other casino—I wouldn't be able to get another job. I told him as gently as I could that I had just been badly hurt by a man and I wasn't ready for another relationship just yet."

"And he said—"

"From then on the pressure increased day by day. He went from firmness to fury. He was not used to being told no, and I should reconsider. I worked for him, did I not, and I should reconsider. I would reconsider or there would be consequences. And so forth. Finally he called me into his office and informed me that his legal department had been going over my papers, which were not in order, and wanted to report me to Immigration. I didn't have a green card, he pointed out. I was in the U.S. on a student visa and I was no longer a student. The Immigration authorities would arrest me, if they knew. I'd be in jail waiting to be deported. For the moment, he was holding off his legal department, but how much longer could he go on doing so. If Immigration deported me, my name would go on a list and I would never be readmitted into the U.S.

"I was in a panic. Half my life was in the U.S. I risked losing the American part of my life forever, my friends, the schools I'd been to, the places I'd lived."

She stopped. She was breathing a bit hard, as if the reliving of this part of her life came with more emotion than she could cope with.

"I went back to my room, got my money, and packed up as much of my belongings as would go into two suitcases. I couldn't pack everything. I left behind a lot of stuff I really liked. I didn't even stop to pick up my paycheck, and I caught the next plane out of there."

"Where did you go?"

"To L.A., where I caught a plane to Paris. There are no borders in Europe anymore. With a Dutch passport I could work anywhere I liked, so after that I worked in a lot of places."

Her story was a soap opera, Conte told himself, neither more nor less. But she had told it as a series of facts, without self-pity. She was not looking for sympathy. She had been a young girl with a problem and no one to solve it but herself. Which she had done. From the bed he looked across at her in the small armchair in the corner, and tried not to feel admiration for her, or any other emotion, tried not to be moved by her story or by her, but felt himself affected nonetheless. How much he could not say. But the strength of his reaction to her continued to surprise him.

It was not in his interest to let her see this. Because he needed to keep her off balance he said: "So you worked in a lot of places. What does the word *work* mean to you?"

"You want to know something, Conte, I couldn't care less what you think of me."

"Just trying to find out who you are and what I can expect from you."

"In Las Vegas a guy from the Folies Bergère had come backstage to ask me if I had ever thought of working in Paris. He gave me his card. So the day after I landed I went to him and he hired me."

"And you went on from there."

"I went on from there."

"Including Monte Carlo," guessed Conte.

"Where do you think I met Georges Grizzard?"

"And you went to Grizzard's house."

"Did I? How interesting."

"What the two of you did there I do not know."

"We did nothing there."

"So what's his address?"

"A pig like that."

"Does he live in a villa or an apartment?"

She did not answer.

"Would you like me to repeat the question?"

"I'll decide when or if I choose to tell you anything, and I haven't decided yet."

He kept pressing her, but she remained silent, and finally he fell silent too.

But a little later she burst out: "If you think I would have anything to do with that pig, then you understand nothing about me, or about women in general."

When it was time they went down to the lobby. As Conte checked out, she stood to one side the way a wife would do. In the taxi out to the airport neither spoke. The plane to Nice was late. In a shop on the concourse Conte bought the *Paris Herald Tribune* and a paperback novel. Waiting, he read first the one, then the other. Gigi studied her fingernails, or else paced in front of him while he watched her carefully, afraid she might run. Also, he admitted to himself, it gave him pleasure to look at her, at the way her jeans fit her, and her blouse, at her bruised face that was beautiful anyway.

In the air in the seat beside him she promptly fell asleep. A little later, dreaming perhaps, arranging herself more comfortably in her dreams, she nestled herself against him, her head on his shoulder. This stirred him. He inhaled the scent of her, felt the weight of her, and wondered if she was really asleep, or only trying to manipulate him in some way.

At Nice they stepped out of the terminal into a balmy Riviera night. The taxi ride to Monte Carlo took about 40 minutes, most of it along the seafront, the sea passing to one side, the towns to the other, Villefranche, Beaulieu, Eze, all of them at this hour half lit. Behind them the great Riviera cliffs rose into the darkness, lighted here and there by the extravagant villas that clung to them. To the other side was the Mediterranean which sparkled and splashed in the moonlight.

In Monte Carlo the taxi came down through the illuminated gardens, through the battery of floodlights shining upward on trees, toward the casino which blazed with light also, and onto the square it dominated, and stopped in front of the Hôtel de Paris, which closed off the square on one side. As they got out of the cab a footman dressed as a pasha ran forward to take their bags.

"You travel first class," said Gigi, looking up at the hotel.

"You've stayed here before?"

"How much do you think they pay girls like me? It's maybe the swankiest hotel in the world."

Conte looked from the casino to her and back to the casino again, which he had never seen before. The baroque, 19th-century facade. People on the steps waiting, perhaps, for cabs. Crowds going in and out, whether gamblers or sightseers he did not know. Ferraris, Rolls-Royces, and the like parked in front.

He realized he was in a world he did not understand. What's a New York cop doing here, he asked himself.

"I'm hungry," said Gigi.

They entered the hotel lobby which was three stories high and filled with antique furniture and statuary. At the end of it rose a marble staircase. Conte checked in, had the bags sent up, and took her across the square to the Café de Paris, which was half restaurant, half gambling rooms, where they ate dinner to the noise of whirling slot machines and cascading money.

"What nationality is Grizzard?" Conte said, making conversation.

"Belgian, I think."

"Why does he live here?"

"In his line of work, wouldn't you? He lives by scandal. Plenty of that here. Someone once called Monte Carlo a sunny place for shady people."

"Tomorrow morning," Conte said, "you show me where the guy lives."

"If I remember."

"What's that supposed to mean?"

"I was only there once. Maybe I can't find it."

"Come on, come on."

She smirked at him.

Annoyed, already standing, he said: "Finish your dessert." He put money down.

A bellboy led them into the elevator. They followed him along a corridor. He opened a door and stepped back.

"Is this my room or yours?" said Gigi suspiciously.

Conte tipped the bellboy. "*Merci beaucoup*," he said, dismissing him.

"Wait a minute," said Gigi. But the bellboy was already gone.

She spun around facing him. "If you think I'm bunking with you—"

"Under present circumstances, that would be rape, wouldn't it? Your virtue is safe. I am not a rapist."

She was breathing angrily.

"Relax, it's a suite. The bedroom for you, this room for me." Having come this far he still feared she might bolt. He did not intend to risk it. He would sleep between her and any escape she might decide on. "You can lock the door between us if you like." Leaving his own suitcase behind, he carried hers into the bedroom, and threw it on the bed. "And in the morning we'll go find Grizzard. Pleasant dreams."

It gave him a start to hear the door slammed violently shut behind him.

CHAPTER

XV

IN THE MORNING he had to knock several times before she came awake enough to call out: "What do you want?"

She lay with the covers pulled up to her chin.

"I'm about to call down for breakfast. Tell me, what would you like?"

"What time is it?"

It was seven o'clock, and when he said so she grimaced.

"I want to be in front of Grizzard's house by eight thirty or before." He did not explain why, but in fact he would have preferred to be there even earlier, in keeping with police theory which was the same all over the world. Catch the suspect half dazed with sleep if possible. Catch him, if possible, literally with his pants down, unready to resist or escape, unprepared for a confrontation of any kind, and likely therefore to answer questions he should not answer.

"I don't normally get up this early."

"Well today you're making an exception, aren't you? What do you want to order?"

The waiter came in, spread a tablecloth, poured the coffee, and went out. Like an old married couple they sat opposite each other with nothing much to say, eating their breakfast in silence, Conte wearing pants and a T-shirt, though still in stocking feet, Gigi in a hotel bathrobe.

"The bathroom is yours," said Conte, getting up from the table. "Don't be long."

He heard the shower running. A little later she came out wearing a towel. Her face looked scrubbed and young, and very nice to him, even though her bruises were a bit more discolored than yesterday. Her arms were bare. The towel was tucked in high, with most of her legs showing beneath it. "Your turn," she said.

On the other side of the door as he shaved Gigi was getting dressed and he knew this, and could hear it. He imagined her putting her clothes on one by one exactly as he had seen her do onstage, exact same order. He imagined this rather too vividly, and had to stop shaving for a moment and admonish himself to get such images out of his head. Think of something else, he told himself.

In front of the hotel they waited for a cab to pull up. The driver, who had come around to open the door for them, said in French: "Where to, folks?"

They got into the cab.

"Give him Grizzard's address," said Conte curtly, not knowing if she would comply.

She did hesitate, but only for a moment. As she issued directions he felt a great sigh of relief well up, which he was obliged to smother quickly, before it could show.

They drove up through the casino gardens, no illuminations at this hour, the casino at their backs locked up tight, and they turned west toward Italy for several blocks, passing posh stores not yet open, the sidewalks crowded with people going to work. Presently they dropped down a few streets where they began to pass apartment buildings that were virtual skyscrapers, the only ones on the entire coast, with Gigi leaning forward in her seat waiting to recognize one of them.

Finally she said: "Driver, stop." Then to Conte: "That one there."

"Are you sure?"

"No."

When he got out of the taxi, holding the door for her, she said: "I'll wait for you here."

"No you won't, get out of the car. Driver, pull over and wait for us please."

He had Gigi by the arm, pulling her along, and they entered the building. He could see that she was furious at being manhandled. Probably she was afraid of being seen by Grizzard as well, and so she was sputtering. The photographer was dangerous, she said. If she were seen leading Conte to him—

The American detective ignored her, concentrating on the *gardien* on duty behind the desk they were approaching. The lobby was marble. Marble floor, marble walls. Many potted plants. The ceiling looked like marble too but was so high up it was difficult to see. From it dangled an enormous chandelier that must be the devil to clean. Chandelier worthy of an opera house. Costly lobby. A luxury building, then. Well, what else had he expected? Probably all of these skyscrapers were the same, the legal residences of tennis players, actors, race car drivers, none of whom actually lived there, people who kept them as mail drops to avoid paying income taxes in their own countries.

The *gardien* sat behind a high counter that curved almost in a semi-circle, facing a bank of closed circuit TV screens that showed, at this hour, empty hallways upstairs.

He was a man who controlled, for the next few minutes, their destiny, knew it, and savored the power this gave him.

"Yes?" he said, eyeing them suspiciously.

"Police," snapped Conte, flashing his shield. "The number of Grizzard's apartment."

The *gardien*'s power dissipated instantly. "Twenty-one C," he said.

Conte pulled Gigi toward the elevator.

"There's another cop up there already," the *gardien* called after them.

"What does he mean?" said Gigi in the elevator.

Conte had felt a sudden chill. "I don't know." But he thought he did.

"They've arrested him. They caught him doing something."

Conte feared worse than that. He said: "Let's wait and see."

They got off the elevator. In front of a door at the end of the corridor sat a uniformed Monaco cop, his chair tilted back against the wall, a folded newspaper on his lap, his cap down over his eyes.

Hearing them coming, he sat up straight, adjusted his cap, and put the newspaper under the chair.

"New York Police Department," Conte said, showing his shield, "what's going on? Where's Grizzard?"

The cop had jumped to his feet. For a moment Conte thought he was going to salute.

"Nobody told me anything, Sir. Guard the door, they told me. Don't let anybody in."

Conte had spoken in English, and the cop answered in English. Later Conte would learn that Monaco, that most international and richest of enclaves, was also the most heavily policed city on earth, with closed circuit television on nearly every corner, and about four times as many cops per inhabitant as New York. Most Monegasque cops spoke English, having been chosen in part for that reason.

The cop said: "They're all up at the golf course at Mont Agel."

"Thank you," said Conte.

"What do you think it is?" said Gigi in the elevator going down.

"Where is this place?" demanded Conte.

"Up on top of the mountain. About two thousand feet straight up."

Conte strode out to the taxi, almost running, Gigi rushing to keep up. Being reasonably certain that Grizzard was not a golfer, he thought he knew in advance what he would find up there.

In the rear of the taxi Gigi sat back comfortably, but Conte stayed on the edge of his seat, leaning forward, urging the driver to hurry. But the road as it climbed had become sinuous, one switchback following another, in some places narrower than two car widths, so that passing was impossible. Elsewhere, other cars inched by. Down below, one could see several of the Riviera towns, their edges etched in the early sunlight, towns that got smaller as the road climbed. Most of the way there was no guardrail. A car that went over the edge would tumble hundreds of feet down the flank of the mountain.

They climbed and climbed, gaining altitude slowly, tortuously.

At length the cab came out onto the high corniche at La Turbie, where the ruins of the monument to Emperor Augustus, after more than 2,000 years, still lorded it over the town. After four or five streets La Turbie was behind them, and there came a small road veering left, which began climbing in its turn, making its way still farther up the mountain. More switchbacks. More breathtaking views below. The road had been carved into barren cliffs, and it took them at last onto a steeply tilted plateau of lawns and big trees, the sculpted fairways and smooth greens visible from time to time through the foliage. But they could go no farther, for the entrance to the golf club was blocked by two gendarmes with their hands up, palms outward.

Conte got out of the cab, showed his shield, and attempted to talk to them, switching to Italian when English failed, but they weren't getting it, or pretended not to get it. They kept telling him he had to turn around and go back. He understood this well enough.

Conte opened the other door and made Gigi get out. He said: "Tell them I'm a New York police officer—"

"But you're not, you said."

"Tell them. Tell them I'm part of the investigation into the crime."

"What crime?"

"If we get past these yo-yos we'll find out. Tell them, for chrissake."

A new element, Conte saw, had been added. The two gendarmes couldn't take their eyes off Gigi. She began to speak to them in French. She sounded convincing to Conte, who did not understand a word, and must have sounded convincing to the gendarmes as well, or else they wanted to believe her so as to go on talking to her, for soon they were nodding and smiling.

Gigi turned back to Conte. "They said we can go through, but not the taxi."

"They're letting you through too?" said Conte, surprised.

"As your interpreter." She smirked at him. "It's clear to them that you're not worth anything without me."

You may regret what you're about to see out there, Conte thought, looking at her.

They walked up the driveway toward the clubhouse, past multiple police vehicles parked in all directions which to Conte, who had seen this so many times before, immediately read *crime scene*. You could measure the importance of the crime by the number of police vehicles, and by how hurriedly they had been not so much parked as abandoned, their drivers jumping out running. So many vehicles meant crime scene long before the yellow tape went up. Did they use yellow tape here? Maybe it was red or blue or some other goddam thing, he would soon find out. As they approached he felt the same chill he always felt at such times, though stronger because of the too curious young woman at his side, him thinking: Whatever you are about to see, Dolly, you are going to wish you hadn't.

"It's on the ninth fairway," said Gigi, hurrying to keep up.

"Don't worry, we'll find it easily enough."

As they came around the clubhouse they could see the crowd out on the fairway, men standing around doing nothing, waiting apparently. This also was familiar to Conte. Waiting for the medical examiner, perhaps. Waiting for the forensic truck, certainly, for he didn't see one ahead. When the truck came it would plow right out there, desecrating the golf course, while any club members present watched impotently, and the grounds crew cringed in a kind of pain.

The fairway was lined with cork oaks, and various flowering bushes Conte could not name. "Stop here," he said to Gigi, "you don't want to come any farther."

And for a moment she did stop, then he heard her come on a few steps behind him.

A man detached himself from the group ahead and came toward them waving his arms and shouting at them in French. "Go back," he shouted. "Who let you out here? Get back."

Without understanding the words, Conte understood the message.

He had his shield out and was showing it, but this had no effect, the man kept coming forward, arms waving, and the shouting continued. He was about 45, Conte guessed, and wearing a shiny suit. From these two clues, and from his bad manners, Conte was able to guess his rank—not high.

Some paces behind him, moving more slowly, much more deliberately, came a second man. He was tall, also about 45. He was well combed, wore a dark business suit that was well cut, and his shoes and the cuffs of his trousers were stuffed into transparent plastic bootees for protection because the grass was deep and it was wet with dew.

Turning to him, the first man said in French: "Preserving the integrity of the crime scene is paramount, *Patron*. That's what I'm trying to do."

The man in the bootees put his hand on his arm. To Conte he said: "Monsieur?"

"Conte, New York Police Department." The American showed his shield. "I have information about your case." He turned to Gigi. "Tell him that in French."

"I speak English," the man said. He had a narrow mustache over a narrow bow tie. The tie was slightly wider than the mustache, not much.

"Who's in charge here?"

The man said: "Commissaire Vidal, at your service." After a brief hesitation he added: "And this is my associate, Inspecteur Principal Dubraine."

"They have no business this close to our crime scene," said Dubraine in French.

"Probably not," conceded Vidal.

"Give the word, *Patron*, and I'll march them out of here."

Conte looked from one to the other, not understanding.

"Perhaps we should hear what he has to say first," murmured Vidal.

The wind was blowing. The air this high up was quite cool. At the end of the fairway began the rise of the great wall of the Maritime Alps. The highest summits, which looked close enough to touch, were snow covered even this late in the year.

"You've got Georges Grizzard here," Conte said, guessing. "I've been looking for him myself."

"Yes, he's here. Right here."

Conte, having advanced two paces forward, Gigi trailing, was close enough to see into the woods beside the fairway. To see what had caught the attention of all these men.

The corpse hung from the branch of a tree. The branch was stout. The corpse's feet were only a foot or so off the ground which, for a man in his death throes, must have been galling. The arms were bound behind its back, but at the elbows, not the wrists, which did not match other corpses of this kind that Conte had seen, but he had an explanation, if asked, or thought he did.

His tone sober, he said to Commissaire Vidal: "Georges Grizzard?"

"Friend of yours?"

"If you only knew how long and hard I've looked for the guy."

"If you had found him yesterday, maybe all this could have been avoided."

"Isn't it nice to think so."

"Save us all a lot of trouble."

The corpse was wearing white overalls, the kind with voluminous side pockets for holding film or lenses or whatever photographers carried these days; and over it a blue blazer which had adapted itself to the lopsided shape a man's body assumes when hanging by the neck from a tree.

Conte and Vidal, Gigi still trailing, continued to advance. Dubraine, chastened, had receded into the background.

"Killer hanged him with the straps of his camera bag," said Vidal.

This news caused Conte to glance up sharply. Memory made him blink his eyes. He moved a bit closer and discerned the straps for himself. It put him in Milan again, and the voice and words of Piccolo played loudly in his ears.

String him up with the straps of his camera bag. That would be fitting, don't you think?

"Hoisted him off the ground and watched him die," Vidal said.

The corpse stirred slightly in the wind. In judicial hangings the condemned man would be dropped through a trap; the drop would break his neck. Death would be instantaneous. That wasn't what had happened here. The corpse's face was blue, and its tongue protruded.

Vidal said: "Diabolical idea, murdering a man with the instruments of his trade. But logical, I suppose. Live by the sword, die by the sword, and all that kind of thing."

The corpse wore a single sneaker. Which meant that when strung up, Grizzard was not only alive but literally kicking. He kicked off one of his sneakers. After that he slowly strangled to death.

Conte's head filled with the too vivid image: the corpse in the final seconds of life, trying to kick its way loose, kick its way to contact with something solid underfoot, and succeeding only in kicking off one sneaker.

Conte said: "Did you find the other sneaker?"

"It's there, about two meters off. We haven't touched it yet. We'll wait for forensic."

"How did you identify him?"

"He's pretty well known around here. Been in all kinds of scrapes. Celebrities smashing cameras over his head. Celebrities filing complaints. One of my men recognized him."

Conte remembered Gigi who had been beside him but now wasn't, and glanced all around, locating her 30 or 40 yards up the fairway and two steps into the woods, bent over, vomiting up her breakfast. He went to her. Retching, her face contorted, she was not beautiful.

When she stood up he handed her his handkerchief. "Wipe your face," he said gently.

She did so and then to his surprise came into his arms. "That poor man," she said, "that poor man. I did that. I'm responsible."

He held her. "You're not responsible. You had nothing to do with this. Whatever happened to him he brought on himself."

She was crying.

He said: "I shouldn't have brought you here. I thought I needed you to identify him." He glanced back through the trees at what he could see of the corpse. "It turns out I didn't." He disengaged her arms but held on to her hands. "I didn't mean to subject you to this. Please believe me."

"Why don't they cut him down?"

"They will in a minute. As soon as their forensic truck gets here."

He let go of one of her hands, but squeezed the other. "Go into the clubhouse," he said. "Have a cup of coffee. You don't need to watch this."

She shook her head, then made a grotesque effort to smile. "I want to stay."

"You're sure?"

When she nodded he led her back to where Vidal, watching them, waited. Seeing Gigi approach, the Frenchman's eyebrows had gone up.

"She's involved in this," Conte told him. "Two days ago an attempt was made to kill her too."

Vidal nodded. "And you think that is connected to this?"

"I think so, yes," Conte said. "Who found him?"

"One of the gardeners. Arab guy. Phoned us and then took off running, apparently. Figured we'd try to pin it on him, no doubt. He's probably halfway to Algeria by now. Locating him could take days, if I know my Arabs. Probably find the killer easier."

"I may be able to help you there."

Again Vidal's eyebrows went up, but he said nothing. He looked like a detective who suddenly hoped that his case might be handed to him on a platter.

Conte was moving forward studying the turf. He pointed. "Those appear to be tire tracks. Your men may be able to bring up a useable impression. If they do, I may be able to direct you to the car that made it."

Vidal gave him another sharp look.

"If the ground is soft under the body there may be footprints. The guy I'm thinking of weighs about two fifty—a hundred fifteen kilos. So if you find footprints, they may be good ones."

"A personal grudge?"

"No, a murder for hire."

"You going to tell me about it?"

"Of course. Let's tidy up here. Then you and I can sit down over a cup of coffee, and I'll tell you what my business is here, and what I think we're dealing with."

From where they stood they had been conscious for some time of voices coming from the parking lot, loud voices, the clamor building.

"Golfers," muttered Vidal, and he called over Inspecteur Dubraine, to whom he gave orders in French. "Go tell those golfers that the course is closed. Then wait out there for the truck. When it comes, bring the men down here on foot."

To Conte he said apologetically: "He's a good investigator. A bit hot-headed, but good."

Vidal was chief of the Nice detachment of the Police Judiciaire, the national investigative police, and when major crimes occurred, the murder of Grizzard for instance, he was under major pressure to solve them. He would accept help from anyone who could give it including, now, Conte.

Later Conte would learn that Vidal was one of those who, having a university degree, and after close to two years of training at the police school near Lyon, had been commissioned a *commissaire*, and had entered the service in a command role. Dubraine, with less education, had started as an *inspecteur* and gone no further. Neither had ever served as a street cop in uniform, as Conte had. Having failed the test for *commissaire* three times over the years, the maximum allowed, Dubraine could not advance in rank, meaning he no longer had to worry about being nice to people. Vidal's chances of promotion, on the other hand, were unlimited. He saw himself one day rising to *sous directeur* and working in Paris. As a result he had to be nice to everyone, even an interloper like Conte, until sure that the person could in no way harm him.

Conte's shoes were wet from the dew, his feet beginning to get cold. Gigi stood some distance off, turned away from the corpse, her gaze fixed resolutely on the snowcapped mountains to the north. She was barefoot, her shoes jutting out of her handbag.

Conte, making conversation, said to Vidal: "I don't know how many hung guys I've seen, but it's usually suicide, not like this."

"Yes, that's been my experience too."

"If you're going to kill someone, hanging him is a lot of trouble."

"Why not shoot him," said the Frenchman. "Or cut his head off. Suicides, on the other hand, often go to more trouble than you can believe."

"They like to hang themselves on the backs of doors, for some reason. I don't know why."

"Sometimes the guy has been hanging a week. Finally the neighbors notify you."

"I had one once," Conte said, "guy had a rubber band tied tight around his cock. Seemed like he was trying to kill himself and jerk off at the same time."

Vidal was laughing.

Meanwhile, detectives on their hands and knees picked through the grass almost blade by blade. Each time they stood up again it was seen that their knees were sopping. From time to time one called out to Vidal: "*Patron*, look at this." Conte too stared down at whatever they had found, which might or might not be significant: possible tread marks, a cigarette, a small penknife which perhaps had been used to cut the camera bag's straps, or the rope that bound the dead man's elbows.

The forensic crew came toward them down the fairway, gear slung over their shoulders, looking much like the golfers they were not. Once in place they curled around the corpse. One man had his tape measure out—he began measuring everything. Two others set up floodlights, making photos that would be shown in court if an arrest were ever made and a trial ensued: close-ups of the ground around the hanging man, the tire prints, the footprints, the loose sneaker. They made close-ups of the corpse's contorted face, of his hands, his feet, of the sock half shaken off, of the straps around his neck.

Wet plaster was mixed and poured into the shoe and tire indentations, making molds.

It was meticulous work, and took hours, lunchtime came and went, but it had to be done exactly as it was being done, however long it took. They were not looking for clues exactly—they looked instead for what the French called *pièces à conviction*. Proofs to use against the perpetrator if he were ever identified and caught.

The *procureur de la République*, the public prosecutor, came from Nice, together with a man named Maurel, a *juge d'instruction*, each with his own entourage, and a bit later came the medical examiner, also accompanied by several other men.

"Murder always draws a crowd," murmured Conte to Vidal.

Conte, watching closely, was getting a course in French police procedure. The *procureur* assigned the case to Maurel, the examining magistrate, who then assigned the investigation to Vidal, who would do the actual work. Maurel would serve as a one-man grand jury, and would sift all the evidence Vidal brought him, then decide when—or if—enough was there for a prosecution. If warrants were needed he would issue them. He alone would decide whether to indict or not indict, and whether to hold suspects in preventive detention until trial or to leave them at liberty.

Conte went over to Vidal. "I'm puzzled about the way Grizzard's arms are tied at the elbows. That's hard to do if the victim has his hands free. I'm wondering if he wasn't handcuffed first. If he was and if he struggled, there may be handcuff burns on his wrists. Why don't you ask your men to check."

Vidal, after still another sharp glance at Conte, went over to the corpse. He came back nodding. "They're there. Are you suggesting the murderer is a cop?" he said.

"The idea makes you sick, doesn't it?" said Conte. "Me too."

"Maybe you're wrong."

"I hope I'm wrong. We'll see."

"An awful lot of people had a motive to kill this man. An awful lot of others would cheer to see him dead."

Finally a body bag was spread, and men positioned themselves to cut Grizzard down. As this was being arranged, two men burst out of the trees along the fairway, one of them a photographer with a camera bag, the other probably a reporter. Ten paces behind came two TV crews.

As Vidal moved to intercept them he was smiling. "How you guys find out about things like this I'll never know," he called out. For not more than five minutes he answered their questions. The photographer and the cameramen, though not allowed close to the corpse, were film-ing everything else they saw. Then, still smiling, Vidal had two detectives escort the group off the fairway.

"Always be nice to the press," Conte commented.

"Or they'll roast you," said Vidal. "I'm surprised there weren't more of them."

"Grizzard was a sleaze."

"But a famous sleaze."

The detectives, one of them on a stepladder, the other two wearing gloves, resumed their grisly work. The cutting down is an awkward busi-ness at the best of times and no less awkward here. The two detectives caught Grizzard and, almost tenderly, laid him out in the body bag.

Gigi, having come close, buried her face in Conte's neck and would not look, and he felt her trembling.

Watching, Conte was trying to imagine Grizzard in the final mo-ments of his life. The guy wouldn't have believed they were his final mo-ments at all until the very end, Conte told himself. As the scene played itself out Grizzard would have been terrified, sure, but also astonished, for what was being done to him would have seemed to him unbelievable. He might even have cried out: "*Wait a minute, you don't kill somebody just because he took some naughty pictures.*"

But sometimes you did. Or, rather, you found someone who was will-ing to do it. Or, in this case, more likely, he found you. And you paid him his price, whatever it was. Your own hand would not show, you were completely divorced from the act itself, and if you were a certain type of man, once the arrangement was made, you wouldn't be troubled by it, would sleep quietly that night and every night.

The medical examiner, called the *médecin légiste* here, came over and examined the body briefly. When he stood up Vidal said: "How long has he been dead?"

"Twelve, fifteen hours," the doctor said. "I'll have a report ready for you by tonight."

Vidal nodded at his men, and the body bag was zipped shut. Two detectives carried the corpse up to the parking lot.

"You can look now," said Conte to Gigi, "it's over." He let go of her.

She looked up at him, and once again her eyes were wet.

"Hey," he said, "you don't weep over a guy like that."

In a broken voice she said: "I don't know what I'm weeping for. For the world, perhaps. The world is not always such a nice place."

Vidal took Conte by the arm. "You and I need to talk."

They sat in the empty restaurant in the empty clubhouse at a table for three, and the manager came over. "I sent the kitchen staff and the waiters home," he explained.

"We're finished here," Vidal told him. "You can open again if you want to." And then: "What are the chances of some sandwiches and a bottle of wine?"

It was midafternoon by then but the manager was anxious to ingratiate himself with the police. "I have a nice Rosé de Provençe," he said.

The wine came first. Vidal poured it out and they began to drink it.

Having been brought up in a restaurant, Conte knew wines, and he approved of this one. "Nice body," he said. "Lovely color."

Gigi said nothing.

"Provence rosés have improved so much in recent years," said Vidal.

So for another five minutes, as if nothing more important troubled their minds or their day, they discussed wines.

Then Vidal said: "You're not a cop anymore, are you?"

"How did you know?"

"If it was official, probably our office would have been notified."

"As easy as that?"

"Also, I asked myself questions. The same ones any detective would ask. 'What is he doing here? What is she doing here with him?'" For a moment he studied Gigi who did not raise her eyes from the table. "I wasn't coming up with any answers."

"I'm sorry if I seemed to deceive you."

Vidal waved off this apology. "You were a cop a long time, I gather."

"Almost fifteen years."

After a brief silence Vidal said: "So what do we have here. What do you know that I don't?"

"The chief suspect is a Milanese cop named Luigi Piccolo," Conte said. "A suspect is all he is at this point, and we don't have much on him.

"He has no motive except money," Conte continued. "This is a contract hit, or else Piccolo didn't do it. If he did do it, who he might be working for we do not know as yet. The word on the guy is that he has hired out his gun in the past, maybe killed a couple of witnesses, but legally speaking that's only hearsay, and of no use in a trial. His rank is *commissario*, same as your rank, same as mine was in the NYPD. Difficult to prosecute high-ranking cops at the best of times. Furthermore he is supposed to have strong political connections, which means that if you go after him through the Milan police you may not get very far. Somebody probably would sell the case so that the evidence disappears, or stall it until the evidence disappears. You have to go after him through their Internal Affairs unit, or through another agency, the carabinieri perhaps." The carabinieri was the equivalent of the French gendarmerie, the police branch of the army.

Both fell silent. In an attempt to lighten the mood, Conte said: "What they teach us in New York is that it isn't enough just to identify a perpetrator, you also have to convict him in court."

The Frenchman laughed, thin mustache twitching. "Is that what they teach you in New York?"

Conte said: "I wasn't sure if they teach that here in France."

They were two cops facing the eternal cop problem. Though they operated in different languages under different penal codes, they were beginning to understand each other very, very well. For both of them the arrest was the easy part, or relatively so. It was the conviction that was hard. "I can help your investigation," Conte said. "But in exchange I need a favor. Tomorrow you will go into Grizzard's apartment. I want to go in there with you."

Vidal studied Conte a moment, studied Conte's offer as well. Finally he nodded, as the American had known he would. With an open murder investigation on his hands, and few leads, he had little choice.

"You have an additional problem I've never faced before," Conte said. "All these borders over here. I don't know what kind of cooperation your different countries give each other. I can place Piccolo in Amsterdam two nights ago ten minutes before he, or someone, tried to kill Miss Meyer here by ramming her against the parapet of a bridge. The Dutch police have her bike, which may have flecks of paint off the car that did the ramming. I have the voucher number, which I can give you. Can you get the Dutch to send you the bike in some way that preserves the chain of evidence?"

"Maybe," said Vidal.

"By itself it's fairly slight evidence. I can hear his lawyer claiming in court that this wasn't attempted murder at all, it was only a hit-and-run case. Maybe so, but that's a crime too. Miss Meyer may be able to pick Piccolo out of a lineup, if one can be arranged. She only saw his face for an instant, but it was a vivid instant and may stand up in court."

Vidal was nodding thoughtfully.

"She is willing to go to Milan and attempt to identify him."

"Am I?" said Gigi beside him.

"He tried to kill her. She is willing to do whatever is necessary."

"I don't know," said Gigi.

"We need Piccolo's car to look for paint off the bike, and also to match its tires against the mold your men just made. The car is a brand-new green Jaguar. I rode in it in Milan a few days ago. It had under a hundred kilometers on it. He's put three or four thousand kilometers on it in the last two or three days: Milan to Amsterdam, then down to the Riviera, then back to Milan. Check the odometer. If the extra kilometers are on there, how does he explain them? He's a cop. He has to answer the questioning of superiors."

Vidal said: "There are no border controls in Western Europe anymore, so we can't track the car crossing borders. To make the mold stand up in court we need to find a way to localize the car and him on the coast last night."

"The way I see it," Conte said, "he waited outside Grizzard's building and when the guy came home kidnapped him, took him up to the golf course, and strung him up. When you question the guard who was at the desk in Grizzard's building last night, maybe he saw something. Canvass the neighborhood around midnight tonight, maybe you find someone coming home who was also coming home last night, and saw something."

Vidal said: "I have men canvassing even now."

"Monaco has all that video surveillance, cameras on dozens of street corners. Do those cameras make tapes? If so, can your men study them? Pick out Piccolo's Jaguar, maybe Piccolo himself. How are your relations with the Monaco police?"

Vidal gave a brief laugh. "Monaco doesn't have a police force of its own. According to its treaty with France, all directors and most of its cops have to be French by law. Most of the ranking guys I know personally. So that's no problem."

"Then there is the matter of Piccolo's shoes. We need to match his shoes to the mold you took. How many pairs of shoes does he have, and how do you get your hands on them?"

All along they had been eating their sandwiches. Into the three glasses Conte poured the last of the wine.

"It's not an easy case," said Vidal.

"No."

And then, after a pause: "What's your interest in this, if I may ask?"

Conte said: "I have a private client who wants to know who paid for certain pictures Grizzard took. Who was he working for?"

Vidal looked from Conte to Gigi and back to Conte. "Pictures of her?"

Conte made no response.

"I see," said Vidal. "So she's the girl." He looked at her and nodded his approval several times. Gigi, meanwhile, studied what remained of her sandwich.

"So who is this private client you're working for?"

"I'd rather not say."

"I can guess."

"Who?" said Gigi.

"Please," said Conte.

Vidal laughed. To Conte he said: "Your secret is safe with me. Perhaps I'm wrong."

"No, who?" said Gigi.

To Conte, Vidal said: "How long have you been out of the police?"

"A few months."

Vidal's expression had turned skeptical.

"I was forced to resign," Conte decided to say, knowing that if you wanted to win someone's trust, it was necessary from time to time to reveal something unflattering about yourself.

Vidal waited.

"I got in a fistfight in a hotel lobby with a superior officer. He had just come downstairs with a woman. The woman was my wife."

"You didn't tell me that," said Gigi.

"Didn't I?"

"You poor guy," said Gigi.

Conte nodded at her. "Finish your wine," he said. "We have to go."

In Vidal's car they descended the mountain, the abrupt switchbacks yanking them back and forth against their seat belts. The conversation in the front seat was cop talk, the two men, each for the enjoyment of the other, describing bizarre cases out of their pasts. They made each other laugh, but not Gigi in back who was silent.

The streets of Monte Carlo again. They turned down through the gardens toward the casino, whose oval turnaround wore its usual necklace of Ferraris, Lamborghinis, Bentleys, and other luxury cars, its front steps busy with individuals and tour groups moving in and out.

At the hotel desk Conte claimed his key. Gigi followed him into the elevator, and then along the corridor. She waited beside him as he opened the door, then followed him inside.

Without advancing out of the foyer, she turned to face him. "I have something to say to you."

"What time is it?" He glanced at his watch.

"Something important."

"I'd like you to go with me to Grizzard's apartment tomorrow."

"I never fucked Murano."

"After that you can go back to Holland, or wherever you want to go."

"I thought I didn't care what you thought of me. But I do."

He looked at her.

"I don't know why I care, but I do."

He said nothing.

"I didn't even stop him from doing what—what he evidently wanted to do. He stopped himself. He really wanted to, too. When a man is wearing only swim trunks, you can tell. Said his wife was waiting for him and he should leave and he left."

"You must have thought you were losing your touch."

"You are such a bastard."

"You tell me one thing one day, one thing another."

"I was angry at you. You thought I was a whore and I'm not."

"With that stage act you do, you could fool a lot of people."

"Nudity is nothing these days. Don't you know that? What age are you living in? I'm not a whore."

"All right, you're not a whore."

"A whore is someone who fucks strangers for money," she almost shouted. "I've never done that. Never." And then because he had goaded her into an admission she had not intended to make she added: "I haven't been to bed with a man in years." Her voice was on a descending note: "Not since my boyfriend stole my money and then got arrested."

"Why not?"

"That's none of your goddam business."

"Why are you telling me all this now?"

"Because I want you to believe me. And because it's true."

They were still standing in the foyer. Conte at last put his key down on the sideboard.

Still gazing at the floor, she said: "Also I thought maybe, if you believed me, you could do something to help Murano."

When Conte made no reply, she added: "I've ruined his life, not to mention Grizzard's, and probably my own. That's all I seem able to do lately, ruin people's lives."

Conte took her hand and said gently: "It's been a long day, and emotionally draining for both of us. I'm sure you'd like to have a bath or take a nap, maybe both. So go in there, close the door, and try to relax for a couple of hours. Then tonight we'll go out and have dinner in a nice place."

She gave him a half smile and nodded. She turned. He watched her go into the other room. The door closed behind her.

Conte sat down on the divan and tried to read. But his head was too filled with Gigi and he could not grasp the words. So he put the book down, and mulled over the many new images of her which the day had provided, but these only clashed with the ones already in his head. Am I falling for this woman, or what? he asked himself. Finally he got up and gazed out the window at what he could see of Monte Carlo and the Mediterranean.

After about half an hour the door opened again, and Gigi stood in the doorway barefoot, wearing a slip, her bra and panties showing vaguely through underneath, her hair pulled back neatly, smiling slightly, her bruised face looking renewed. "The bathroom is free, if you'd like to have a turn," she said.

He said: "Thank you," and got some things out of his bag and went past her and across the room. When he came out a bit later she reclined against the headboard watching television. She was still in her slip, her knees up, the remote in one hand. This place is a hotel, he told himself passing through. It is personal to nobody. Why then did it make him feel peculiar to move back and forth through what, temporarily at least, was the bedroom of this woman he hardly knew? I should have asked for a second room for tonight, he thought, I don't think she'll run now. She should have asked me for a second room. But he hadn't and she didn't, he did not know why.

"I'll reserve a table," he said. "We'll go out about eight o'clock."

When he knocked on her door later she opened almost at once and, seeing her, he wanted to whistle, though he did not. Because the way she looked, though it demanded a strong reaction, left him momentarily unable to talk at all. Again she had surprised him. Her hair was down to her shoulders as he had not yet seen it, more curl to it than he would have thought, framing the perfect oval of her face. She wore a simple black dress and shoes with thin high heels. A cocktail dress such things were called, he believed. It was in no way formfitting, did not at all accentuate her bosom or hips, her fine waist, her fine long legs, and yet it did. She carried a small beaded bag, and wore no jewelry except for a thin gold chain around her neck.

"You look very nice," he said finally.

"Thank you."

"I didn't know you had anything like that with you."

"The hard part was ironing it on the bed," she said.

"You could have called down and had the chambermaid do it."

"Well, I'm not used to chambermaids."

He took her to the Reserve de Beaulieu, a small, elegant, and very expensive restaurant a few miles down the coast. When they sat down he could feel the tablecloth against his knees. It was a warm, calm night and they were outside among other tables, with the Mediterranean glittering before them. She had turned heads crossing the terrace. Men dining with their wives, most of them older men in a restaurant this expensive, were still staring covertly from other tables, glances thrown and held in her direction. It was almost funny. She did not seem aware of such attention, or perhaps she was used to it. If I were a different kind of man, Conte thought, I would be puffed up at myself for being seen with such a woman on my arm. But he was not puffed up because, with a detective's hard-eyed reality, he realized two things: that she was still a stranger to him, and that she would soon be gone out of his life, probably by noon tomorrow.

For such a woman, he decided, one should start by ordering champagne cocktails. So he did, and when the waiter set them down they toasted each other and sipped them and listened to the murmur of the voices around them and to the lapping of small waves almost at their feet.

At first the conversation was tentative, as if on a first date, which in a sense this was. From where they sat they could trace the lights of the Cap Ferrat, a two-mile-long finger of land pointing out into the sea. Very expensive real estate out there, Gigi commented. Really? said Conte. Maybe the most expensive in the world, said Gigi.

In the bay formed by the cape were anchored a number of yachts, so they talked of yachts as well. Some of them were dark, some were floating Christmas trees, including a number that floated on the ladder the moon had made.

Later the conversation became more personal. Gigi described the countries she had grown up in, the boarding schools she had been put into, the classes she had sat through in languages she did not at first speak, and the words she would misuse, causing the other children to laugh at her, sometimes uproariously. Ridicule of this nature sometimes made her cry. She recounted some of these misused words now, making him smile, though they did not quite translate into English. Always she had been the odd girl out. "So I learned to play the clown, make them laugh on purpose. After that it was better."

Even then, he saw, she had been a survivor.

In his turn he talked of life in a restaurant where, over time, all kinds of crazy people came in. Film stars with their entourages and their absurd demands. Opera singers who suddenly started singing, a blast of sound which, in such a closed space, rattled plates. Once a man came in with a monkey on his shoulder. At first the monkey appeared to be sedated, but this wore off and it jumped up onto the table and from there to the nearest wall fixture where it decided to circle the room, swinging from sconce to sconce with all the waiters trying to catch it, until finally it landed with a splash in somebody's soup.

He told stories well, she said. Every cop did, or learned to, he said. Cops were men who could turn even grotesque events into comedy.

He said: "After that monkey the restaurant had a rule, no pets of any kind."

This started her laughing again. She had tears in her eyes, and he was pleased with himself.

She said: "Sounds like fun, your restaurant."

The family had an apartment one flight up, but used it only to sleep, he told her. They ate all their meals in the restaurant, even on Sundays and holidays when the restaurant was closed. He did his homework at a table in the back. He couldn't wait to get out of school, get a job, and live like other people.

"At least you had family," she said. "I didn't even have that. After my mother died my father brought women home. Two of them he married. They saw me as a nuisance. So did my father. From the age of ten I had no one. One boarding school after another."

By then they were sipping a 1995 Barolo, the sommelier keeping their glasses full. Gigi said: "And you know wine."

"Italian wines, certainly. The best of which are the Barolos."

"This one's very nice."

"It's a Monvigliero from Sebaste. Those are two of the best names up there."

"You keep surprising me. I mean that as a compliment."

"Not half as much as you keep surprising me. I mean that as a compliment too."

A trolley was wheeled toward them, and they watched as their dinner was carved, deboned, and prepared by the maître d'hôtel beside their table, the waiter standing by and then serving.

It was a long languorous dinner. By the time a taxi brought them back to their hotel it was nearly midnight.

CONTE LAY IN THE DARK, the hours passed, and he felt as alert as he had ever been. The French doors were open onto his balcony, and he got up and stood out there barefoot in T-shirt and boxer shorts, which on this trip served him as pajamas, and listened to the muted sounds of the city. A car starting up close by. A dog barking many streets away.

He came back inside. He looked at the door to the room in which she slept. He looked at his watch and saw that it was past two in the morning.

Back in bed he again tried to sleep, and again could not. Finally he put the light on and sat up and tried to read, but couldn't do that either, so he sat there staring at the wall, and the door opened and Gigi stood in the doorway backlit, the light behind her showing her legs through her nightgown.

"I saw your light on," she said in an agitated voice. "I can't sleep."

Conte put the book down.

"I keep seeing that man."

"Which man?"

"Both men, one of them hanging from a tree with his swollen tongue sticking out, the other, grinning, all his teeth showing, close enough to touch except that I'm in the air, and then I'm in the canal drowning."

"We could call down, maybe get something to help you sleep."

"I never saw anybody dead before today."

"It wasn't pretty," Conte agreed.

"My first dead guy was him dangling. How's that for a first? Makes you want to laugh, doesn't it?"

"No."

"His face blue, his tongue all swollen. It was horrible, horrible."

He watched her.

"I keep telling myself I'm not responsible, but it doesn't work, because I am."

"You're not responsible."

"I can't help it."

"It's not your fault. It had nothing to do with you."

"The blue face, the thick tongue. His face is torturing me. It's stuck in my head torturing me."

"Dozens of people wanted to kill him, and one finally did."

"It's as if he's talking to me. Blaming me. When it gets to the point where I can't stand it anymore, his face goes away and it's the other face, the man who tried to kill me. And then I'm not only guilty, I'm terrified, and I tell myself he may come back to finish me off."

She had begun pacing. "And if he does, it's because I deserve it."

"He won't come back."

"How do you know? How can you possibly know?"

"He's in Milan."

"You're just saying that."

"I called him up before dinner."

"Why?"

"Because I wanted to be able to reassure you, if necessary, that he was there."

"You did that for me?"

"Yes."

"You called him?"

"He came on the line. He said: '*Pronto*,' and I hung up."

For a moment she was silent. Then she became agitated again. "That doesn't mean he's still there. He could be here by now."

"You're safe here, Gigi."

"How far away is Milan, four hours? He could come in through the window. And if he kills me, it's because I deserve it."

He saw that she was shaking.

"I'm exhausted and I can't sleep."

He reached for her hand. She let him take it, and he drew her over until she had sat down on the bed.

"I'm not safe anywhere."

He sat up and held her. "You're safe in this room."

"I'm cold and I'm scared and I've got to get some sleep and I can't."

In the face of such anxiety he lifted the covers up and said: "Get in."

She got into bed the way a child would and snuggled up against him and buried her face in his shoulder, and she was shaking. He held her against him. "Stop," he said. "You're safe here. Stop."

"I'm sorry."

"Is it fatigue or fear?"

"Both, I guess."

Finally her body stopped shaking. She lay against him and was quiet.

Now what, he asked himself. Here he was in bed with a woman he was half in love with, and he did not know what to do. In his experience, a woman who came to a man for comfort would get annoyed if he tried to caress her sexually. If Conte now made an advance of some kind, if he touched her that way she might say, probably would say: I didn't come in here for that. And she would jump up. All men can think about is sex, she would say, and go back to her room.

Greatly embarrassed he would say:

Sorry.

Say it probably to her back.

Trouble was, he didn't know how she would react, any more than he knew what it was she wanted from him. She wanted comfort, obviously, and he was giving it. Anything more than that? He found her impossible to read, for she had surprised him at every turn so far.

There were rules of conduct governing situations like this, and he considered them now, rules drummed into him at the Police Academy and since, principal among them this one: A detective does not fool around with female informants.

Is that all Gigi was to him, an informant?

He himself was no Romeo. He had had little sexual experience before his marriage, none during it apart from his wife, and none at all since well before the fight in the hotel lobby. After leaving the police department, preoccupied by the need to find a new job, he had been unwilling to risk rejection from the few women who had crossed his path, and so had been celibate for months now. He considered himself inexperienced at the love game — if game was what it was. He had proven this with the fiasco that his marriage had turned out to be, and he did not want to embarrass Gigi now. Or himself.

He did not want to risk still another rejection.

She lay with her head on his shoulder, one hand lying loosely across his chest. He had one arm under her, so that his hand rested lightly on her silky forearm. For a long time she didn't move, and neither did he.

There was still another possible source of embarrassment. He could control his movements, but not his thoughts. He was wearing only the T-shirt and boxer shorts which in no way concealed the effect she had on him.

"I think I could fall asleep here," she murmured after a time.

"Go ahead, if you want to. But it's a divan. It's not very comfortable compared to your room."

"Are you kicking me out of bed?"

"Not at all."

"Because if you are," she murmured into his shoulder, "it's something that's never happened to me before." After which she was again silent, unmoving.

"How old are you?" he asked.

But she laughed and would not tell him.

Feeling her weight against him, her nightdress against his arm, he was not sure what to do, and he worked the situation over in his head. If she thinks of you as her protector, then you can't very well assault her sexually. Or at least he couldn't, and he said so finally: "I want what you want, but I don't know what that is."

"Obey your instincts, I always say."

So he lifted her chin and kissed her, a deeply satisfying moment, as if he had been holding his breath, knowing that a surprise was coming. It was a kiss that lasted, after which he said: "My instinct has been telling me to do that for the longest time."

"Why did you wait?"

There were many more kisses, deep ones, deeply felt on both sides, it seemed to him. At first they behaved like teenagers in a car, as if this encounter might go no further than kissing, but there began to be caresses soon enough, and a certain amount of squirming, until Gigi said finally: "Something keeps poking into me."

"Why that's disgraceful."

"But there is a place, if it poked me there, I wouldn't mind."

And so it started. When they came apart some time later, both of them a bit breathless, Gigi said: "I had forgotten how nice it could be."

"Yes," said Conte, "me too."

"Sometimes sex is nothing. Other times it's like —"

"— a kind of heaven."

"It's being as close to another person as human beings can get," she said. "It's wanting nothing more from life or the world but this person and this moment."

"It's being happy."

"I'm thirty years old."

"I'd like to make love to you once for every year. May I?"

"Thirty is a lot, but I wouldn't mind if you tried."

It went on almost to dawn. From time to time they would doze, until one of them, not always the same one, would wake the other and it would start again.

At a certain point they had moved to the other room where the bed was more comfortable. There were many conversations. Confessions too, at times.

Once her finger traced the scar over his eye, the thickening of the bridge of his nose. "Are these from the fight in the hotel lobby?"

He caught her hand and kissed it.

"What were you thinking of, to do such a thing?"

"When I hit him I was so surprised. I had no idea I was going to do it. It was so crazy."

"He was even more surprised, I imagine."

"He was the number two man in the department. There's only one of those, and I was a captain, of which there are hundreds. He was such a supercilious, priggish kind of guy, and here he was getting slugged by a captain, and he had to hit me back to preserve his macho status in the eyes of my wife. Who was already gone, by the way. One squeal and she was out the door, scandal averted."

Gigi was laughing. "Forgive me," she said, "it's really not funny."

Telling the story Conte had tried to make it funny. He loved to hear her laugh. But now the joke was over, for there was something he felt obliged to tell her. He said: "After that I never even looked at another woman until you."

"But you did look at me."

"I had to. For business reasons."

"And what's going on between us right now is business, right?"

"Strictly business."

It made her catch her breath.

"You're a very good," she said, "good businessman."

SHE TALKED OF THE ART of the striptease. "The sexiest part of any seduction is the prelude, right? Will she or won't she?"

The promise of sex was sexier than the sex itself, she said. The striptease artists of the past imposed a discipline on this prelude, and prolonged it, turned it into a ritual. At the same time they kept themselves at a safe distance. It called itself a tease, and that's all it was. Where the stage ended there stood an invisible wall behind which the girls were safe. No one could cross. The striptease was based on the basic weakness of all men. It worked, because their erotic needs were so close to the surface.

Now, of course, you had nude beaches, nude cocktail waitresses, nude lap dancers, men could grab a handful if they liked, and the striptease was dead. She herself had not invented anything new or different. She had merely put the ritual and discipline back where it belonged.

The first stripper was Salome, she said. The first we know anything about. The dance of the seven veils was thousands of years ago—the art itself has existed that long.

What was it like to be naked onstage? he asked.

At first, she said, she had felt all the anxiety, all the fear of derision any woman would feel at denuding herself. Nowadays she feels a kind of split personality, pleased by her skill and timing, excited by the risks she is taking, and by the absolute silence of her audience, and at the same time she feels almost totally disassociated from herself and from them. "It's an out-of-body experience," she said. "It's a kind of ecstasy. It's almost like being drunk. You're not really there."

HE STROKED HER still puffy cheek, the blue circle under her eye, and they talked about physical beauty. As you got older, Conte said, you acquired scars. That was a fact of life. He could live with his slightly damaged face. "I was never a beauty anyway."

"You're not movie star beautiful," Gigi conceded. "But that's not important unless you actually are a movie star. You're a very attractive man."

"Nice of you to say so but—"

"Don't worry about not being beautiful. Look where looks have got me. Not very far. The women I meet hate me on sight, and the men are so dazzled they can't behave normally. Half of them treat me as a goddess, and the other half as a slut."

"Is it that bad being beautiful?"

"You look honest, or perhaps honorable — is there a difference? You have a strong face. You look dependable. And your feelings show in your face. Your feelings for me, for example. You never really believed I was a slut. You didn't know what to believe, did you?"

"No."

"Your feelings were ambivalent. They switched back and forth from one minute to the next."

"Was it that obvious?"

"But at the moment you're not ambivalent at all, are you?"

He laughed, and put her hand down where he wanted it. "That feel ambivalent to you?"

THEY TALKED OF SEX and of love. Conte saw sex as a long fuse leading to love. If you lit the fuse it could lead to an explosion of love. But the fuse could be smothered anywhere along the way. "Tonight it did lead to an explosion of love," Conte confessed. "It did for me."

"For me too."

"At the moment I'm totally in love with you."

"And I with you."

"Will we still be in love tomorrow, next week, next year? We'll have to see."

"It would be a shame," she said, "if it were just tonight."

And they looked at each other as best they could in the dim light, both of them vulnerable, both suddenly, surprisingly, emotionally naked, exposed one to the other to a degree that neither had intended, or imagined could occur.

IN BETWEEN EACH OF THESE conversations he was on top of her, or she was on top of him, or they were in some other contorted position, the clinical mechanics of love, love manifested by contortion one might say, the mechanics bearing no resemblance to the smoothness of skin, the emotion produced, the delight they took in each other, the sensation of oneness that came from it, and which, among the many sensations they experienced that night, was to both of them the most delicious of all.

In the morning in the big bed they awakened almost simultaneously and gazed at each other somewhat sheepishly, as if embarrassed at all that had happened during the long night, all they had showed of themselves, each to the other.

Conte kissed her on the forehead, then the lips, for he was brimming over with affection for her, then said: "What do you want for breakfast?"

Back to the business of living. He picked up the telephone and called their order down.

THE COURTHOUSE, CALLED the palace of justice here, was small, and the courtrooms in it were small, because nothing bigger was needed. Serious crimes were rare in this small and favored place, and those that did occur were almost always perpetrated by foreigners. What was left were misdemeanor trials, civil trials, property disputes, and divorces.

On the appointed day as ordained by law, Maria Cristina and Antonio Murano were called into court for the "reconciliation meeting" which took place in one of the small courtrooms in front of a judge who was unknown to either of them. Maria Cristina wore pale yellow, a linen suit over a black silk blouse. The hem of her skirt reached just above her knees. Her medium-heeled shoes were in the same yellow, and she carried a matching yellow handbag. It was as if she was about to go out on a date and wanted to look her best. Murano wore his best blue suit — well, he only had the one — but the creases were sharp, for it had been ironed by his mother last night. The judge wore a red robe with its accompanying white bib, and the traditional red cap.

Both parties had waived the right to be represented by lawyers, and the sovereign had waived his right as chief magistrate to preside over the proceedings. He stood between the two soon-to-be ex-spouses, though one step back, and since reconciliation meetings were not open to the public, was the only spectator.

The two parties had entered by different doors. Murano's eyes were fixed on his wife's face but Maria Cristina's were fixed on the floor. As she made her way to her place, she never looked up.

They stood now in front of the dais, and as the judge read the mandatory tract about the sanctity of marriage, Murano threw ever more glances in Maria Cristina's direction, none of which she returned. Finally he too stared only at the floor.

He had phoned her repeatedly over the past weeks, at first on her cell phone, but an intercept came on saying the number had been disconnected. Had her father taken the cell phone away from her? He tried the palace switchboard and, when his calls were not put through, had each time left his name, asking that she call him back, which she had not done. He could not be sure she ever received these messages. He had written her letters, asking to see her. But perhaps she had not received his letters either, for they too drew no reply.

The courtroom ritual continued, the judge turning now to Maria Cristina to pose the specific questions the ritual required. Some of these were couched in formal language, but the import of all was the same. Did she consider her marriage beyond saving, was the bond that had united her to this man here present irretrievably broken, did she wish for her marriage to be dissolved? There were seven such questions in all. Murano was leaning forward, his eyes fixed on her face as she replied. But she never glanced in his direction, or even looked up, and to each question, in a voice so low it could barely be heard, she answered: "Yes."

The judge turned to Murano. By this point he knew only that his phone calls had not been returned, nor his letters answered. His wife, though she stood only a few feet away, would not look at him, and she had answered yes to all those terrible questions. It was clear to him that no one wanted to hear his apologies or explanations. There seemed to him nothing further he could do, and so to each question he too answered: "Yes."

The ritual ended there. The judge stepped down from the dais. The two parties left by separate doors. Murano looked back as he went out. Maria Cristina did too, and their eyes finally met. But her father, who must have been on his guard for just this, stepped quickly in between. The moment ended, and the door closed.

In silence father and daughter returned on foot to the palace. Having exited from the opposite side of the courthouse, Murano could not see them. He stood in the street meditating about that final glance, clinging to it as one might cling to a rope, and tried to read into it messages that were perhaps not there.

The official papers were ready about an hour later. The judge sent them across to the palace, and the feudal lord signed them.

The marriage was over. Maria Cristina and Murano were now legally divorced.

The girl in her room did not come out for the rest of the day, except once to refill and heat a bottle for her baby. Lady Charlotte prepared food on a tray, and carried it in herself, but the young mother did not touch it. Antonio Murano did not know this, and had he known it, he would not have been able to say what, if anything, it meant.

For two days, the divorced man did not leave his childhood bedroom in the apartment over the butcher shop except to go into the kitchen from time to time to find something to eat and, later, to sit at dinner with his parents at the kitchen table. His mother prepared these dinners and said nothing. The butcher mocked and jeered. His contempt, it seemed, was total. This reaction was perhaps more normal than any of the three realized. Not only had the son's social standing been dissolved by these recent events, but so had the butcher's.

For two days, having been savaged by life in ways he was unable to comprehend, the young man took his father's abuse and did not raise his head.

On the morning of the third day he left the apartment and went looking for a job. He knew he would draw stares, and he did, that people would titter behind their hands, and they did. But if he was to win his wife back, if he was even to stay in the duchy, he first of all needed a job.

Because of the duchy's business boom, not to mention the hordes of tourists who needed servicing, he thought finding one would be easy.

He went first to the tennis club where he had worked as assistant pro.

The head pro seemed glad to see him. His handshake was warm, as was his smile. He was entirely commiserative and understanding. Murano had had some bad breaks, he said. But the duke was not a nice man. In fact, he was a bastard, as everyone knew. "Getting mixed up with people like that was a mistake because you can't trust them to behave like human beings."

The head pro said he'd love to have Murano back as his assistant. "You were good, the clients liked you. Just let me clear it with the club president. Come back in an hour and be ready to start."

For an hour Murano wandered around the town. He did not have enough money even to sit in a café over coffee.

The hour up, he returned to the club. The head pro was embarrassed. "He said I can't hire you," he said.

"Did he give a reason?"

"No, no reason."

Murano went to the municipal swimming pool where he had once worked as a lifeguard.

Same result.

One by one he tried the several construction companies active in the city. "We can always use young muscle," said the first foreman he talked to. "When can you start?"

"Immediately," said Murano.

"Just let me check something first."

But when Murano came back the foreman shook his head sadly. "We have a hiring freeze on right now that I didn't know about."

He tried the next construction site which, according to a bulletin board posted outside, needed masons, carpenters, and an electrician's helper. Murano was not a mason, but knew how to work with concrete. Given the right tools he was a good carpenter. He understood electricity. The foreman went into the office, which was a trailer parked on the site, but when he came out he said: "Bad news, we have no openings right now."

The divorced man tried one more construction site, and then the two national cab companies. He was refused by all of them. By then he understood that no one who depended on contracts or permits from the palace was going to hire him, and that meant nearly everybody. He understood also what his ex-father-in-law was trying to do — drive him out of the duchy altogether. The message was clear. He must emigrate. He was not to be allowed to remain in the city in which he had been born.

All of this searching took two days. On the third day Murano tried the bus company that ferried passengers to and from the airport 50 miles away across the border. This was almost his last hope. The company was not owned by the duchy but by a consortium of airlines, and one of their drivers had just been fired for drunkenness.

He was fitted for a uniform and hired at once.

It was not the career he would have envisioned for himself; he would need to find something better. But it would do for the moment. He borrowed money from his mother to carry him to his first paycheck, then set about trying to contact Maria Cristina. He could not go through the palace switchboard or write any more letters. The cell number he had for her no longer worked. Probably her father had confiscated her phone, precisely to prevent a call from him. If so, by now she would have bought herself another.

There must be ten people who would know this number, friends of hers. Friends of both of them until a few days ago. So who should he go to who would know the new number — and who would give it to him?

GIGI STOOD IN THE BATHROOM, dressed, not primping exactly, but arranging her hair in the mirror.

He watched from the doorway. She was wearing jeans, a blue blouse, and flat shoes this morning. Her bruises were healing fast. If her face was a bit red, it was from rubbing against his stubble, he imagined, feeling a bit proud. To him she looked delicious. She was smiling and talking over her shoulder. She wanted to go out and see the shops, she said. She seemed gay, lighthearted, eager to see what the day would bring. So was he. He was brimming over with an emotion that was perhaps love, and with the hope only half admitted to himself that in the weeks to come they might be able to make something together.

This image of her at the mirror would stay with him a long time.

Did he think it would be all right? she asked, turning. I mean, to go out alone? Nobody knows I'm here, she said. How could anyone find me? Even if someone was looking for me?

"You're not scared anymore?"

"For the moment, no."

In his head he added to her arguments a few cop observations. In Monte Carlo the sidewalks were as crowded as midtown New York, the streets too, cars inching along. A gunman, if any, would see mountains to the north and sea to the south, meaning too few escape routes for himself—none at all in two of the four possible directions. He would see manned police booths on many of the corners. This place had more cops than anywhere else Conte knew.

No one in his right mind would risk fulfilling a contract on streets like this.

Conte had calls to make and receive that would tie him up all morning. The first several would be to Italy. Later he would call Prescott at home in America, and most probably, given the time difference, wake him up. But it was time to report on where the investigation had taken him so far, and where he thought it would go next.

It wasn't fair to make Gigi sit here all morning watching him dial numbers.

So he decided to indulge her. He was like a father allowing his daughter out alone. "Sure, go do the shops," he said. He might as easily have admonished her to be a good girl and look both ways when crossing the streets.

"Don't worry," she said, as if reassuring a husband. "I'm not going to buy anything."

As she opened the door to the hall he said: "If you see anything that costs only one or two million, call me and I'll come buy it for you."

"I wouldn't buy anything in this town. Have you seen the prices? During the three months I worked here I never bought a thing. I'd go to Nice or across into Italy. The shops here are lovely to look at, though."

Then she was gone.

He sat by the telephone but instead of lifting it he brooded.

His investigation, so far, had not got very far, his major questions unanswered. Who had commissioned and financed those photos of Gigi and Murano, and why? It had always seemed clear to him that if he could find out who, then the why would be obvious. He had started out believing there were three possibilities: the magazine *Secrets*, or Grizzard himself, or those two mystery men from Italy whom he had so far not investigated at all. There was a fourth possibility that he had also considered, for he was not stupid, and he had absorbed over the years a good deal of police cynicism which held that everyone's motives were probably impure, and were often unclear even to the person himself;

and that everyone, given the proper circumstances, was capable of horrendous acts.

The fourth possible culprit was the duke himself.

But Conte had discarded this idea almost as soon as it occurred to him. That any father would betray his daughter to that extent, especially a daughter who had just given birth to the royal heir, seemed to him inconceivable.

Therefore, three possibilities. Plus who knew how many others that he hadn't even guessed at yet, and that, if they existed, would be buried much deeper down.

He had thought of Gigi and Grizzard as the keys to the mystery. That once he had identified and located them, all would become clear to him. But this hadn't happened. Gigi knew little of value and Grizzard, now, was not going to answer the questions of Conte or anyone else.

Was the murder of Grizzard connected to those photos? Conte's cop instincts told him it was, but he had no proof. As Vidal had kept suggesting, the crime could just as well be connected to some other scandalous photos in Grizzard's past; God knows there had been enough of them.

Were the murder of Grizzard and the attack on Gigi connected? Was Piccolo the perpetrator of both?

Again Conte's instincts answered yes to both questions. But again he had no proof. Whatever proof might exist would be difficult, perhaps impossible to get at: Piccolo's car, Piccolo's shoes, Piccolo's movements. These proofs, if they existed, were 200 miles away in another country, and probably would be made to disappear before anybody could get at them. But if Piccolo was indeed involved, then who was paying him and why?

Was the same person or persons behind both the scandalous photos and the murder of the photographer who took them? If so, how did that person or persons and the murderer, presumably Piccolo, find each other?

Which brought Conte back to his original starting point. He seemed caught in a circle from which there was no way out, the mystery no closer to being solved.

This job was giving him a headache.

He began making calls. The first two were to the two other Italian cops he had met at FBI school. He had kept in touch with them in the years since. Both, separately, had later come to New York with their wives, and Conte had shown them around the city. He had taken the first couple to Yankee Stadium where he had attempted to explain to them the game of baseball. Unfortunately it was a 1–0 game with only three hits on each side. He realized after a while that baseball could never be explained to a foreigner, and so had taken the other couple the following year to a Giants game. But pro football proved not much easier to understand, apparently. In both cases, when they discussed the games at dinner afterward, they had all had a good laugh, and Conte had promised that the next time they came to New York he would take them to the opera.

Now, reading the numbers from his address book, he phoned the first of these men, Dante Marino, in Rome, and then the second, Franco Cortile, in Modena. Neither was in and he had to wait to be called back. Finally he did talk to them, first one, then the other, two very long conversations, for he hadn't seen them in several years and so small talk came first, followed by explanations of why he was not a cop anymore, and only then the reason for his call. He was on a case of some delicacy, he told them. A client had asked him to vet two possible investors — he gave their names. What could Marino in Rome and Cortile in Modena find out about these men? Were they legitimate businessmen? Any police record? Were they likely to be looking to launder money? Any suspicion of wrongdoing at all? If crossed, were they likely to have people roughed up?

"You don't want much, do you?" said Marino.

"I took you to a baseball game," said Conte, "you never had so much fun in your life. You owe me."

"My wife still talks about it," said Marino.

"You must have the equivalent of Dun & Bradstreet there."

"Yes, we do."

"So what kind of credit rating do these guys have?"

"I'll call you back."

Conte left the hotel's number and hung up. A few minutes later he held virtually the same conversation with Cortile.

Almost immediately his phone rang and it was Commissaire Vidal. The search warrant on Grizzard's apartment would be ready about noon, the Frenchman said. He would pick Conte up at two P.M. sharp. "Did you see yourself on television last night?"

"Me?"

"Story led the newscasts on all the channels, just as I said it would. From a distance it showed Grizzard hanging from that tree. Very tasteful. And then the rest of us standing around."

French newscasts start at eight P.M. "We were in a restaurant by then," Conte said.

"They had some nice shots of your bimbo, too."

"Jesus," said Conte.

"What's the matter?"

Gigi out in the streets alone. "She's not my bimbo," he said.

"Your pictures are in most of the papers too."

"Hers as well?"

"Both of you. The *Nice Matin* must have sold the photos all over Europe."

"I've got to go," he said, and hung up.

In the hall he rang for the elevator but when it did not come he turned immediately to the stairs. The banister was polished oak under his hand. He descended two steps at a time. The stairs were carpeted. His feet made no noise.

At the newsstand in the lobby he grabbed a *Nice Matin* off the pile, seeing its big front-page photo, then noticed the same photo on other papers and bought them too, Italian, French, Spanish, he didn't know what or how many, four or five. He was reading the *Nice Matin* as he crossed the lobby, trying to, the rest of the batch under his arm, other patrons forced to step out of his way, or him avoiding them at the last moment. He saw his own name under the photo, Gigi's too. He was identified as a New York detective present on the Côte d'Azur on a related case. Gigi's name was given as Georgette Meyer—they even got that right. She was said to be his fiancée—wrong there.

The *Corrierre della Sera* from Milan had the same photo, same information, they all did, where did they get it from? Yesterday, during Commissaire Vidal's impromptu press conference, Conte had heard many questions asked, few answers given, and no names mentioned—the American standing close enough to hear all this clearly. Of course the names of all persons present at this crime scene or any other had had to go into the police report, same as in New York. But the crime scene report was not a public document. No one would have access to it but cops and prosecutors. So how had their two names, his own and Gigi's, got from the police report into the papers? But he answered the question himself. Reporters are detectives too. Reporters have contacts in the police and elsewhere. They have favors owed them. They have ways of finding things out, don't be so surprised.

To Conte the Milan paper seemed the most threatening, because Piccolo in Milan would have seen it, couldn't have missed it. It proved that Gigi was not dead, not even injured, and was in Monte Carlo with Conte. A single phone call to some contact in the Nice police would give him—perhaps had already given him—the name of her hotel.

So Gigi, at this moment, as she moved blithely along a sidewalk somewhere, the shop windows like a series of cards flipping over, one after another, each one revealing a new surprise, was at immediate risk. He was perhaps at risk himself if the paid killer, Piccolo or whoever, saw him as getting too close. But he shrugged this off. He knew how to defend himself or so he believed, whereas Gigi did not, was nothing if not an easy target. She had perhaps been followed from the hotel and now, even in crowded Monte Carlo, could be picked off from a motorcycle or scooter as she ambled along. Or, if there were now two assassins in a car, even a car hampered by traffic, she could be forced into the backseat and disposed of elsewhere.

In front of the hotel waited a line of taxis. He got into one and instructed the driver in a mixture of English, Italian, and pidgin French to drive him along the Boulevard Princesse Charlotte, which he thought to be the principal shopping street of the town, the street Gigi might have chosen, his best bet. But within a hundred yards the cab was immobilized behind two tour buses slowly disgorging their passengers, people of a certain age for the most part, mostly wearing short pants and sneakers. Conte threw money at the driver, left most of his newspapers on the seat, and went up through the gardens not quite running.

On the boulevard he could not see very far ahead. Even the opposite side of the street came to him only in glimpses between cars. He tried to glance at all the faces in them, to glance into every store. Gigi had said she would buy nothing, but she might be in one of them, having changed her mind. Cars went by from all parts of France, all parts of Europe, Conte saw, for he knew how to read the license plates, some of them. But he did not see her in any of the cars, or any of the shops. He did not come upon her on the sidewalk.

He reached one of the police booths, the cop on duty standing half in, half out, his blue uniform with the red piping and his white cap looking brand new, him looking like an extra out of a comic opera. Probably he had never in his career seen anything more traumatic than a purse snatching. Conte approached him, asked if he had seen a tall young woman wearing flat shoes, jeans, and a blue blouse. Even as he spoke he realized he had described half the girls on the street. Even a real cop could not have noticed Gigi, except perhaps sexually, and then only if she came close. Real cops constantly eyeballed the street but what caught their eye was the unexpected, the bizarre, something out of sync, not a young woman window-shopping. Conte turned away even before the cop had managed to think up an answer.

Up and down that street and most of the intersecting streets Conte searched but did not find her, and many times he cursed himself for having let her out alone. Finally with slow steps he turned back toward the Place du Casino, where they had agreed to meet for lunch at twelve thirty sharp.

And there she was, exactly as planned, standing in front of the Café de Paris, smiling, unconcerned, waiting for him.

So this was the second image of her that day that would stay with him.

He grabbed her arm. "Where were you? Where did you go? I couldn't find you. How dare you disappear?"

She jerked her arm loose. "Don't you talk to me like that. What's the matter with you?"

"Something's come up." He had her arm again and was half dragging her toward the café.

"What's come up?"

"Have you seen the paper?"

"What paper?"

The *Nice Matin*, furled, jutted from his back pocket, and he yanked it out and thrust it at her. "This."

Seeing her picture she stiffened.

In a calmer voice he said: "We were all over the TV last night as well. In every country, probably."

The maître d'hôtel approached. "Monsieur, Madame," he said, "inside or outside?"

It was a warm, sunny day. The tables on the terrace were beginning to fill up. The dining room, they could see through the window, was empty.

"Outside," said Gigi.

"No," said Conte, "inside, please. My wife," he explained to the maître d'hôtel, "is allergic to too much sun."

The maître d'hôtel led them to a table. Gigi hung her handbag over the back of the chair and they sat down.

"So now I'm your wife," said Gigi.

"Sorry. I said the first thing that came into my head."

"There's not a soul in here. Outside might have been safer. More people."

"No, too visible."

"You're really upset, aren't you?"

"I looked for you everywhere," Conte said.

"You were that worried about me?"

"I couldn't find you."

"That's a first for me," Gigi said. "Someone worried about me."

She put her hand over his on the tablecloth, the two hands became one, and they sat in silence until the waiter came to take their order.

It was a short, nervous lunch. They watched the door rather than the food. Conte pointed out that the sun was on the windows. Therefore they were invisible unless somebody cupped his eyes against the glass. They watched the door anyway. Gigi picked at a *salade niçoise*, finally pushing it away saying: "I ought to be hungry, all the exercise I had last night." She gave him a weak smile that faded. "But I'm not."

Conte did a bit better with the lamb chops and fries he had ordered. They drank a bottle of rosé, and talked of what they should do. Check out of the hotel certainly. That was the first decision. But go where? He would ask Vidal for suggestions when he came, Conte said. He called the waiter, and paid, and they crossed the Place du Casino to their hotel where Gigi went up to pack while Conte at the cashier's desk asked for his bill. This took longer than expected, with the result that he went up in one elevator while Gigi, carrying her small suitcase, descended in another. She peered around the lobby for him, found no one she knew, and so stepped out onto the stoop. Vidal's unmarked car should be there by now, and perhaps Conte as well.

Wrong on both counts.

A doorman in his elaborate uniform asked if she wanted a cab. She shook her head and prepared, for safety's sake, to step back inside the hotel.

It was at this precise moment that a dark green Jaguar entered the Place. It passed close in front of her, perhaps ten feet away, perhaps a bit more. She could have thrown her suitcase at it and, if her aim was good, it would have hit the driver in the eye. There was a flash of recognition on both sides. If she was who the driver was looking for, then he had found her. They stared right at each other, and Gigi gave a gasp.

The driver was as startled as she. He stomped the accelerator into the floor provoking a squeal of wheels, and within 50 feet jammed on the brakes, causing the same noise again. The car shivered, but stopped. It was either that or mount the front steps and enter the casino without paying. Now the steering was wrenched again. The driver got the car straightened out and came back up the other side of the square at equivalent speed. Then he was gone.

Elapsed time? Not more than two seconds, perhaps less. Two seconds that left Gigi trembling.

When Conte came out of the hotel a moment later she threw herself at him, crying: "It was him, it was him."

"Who?" said Conte. "Who?" But from her agitation he had already guessed.

"The man who tried to kill me in Amsterdam. He just went by in a car."

"What kind of car?"

"A car."

"What color?"

"Dark. It was dark."

"Dark green?"

"I don't know."

"A Jaguar?"

"It was a car."

"All right, calm down, calm down."

Conte's eyes were darting around. He was trying to glance in all directions at once. "He's gone now. Which way did he go?"

"Up through the gardens."

"Fast?"

"The car was squealing like an animal."

Vidal's car drew up in front, and he got out waving a paper. "I've got the warrant," he said. And then seeing the two suitcases he came around and opened the trunk. "Checking out?" he said. "Where are you going?"

"How far are we from the Italian border?" Conte interrupted.

"Ten or twelve miles."

"How many roads go across?"

"Two. Why?"

"How long does it take to get there?"

"Along the front through the towns, a long time. If you go up to the *autoroute*, maybe thirty minutes. Once on the *autoroute* you can go like the wind."

Conte visualized the switchbacks that had to be climbed. "Are the border crossings manned?"

"With customs guards, yes. But cars go through without stopping these days. Normally they do. Unless the guards get a tip of some kind."

"Two crossings. Can you close them?"

"What's this all about?"

"Our suspect just drove past the hotel."

"How do you know?"

"I saw him," said Gigi.

"Maybe you're mistaken."

"I recognized him and he recognized me."

Vidal looked dubious.

"If she says she saw him, she saw him," said Conte. More and more he saw this young woman as observant and reliable.

Gigi said: "The right front fender was dented where he knocked me into the canal."

"Come on, come on," said Conte, "we're wasting time. Can you close those two crossings?"

"Do you realize the traffic jams you'd be causing?"

"Close them for an hour. If he doesn't come through in an hour, open them again."

"Even if it was him, you have no idea which direction he'll go in."

"Seeing Gigi with a suitcase startled him," Conte declared. "It meant that in a few minutes she will have gone somewhere else, he won't be able to find her. Being recognized by her shocked him even more. Whatever plan he had, he has to redo it. He needs time. And he needs to feel safe. For him that means Italy."

"Maybe."

"If I was him, I'd try to get back to Italy where I have some protection, wouldn't you? Can you close those crossings?"

"I don't know. I can try."

"Try, then. Quickly."

Vidal held the car keys in one hand, his cell phone in the other. Conte took the keys and went around to the driver's side. "I'll drive, you call," he said. "Get in."

"Wait for me," said Gigi.

They both looked at her.

"If you think I'm staying here by myself, you're crazy."

Conte nodded.

The doors slammed. Conte with his two passengers took off with a squeal to match Piccolo's a few minutes earlier.

"May I ask where you think you're going?" said Vidal.

"Up to the *autoroute*. That's the most likely place. See what we find there. You got a siren? Where is it?"

"Put the blue light on the roof," said Vidal. He was punching numbers into his cell phone, from time to time directing Conte which turn to take. Conte was using the siren when needed, but for many minutes progress was slow. The route led out through the streets of Monte Carlo into the streets of Beausoleil, both towns crowded with cars, and only then began slowly to climb, reaching the streets of Roquebrune and coming out the other side.

"It's a dark green Jaguar," Conte said. "Milan plates. MI 6688. Tell them that."

"You sure of that license number?"

"Of course I'm sure. I memorized it."

The switchbacks began, short sharp climbs doubling back on themselves, the road a series of narrow ledges. To one side rose sheer cliffs so high and steep one could not see the tops of them, and to the other was the sickening void that dropped almost straight down to Monte Carlo and the sea. Conte was sliding all the corners, driving much too fast for roads like this, so that Vidal beside him, removing the cell phone from his mouth, cried out: "Slow down, for God's sake, you'll kill us all."

"I figure he's got a seven- or eight-minute head start on us."

"He can't make good time. He's not from here so he doesn't know the way."

"He found that golf course easily enough."

Though repeatedly thrown into his seat belt straps, Vidal was still on the phone, sometimes cajoling, sometimes shouting impatiently, using whatever tone he thought was needed to convince men to close the border.

Gigi, silent in the backseat, was holding on with both hands.

"Tell them he's armed, and must be considered extremely dangerous," said Conte.

Finally Vidal clapped the cell phone shut. "Customs say they'll do it. Maybe they will. If so, will they do it in time, that's the question."

The Vista Palace Hotel squatting on top of its spur of rock came into sight ahead and above. The road crossed in front of it, then swooped down onto the *autoroute* into traffic running at a legal 81 miles an hour, and sometimes much more. Conte never slowed down, and once in the fast lane increased his speed to 90, then 95, finally holding it at an even 100, passing everybody. Even this high up there were many tunnels, the car plunging from bright sunlight into darkness, no one able to see in there except hopefully the driver, and then erupting into sunlight that each time seemed blinding. Between tunnels they were treated to spectacular views, high mountains to the north, the sea far below burnished the color of Bronze Age armor, the steep coastline ragged and broken as far as the eye could see.

They came into the final tunnel where the traffic first slowed, then clotted, brake lights shining for 15 or 20 cars ahead. The tunnel's exit, that small halo of daylight, was some distance farther ahead still.

"There's your answer," Vidal said. "They've closed the border. They're checking the cars."

Since there was no telling how long they would be stalled there, Conte got out of the car. "If they catch him, they'll need an identification," he said to Vidal. "You don't know what he looks like, and I do." As he started forward on foot he called over his shoulder: "You take the wheel from here."

"Don't get yourself shot," Vidal called after him.

Walking between the tunnel wall and the cars, eyeballing every driver he passed, he heard the car door slam again, and looked back, and it was Gigi following him. He waved her to go back but she ignored him. He was halfway to the tunnel exit by then.

When she came up he grabbed her shoulders and shook her. "Go back to the goddam car."

"No."

"Do you have any idea how dangerous this could be?"

"I'm staying with you."

Muffled detonations from outside. Shots fired, thought Conte, who had heard plenty of gunfire in his career, though never before from inside a tunnel. But he had been expecting gunfire any minute, so that's what he thought he heard now, and he started running. He came out into daylight into a vast open area, ten lanes wide or more, the long, narrow customs shed in the middle — into which until not very long ago people had had to drag their suitcases to be searched, their passports to be stamped. Today's traffic moved normally, quickly, past one side of the shed, not even slowing down, but on the other it was stopped dead, with all that space to one side that, in this age of open borders, was empty, no longer needed.

Conte was concentrating on the commotion he expected to find ahead, but somehow could not locate, at the same time peering into each of the cars he passed, an instant's study of each face, none of them recognized by him. He had forgotten Gigi, certain under the circumstances that she would have stayed in the tunnel. But she had not. She was about ten paces behind him and advancing.

PICCOLO HAD BEEN STUCK in the line ten minutes, perhaps longer. He had come out of the tunnel, the traffic moving fluidly, and had seen the roadblocks go up, and he had cursed. Who knew how much time this was going to take. If he had arrived 60 seconds earlier he would have been through, the roadblock behind him. The French *douaniers* had come out of the shed and spread out across the area, the cars all slowing down and then funneling as directed into a single lane, all trucks into another, all of this happening in front of him. A few of the trucks had been stopped too, drivers handing down their papers, but most had been waved through at speed.

It was cars the *douaniers* were interested in, obviously, not trucks.

At first there had been 60 or more stopped cars ahead of Piccolo, a number of drivers getting out to stand on the pavement in the crook of their door watching what was happening ahead and wondering what the *douaniers* were looking for, why the traffic was being held up. Piccolo wondered also but was unworried. Impatient, yes, but these things happened, it had nothing to do with him, could not possibly have anything to do with him. Maybe a tip about drugs going through, or some other contraband. In a few minutes he would be on his way.

The line moved ahead deliberately, almost imperceptibly, first one car lurching into motion, then another, the queue advancing only one car length at a time.

A few drivers, each in his turn, were made to get out of their cars and stand there while the *douaniers* studied their papers. Whenever this happened the wait was longer.

For the first time in many years the frontier post was behaving like a frontier post.

Behind him, Piccolo could see in the mirror, more and more drivers were standing beside their cars.

Then came the detonations Conte had heard. It startled Piccolo, lifted him out of his seat. It wasn't gunfire, though at first he too had thought it was, for he was strung much tighter than he had admitted to himself. In actual fact it was a truck starting up, energetically blowing smoky farts out its rear.

When Piccolo looked up there was a *douanier* standing beside his door.

"Papers."

The man was in uniform, blue tunic, kepi on his head. Piccolo got his wallet out and showed his police credentials. "I'm in a bit of a hurry. I'd appreciate it if you'd let me through," he said in credible French, thinking this would be the end of it, professional courtesy would be shown him. But it wasn't.

"Papers," the *douanier* said.

"What seems to be the trouble?"

"Papers."

This was a customs guard, not a cop, Piccolo realized, nothing to get alarmed about. And he handed over his passport.

"Registration as well."

He handed this over too. Without looking at the papers, or giving them back, the man walked away, walked to the shed and inside, Piccolo telling himself he still wasn't alarmed, though by now he was.

Another *douanier* signaled him to pull out of line and park here, indicating the spot. Piccolo did as ordered, and the car behind him was signaled to come forward, and then was waved through.

Nobody looked at Piccolo, or disturbed him in any way.

In a mood of increasing tension he too got out of his car and he too stood in the crook of the door. He then heard a siren back in the tunnel. This was Vidal trying to carve his way through the massed cars in there. Piccolo didn't know who it was but did sense what it was, that the siren had to do with himself, and that was when he glanced back at the tunnel exit and to his surprise saw Conte and the stripper woman striding toward him.

They were still a hundred or more yards away. Hurriedly Piccolo jumped back in his car, knuckles tight around the steering wheel. He was wearing big dark glasses, so perhaps they hadn't recognized him from such a distance. But in a moment they would be alongside the car. Clearly this roadblock here at the edge of Italy had been set up for him personally. And once the French got their hands on him, perhaps they wouldn't let go.

Italy was about a hundred yards ahead.

Customs' cars had been parked broadside across the very wide space, but there was a gap he thought he could get through. Beyond that were the tollgates with their barriers down. Those barriers would stop nothing, he believed.

The big engine was purring softly. He put the car in gear, wrenched the wheel around, and stomped on the gas pedal. He had to line the car up to fit through the gap he had spied, and he did so, three maneuvers only, a few seconds. The big, beautiful car was making 60 mph as it shot through the gap, and faster still as it approached the tollgate barrier. Behind him he could hear whistles blowing, see waving arms. In a hundred yards he would be in Italy. This was the only concrete thought his head could handle at the moment, but others were in there, unarticulated but real. He was leaving his passport behind; he would have to get a new one. Car registration, the same. A nuisance, but for a man in his position no more than that. In Italy he could blunt any inquiry that came his way. If the French wanted to blame him for something, interrogate him, they would have to extradite him first. Him, an Italian *commissario*.

It couldn't be done. In Italy he might have problems, but none that were insurmountable.

So all his thoughts led in one direction, and that direction was Italy. And Italy was only a few more yards away.

ALMOST IMMEDIATELY BEYOND the row of tollgates the road begins to narrow down to the normal four lanes, two in each direction. On the Italian side it goes on to Milan, Venice, Rome, and many other places. But in the wide part on this particular day—most days, in fact—waited a customs sedan, which was empty, and two guards in their gray uniforms, the straps of their submachine guns over their shoulders, the weapons pinioned under their elbows. Although customs inspections for most tourists were a thing of the past, could almost be considered quaint, nonetheless people still felt a slight twinge of fear to see them there. When clearing the toll booths one passed within a few feet of them, the car in back of them ready to engage in pursuit if one disregarded orders to stop.

One of the guards today, Aurelio Manfredi, had been a member of the customs service for just over ten months. He was 23 years old and newly married. He lived with his wife, who was eight months pregnant, in a one-room apartment in one of the poorer sections of San Remo, and he traveled to work each day on a Vespa motor scooter. Manfredi had quit school at 16. He spoke no language but Italian, but he knew many equivalent words in French, *autoroute* for *autostrada*, *douane* for *dogana*, and so forth. He also knew something of the history of the Italian customs service.

In the past it had always been thought of as a place to make money. This was true in most of the European countries, Italy no different, especially at its many isolated, mountainous crossings, manned sometimes by a single guard. Contraband trade had always flowed over such borders, and it was believed in criminal circles, and by truckers and tourists as well, that almost any goods could pass, but for a price.

But these days Europe was virtually a single market. The words Common Market meant just that. With hardly any product still counted as contraband, and with the borders open in every direction, it had become much more difficult for dishonest customs agents to turn a profit. Aurelio had been glad to find this out. He was an extremely religious young man. He had no intention of breaking the law himself, or letting others do it in his presence. This presented a bit of a problem because the young man beside him, Nino Benvenuti, had leanings in that direction, Aurelio knew. Nino was the same age as himself, they had grown up together, entered the service together, and in addition Nino was his wife's brother. Aurelio saw it as his job to keep his brother-in-law straight.

At this moment the two of them lounged against the customs car, about 50 yards past the tollgates, only one of which was doing any business at all, for the cars were still trickling through one by one. The young men had been briefed, vaguely. They knew that the French were trying to catch some guy who was armed and dangerous, supposedly.

They had no great interest in what the French did or did not do. Let the French handle their own problems. Their job was to protect Italy.

Suddenly there was a vast commotion on the French side. They could not tell what it was, but they could see through the row of tollgates the frantic arm waving, and they could hear the whistles. Aurelio Manfredi knew immediately that someone, presumably the guy who was armed and dangerous, was about to try to crash through. This caused two half ideas to fluctuate in his head: 1. For the sake of Italy this could not be permitted; and 2. He was supposed to do something. The two half ideas were heavy, and they began to alternate behind his eyes without him being able to grasp either one of them. He raised his submachine gun. Perhaps he thought that the simple threat of this awesome weapon would be sufficient. Perhaps he was imagining himself a hero. Who can say?

From about 50 yards beyond the tollgate the car was coming straight at the barrier. It was already moving at great speed. It was coming straight at Aurelio Manfredi with only the barrier between it and him. At some point he recognized the oncoming car as the dark green Jaguar the French were trying to stop, its driver armed and dangerous. Somewhat frantically Aurelio wagged his submachine gun so that the driver would be sure to see what it was. But this had no effect whatever. The threat of his mighty weapon stopped nothing.

The Jaguar shattered the barrier. A section of it—about three feet long and jagged—landed almost at Aurelio's feet. It startled him so much that he pulled the trigger.

He shot off 15 or 20 rounds, no one knew how many, least of all him. Although he maintained the next day, when at last he could talk coherently, that he had aimed low, trying to disable the vehicle, not kill anybody, the weapon had paid no attention to his wishes, if in fact he had had them.

Instead it seemed to have a mind of its own. The first two rounds were not low at all. They hit the Jaguar in the windshield, which turned instantly opaque. After that the weapon climbed. From the first shot it was already climbing, for Aurelio had never fired it before even in training and he could not control its rate of climb, nor its incredible power either. The noise deafened him. The recoil almost instantly numbed his hand. That he kept firing was not even his doing—his finger was stuck tight to the trigger as if by centrifugal force. He was unable to lift it. Also, by the end he was firing and trying to jump out of the way of the oncoming car, both at the same time and neither he nor anyone else knew where those bullets went. Into the cliff above the tunnel, presumably. Starting tomorrow, carabinieri on ladders, and on their hands and knees where possible, would be searching there for spent bullets. The search would last days.

Of the two shots that pierced the windshield, one drilled through front and rear backrests and then through most of the clothes packed into a suitcase in the trunk of the car. But this same bullet, it was later theorized, had sent forward a thumbnail of glass that took out the driver's right eye. Of course he might already have been dead by then, for the other round, either the first shot or the second, entered his mouth, driving two teeth into the back of his throat and destroying the third cervical vertebra—in effect it broke his neck. Death appeared to have frozen his foot on the accelerator, however, for the car, traveling now in a straight line, continued on, its speed even increasing slightly, and it was as if the dead man had aimed it directly toward the two customs guards. It missed Aurelio but not Nino. At the last second he had tried to jump out of its path but had opted, it appeared, to jump the wrong way. The Jaguar's bumper, which had lifted, caught him in the chest, driving him backward into the door of the customs car, half crushing his chest so that he could no longer breathe. He was still standing but pinned there, his face contorted, a man trying to scream, but with no noise or breath coming out. Realizing at once what had happened, Aurelio threw down his gun and tried single-handedly to lift the Jaguar off his brother-in-law, all the while shouting for help. The first to realize what had happened and also the first to reach him was Conte, who came running. The two of them pulling together at the heavy steel were slightly more effective than one man alone, not much. Everyone else had taken cover, was still crouched somewhere expecting or fearing another fusillade. It was several minutes before additional help got there. By then Nino was dead. He was laid out on the ground where the first of a succession of men in uniform tried mouth-to-mouth on him. They worked on him for 20 minutes before they gave up, and someone found a tarpaulin and covered him.

Conte had gone over to the wrecked Jaguar and peered in. The corpse wore a red bib, one eye open, the other missing. Conte thought: He's not going to tell me who hired him either. First Grizzard, and now this guy. Meaning that Conte's case had again come to a dead end.

He was still chewing on this notion when he was joined by Vidal.

"Is that the guy?"

"Yes," said Conte. He went to get Gigi, who was standing some distance off, shoulders stiff, staring down at the sea far below, refusing to look at anything nearer at hand.

He went over to her.

"I'd like you to identify him, if you can," he said gently. "You don't have to do it, but it might relieve your mind to know he won't bother you anymore, and it might help the investigation as well."

When she nodded he brought her over to where Vidal waited.

"He isn't pretty," Conte warned. "You don't have to stare at him. A quick glance is enough."

She leaned over enough to see into the car, straightening up almost instantly and looking away.

"Is this the man who tried to kill you in Amsterdam?"

Her shoulders were shaking. "Yes," she said.

He led her back to where she had stood, and left her standing there, shoulders stiff but controlled, concentrated on the same view as before. "I'll be as quick as I can," he promised her, and went back to Vidal.

"I sense we have a problem here," he said to him.

"Yes, we do."

"We need the corpse and we need the car," said Conte.

"The other side of the tollgate, we could claim we were in France. Here we can't."

"The Italians will say the corpse and the car are theirs," said Conte.

"The Italians'll take over the entire case. Probably won't even tell us how it came out."

"Morally speaking, it's our case," said Conte.

"And legally speaking?"

"First one up here with a tow truck, legally wins," advised Conte. "An ambulance the same."

"Kidnap the lot," said Vidal.

"I can see you're a cop with a keen interpretation of the law."

The Italian ambulance arrived first, but busied itself with Nino Benvenuti, and with Aurelio Manfredi who by then was incoherent, verging on catatonic. A few minutes later the French ambulance and tow truck arrived simultaneously. The corpse was loaded into the one, and the wrecked car was winched up onto the bed of the other, almost before the Italians noticed. When they did notice there was much bleating and pushing. Violent curses erupted, the two sides threatening each other with hands on their guns. Conte had seen similar scenes in the past. Cops from neighboring precincts fighting over prisoners. NYPD cops trying to hold on to prisoners over whom the FBI claimed federal jurisdiction. These things happened, and sometimes it got violent.

This time the accusations and curses were, for the most part, incomprehensible to both sides for they had no language in common. The result was almost funny, but scary too. Cops with guns, in Conte's experience, were capable sometimes of acts of unimaginable stupidity. He did not see where these cops would be any different just because they were European.

Gendarmes arrived in a bus. A big bus, and full. The men spilled out and this settled the issue. Some carabinieri had come too, but only a carload. In the face of such superior force the Italians seemed to recoil a bit. Then Vidal drew aside their commander and, using Conte as his interpreter, spoke to him gently, and got him calmed down. The Frenchman explained the case, promised to keep the Italian informed, and at the end they exchanged business cards. The Italian then waved his men aside, and the burdened French vehicles started back into France.

Vidal said to Conte: "I'll finish up here. Take my car." He looked over at Gigi, still standing off by herself. Even from this distance she looked tense. "Take your lady down," he said. "We've seen this kind of thing before, but she hasn't. Today hasn't been easy for her."

Conte went over to her, took her hand. "Come," he said. "We'll go back to the hotel."

She said, "I'm the one who started all this. The result is two men dead. Plus that poor Italian boy, the customs agent."

"The customs guy you can feel sorry for, but not the others. I told you something yesterday, remember. They were not nice men, either one. They played a dangerous game. You're not responsible, they are."

In Vidal's car, behind the driver, Gigi clung to his hand. There had been steady traffic coming from Italy, and they joined it. As they proceeded into France, they saw that the other side was jammed up for miles.

Gigi gave a broken laugh: "I must say you're a man who tries not to bore his dates. Two corpses in two days."

"Most men trying to impress a woman take them to nightclubs or Broadway shows. I take mine to crime scenes, the gorier the better." Neither laughed. "I'm sorry," Conte said.

She did give his hand a squeeze, but she said nothing more all the way down into Monte Carlo. With traffic backed up from the *autoroute*, all the streets were clogged and it took a long time.

As they approached the hotel Conte realized that he would have to check in again, and he worried about it. One room or two? When Anna left she had taken with her most of his confidence with women. Perhaps now Gigi wanted only to be alone. He was not sure of himself. Perhaps Gigi was already regretting last night. They didn't know each other well. I mustn't presume on this woman, he told himself. I could ruin everything.

As the car drew up they were seated on opposite sides of the backseat, not touching.

She said: "I'm sorry I'm so morose. I keep telling myself to smile."

He said: "When I check in, well, you're entitled to your own room tonight, if you like."

She seemed to tense up, then saw how tense he had become beside her, and just as quickly she relaxed. Onto her face came a half smile that was almost a smirk. "I'm afraid if I'm alone I might have nightmares."

Conte gave a vast interior sigh of relief. With a smile he said: "I'm good with nightmares. Maybe I can help you block them out."

"It's worth a try."

The driver handed out their bags. "Vidal invited us to have dinner at his house tonight. I told him I didn't know how you would feel."

"Sure," said Gigi. "Get my mind off what I've been up to lately."

They sent the bags up, then sat in armchairs off the lobby and a waiter in a white jacket came and they ordered tea. The tea came in silver pots, together with finger sandwiches, so they lingered there a while. Afterward they went out into the streets. Conte bought a bottle of wine to bring with them that night while Gigi stopped at a pharmacy.

Later in their room Conte watched her re-iron her black dress on the bed, still another vivid image of her that day, and one with a surprising sense of domesticity.

They were six at dinner, two French cops and their wives, and a de-frocked American cop accompanied by a woman who performed nude in nightclubs. The apartment was small. It was high on one of the hills be-hind Nice. It had a terrace but no view, a cop's apartment, not the apart-ment of rich foreigners. It was furnished partly in antiques inherited from the wife's family, or his.

The two wives were both schoolteachers and neither spoke English. Gigi spoke to them in French which, thought Conte who eavesdropped from time to time, she seemed to speak as well as they did. Also she seemed able to make them laugh at will. They seemed charmed by her. And of course the two men were. From time to time Conte attempted to speak French himself. Mostly he talked to the two cops in English, sometimes about the case, sometimes about the international situation, even more often about the food which, especially when compared to what one was likely to be served at a cop dinner party in New York, was exquisite: foie gras and toast, followed by roast quail with roast potatoes and tiny string beans, then a salad tossed with walnut oil and balsamic vinegar, then a tray of cheeses, then a homemade apple tart. Madame Vidal, judging from the evidence, was a fine cook. Conte had brought with him a 1995 Chateau Figeac, which is a famous label, but the other wines seemed to him equally good even though the names were un-known to him.

At the door, his guests departing, Vidal said to Conte: "We'll serve the search warrant on Grizzard's apartment tomorrow morning. We'll come back to my office with what we find, and put it together with what-ever has come out of Piccolo's pockets and suitcase. We'll lay it all out on a table and see what we've got."

Conte and Gigi got into the car of the other cop and his wife, and were driven back to their hotel.

Then they were back in their room.

That afternoon and early evening, though knowing what would happen between them before the night was over, Conte and Gigi had moved carefully about the room, each intensely aware of the other but without touching, each behaving as if the other might break in two if touched, not even brushing together in the narrow parts of the room, turning sideways to pass. The sexual tension between them had seemed to increase moment by moment, but still they did not touch each other, holding it off, as if to make eventual release all the sweeter. For Conte the tension had become almost insupportable, though delightful too, in its way.

Now they came in the room and fell on each other, mouths first, then the rest. The floor became strewn with clothing and in a moment all the tensions of the day dissolved, the sexual ones certainly, but also all the ugliness, horror, and fear that the day had brought, all dissolved, and although what they were doing was not a bit peaceful, they were at peace.

THEY WAITED FOR VIDAL on the sidewalk outside the hotel, Conte reading a newspaper folded lengthwise the way standees do in New York subways, Gigi studying the ornate, 19th-century facade of the casino at the bottom of the square.

"The most famous casino in the world," she said, "and you haven't even been in it."

Conte said: "Well, I'm not here as a tourist."

"You've got time only for your job."

He gave her a smile. "Only for my job."

"I see."

"I may have taken off five minutes now and then. To relax."

They were smirking at each other. She took his hand.

"Don't do that," he said, but did not let go. "Suppose someone sees us."

"You think it will make Vidal suspicious?"

"He may come to the conclusion there's something between us."

"Where would he get that idea?"

"He's a detective."

She said: "I see him looking at us, trying to figure us out."

"He hasn't asked me a thing about you. But I think he's about to."

"What will you tell him?"

"The truth."

"Which is?"

"That I'm nuts about you."

He thought she may have looked pleased, but he himself felt suddenly as soppy as a teenager. Dropping her hand, he thought: Why did I have to tell her that? He was old enough to realize that such confessions, confessed in cold blood so to speak, weakened a man's position with a woman. He had said such things to Anna often enough, and look where that had finished. What you said in bed was one thing, cold blood was another. He had no idea how Gigi would feel about him in a month's time, or he about her, and meanwhile she was still the key to his case. He felt her touch his shoulder, but did not respond, and instead looked uphill in the direction from which Vidal would come.

By the time the Frenchman's car entered the Place they were separated by a yard of air.

Vidal came around the car, shook hands with Conte, and kissed Gigi on both cheeks in the French manner. Drawing the American slightly aside, he said in a low voice: "She can't go with us, Old Man."

"Why not?"

"Well, we're serving a search warrant."

"So?"

"That's a legal procedure. There's no way I can justify her being there."

Conte said: "Neither you nor I knew the guy. The only time we ever saw him he was hanging from the branch of a tree. As far as the search warrant is concerned, we don't even know what we're looking for. We're going to flounder around in there. Whereas she did know him. Maybe she can point us toward whatever it is we wouldn't be able to see by ourselves."

"I don't know."

"When you come right down to it, you can't justify me, either."

Vidal looked doubtful. "That's true."

"We need her. Get in the car. Let's go."

Grizzard's building was a 24-story tower on the Avenue de l'Annonciade, one of a number of towers on that street, the towers being in tiny Monaco, the street behind in France. There were other more recent tow-

ers in front of them, cutting off their view of the sea. These were in
Monaco also, built after the apartments behind them, including Grizzard's, had all been sold, depriving the old owners of the view they
thought they had paid for, something they had never imagined could
happen, or be allowed to happen.

Two of Vidal's detectives, one of them Dubraine, were waiting out
front carrying cardboard flats that would become boxes. As Vidal showed
the warrant to the *gardien*, they trooped past him to the elevator.

Grizzard's apartment had been sealed. Vidal broke the seals and they
let themselves in with Grizzard's keys.

Conte saw that this apartment was as slovenly as the one in Milan, except that here the sinkload of encrusted plates looked more recent. Although obviously this was a luxury apartment, Grizzard seemed not to
have treated it as such. Again the wall over the telephone bore scribbled
numbers, and when the American went into the first of the bedrooms he
had to kick the soiled laundry out of the doorway.

Gigi beside him wrinkled her nose. "What a slob," she said. "It was a
mess the last time I saw it, too."

The two detectives, Conte saw, had pulled on white gloves. Dubraine
said to Vidal: "What are we looking for, *Patron*?"

Vidal said: "Checkbooks, bankbooks, address books, bills, letters.
Money. The usual."

Both detectives grinned. "Money," the other one said.

"Cameras too. There could be undeveloped film we would want to
look at. Plus anything out of the ordinary, of course."

"When were you here last?" said Conte to Gigi.

"About a year ago."

"What was the occasion?"

"Don't go getting jealous on me."

"Notice anything different this time?"

"He offered to take some publicity shots of me, if you must know."

"But he didn't."

"Instead he came out with this crazy scheme for me to seduce some guy. I told him no, and I left. The place was a little less unkempt that day than now. He must have cleaned it up specially for me."

She had begun to move slowly, carefully through that room and the others. "Otherwise it looks much the same," she said.

There were two bedrooms. A bed and dresser in one. The other fitted out as an office, its desk piled with papers. Various cameras, scanners, computers, monitors stood on an adjacent table or on the floor. In an adjoining bathroom the tub was once again stained from chemicals.

"Don't touch anything," said Conte. He had come up behind her, his hand on her arm.

She turned and smiled at him.

"If you want to point something out," he said, "call Vidal over."

Vidal too was looking into rooms, but at the opposite end of the flat.

There came a banging on the front door.

Vidal opened to two men in business suits, one dressed in blue, one in brown, both about 40, their manner truculent. They pushed past him, glancing all around.

Blue suit said: "Who are you and what are you doing here?"

Vidal identified himself.

"This apartment is sealed, so get out."

"Was sealed," said Vidal. "I unsealed it."

"This is our case," said blue suit. "Out."

Conte, who had turned from the bathtub, watched from the doorway, not understanding the French words but understanding turf battles well enough, having been in so many, and he stayed clear of this one.

The detectives in their white gloves had come to stand behind Vidal.

"Who are these two guys?" brown suit demanded.

"Two of my men."

Gigi, who at the start of the confrontation had stepped out onto the terrace, came back inside. Blue suit gestured with his chin. "Who's she?"

"A witness in the case," said Vidal patiently. "I have a search warrant."

"Let's see it."

Vidal went to get it out of his briefcase.

After looking at it briefly, blue suit handed it to brown suit.

"This warrant is no good here. Monaco is our jurisdiction, not yours."

Vidal was becoming annoyed. His words when he spoke were both measured and hard: "This is a murder case," he said. "The murder took place up at the Monte Carlo Golf Club, which as everyone knows is in France, as are the Monte Carlo tennis club and the Monte Carlo cemetery. Monaco isn't big enough even to have a police force. You guys are all French. I cleared the search warrant with your boss last night. *Arrêtez les coneries.*" This last phrase, which was spoken harshly, might be translated: "So stop the horseshit."

Blue suit got a cell phone out of his pocket and punched in a number. When the connection was made he stepped out into the corridor. He was back almost at once, folding the cell phone, and gesturing with his chin at his partner. Without another word, both departed.

Gigi had begun studying the phone numbers scrawled on the wall.

Conte said: "Do you recognize any of them?"

"My own." She pointed to it.

"Any other?"

"I recognize a name," said Gigi. Most numbers had only initials attached. She pointed to one of the few names. "Renzo. I had forgotten about him. If it's the same guy, he was at the villa when those" — her voice stumbled a little — "those photos of — of Murano were made." Nervously she hurried on: "I never spoke to him. I don't speak Italian and so far as I know he doesn't speak anything else."

"His number has no area code," noted Conte. Most numbers on the wall had none. "Where does he live?"

"In Italy, I imagine. The code from here is 0039."

In his notebook Conte was copying down this number and the others as well. "Did Grizzard ever say anything to you to suggest who was financing this thing?"

"No. He was waiting to get financing from somewhere, though. Even when the money he was offering me got so high that I agreed, though with conditions, we were still on hold. Then one day he called and said he had the money, come on down."

"What were your conditions?"

"That my face and name would not appear. He told me not to worry, the photos were only to 'influence' somebody and would never be published."

"Influence who?" Conte asked.

"I have no idea."

Influence, thought Conte. Another name for blackmail. If you threaten to publish them, and the concerned party does what you want, then you don't need to publish them.

It's still blackmail.

"If I had known he would sell them to all those magazines I would never have agreed. No matter how much he offered."

Conte contemplated the possibilities. If publication was not in the original plans, but Grizzard did publish them, what did this mean? That the threat didn't work? Maybe the threat did work, but Grizzard couldn't bear to see his handiwork sit in a drawer unseen by the world. Great art demands to be seen. The artist couldn't resist publishing them anyway.

If that is what happened, somebody would have got very mad at him.

Mad enough to order him killed?

Well, he did get killed.

You don't have many answers, do you, Conte told himself.

"So as to who paid him," he said to Gigi, "we still have no idea."

She said: "Ask Renzo, he might know."

His white glove waving a handful of eight-by-ten glossies, Dubraine called out to Vidal: "*Patron*, what do we do with all these photos?"

They were finding photos everywhere. Some had come out of a chest of drawers, every drawer crammed with photos. Now, as Vidal began to look through them, Dubraine's handful first, then the contents of one of the drawers, Conte went over there.

"How did he ever get this close to the queen of England?" Vidal asked Conte, passing him the photo.

A close-up of the queen laughing, showing all her fillings.

This one Conte had seen in Grizzard's flat in Milan.

They began handing photos back and forth the way families did every few years when they got out the albums.

There were photos of film stars in supermarkets pushing shopping carts. Supposedly glamorous actresses had become drab, colorless women with their hair in curlers, looking no different from housewives. Some of them in fact looked hungover. Others were shown topless on boats and beaches. There was a series on a male film star picking his nose. In the first of them his pinky was halfway up his left nostril, and in the last he was examining what he had found there. Next came a woman of a certain age wearing the bottom of a swimsuit, with one breast hanging out of her bra which she seemed frantically trying to tie back on. Conte had no idea who this mortified 50-year-old individual might be but assumed she was famous in this country or another.

"This guy was really good, wasn't he," commented Conte grudgingly.

Another photo showed a female TV journalist, every hair impeccably in place but nude, laughing at something said by a half-dressed male journalist in what looked like a motel room, the photo apparently having been shot through the motel room window from outside in the garden.

"I remember that one," said Vidal. "I was in London at the time. Caused quite a stink."

"Both of them married to others, I assume," Conte said.

"Of course."

Vidal looked up from the photos. "You could sell these things. Get quite a lot for them, I imagine."

The detectives in their white gloves were leaning close too. "Money," Dubraine said.

"Collectors would buy them," said the other detective.

"A gallery owner could mount a show," said Vidal.

"A Grizzard retrospective," said Conte.

"Charge admission," said Vidal.

"People probably would pay to see them," admitted Conte.

"Right."

The American, who had come of age with police corruption all around him, wondered where the Frenchman was going with this line of reasoning.

"We don't want somebody breaking in here and stealing them, do we?" Vidal said.

"No, *Patron*," said Dubraine.

Vidal, who had been holding a stack of 20 or 30 photos, dropped them into the cardboard box at his feet. "Put them all in this box," Vidal said. "And when you get back to the office voucher them as evidence, and inventory them."

"That's a big job, *Patron*."

"I'm sorry, but it's got to be done." And he moved away before the crestfallen detective could protest further.

An hour later, the two detectives having pocketed their white gloves, they all left the building, the detectives embracing cardboard boxes that were stuffed full, stepping carefully off the stoop because they could not see very well around or over the boxes.

Conte and Gigi got into Vidal's car and he drove them back to their hotel.

"Take the rest of the day off," Vidal advised Conte.

"Good," said Conte, "I'll finally get to see the casino."

"Maybe we'll just walk along the harbor," said Gigi. "We don't need any more excitement this week."

The three were standing in front of the hotel.

"By tomorrow the inventory should be completed," Vidal said. "Come in about ten, and we should be ready for you."

HEADQUARTERS OF THE Police Judiciaire for Nice and much of the coast was at 1 Avenue Maréchal Foch. The following morning Conte sat with

Vidal at a table in an office on the fourth floor. The box containing the photos had been pushed under the table, and for the moment was of no interest to either of them. The second box was at their feet, and they up-ended it on the table. It made for a high, unstable pile. As they picked slowly, carefully through it, they were constantly having to lunge for large sections of it that had started to slide toward the floor.

Each piece as they finished with it was dropped down into the box.

They sifted through address books, check stubs, paid bills, and what-ever else came to hand. This was scant evidence, but it was all they had, and they worked backward through a man's life seeking patterns in the scraps of paper he had left behind.

The Piccolo inventory was complete as well, but there was much less of it: an address book, a checkbook, and the various cards out of his wal-let, all of which Vidal had had photostatted front and back. The originals were in the French equivalent of the property clerk's office, and the photo-stats were what was left to work with.

Still to come was a report on the contents of the hard drive from Grizzard's computer, and the lab results on Piccolo's shoe prints and tire prints.

Conte worked the rest of the day, much of the time alone, once because Vidal had been called away to deal with some other case, and another time because two detectives from Milan showed up wanting in-formation about the death of their colleague. Two hours passed before Vidal was able to get rid of them.

Conte, meanwhile, studied bank statements for suspicious deposits and payouts, and charted them by date; he charted as best he could Griz-zard's movements in and out of Nice airport, and was sometimes able to pinpoint each flight's origin or destination; and he sought to put names and places beside every number listed on Grizzard's phone bills. He made notes, covering many pages of a yellow pad.

Late in the day something clicked over in his mind and he went to find Vidal.

"Look at this," he said.

He had found a certain phone number in Grizzard's address book, and the identical number in Piccolo's.

"Up until now," Conte said, "we've assumed that these two guys had nothing whatever in common, never met until the night one of them strung the other up."

"There's no country code with those numbers," said Vidal skeptically. "They may not be the same at all. They could be in two different countries. One in Germany, say, one in Spain."

"I have a hunch the two men had the same country code in mind. They didn't put it down because they knew very well what it was."

"You mustn't push this too far. You need a lot more than just a hunch."

But Conte was ebullient. He thought he might have come upon the key to the case. "That number goes into the duchy," Conte said. "Someone in the duchy is behind all this."

"Maybe."

"I'd bet my house on it. Assume for a moment the number does go into the duchy. Can you trace it for me?"

Vidal was back an hour later. "Unlisted," he said. "You'd need a court order, and even then —"

"That seems like further proof to me."

"Slow down, slow down," the Frenchman cautioned him.

Returning late to the hotel Conte found Gigi at a table on the terrace. In front of her was an empty espresso cup and a book she was not reading.

He was full of good humor. Late as it was, it was too early to take her to dinner, so he said: "Would you like an aperitif?"

"Sure." But she had not smiled at him and, now, did not meet his eyes.

The waiter stood beside their table. "What would you like?" he asked her.

"Anything," she said, still not looking at him.

Conte ordered a Cinzano for her, Campari for himself.

"What have you been doing all day?" he asked.

"A number of things."

He had planned to tell her with some excitement what he had found out that day, how much closer he had come to determining who had financed those photos. Who had hired Piccolo as well. But now he did not do it. Something had gone wrong between them, he saw, he did not yet know what. His world had just been reduced in size. Suddenly it was no bigger than this table, and he waited for her to speak.

"I've been thinking."

He tried to make a joke of it. "All day?"

"Yes, all day."

He experienced a sinking feeling in the chest. "What about?"

"About us."

Once when he was a teenager a girl had jilted him, the final conversation starting with much these same words.

"What about us?"

"We're going much too fast."

"You think so?"

She said: "We have to back off a little."

"Back off?"

"Get away from each other for a time."

"How long a time?" he asked.

"I'm falling for you and I don't even know you. It makes me very uncomfortable."

He tried a joke. "When you know me better you'll love me even more."

But she did not smile.

At this point he still hoped the situation was reversible. Perhaps she was only nervous. The life she had lived had made her skittish. She had not had much success with men. She had spent years avoiding entanglements with men at all costs. Men such as himself. This could be got around, he told himself. All he had to do was be careful.

He said carefully: "You don't trust me."

She did not answer.

"You don't trust men in general."

"Over the years they haven't given me much to trust."

"I'm not that kind of guy, honest."

Again she did not smile. She said: "I think we need some time apart from each other."

"Beginning when?" He tried to say this lightly too.

"What would you say if I went back to Amsterdam?"

He did not know what this meant, nor what reply to make.

"Because I have things I need to do there."

"When would you go?" he asked.

"Well, soon."

"I have to go to Italy next. To Rome, then up through Florence to Bologna, maybe one or two other places. I was hoping you would come with me."

She did not answer.

"Rome, Florence. How does that sound to you?"

She gave a brief laugh. "You're trying to bribe me."

"I have to see a few people there, but it won't be like today. I won't leave you alone. Short interviews. Shouldn't take too long. We'll have most of the time to ourselves."

"I'm not blaming you for leaving me alone today. I was happy to be alone."

"We could see the sights, try some of the restaurants."

"Thank you for the invitation, but I've been to Rome. I've been to Florence. I wouldn't mind going back someday, but not right now."

"What's so pressing about Amsterdam?"

"Things."

"What things?"

"Things I've been neglecting."

"No, tell me."

"They're, well, personal," Gigi said.

They weren't personal exactly. Not in that sense. But nothing any-more was very clear in her head. She needed to see her father, decide if she wanted to live in a consulate in Philadelphia—a decision she could not put off much longer and that seemed too big to make at this distance. But she could have talked to her father on the phone, and the decision was easy compared with understanding what had happened to her in the last few days. She had given too much of herself to this man here. For years she had lived in an almost comfortable aloneness, which was now being threatened in ways she did not comprehend. She needed time.

Some of this Conte divined. He knew nothing about Philadelphia, of course, but he sensed a good deal of the rest. He just didn't know what to do about it, what sort of stand to take.

Personal, she had said. A word that erected a barrier between them. Her intention, no doubt.

"You going back to that nightclub?"

"Only to collect my last paycheck. I think you've weaned me away from that line of work. I'll grant you that much."

"How much time do I have?"

"Time for what?"

He smiled: "Well, to get you to change your mind."

"I don't think you can change my mind."

"The press might find you there."

"The press might find me anywhere."

The surest way to lose her definitively was to tell her truly how he felt about her, he believed. Look what had happened with Anna. Let a plead-ing note come into your voice, he told himself, and you are finished with this woman. With almost any woman.

"So if I go back to Amsterdam would you be really broken up?"

"Well, I'd like it better if you stayed. For a little longer at least."

"A little longer?" After a moment she said: "I'm living off you. I feel like a kept woman. These swanky restaurants we go to. This swanky hotel. I'm not paying my way. Except perhaps sexually."

This was just another way, they both realized, of saying how uncomfortable she had begun to feel.

He decided to try another joke. "Okay, from now on you can pay every other restaurant check and half the hotel."

"Unfortunately I don't have that kind of money. And since this thing started I've had no money coming in."

He did not know what to say to this.

"I want to be on my own again." Did she? She wasn't sure herself, and he didn't know what to believe.

This conversation, in one form or another, continued through dinner, and also in their room as they got ready for bed.

"When were you thinking of going?"

She sat on the bed tugging off her jeans. "I have a plane reservation for tomorrow morning."

He felt betrayed. Her departure was already booked, had been all along, and this evening's conversation had been just that, conversation.

She stood up, folded the jeans in half, and draped them over her suitcase. "How long has it been since you pulled me out of the canal?"

"A few days."

"If you wanted to," she said, "you could count the time in hours."

"They were good hours," Conte said.

"Sometimes they were."

He said: "Will I see you again?"

"If you want to."

"No, I think the choice is yours. Do you want to?"

"Sure."

"When?"

"I'll be in Amsterdam for a while. You could stop off on your way back to America."

"Would that be enough for you, one more weekend?"

She was standing in underpants and bra, not looking at him. "Well, we haven't talked about anything permanent, have we?"

He said: "Not yet, no."

"Another weekend might be nice."

"Instead of a one-night stand," Conte commented, "you could call it a ten-day stand, or however long the total turns out to be."

"That's not a very nice thing to say."

"I'm sorry."

"But you're right," she said, "the sex was great."

"I don't like to hear you describe it that way."

"How should I describe it?"

Now they were quarreling. He said almost doggedly: "It was more than sex, I thought."

"You're the one said that, not me."

"You agreed," he said, "or so I imagined."

She said: "You're a good lover."

"Thank you."

"I told you that already."

They had come too far too fast and other emotions had begun to separate them: uncertainty, a fear of commitment. Strongest of all, perhaps, was embarrassment. They had exposed too much to each other too fast, and both were embarrassed by it. Embarrassment was pushing them farther and farther apart but either they did not recognize this, or were unwilling to risk further embarrassment by mentioning it.

Conte too was getting ready for bed. Standing in T-shirt and boxer shorts he gestured toward the divan. "Would you rather I slept there?"

"That's not a very comfortable bed."

"It's adequate."

She shrugged. "Do what you like. It makes no difference to me."

Turning away from him, she unhooked her bra, and stepped out of her underpants. She pulled on her nightdress and got into bed. Propped on one elbow, she reached to extinguish the bedside lamp. In the penumbra he saw her head drop down into the pillow.

He said: "Good night, then," and he bedded down on the divan in the dark. For a long time he could not sleep, and wondered if she could. She had not closed the door and he thought he could hear her breathing.

Finally he did fall asleep.

He was awakened by her tugging on his hand. When he sat up he saw her there, standing in what fragments of light came through the window, the fragments raking her body through the thin nightgown. "Come to bed with me," she said.

He allowed her to lead him back to the big bed, and then, with only a sheet over them, she was clinging to him in the dark, and he to her.

But in the morning nothing much had changed. He rented a car and drove her to the Nice–Côte d'Azur airport. She hardly spoke during the 40-minute ride along the coast. Neither did he. The Riviera cliffs passed to one side of them, the sea to the other. At the airport he handed over her small bag, realizing that when he got back to the hotel there would be nothing left of her there.

Strangers milled around them. "Time to go," she said. They looked at each other, and were consumed by silence.

It was a moment during which he might have told her what he felt, might have begged her to stay. But his own wounds were still too raw, and he was unable to say the words.

She kissed him briefly, then turned and fled. He watched her go through security. She did not look back.

He changed hotels, moving to Nice to be closer to the commissariat, and worked two more days there, returning each night to his empty room.

Grizzard's hard drive showed nothing of interest.

Piccolo's tire track and shoe print checked out. Considering that this virtually closed his murder case against Piccolo, Vidal put Dubraine on what was left of it, and went on to something else. From then on Conte saw him only in passing, except for the farewell drink they shared on the eve of Conte's departure.

They sat on a café terrace on the Rue de Lépante while people hurried by on their way home from work.

"What's happened to Gigi?" Vidal asked.

"Gone back to Amsterdam."

"I couldn't figure out what, if anything, was between you two."

"Well, I can't either."

"She's certainly a beautiful girl."

"Yes, she is."

"And bright, too. Very bright. Is she really the girl in those photos?"

"Yes."

"You certainly hid her well. Every journalist in Europe has been trying to find out who she is. Half the police departments as well."

"But not yours."

"No, not ours. She didn't commit any infraction here."

"I appreciate your keeping quiet though. If I had had all those people on my neck—and hers—the media, the paparazzi, and so forth, it would have screwed up my case."

"Are you going forward with what you have?" Vidal asked.

"I have to," said Conte. "I don't have any choice."

"You need more evidence. What you have is not actionable. You couldn't go to court with it."

"Unlike you, I don't have to go to court with it. All I need is enough to convince certain people."

After a pause, Vidal said: "Where do you go from here?"

"I have a few stops to make in Italy."

"Maybe you can pick up a bit more."

"Maybe."

"I liked Gigi. I liked her a lot."

"So did I."

"I can't believe such a woman would get mixed up in something as sordid as those photos."

"I don't understand it myself," Conte said. "I'm not sure she does either."

They had been sitting more than an hour. Vidal said that he had to get home, and signaled the waiter for the check.

"I'll take that," Conte said when it came, and he put money down. The two men rose and made their way out through the tables.

On the sidewalk Conte said: "I couldn't have done a thing without you. I want you to know how grateful—"

"Grateful? What for?"

Conte was embarrassed. "For your kindness and cooperation."

With a smile Vidal shrugged this off. "It was just one cop helping out another."

They shook hands.

"Any cop would have done the same," Vidal said.

"You really believe that?"

"Well, maybe not every cop."

"Some would. You're right."

Vidal smiled again, mustache twitching. "Besides, you helped me just as much. More even."

They were two members of the same club who, now, might never meet again. Vidal gave a brief wave, and they moved off in opposite directions.

The next morning Conte drove to Ventimiglia, the border town, where he had arranged by telephone to take Renzo to lunch. They dined on the balcony of a restaurant in a row of restaurants, all standing on piers planted solidly in the stony beach. Below them the sea played its constant song, rushing up to surround the posts, then being sucked back over the stones. It was an almost musical accompaniment to a lunch that was pleasant, but to Conte not particularly productive. Renzo seemed willing enough, he just didn't have much useful information. He said that Grizzard wasn't sure until the last minute whether he had the contract or not. No, he had never said who had hired him. Somebody big, apparently, or so Grizzard had said, but with him you could never be sure.

"Did you meet the girl?" Renzo asked.

"I've talked to her, yes."

"What a piece," said Renzo, suddenly animated, and he began to describe Gigi at the swimming pool, the way she had stripped off her clothes, the way she had swum around totally nude, "backstroke and everything." The way her tits moved as she swam, her rounded ass, the way the bush between her legs, wet, flattened down, had almost glowed. "Made you want to drink off of it," he said. All this he described giggling, using vulgar words where possible, his face and voice alive with excitement.

"When she did the frog kick you could see everything."

This part of the interview upset Conte, made him want to slug Renzo's stupid face, though his own face, he believed, showed nothing.

"What else can you tell me about Grizzard?"

But Renzo was still talking about Gigi. "What I wouldn't give to fuck a piece of ass like that."

Conte told him to change the subject, he was here to talk about Grizzard, wasn't interested in the girl. To his credit Renzo tried for a moment or two, but he had nothing to add about the photographer. It was Gigi he was enthusiastic about, and he kept coming back to her, Gigi nude, Gigi's glorious—

Until Conte suddenly stood up, strode to the desk, paid, and walked out.

He drove on to Modena where he met with Commissario Cortile who handed him financial and other papers on Crespi, the younger of Antonio Murano's prospective buyers, which he studied that night in his hotel room. The following day, Cortile beside him, he drove to Bologna, which is nearby, and which is a university town; like other university towns in any country it had trash blowing up and down its streets, and its main square was filled with students sitting on backpacks. Together they met Crespi for lunch. The ex–soccer player turned out to be a heavily muscled, slow-speaking young man who kept asking: "What's this all about?" in between answers to questions. If guilty of anything, his answers should have been more guarded, Conte thought. They weren't.

And some hours after that Conte was in Rome where his friend Commissario Marino handed him another batch of printouts, and told him that a luncheon meeting with Signor Balducci had been arranged for the following day. Conte had booked himself into the Hassler Hotel above the Spanish Steps, where that night he pored over the papers in his room. He met Balducci at noon in the hotel's rooftop restaurant. The luncheon was pleasant enough. During business trips to New York, Balducci said, he had dined several times at the Conte restaurant in Little Italy. "Good restaurant," he said. He was not a loquacious man, and his answers were hard to read.

According to Conte's police friends, neither man had known criminal ties to anyone.

There was nothing for Conte to do now but write his report, and then go to the duchy and present it, and he called down to the desk and asked that a computer be sent up to his room. While waiting he phoned Alitalia and reserved a seat on a plane.

The next morning he read over the material he had gathered, and studied his draft report. He was at 30,000 feet in brilliant sunshine by then. He knew that he had one small point still to check out when he got where he was going, but he did not expect any surprises ahead, and he was able to convince himself that the case was virtually over.

He had not yet phoned Prescott in New York to explain where the case had led, and that he planned now to end it.

CHAPTER

XIX

ONLY TWO ROADS entered the duchy, one of them over Valiro Pass, 8,212 feet high. At the start of the reign of Augustin II Valiro Pass had been two lanes narrowing to one, the top part unpaved, and it had been closed by snow six months of the year. Not anymore. These days it was a four-lane highway wherever the terrain permitted, meaning plenty of passing zones, and it was wide enough elsewhere. It was paved all the way of course, and at great expense to the duchy it was kept open year round.

Except today. Conte's rental was turned back by what he took to be gendarmes, or whatever they were called here, cops anyway, who told him he would have to go around. The road was closed to accommodate the Tour de France, which these days made regular incursions into neighboring countries in search of lung-busting climbs, plus authorities willing to close 150 miles of roads for six or seven hours—not easy to find in modern times, either one—not to mention the host city's willingness to pay the hefty fees the Tour demanded. The duchy had never hosted the Tour before, and Conte realized that today counted as still another triumph for Augustin II as he pushed his so-called nation to the forefront of European events.

The Tour's first cars and trucks would arrive momentarily, Conte was told. He knew what this meant: three hours of advertising floats and gear trucks, to be followed by the press and team cars, by gendarmes on motor-cycles and then, the pace quickening, by the riders themselves, 150 of them or more who, given the length and difficulty of the climb, would soon be strung out on the mountain, some going over at a good pace, some struggling all the way up. So the road would be closed all day. Tens of thousands of fans were already up there waiting to cheer for their favorites as they pedaled over the top and then plunged down into the duchy, but Conte was not going to be permitted to join them.

Small as the duchy was, going around it was not easy. This was mountainous terrain, the route was tortuous, and it took him more than two hours. If you ironed this place out, he thought with increasing irritation, it would be the size of Kansas.

He came into the city by the other road, which was not nearly as high, and found himself crawling through streets jammed with still more fans. He located his hotel, parked in its lot, and checked in. Going out into the street he found the finish line easily enough, and also the stand built of white lumber and resembling a gallows that had been prepared for the victory ceremony. On it the stage winner and the overall leader would be raised above the crowd. The ceremony, he had learned at the hotel, would be presided over by the young Duchess Maria Cristina, formerly the wife of Antonio Murano. This was fine with Conte who, before he could lock the case up, had questions about her that he needed answered, and he found a spot with a good view of the stand, and watched the last of the publicity floats come in, and then the press cars hurtling through, some of which skidded to a stop 50 feet farther on and hovered there for the time it took reporters and photographers to bail out, before continuing on.

He watched Maria Cristina driven up in a car. She was dressed in a pale blue summer suit, had just come from the hairdresser's apparently, and was all smiles as she shook hands with a number of officials — race officials, Conte supposed. She was accompanied by two young men with buttons in their ears who faced outward as she did this, and they watched carefully that no one molested her as she was led up onto the gallows. One of them had seemed to touch her rather a lot, his hand on arm or shoulder on any pretext, as if she was unable even to climb a flight of stairs without help from him. He was often rewarded with a soft smile, for which he looked each time absurdly grateful, before sending her the same smile back.

And some minutes after that the day's leaders crossed the finish line, eight or ten men who had come over the pass well in front of the pack, the winner throwing a victorious arm into the air. Conte was watching her, not them, and also the favorite bodyguard who had taken up station beside her and often talked into her ear, probably only explaining details about the race, though the tableau itself was intimate enough. They were certainly at ease with each other.

How much at ease?

He didn't know, but it set him back a pace. This case was perhaps not closed at all.

More riders crossed the line, then a pack of about a hundred. During the next ten or fifteen minutes most of the remaining riders dribbled in, followed much later by the stragglers, the badly defeated.

Finally came the victory ceremony, Maria Cristina performing her role graciously, perfectly, making a little speech into the microphones, planting kisses on the winner's dirty cheeks, jumping back just in time as he sprayed the crowd and also his colleagues with champagne. Through all of this she smiled in what seemed an assured, happy way.

It looked to Conte as if she had got over the loss of her husband, and he thought about this for a time.

He was reasonably sure she had never noticed him in the crowd. There was no sign of the duke, nor of Murano, though with 5,000 people milling around, the ex-husband might have been there, perhaps even gazing longingly at his former wife. If so he was invisible to Conte.

Maria Cristina was driven away, the favorite bodyguard helping her into the car though she was an able young woman who had no need of help. Conte did not get close to her, couldn't have got close if he had tried, which he did not.

He went back to his hotel where he sent one of his suits down to be pressed, then took a long shower. Afterward he lay on the hotel bed with a pen and yellow pad, and once again tried to work out exactly what he knew and what he didn't know, and which of his theories were incontrovertible and which were guesswork.

On the esplanade opposite the palace at a restaurant that, he had been assured, faced the gate that the family came out of, when they came out, he sat down and ordered dinner. He had asked around, and that particular gate out of several had been pointed out to him. He made the dinner last, sat long over coffee, ordered a cognac which he also lingered over, sniffing it from time to time, not drinking it. He sat there till the restaurant closed at past eleven o'clock, and nobody went into the palace or came out.

He went back to his hotel.

In the morning he bought the local newspaper, having been told that it would list the day's activities of the so-called royal family. Reading, he noted that the duke and duchess were in London to take part in something or other at Buckingham Palace, and would be gone for two more days. As for Maria Cristina, she was presiding at the opening of a new hotel that morning, and in the afternoon was cutting the ribbon on ski lifts in a newly opened area five miles up the valley.

So he attended the hotel opening. He was in shirtsleeves, dark glasses, and a baseball cap, and he stood well back, not wanting Maria Cristina to notice him. A hundred or so people were present, many of them foreign tourists obviously, which was what he was trying to pass as himself, and the young woman smiled a lot, and shook many hands. After posing for photos with an enormous scissors in both hands, she cut a ribbon there too, meaning that the ski lift ribbon later would be the second of the day, not the first. The two bodyguards were with her again this morning, sturdy young men in ill-fitting suits, one of them yesterday's favorite who again managed to handle her whenever he could. She seemed to like the attention well enough. Conte was trying not to be judgmental. Her husband had been exposed worldwide fondling the breasts of another woman. Maria Cristina was perhaps in need of sexual reassurance and if it was from this particular bodyguard that she was getting it, this was normal enough, was it not?

For lunch she went into the new hotel with some of the men. From the hotel bar Conte watched the start of the banquet that ensued, then went back out into the street, found a restaurant, and had lunch himself.

In the afternoon he watched her perform her function at the base of the new ski lift, watched the second of the stupid ribbon cuttings, after which he followed her back to the palace. In the souvenir shops opposite he wandered up and down aisles fingering statuettes and ashtrays, all the while watching the palace gate. But she did not come out.

At night, wearing his newly pressed brown suit and newly shined wingtip shoes, he sat down in the same restaurant at almost the same table as the night before, and was prepared to linger there till closing if necessary, but about ten P.M. she came out at the wheel of a little green sports car. Immediately he put money down and ran for his rental, parked nearby. He followed her through the town and then up the mountain, realizing after a time that she was headed for the villa she had shared with Murano, and passing her and getting there first. He continued around a curve in the road where he parked, got out, and hurried back, skulking, staying close to the wall. He was just in time to watch her drive in through the big wooden doors, and he ran up as they began to close, and slipped into the garden without being seen, and hid behind some bushes. In New York in the past he had twice performed similar acts of illegal entry in the hope of gathering evidence. Such evidence, being acquired illegally, could never be used in court, but it could tell him which way to take each of those particular cases, and in fact had. Then as now his heart was trip-hammering in his chest. He did not like being a lawbreaker. In New York, if caught, he would certainly have lost his job, and possibly gone to jail. Here the stakes might be even higher. As a foreign national they could do anything they wanted with him. To him. He would have no recourse at all.

The night was dark. Conte was crouched behind a small shed which probably held gardening tools, but from there he could see nothing, nor hear either. He was about to move closer to the house when the wooden doors began to hum, a gear clicked into place, and they began slowly to swing open. He had heard no car pull up. When the gap was wide enough, a man slipped through into the garden. He was about the size of the favorite bodyguard, and was dressed all in black like a burglar, with a dark hat of some kind pulled down to hide his face. He went straight to a door in the side of the house, leaping up onto the stoop and yanking it open. He had not paused to orient himself which meant, assuming he was not a burglar but a lover, that a tryst of this kind in this place was not new to him. He had not gone toward any of the other doors but straight to this one as if he knew in advance it would be unlocked.

The briefly open door had given Conte a glimpse of cabinets and a refrigerator—a kitchen, then. During that same brief moment he had glimpsed Maria Cristina as well, her eyes tense, her knuckles at her mouth. Then the door had closed.

Conte crept to the back of the house and peered in the kitchen window. Though still lighted the room was empty. Continuing along the back wall, ducking under windows, he came to another lighted room but this one gave onto a terrace. The windows here were French doors, meaning that to see in without being seen he had to stand well back in the garden.

Maria Cristina and the man were locked in a passionate embrace, the man kissing her all over her face, she kissing back. Already the man had her partly undressed. Even as Conte watched, the man's attention switched away from her mouth and he began to nuzzle her breasts, first one then the other. Her eyes were closed, a beatific expression on her face, and her hand on the back of his head held his mouth where it was.

A baby cried out.

Breaking the embrace, she led the man by the hand to a straw bassinet which at first Conte had not noticed, and which sat on one of the sofas. Lifting the baby out, she presented it to the man who had finally turned his face in the direction of Conte, and of what light there was in the room. It was not the bodyguard at all, he now saw. It was her ex-husband.

Grinning foolishly Murano gazed down on his son, but when the baby continued to whimper he handed him back to the young woman, who sat down on the sofa and put their son to her breast. Murano had sat down on the same sofa. Maria Cristina had her legs in his lap, and was suckling the baby while gazing adoringly (or so it seemed to Conte) at her ex-husband, who was gently stroking her legs. It was a scene of intense domesticity, one hungry mouth had replaced another, an intensely private scene, one Conte had no business watching, and he stepped back into the darkness and from there made his way to the front of the house.

He found a switch which he supposed was there to work the wooden doors from a car waiting to go out, and when he pressed on it, the doors opened, and he slipped out into the street. He assumed they would close by themselves and he waited to make sure they did, not wanting the young couple in there to be surprised by someone else. Then he returned to his car, coasted noiselessly down past the house, drove back to his hotel, and went to bed.

When he woke up in the morning he looked out and it was raining. Heavy at times, the rain fell all day. Mostly he stayed in his room and waited for the duke and duchess to return to the palace. He had done all he could. The case was over. He could go no further with it, and wanted only to get away, to leave it behind, for it seemed to him more unsavory than anything he had ever worked on in the NYPD.

He phoned Augustin's office and demanded an appointment for the next morning. Impossible, the secretary told him. Not before a week from now, she said.

As she spoke he could visualize her, the tall, prissy woman who sat in Augustin's outer office.

"Tomorrow," he told her. "Say ten A.M. Clear his calendar for me. If he protests, tell him that his reputation, and the reputation of his duchy, is at stake."

"But—"

"No buts. Ten A.M. Tell him. I'll be there at ten sharp, and I don't want to be kept waiting." He hung up before she could protest further.

He knew he should phone Prescott in New York, explaining where he was and where the case was, and why he believed he had taken it to the end. He should explain what he planned to say to Augustin. But knowing Prescott would oppose him, he kept putting this call off. It was a call he could not bring himself to make.

So he phoned Gigi in Amsterdam instead. But there was no answer, and no answering machine either.

He stood at his window and watched the rain come down. His head was churning, his stomach too. He could not see the mountains, and drifts of fog obscured the lower slopes. Eventually he went back inside and phoned Gigi a second time with the same result, and then, after a moment, dialed his boss's number 4,000 miles away.

Prescott came on the line sounding cheerful. "So was there a plot?" he said. "And if so, who was behind it?"

"There was a plot," Conte said, "and the one behind it was the duke himself."

Into a shocked silence Prescott said: "Our client?"

"Yes, our client."

"I don't believe it. No father would do something that humiliating to his own daughter."

"What do you love most, your daughter or your duchy? Story begins thirty-five years ago when he inherits this moribund place from his worthless father. One by one he invents the ski stations, opens up the mountain lakes, brings in the hotels, the banks, the casino, the roads. He invites journalists to write articles, all expenses paid. The crowds begin to come. The place booms. His subjects adore him—they have the highest per capita income in Europe.

"Then he acquires a son-in-law, an uneducated lout, a butcher's son, who embarrasses him for two years prior to the wedding. His work of art is being besmirched. He waits until he has his heir, then moves to rid himself of this supreme irritant—and never mind any pain to his daughter. Some genius, probably not him, thinks up the photographer, the nearly nude woman, the plot. He okays it. Once in motion the plot takes off by itself. As a result three people are dead, there was an attempt to murder the woman involved, and for all I know, I was supposed to be next. He's responsible, and he ought to be in jail."

After a moment, Prescott said: "Can you prove any of this?"

"In a court of law?"

"In a court of law," said Prescott.

"No."

"So you're guessing."

"I've eliminated every other possibility—"

"Not good enough."

"—and I've got a phone number linking the client both to the photographer and to the hired assassin, the dead cop."

There was a long silence in which Conte thought he could hear wheels turning inside Prescott's head in New York.

Prescott said: "I've explained to you how important this case is to the firm, did I not?"

"Yes, you did."

"We're not in business to embarrass clients. Our job is to make them happy. Embarrass them and we won't stay in business long."

"This client deserves more than embarrassment."

"Not from you."

"I hate for a guy like that to get off scot-free."

"You can't prosecute him, for chrissake. Even if you had the evidence, which you tell me you don't. No court has jurisdiction. This particular client has his own country. He can't be touched."

Conte said carefully: "I've been trying to figure out the best interests of everyone involved. What do I do next?" What he wanted to do next was immaterial. This job was the only one he had and he needed to keep it.

Prescott said: "You walk away, that's what you do next. Anything else would accomplish nothing and it would destroy any chance of our company moving into Europe."

Conte said carefully: "That's why I called you. How do you want me to handle it?" He saw no way around the orders he knew Prescott was about to give him.

There was another long silence. When the ex-prosecutor's voice returned it was as firm as ever, but now he sounded cheerful again. "Here's what you do, Vince. You write out a report saying you've conducted a thorough investigation and you have concluded there was no plot, that the photographer set up those photos to sell them to magazines, and no one else was involved."

Prescott laughed. "That way we might even get paid the rest of the money they owe us."

"My expenses, you mean."

"I imagine you've spent plenty. How much have you spent?"

Conte told him.

It made Prescott whistle. "As much as that? Well, then you justify it in your report. You write it long and flowery. You give all the details of all the leads you checked out, how hard you worked, blah, blah, blah. You leave out anything that might embarrass the client."

The world saw truth as relative, Conte well knew. Justice, too. Whether he did or not was, to anyone else, of no importance whatever.

"Tomorrow," Prescott said, "you smile, you hand over the report, and then you get the hell out of there fast. As soon as you get home, you send them the expense account."

Conte was silent.

"That's not so hard to pull off, is it, Vince?"

No, Conte wanted to say, but it is not what I was trained for from the police academy on, nor what you were trained for either. It's not what both of us once swore an oath to uphold.

Prescott said: "I sense you're feeling righteous."

Not so much righteous as afraid. Tomorrow, Conte saw, in the presence of these people, and with his future riding on it, he would have decisions to make. What he feared was making the wrong ones.

"Stop thinking about justice, Vince. This isn't law enforcement anymore, it's business."

Prescott had used the word as casually as most people did. Business was not only a law unto itself but was protected by respectability. "Yes," Conte said, "business."

"I'll make it easier for you," Prescott said. "A week or so ago you told me you had two employers there, not one. The duchess seemed like a nice lady, you said. So give her your report. Skip the duke. Tell her what she wants to hear, and then, as I said, get the hell out."

And on that note Prescott rang off.

From his briefcase Conte withdrew the report he had written two days before, and paced the floor holding it in its manila envelope in his hand. He did not need to reread it. He knew what was in it. Presently he sighed, put it back in the briefcase, and went down to the hotel office where he wrote and printed out the report Prescott wanted him to write, one that would please the duchess, and that the duke would receive with, most likely, a vast sense of relief.

Back in his room he phoned the palace, was put through to the duchess's secretary, and requested an appointment. The duchess would see him at ten A.M. tomorrow, he was told. Then he called the duke's office to cancel his appointment there. But Augustin had phoned in, the secretary told him, and was looking forward to seeing him, asking only that their meeting be moved from ten to eleven.

Fine, thought Conte as he hung up. His time with the duchess would be short, 15 minutes, no more. He would leave the castle immediately after. He would be gone long before the duke expected him. By the time Augustin realized he wasn't coming, he would be halfway out of the duchy.

Outside, the rain had stopped. He went for a long walk in the town to quiet his nerves.

———

"GOOD OF YOU to see me on such short notice, my lady."

The detective had decided to try this title out, see how it sounded coming from his own lips. In fact, he thought it sounded ridiculous.

"Sit down, sit down," she said, waving in the direction of one of her chairs. She wore a red dress and much jewelry, including a necklace that seemed to be principally diamonds, and bulky rings on several fingers.

Conte sat. It was more a sitting room than an office: sofa, armchairs. A very small desk. Her husband's portrait on the wall. No electronic equipment of any kind. One window: it had been cut through a wall that was more than three feet thick.

"Well, the investigation is over," he began. "I have all the answers you asked me for, and the duke asked me for."

"The men in Italy and all that?"

She was a very plain woman, he decided. Slightly buck teeth, fleshy nose. She must always have been plain, even as a girl. But there seemed a sweetness about her, or so he imagined. "Even the men in Italy," he said.

"Well, good. Tell me, I'm all ears."

"Possibly I should be talking to your husband first, but he's not available until later, and I thought that technically, since you're the one who hired us, I'm really working for you. So it's not wrong that you should be the first to know. I hope you agree." A long nervous speech.

She stood up and to his surprise came around the coffee table. "I'm very pleased with you." She was wringing Conte's hand. "Well, don't keep me in suspense, Mr. Conte, what did you find out?"

"The purpose of the investigation," said Conte, "was to discover if your son-in-law was set up in some way as part of a plot." He gestured in the direction of the window, and by extension toward the city outside it— "thereby causing the divorce and the embarrassment to you and yours." He handed her the manila envelope containing his revised report. "Here's my official report. I think you'll be pleased."

"No ugly surprises?"

"My report says the incident was exactly what, on the surface, it seemed to be, that the only plotter was the photographer himself. That there was no plot by an outsider against any of you, or against the state."

"I'm much relieved," she said. Then: "No possibility of error?"

"My investigation was very thorough, my lady."

"Well, good."

He noted that she put the report aside without reading it.

"We can all sleep easier tonight because of you," she said. "Thank you."

"And how is your daughter doing?"

"Much better. I think she's over the worst of it."

"I'm very glad to hear that."

"I was worried sick about her for a time. In fact, that's mostly the reason I wanted you to do your investigation. But in the last few days she seems to have returned almost to normal."

"Any chance of the young couple getting back together?"

"I don't think so."

"My investigation indicated that they both still care about each other."

Lady Charlotte looked surprised.

"Very much so, in fact," Conte said. "The marriage could be saved. Maybe you could do something to help."

"I wish I could, but my husband would never permit it."

"But she's your daughter too."

"You don't really know my husband."

"I know him perhaps better than you think."

While she puzzled over this remark, Conte again reached into his briefcase, his hand coming out with pages attached to bills — his expense account. He said with false lightness: "Before we go on, can I ask a favor of you?"

"Of course."

"Here are my expenses, all worked out, bills attached. Can I submit them to you now?"

The duchess took the papers, thumbed to the last page, the total sum, nodded, and dropped the papers on the coffee table.

Conte said: "I'm leaving the duchy almost at once, and —"

"Can't you stay a few days? We have some wonderful attractions to show you here."

"I wish I could, but I have to get back."

"Well, all right, but it's a shame."

"The favor I want to ask of you is this. Could I possibly be reimbursed for my expenses right away?"

The duchess seemed to hesitate.

"As you can see, my lady, they are higher than any of us would have liked. But the trail led to Milan, Amsterdam, the French Riviera, and finally to Rome, Modena, and Bologna. That's a lot of airfares and car rentals, a lot of hotels."

Still she hesitated.

"The money I've laid out is my own," Conte said. It wasn't. His credit card bills went to and were paid by his firm. But in truth his expenses amounted to a substantial sum, and if he could leave here with her check in his pocket he would be in the clear with Prescott, or so he hoped, whatever else happened. "Of course I'll be reimbursed eventually," he said to the duchess, "but it will have to go through your accounting department, and then ours. It will take time, and on a personal level I've got a lot of major bills to pay when I get back to New York."

She picked up the expense statement and looked at it.

" — And I don't have the money to pay them."

She carried the sheaf of bills over to her little desk, which she opened. Having found a checkbook inside, she leaned over and wrote out the check. "I don't normally write checks at all," she said, handing it across. "But this is private, isn't it. Just between you and me."

"Thank you," said Conte, slipping the check into his billfold. "You've helped me a lot."

The door was open onto the corridor, and now they could hear footsteps coming, not running but heavy, coming fast, coming with purpose, two men, one in rubber-soled shoes that squeaked on the marble floor. When the shoes turned into the duchess's small office, Conte saw that it was the duke, looking angry, followed by the one-armed man, De Blondin, who quietly closed the door, then took up station beside it.

"What do you think you're doing?" the sovereign said to his wife. It was a barely repressed shout. "You're meddling again. How many times have I told you not to meddle in my affairs?"

The door was thick wood and looked well seated, soundproof, or virtually so. Nothing that went on in here could be heard in the corridor outside, Conte supposed. He felt oppressed by the weight of the walls surrounding him, this thick-walled room and the even thicker walls of the castle itself. It was like being locked in a medieval dungeon. There was no escape.

"I'm sick of you meddling," said the sovereign. "Sick, sick, sick."

"I'm not meddling," the duchess said in a small voice.

Conte hated to see men abuse their wives in public.

"Oh, no? What do you call it then?"

"What are you blaming her for?" the detective interrupted. "If you want to blame somebody, blame me."

Augustin turned toward him. "You were ordered to report to me, and to me only."

"I have an appointment with you in about thirty minutes. Isn't that soon enough? In the meantime, I saw nothing wrong with talking to your wife. She's the one hired us and paid us."

"In a minute nobody's going to pay you."

"All right, calm down," Conte said.

"I have his report," the duchess offered. "It says it's just as you thought, no plot, nothing."

"A total waste of money," the duke said.

"Not totally," Conte said, "I did find out a few things."

The duke glared at him.

"—If you want to hear about them," Conte said.

The duke said: "Go on."

"I started in Milan, as you suggested."

"Oh, yes, the photographer." With what Conte took to be pretended nonchalance, the duke walked to one of the armchairs and sat down. "I saw where the fellow got himself killed."

The duke might have seen a story about the killing, but he was not supposed to have known Grizzard's name.

"Dead, yes," said Conte, "and before he could tell me who had hired him, unfortunately."

"I'm sorry to hear that."

"Someone strung him up by the straps from his camera bag."

Augustin said: "Did they, indeed. Fitting, in my opinion." He nodded several times, then added, his voice slowly rising: "Men like that are a blight on Europe." His voice got harder, angrier. "If they hound film stars and the like, who cares. But when they stick their cameras into the faces of people of standing, preying on us just because we are someone of standing — I draw the line. The reputations of families that go back hundreds of years, spotless reputations hundreds of years old — all that means nothing to them." There was a pause in which he seemed to calm down. He shook his head sadly. "The things they did to my daughter."

"Yes, it was terrible," agreed Conte.

"Well, that particular paparazzo won't be bothering her anymore, will he?"

"No, he won't," agreed Conte.

"Unfortunately, there are so many others just like him still out there."

"We can't kill them all," Conte said, "can we?"

Augustin looked at him.

"More's the pity," said Conte, "wouldn't you say?"

Watching for a reaction, Conte said: "The guy who hanged him got killed too."

"That I hadn't known." There was a brief hesitation before Augustin added: "Who was he?"

"Oh, just your everyday hired assassin."

"How did he happen to get killed himself?" A rhetorical question. There had been another pause before he even asked it. Conte was satisfied the sovereign already knew the answer.

"A customs guard shot him."

"Oh, yes," said Augustin. "I read about that." He added quickly: "Without knowing there was a connection, of course. Customs, you say?"

"You don't look too shocked."

"Of course I'm shocked," Augustin said calmly. "Because in Europe," he added, "we don't take customs very seriously anymore."

"Well, that particular guard took it seriously, didn't he. The assassin he shot took it seriously too, we must assume."

Augustin was no longer looking so confident. He sat with his knee twitching, fingernails drumming noiselessly on the arm of his chair. His antennae are up, thought Conte. He wonders why I'm dragging this out. He's worried about what's coming. Which was fine with Conte. Let him suffer, he thought. He risked a glance at the other two people in the room. Lady Charlotte looked perplexed, which was to be expected. She didn't know what any of this was about. De Blondin did know. Like the duke he had begun to look off balance.

Augustin said: "Perhaps we should get down to business."

"Good idea," said Conte.

Turning to his wife, Augustin said: "You can go." When she seemed to hesitate, he said: "I said you can go. You're not needed. Go."

"If you don't mind," said Conte, "I'd like her to stay."

Augustin turned to Conte, his face hard.

Conte said: "The girl is her daughter too, as I understand it. She should listen to what I have to say."

But I have nothing to say, Conte reminded himself. He lifted the phony report off the coffee table. I'm supposed to give them this and leave, he reminded himself.

But already he was losing patience and wondered how far he was from losing control. He began to page through the report, stalling.

"Okay," he said. "Let's begin, shall we?"

"The photographer," said Augustin.

"The pictures," murmured Lady Charlotte.

"Guy's name was Georges Grizzard. What you wanted to know was who financed him. If it was a plot, who was behind it. I started out with four possibilities. Grizzard himself. Or his magazine. Or those gentlemen from Italy you advised me to look into."

"And the fourth?" asked Lady Charlotte.

"Person or persons unknown, as we say in the trade."

Augustin hesitated, then said: "The photographer financed himself, you say."

"Did I say that?"

"I thought you did," said Lady Charlotte.

"I'll come back to that in a moment."

"What are you trying to pull here?" the duke demanded.

"Bear with me, please."

"I've had enough of you beating around the bush."

Conte tapped the pages in his hand. "It's all in here." Of course it wasn't, and he was having trouble ignoring the voice in his head that, with increasing volume, urged him to throw this report in the duke's face and bring out the other.

Which would not be a good career move, he reminded himself. In fact it would be incredibly stupid, and for a number of reasons. You have no choice but to end the case according to your orders from Prescott, he told himself. Anything else, he told himself, made no sense at all.

But he could not resist working on Augustin's insecurities a while longer, see what developed.

He said: "You'll understand everything when you read it."

"Give me that thing."

"Not just yet," Conte said. "I want you to understand how I came to the conclusions that are in it."

Augustin was silent.

"Do I have your permission to continue?"

The sovereign, tight-lipped, said nothing.

Conte said: "I was able to make contact with three of the principal actors involved in this case: the girl, the photographer, and the assassin. Unfortunately two of the three were dead by the time I got to them."

"You found the girl?"

"Please let him tell it his own way," said Lady Charlotte. She's got sharp instincts, thought Conte. She's picking up vibes from somewhere. By now she looked as tense as her husband and De Blondin.

Augustin snapped at her. "Stay out of this," he told her.

Conte said: "Let me start at the end of my investigation, if you will, rather than the beginning. Perhaps it will be clearer that way."

The American realized that for the last several minutes the duchess had not taken her eyes off him.

"Get to the bottom line," ordered Augustin. "I don't have all day."

De Blondin said: "If there's something you'd like me to do, my lord—"

When Conte and the sovereign both looked at him he fell silent.

Conte continued: "I went to Italy. The older of the would-be investors, Balducci, is the uncle of the younger one, I learned. The younger one, Crespi, is much like your ex-son-in-law. He was once a promising athlete. A footballer. Played for Juventus of Turin, then got hurt. Now he's trying to get something going in a business way, just like Antonio Murano. His uncle was ready to help him, if he could. I studied confidential financial statements on them both, and I interviewed them both. They were quite frank with me. The uncle has a little money, not nearly enough to blow a wad on Grizzard and his photos, and the nephew has no money at all. So they weren't trying to get into your duchy to launder fortunes or for other nefarious reasons."

Conte was tense himself. He was used to having the law on his side, but in this place the law was elsewhere or absent, and he was powerless. Even so, his sense of justice was outraged, and he was increasingly close to the edge.

"So scratch the two Italians as suspects," Conte said, and in his tension he looked up and grinned at the royal couple, as if expecting applause.

Fingers still drumming, Augustin watched him.

"It's as Mr. Conte has told me," murmured Lady Charlotte to her husband, "the photographer financed it himself." But now she sounded uncertain. This interview was not going the way she had expected. Perhaps it was the sovereign's fault for being so disagreeable. She hoped that's all it was, but was no longer sure.

She kept imagining that something terrible was about to be disclosed.

"In Milan I went to the magazine. They would tell me nothing about Grizzard or the photos, citing freedom of the press. I sat around in the bar across the street and talked to staffers when they came in. The staffers described Grizzard as a tightwad who wouldn't make a move until he had his financing. I went to two photo agencies. Both guessed at the fee Grizzard would have commanded for those photos. It matched with bank statements found later in Grizzard's apartment in Monte Carlo. A nice fee, but not enough to cover the expenses of the shoot."

"This is getting long," said Augustin, his voice cold, but not as firm as it had been.

"I became satisfied that the magazine did not finance those photos either. But maybe this time Grizzard had made an exception and had financed them himself. I couldn't be sure because I had not yet been able to find him."

Conte was toying with them now, but he was toying also, whether he realized it or not, with himself.

"I did find the girl. She led me to Grizzard, but too late. The two of us watched the Nice police cut him down from that tree. A day later the man who hanged him was machine-gunned to death by the customs guard, and the two of us watched that as well. And then we watched the other customs guard get crushed to death by the assassin's runaway car."

Motionless, silent, his face dark, De Blondin stood beside the door.

To Conte he looked like a cop guarding the door to a room in which a suspect was being interrogated.

After a brief pause the detective said: "On the whole, this has been not only a difficult assignment but, shall we say, a messy one." But his outrage was reaching a critical point.

Augustin said: "You found the girl, you say?"

"Yes."

"A prostitute, I assume."

"And spent considerable time with her, as it happens," Conte said, and Gigi's face and voice filled his head. For a moment she became more real to him than these people, this castle, this case.

"Who is she?" demanded Augustin.

"The assassin tried to kill her too, but missed, barely."

"Who is she?"

"The papers and magazines are still trying to find out, aren't they?" said Conte. "I still see all the stories. The police of several countries are looking for her too, I believe."

"I said, who is she?"

Conte, holding the manila envelope, looked at Augustin over the top of it. "I took her out of circulation so that no one could get to her."

"And her name is in your report?"

"In exchange for her cooperation," said Conte, "I promised confidentiality."

"It's not in your report."

"Unfortunately, no," said Conte.

"But you'll tell me."

"As a matter of fact I won't."

"You are working for me."

"If he promised her —" murmured Lady Charlotte.

"If you are going to keep interrupting, you can leave."

"Madam has a point," said Conte.

Augustin's nostrils quivered. "Who is she and where is she?"

"At present she is in a safe place." Was she? Conte hoped so.

"I want her name —"

"You won't get it from me."

"—and her whereabouts," said Augustin.

And there Conte's resolve broke. "Why? So you can have her killed? Have someone finish the job your assassin muffed?"

He had not meant to say these words, or so he believed. He had been determined to obey Prescott's orders, or so he believed. Any other conduct, from any point of view, was madness. But suddenly, clearly, he saw that this man was more dangerous even than he had imagined, and Gigi in terrible danger from him, and the words had come out almost of their own accord. The sovereign lived by his own laws. Once his men found Gigi, killing her would be easy.

The solution ordained by Prescott had just gone out the window, and now, pushing aside anything of it that remained, Conte gave vent to his outrage. He would go where truth and justice led him, whatever the consequences, and with this decision he felt strangely comforted, and a great calmness came over him.

He said: "Which leaves only the fourth of my possibilities. Person or persons unknown."

Lady Charlotte's eyes were fixed on her husband. By now, Conte judged, she must be suspecting the worst, fearing what was coming, for the expression on her face could only be called tragic. She said: "Go on."

This time Augustin failed to rebuke her.

"Grizzard had an assistant. Man named Renzo. An Italian. Lives in Ventimiglia. I went to see him. He confirmed for me that whoever financed Grizzard had dragged the thing out for months—Grizzard waited months for his financing to be confirmed. Renzo also told me what Grizzard had told him. Where the financing was coming from."

Renzo had told him no such thing, but Augustin didn't know this.

"From where?" said Lady Charlotte.

"From here, my lady, from here. Grizzard's sponsor was someone right here in this duchy. In fact in this very palace."

De Blondin, Conte saw, had taken half a step forward, and stood now as if frozen in midstride. Augustin had not moved, but his fingers had stopped drumming. From across the coffee table he and Conte glared at each other.

Then Augustin's left foot moved slightly. It was the only movement on either side.

"You don't look too surprised," Conte said. "If you're not surprised at where the financing came from, at least you could show some surprise that I found it out."

"You found out nothing." Augustin's fists were clenched, and he had jumped to his feet.

Conte, looking up at him, continued calmly: "Grizzard had a habit of writing frequently called numbers on the walls of his apartments above the phones. Saved him looking them up, I guess. Among the numbers I found on the wall in his Milan apartment, and again in his Monte Carlo apartment, was this one." Conte recited the number, adding: "Recognize it, Duke?"

Augustin looked away.

"It was in his address book too," Conte said. "Same number. I called it to see who answered. It turns out that the number rings here in this very palace. Imagine that. In the office of a member of your personal staff. Fellow usually described in the press as your troubleshooter. Sometimes as your right-hand man, although he doesn't have a right hand himself. Does all the jobs you want done, but don't want to be seen doing." Conte turned to look at De Blondin: "That man there."

When Augustin did not respond, Conte said: "One other possibility occurred to me. Could your daughter be behind the photos? I don't know her very well. When I talked to her a couple of weeks ago she seemed broken up, but that could have been an act. It occurred to me that she might have engineered the plot herself to get rid of a detested husband. Just a possibility, you understand, but it had to be disproved before I talked to you. So I decided to devote some time to it. I came here three days ago. I tailed her through the streets. Waited outside the palace and followed her when she sneaked out at night. I found proof that she was not behind this thing."

"Proof? What is that supposed to mean?"

"Proof," said Conte.

"I've had enough of these insinuations, this claptrap."

"So as a suspect, that leaves only you, Duke. Only you. You were the one who set up this whole charade."

Augustin's face was flushed and he gave off that emanation of guilt with which Conte was so familiar from past cases. Augustin controlled this duchy and everyone in it, but once accused of his crime was no more able to control his physical reaction than petty thieves in a meat-packing plant.

"Anyway," said Conte, "that's what my report says. This report here." He replaced the revised report in his briefcase, and tossed the original one onto the coffee table.

"If you publish that thing I'll sue you for libel in every court in Europe."

"Well, we're not in the habit of publishing our reports—"

"What do you want, money?"

"—but in this case we might make an exception."

"How much do you want?"

"How much," said Conte equably, "is my silence worth to you?"

"Name your price."

Well before talking to Prescott the detective had indulged in a dream scenario of his own. In it, not having enough evidence to prove his case, he would goad Augustin into a reaction of some kind that would stand as proof. This had seemed to him his only chance. And it was what he believed he had now both seen and heard, the only proof he was likely to get.

"My price?" he said. "Now we're talking value. One always likes to get value. Even someone as rich and powerful as you. When you give orders, everyone obeys—everyone but your own daughter, who marries a boy whom you see as not worthy of her, not worthy of you. What do you do? You suffer him for a while, you permit a wedding rather than allow your daughter to give birth to a bastard heir. Then you decide to disgrace him, get rid of him. Whose idea was the photos? Yours?" Conte stared across at the one-armed man. "His?"

Augustin did not answer.

"Doesn't matter," said Conte. "You acquiesced, and someone working for you went out and hired Grizzard, hired the best. Grizzard put a half-naked woman in front of your son-in-law, and photographed what happened. What happened was your son-in-law failed the test. Suppose he had passed it? You would have been out all that money, wouldn't you? Technically speaking, adultery never took place that day, by the way. Both parties told me that separately, and I believe them."

Conte continued: "It's my guess that you never intended for those photos to be published. You thought that showing them to your daughter would be enough. But Grizzard double-crossed you. He blackmailed the young man, which you hadn't intended, and he went and published the photos which made an international scandal — the last thing you wanted. Well, when you deal with slime, slimy things happen. Was he blackmailing you too? My guess is that he was. How much money did he ask you for?"

Conte studied his report a moment, making Augustin wait for what came next.

"Blackmailers never stop blackmailing," the detective said. "Grizzard threatened to tell your daughter what her father had done to her, and then tell the world. And he wanted money. He had to be got rid of, but how? And then a corrupt cop from Milan enters the picture." Conte stopped. He did not intend to mention his own meetings with Piccolo, but he regretted them. "The corrupt cop offers to do the job, possibly for less than Grizzard was already demanding." Conte scratched his head in puzzlement. "How he made contact with you I don't know exactly. Did he call you directly? Was he recommended by someone you had already done business with? You checked him out. You learned that he was absolutely reliable. Unfortunately, he managed to do only half the job, killed the photographer but not the girl. But at least it was the more important half, you thought. And getting himself killed was probably a good thing too, because that was the end of it."

Then Conte added: "Except that I was still out there."

"Your fairy tale is just that," said Augustin. He was quivering with rage. "A fairy tale."

"More than that, I think."

"What can you prove in court? Nothing, nothing."

"I don't have to prove anything in court. I can ruin you in the court of public opinion."

Augustin's fists were clenched. A pulse throbbed in his neck.

"I can't prosecute you," said Conte. "You are sovereign here, immune. No one can touch you."

Augustin said evenly: "If I have offered to pay you it is strictly and solely to avert another scandal. When you reach a certain level in the world, people will believe any nastiness about you."

"What sum were you thinking of?" said Conte. He had got up and had moved toward the door.

Augustin named it.

"Not enough," said Conte.

Augustin doubled it.

Conte reached for the doorknob. "My silence is not for sale."

The one-armed man, he saw, was looking from one to the other as if awaiting instructions. What Lady Charlotte's reaction might be no longer concerned him. He gave her only a glance. She was suffering, obviously. Those big rings were at her mouth. What would happen between her and her husband when he had left the room he could only guess.

At the door, Conte said: "One or two other things before I go. If you try to prosecute the woman in the photos, if you allow anyone else to prosecute her, or if any harm should come to her, if anyone even goes near her, I'll ruin you. You stay away from her, is that clear?

"And your second job is this—consider it part of our new agreement. You are to find a way to make this up to your daughter and her ex-husband. They have been through a terrible time, and they love each other still. That much I have seen with my own eyes. I have an idea for you. Let them remarry, if that's what they want, and move to some other country—something like that."

He pulled open the door. "I'll be watching to see how you work it out. I'll give you two weeks. If you don't work it out, someone might leak our report to the press."

The door closed behind him.

Now he had to get out of the castle, and out of the duchy, and as he made his way along dark, high-ceilinged corridors, stone walls to both sides, the fear came up strong. Would someone try to interfere with him, before he reached the street? His brave words just now were stuck in his mouth like paste, not brave at all, only stupid. He descended one stone staircase, then another, unsure of the way out. He listened to his echoing shoes. He saw the castle as huge, unknowable, with himself lost in it. While making his little speeches upstairs, he had been pleased with himself. His righteousness. His high moral tone. What an honorable person he himself was, which this other man, this reigning sovereign, was not. Another corridor. Another stone staircase. Now he was on what he hoped was the ground floor, though he was not sure. As an actor, he had spoken his lines perfectly. Had he listened for applause? Maybe. But it was his foolishness that struck him now. He had left himself no weapons, no protection. He was in someone else's house and country, and for as long as he remained there he was defenseless.

CHAPTER

XX

AHEAD WAS A DOOR, daylight showing through. He hurried toward it.

Then he was outside the palace gate, striding toward his hotel, the sun shining, safe for the moment, but for how long? People moved along the sidewalks on both sides. Augustin had already had people killed. Cars went by. Conte was aware of towering mountains all around him, around everybody. He was hurrying. Had he goaded this reigning sovereign into some new act of unreason? He was consoled by the notion that any such act took time to set up — usually it did, but perhaps not always. I've got to get out of here fast, he told himself.

He was not fast enough.

He thought of the check in his pocket which the sovereign would block as soon as he found out about it, as he surely would, because that woman would not dare stand up to him. Passing a bank, he went in and had it turned into a certified check which he put in an envelope ad-dressed to himself in New York, and dropped in a mailbox by the door. This protected the money. Did it protect him against Prescott, as well? Maybe. He could hope so.

The bank was about six blocks from the palace, his hotel another two blocks farther on. He was in the bank only a few minutes. When the hotel came in sight he noted two men idling under the porte cochere, one taller than the other, both of them brawny. Cops? Goons?

Did it matter?

The belongings in his room, his shirts and underwear, his other suit, his toilet kit, would have to be abandoned. He would have to go directly to his rental, jump in, and just go. Drive away from the goons and from here. And he started around the building toward the hotel parking lot in back. There were still only two roads out of the duchy into neighboring countries, two border posts that were scarcely manned, one north, one south, and he was trying to calculate which was closer, and how long it would take him to get there. If the sovereign should decide to shut the borders, could he get across before this happened? He had left the palace not ten minutes before. Given that Augustin already had men at the hotel to arrest him, perhaps not.

He was trying to calculate also what the risks to his person might be. He did not think Augustin would have him killed, principally because he did not need to, and it was this latest notion that caused the American detective to start sweating. He could feel the sweat on his forehead, and running down his backbone. Why kill him when it was so easy just to arrest him, plant some evidence, jail him for a year or two, and disgrace him forever? Under such circumstances as that, any countercharges he might make, especially considering what little hard evidence he would be able to present, would convince nobody. Imagine charging from jail that the sovereign, or one of his agents, had hired a corrupt Italian cop to murder Grizzard. People would laugh at him.

He continued past the hotel and around the block until the hotel parking lot came in sight. When he was close enough, he saw that two other men idled there. One of his first reactions was to feel ashamed of them, and of the two out front as well, ashamed of such inept police work. When detectives stake out a place, they don't stand in plain sight advertising their presence, they hide themselves and wait for the subject to show up. When he does, they spring. Of course this wasn't New York. One couldn't expect competent police work in such a backwater as this.

Conte's next reaction was more personal. It came as a question. What do I do now?

If it were winter, and if he had skis, he could perhaps go up to one of the high passes and ski down into the next country. But it was not winter, and he had no skis. Then he thought that he could perhaps go out over the mountains anyway. He did not know if, at this time of year, and at such altitudes, a possible escape route existed. But he had no other choice. If he meant to keep his freedom and reputation intact, nothing else was open to him, and if he did not hurry even this would close up, so he strode down the street until he came to the one *téléphérique* station that terminated in the city itself, where he bought a ticket all the way to the top, then stood alone in the otherwise empty cabin for ten increasingly nervous minutes until other passengers began to board, and it was time for the car to climb.

It was then about eleven in the morning, the sun was high, and he shared the car with two pairs of hikers, and two young couples who might be honeymooners, and some tradesmen bringing crates of bottles and produce to the restaurant up there. He had heard of this restaurant, for it bragged of its great food and panoramic view. The city was at about 3,000 feet, and the ten-minute ride—tense minutes for Conte—lifted them up to the restaurant at about 6,000 feet, where all passengers disembarked. To go any higher, one transferred to a different line, which was what Conte intended to do.

Thirty years earlier, at a time when he was trying to establish his duchy as one of the premier tourist attractions of Europe, Augustin had declared that his frontier passed through the middle of the peak known as Piz Nero which, at 11,800 feet, was the highest summit in that part of the Alps, and possibly the most inaccessible, too. There was no way to disprove his claim except at great expense and, apart from Augustin himself, who cared? So the surrounding countries did nothing, and the claim was allowed to stand. Almost immediately Augustin began to build a *téléphérique* up to the peak, having announced it in advance as the highest in the world. It turned out to be an engineering marvel as well, because only a few steps behind the much lower restaurant the mountain turned into an almost sheer cliff. This had to be scaled with tools and gear, and the result, when the work was finished, was a set of pylons and cables that hoisted the cabin, which held 40 people, almost straight up.

The cabin hung rarely more than ten feet from the face of the cliff, and most days it swayed in the wind, approaching much closer than that, threatening at any moment to dash out its brains against the rock, and the brains of everyone in it as well.

The construction was considered a fabulous achievement and there were spreads about it in the ski, tourism, and architecture magazines. This brought mainstream reporters and TV crews, and stories about it appeared all over the world. Augustin had won his great gamble, had reaped reams of publicity celebrating his duchy, and his goal of attracting millions of tourists began to seem achievable.

In the restaurant, which was empty at that hour, Conte bought a sandwich and a bottle of mineral water to take with him, for there would be nothing to eat the rest of the way. Even though he did not know what the terrain would look like up on top, or how long it would take him to work his way down the other side, he was aware that he had a difficult and possibly dangerous trek ahead of him. It might take him all day, it might take him close to exhaustion, and he would need to keep up his strength.

This lunch went into his briefcase, bulging it, and he stood in a corner of the cabin, trying to look inconspicuous as he waited for it to leave. More than 30 minutes had now passed since he had left Augustin, and he fretted about those men — cops or goons or whatever they were — waiting for him back at the hotel. How long would they wait before they came looking for him? he asked himself. How long before their attention zeroed in on the bottom *téléphérique* and they went to question the ticket agent? *Seen any American detectives lately?* Any New York cop, he believed, would have thought of this, and done it, long ago. A New York detective would be up here already, not waiting for him down there.

At last the cabin, by then half full of tourists, began to lift. At first it approached the cliff face on a slant, but upon reaching it, its direction changed, and it began to ascend almost as straight up as an elevator, though one with no intermediate floors. As it rose it got closer and closer to the face of the cliff, out of which at this level there protruded here and there small bushes struggling to live, even small starved trees. But as the altitude increased these dropped below, for nothing could live this high up, and the cliff face became barren. Also steeper, and it changed color constantly, Conte saw, depending on how the light struck it. It could look white, red, even purple. At times it was laced by thin blue lines like varicose veins. There were fissures, some of them profound, and in one place they extended outward from a central point like the segments of a grapefruit. If he stared at the rock long enough it came alive, and he discerned its features, its nose, its mouth, its teeth. But such fanciful ideas did not last, for the cabin was buffeted by wind, and he had to hang on to remain upright, as if riding the subway. At times it seemed to him that the car would scrape its skin against the cliff's rocky face, leaving behind paint at least, or perhaps doing itself real harm, but it never did.

The halfway point. For a moment the other car, on its way down, was alongside, swaying. The two groups of passengers waved to each other. Then the down-car was far below and receding. Outside the window there began to be snow atop the outcroppings, snow in some of the fissures.

There were more than 5,000 feet to climb which took considerable time. Time that seemed interminable to Conte. He talked to nobody, soon lost interest in the cliff, and from then on only gazed out the window at the rest of the world below. It was getting smaller, the city a toy city, the down-car the size of a teardrop. How long, he wondered, before one or more of Augustin's men rushed into the *téléphérique* station below, and ordered all machinery shut down? Or gave the order from a distance via cell phone. How long before the electricity was cut off? Were they too stupid to think of this? Well before the summit, he expected to feel the car stop, dangle briefly, the wind sucking it back and forth, then start back down. If this happened there would be, for him, no way out. As each minute passed and it didn't happen he was surprised. The world to all sides of him was not only hostile, but closing in, the hostility was of his own making, and he could do nothing about any of it but wait for the car to dock, at which point he would face only more perils, probably greater ones.

What would the summit look like? He saw himself standing on it looking down the other way. The snow would be deep. How deep? Was it possible for a man in a business suit and business shoes, and carrying a briefcase, to slog down through it? Supposing Augustin's men came after him? He had his passport in his pocket but was otherwise unarmed. If these people were serious, and he supposed they were, his passport would not help him.

Suddenly the car slowed in its ascent, which gave him a bad moment, but it was only so that it could settle itself into its dock. Miraculously, it did dock. Miraculously, its doors slid back, and everybody exited onto the platform, and then out through the door into the snow and the clear, cold air. The station, Conte saw as he passed through it, contained two docks, the other one empty, but otherwise was small and smelled foully of oil.

He stepped outside into the dead of winter. The cold stung his nose, his lungs. The snow, at least where there were drifts, was deep — yesterday's rain down in the town must have been a heavy snowfall up here. There were drifts of snow against the wall of the *téléphérique* station, and the snow was high against the various projections on its roof.

The summit, Conte saw, was a snowfield the size of a tennis court. The wind was blowing. There were concrete benches here and there half buried in drifts. Close to the station, the snow had been tramped down by shoes. Elsewhere it was mostly smooth crust, the wind scouring the surface, the snow blowing in gusts off the crust, blowing sharply with a texture to it that felt almost like sand.

The air was extremely clear. Conte could see for a hundred miles in any direction. To the west rose mountains that were higher than here, but this one was built more sternly than any of them. To the east the world tilted down.

Most of his fellow passengers, he saw, stood around taking deep breaths and grinning. Chests expanded and contracted. Air was sucked in and blown out again.

"That's some air," one man said.

"Is that air pure enough for you?" said another.

This subject exhausted, they gawked at the view, and began pointing out distant, famous peaks.

But presently they would become cold, most of them being dressed for summer, and would reboard the cable car and descend, the day's adventure ended.

For skiers in season, Conte knew, there was only one route down. It went off the south edge of the peak, descending for miles in that direction, before circling around in front and continuing down to the level of the city where taxis waited in the road to take skiers back to their hotels, or to the *téléphérique* station to go up again. The descent was one of the longest and most famous in Europe, about a ten-mile run in all, some of it steep, some intermediate, some barely tilted — the skiers poled themselves along.

Conte was not interested in the view, or the sharp taste of the air, and the skiers' route down would only have taken him back where he came from. His way out was off the northeast edge, and he went over there. The snow underfoot was coarse, granular. It looked as if it could rub a man's skin off, like sandpaper. He stood on a kind of cornice, and peered down at the slope he would have to descend. The wind was at his back. It cut through his summer-weight business suit and chilled him.

Below him was a snow-covered depression wider than two football fields, a shallow valley, almost a gully, that ran downhill for a thousand yards, perhaps more, bordered all the way by ragged rock ridges on both sides. He could see a chairlift far below, though it did not appear to be running, and there would be other lifts elsewhere, also probably not running. There were no lifts reaching the summit on this side, and none up the gully at all. The angle of descent did not look severe to him. A skier might rate its difficulty as intermediate, Conte supposed. Getting down on foot would not be fun, but if he was careful he thought he could do it.

Because he was not a stupid man he considered the possibility of provoking an avalanche, but he did not have enough knowledge to see any particular danger — to make a judgment one way or the other.

In fact the slope below him was a classic avalanche chute on a day of classic avalanche conditions. Any mountain man would have recognized this in a minute. The heavy snowfall of the day before. The violent day and night temperature fluctuations of this time of year. The prevailing west-to-east winds of Europe which scoured summits and deposited unstable granular snow on lee slopes such as this particular northeast face, which got relatively little sunlight anyway, and on which new snow did not bond properly. And the gully itself. A slope that, to any experienced eye, looked stressed out and near the breaking point.

Conte was not a mountain man, and saw none of this. There were other clues he might have picked up on, though he did not. The absence of ski lifts on a slope that looked skiable enough was one such clue. But this could be due to financial or engineering problems, he told himself. Perhaps lifts had been scheduled but not yet built. Also there was a debris field far below where past avalanches had piled up, another clue. But Conte couldn't discern this. It was too far distant, and the light was wrong. From where he stood the angle of the sun had blurred all definition.

Conte had once watched a documentary on avalanches, but very little had stuck beyond the title of the show: *The White Death*, plus certain of the grim statistics. Small avalanches were sometimes detonated by ski patrols to protect skiers — this was almost the only good news the show had offered. Big avalanches could be massive. Half the mountain could start sliding, an expanse of snow twenty football fields in length and ten feet thick, all of it sliding down the mountain at increasing speeds that reached sometimes a hundred miles an hour, the weight of snow obliterating whatever was in its path, flattening houses, even hotels, overwhelming everything before it including the puny hiker or skier, puny you, and at the end burying you under tons of snow. Once buried, a victim had from one to three seconds to make himself an air pocket, make room in which his chest could expand, before the snow set like cement, and became almost impossible to budge. If he failed to do this, he would be unable to breathe, the weight of snow on his chest would suffocate him, and in a few seconds or minutes he would be dead. Even assuming he managed to create a bit of space, and could breathe at least in shallow gulps, he either got dug out within 15 or 20 minutes, or else he died anyway. Some victims lasted 30 minutes, and were rescued. No one lasted more than 45. In actual fact nearly everybody, once buried, died. The few who survived were usually wearing transponders that pinpointed their location, and they had colleagues nearby with emergency gear, particularly shovels, with which to dig them out. People alone, as Conte was alone, had little or no chance.

Some of the above, as he peered over the edge, Conte did remember. He did consider the possibilities. But he did not expect to get caught in any avalanche. He was a New York City boy grown a bit older. He did not really believe that one man alone could dislodge that much snow. In any case he had no choice. There was only the one way out of the impasse in which he found himself: down the gully.

So instead of worrying about the White Death he tried to settle on which route to take, tried to judge his chances of controlling his descent. The snow close enough to appraise looked to him as granular as the surface of the summit. His shoes would have to penetrate this snow if he was to stay on his feet. How hard was this crust? How deep was the snow under it? How did he catch himself if he fell and started sliding? He could see the tree line far below — how far he could only guess. If he could reach it he would be okay, he supposed. But could he reach it? He told himself he could. And then: Would there be a restaurant partway down that would be open? He decided to save his lunch as long as he could. After his bottle was empty, he would have to eat snow.

Behind him strident bells rang out, and he heard the doors of the cable car bang suddenly shut. Some of the tourists ran for the station but were too late. Without warning, the cabin had suddenly started down.

Conte knew what this meant. The goons had localized him and were on the way up, probably in an otherwise empty car that they themselves had emptied out, and perhaps there were enough of them that, once they got up here, they would herd all the tourists into that same car and send them down, denuding the summit of witnesses. After that, if they could catch him, they could do with him as they liked.

The time for terrain study, the time for calculation, was over. Conte stepped off the edge of the cornice on which he stood, and began his descent, the other tourists unable to believe their eyes and rushing over to see what this crazy man was doing.

Almost at once he crashed through the crust, fell, and started sliding. About 20 feet farther down was a rocky outcropping against which he lodged, and he got to his feet and attempted to shake the snow off himself. He had snow in his pockets, snow inside his shoes and his shirt, snow under his belt. It was wet snow, heavy, melting quickly. His socks and pants were already damp — worse than damp — but he had not hurt himself, he had been lucky after all.

"Are you okay?" someone called out from on top. An Englishman from his accent.

Conte gave him a wave, and looked around for his plump briefcase, but did not see it. Buried under the crust somewhere, obviously. He did not have time to look for it, and so continued down, moving out of the sun and into the deep shade of this side of the mountain, the air suddenly colder, the surface thinly crusted, the snow under it colder, fluffier. He was stepping more carefully this time, more slowly, knowing he could not afford any more falls, moving sideways across the mountain, a series of traverses, trying to stick to one side of the gully, staying out of the center, which was the only anti-avalanche precaution available to him. He was descending now on a lesser angle than before, gaining ground with each step but not very much ground, each time testing the footing as best he could before he put his weight down, and in this way staying on his feet.

He could not see the cable car, but he could hear it coming fast, and then it slammed into the dock harder than he had expected, and he judged that they must have a high gear for that thing for use in emergencies — an emergency such as solving the problem that was himself. In any case they were here, and he did not know what to expect next. He was hurrying again and when he looked up he saw a face peering at him over the edge, heard a voice calling out to him in a language he did not understand. Orders probably. Stop. Come back. Something like that. Orders he did not intend to obey.

Presently that man or another stepped over the edge and started after him. But he too fell almost at once, slid farther than Conte had, most of it on his face, and crashed into a different rock outcropping, and lay there moaning. If he had had a gun he could have used it, Conte was close enough. Even a snub-nosed revolver, what New York cops called an off-duty gun, might have been sufficient. Even now he could have raised up and fired, though he didn't, and in this respect he resembled, in Conte's experience, the way gunshot victims always behaved. A bad fall was apparently no different. Even the slightest of wounds took a man out of the fight, took the fight out of the man.

He heard the cable car start back down, all the tourists forced into it surely, leaving how many men on top? He did not know, two anyway, for when he again looked in that direction that's how many he saw. They were up to their knees in snow and coming after him. He kept looking back at them as he descended. When they reached the level of their injured colleague, they talked to him briefly, apparently, but did not stop. Well, he had not expected them to. They were coming down the center of the gully, making steeper traverses than Conte had made and therefore gaining on him, meaning that to stay ahead he had to open up his own, go faster than he liked, increase the risk of falling.

In some places the snow was deeper than he was ready for, thigh deep when he broke through to it, and it occurred to him that he could step into a hole and be unable to get out, a prisoner waiting for them to reach him. When they came up they would do with him — what? Kill him probably. Why not? Who would know? Shoot him and toss him into a crevasse. Winter when it came would pile another ten feet of snow on top of him. He would become part of a glacier moving inexorably downhill, not to resurface until the glacier reached the road 50 years from now. Earlier this morning they had merely been obeying orders, but it would be personal now. He had frustrated and thwarted them, and his escape by *téléphérique* had shamed them in front of their superiors. He had them slogging down the mountain after him at great risk to themselves, their clothes getting ruined. He had caused serious injury to their colleague who, when they finished with Conte, would have to be rescued. By now they would be mad with rage. Of course they would kill him if they caught up. He didn't have to worry about losing his freedom now, only his life. But this thought, instead of panicking him, cooled him down. Don't lose your head, he cautioned himself. Step carefully. If you panic you are lost. If you fall you are lost.

The air was thin this high up. It was hard to breathe, he was unable to draw in as much oxygen as he needed, and his thighs felt on fire. He was sweating heavily, his clothes soaked inside and out.

His body, as he descended, was moving great quantities of snow, and now he did begin to worry that he might start an avalanche, or that the men above him might start one. He imagined being buried under tons of snow. If still alive he would be almost impossible to find, even if search parties dared to clamber out onto the loose snow and start probing — but in his case, since no one knew he was up there except the two men who wanted him dead, there would be no search parties.

The two goons started shooting. The distance between him and them was about 200 yards. The shots rang out and the detonations reverberated all around. From the noise he recognized the caliber, or thought he did, .38s, the classic New York police gun, and as near as he could tell from his quick glances up to where the bullets were coming from, the short barrel model, totally inaccurate at the present range. Conte wondered who the two men were. If experienced mountain men then most likely they had read the slope accurately and had seen no avalanche danger either to themselves or to him. But perhaps they were city boys too. Perhaps they were too enraged to think straight. Or perhaps they were just fools. Conte had no way of knowing, but it made him move even closer to the edge of the gully, to crowd the edge as much as he could. This was instinctive, a move that seemed sensible. If something happened, would it save him? He did not know. There were more shots. The bullets made popping noises as they passed over his head. In the past he had been shot at from much closer range than this. The two men were close enough for their guns to seem threatening, not nearly close enough to hit him, and their shots went wild. Finally they seemed to realize this. Holstering their weapons they resumed their descent, but their thighs must be burning too, their breath coming in gasps just like his, descending was hard, hard work, so that one of them soon stopped and resumed firing, and after a moment the other did too.

And then with a sharp crack the snowcover fractured. The sound was sharper than any gunshot, sharper than a crack of thunder, like boards falling off a truck but magnified, and it reverberated longer, echoed from peak to peak. The avalanche had signaled itself, had already become irreversible. Conte, though innocent of mountains, recognized instantly what had happened. Oh my God, he thought, even as the fracture raced in a jagged line across the gully until it had reached from one wall almost to the other. He couldn't see this, though in his sudden panic he strained his neck trying. Then came a rumble, the noise building, the fracture opening at great speed, opening wide, wider. The rumble got louder, then louder still, and then here it came, a cloud of cold white dust with the wall of snow under it, coming fast, tons and tons of snow, the mountain voiding itself.

Conte had no time to think anything further. In the frantic seconds left before the world slid out from under him he managed three or four additional steps to the side, hoping that's where safety was, hoping the avalanche would miss him. Not enough time. Not enough steps.

It sideswiped him, swept him up, swept him downhill tumbling. At times he was riding on top as if on a great fat pillow inside a cloud that was like a blizzard, a whirl of snowflakes inside of which he could not breathe. But almost immediately he was deep down, swallowed up and half smothered, trying to swim to the surface, to get his head above water and keep it there. He began somersaulting like a diver, while trying to tuck himself into the smallest possible package, the best way to avoid injury in any contact sport, as he had been taught by coaches as a boy. He became completely disoriented. Faster and faster the avalanche moved him. He was being banged into things, being battered. His mouth became clogged with snow, so that for what seemed minutes at a time he was choking. He protected his face and head as best he could, while worrying about what was happening to his hands. To hold himself in a fetal position took all his strength, arms and legs kept getting yanked loose, flying away from him. They took a terrific beating, and so did his ribs, and he worried briefly that if he survived this at all he might not be able to stand, much less walk. He might be hardly able to breathe too, might be too injured to get down off the mountain. If so, then he would die up here on top of the snow. When night came he would freeze to death. Or else, another possibility, one of the goons would have survived the avalanche also, and would stroll over and kill him.

Either way the end of his life was close by and he could see it, almost touch it. You have really done it to yourself this time, he told himself. His small knowledge of avalanches filled his head with images that were vivid, new, and he shuffled through them looking for instruction, looking for a way to survive. But they were no help. Hardly anybody gets out of these things alive, they told him. You're dead, Conte, he told himself. Buried alive. How does the satisfaction of telling off Augustin measure up against being buried alive? Why did you have to show off your moral superiority? If you had done what you were supposed to do you wouldn't be here, living out the final minutes of your life.

But even thoughts like this were fleeting. He did not have time for them, or energy. He was carried downward for hundreds of yards, for how many minutes or seconds he had no way of knowing, he lived an entire lifetime compressed into that small window of time, him fighting the avalanche from inside it, trying to hold himself together against forces that were pulling pieces of him in several directions at once, fighting for control where there was none, fighting to stay as close to the surface — what he hoped was the surface — as he could.

It was not a major avalanche, as avalanches go, there being less depth of snow on the mountain now than in winter or spring, and he was caught only by one side of it. It was a great heavy slide nonetheless, and at the end he was again trying to swim to the surface, riding the snow like a man bodysurfing, the wave speeding him along until such time as it dumped him onto the beach.

But at last the snow around him came to a stop, and some of the noise died away, not all, for elsewhere the principal mass of the avalanche, though slowed, kept plowing downhill a while longer.

There was no beach. He was buried. He remembered that he had only a few seconds to work in, and got his arms up and cleared his face, and got his knees up to his chin, and expanded his chest as much as he could. He was no longer sure which way was up. Where was the sky, where was the mountain itself — which way should he start digging? How many feet of snow would he have to dig through? The most basic realities of life had been lost to him, his panic was very nearly total, and he thought of all he had loved in life and would never see again, his mother who was sick and probably dying, and would need him there at the end, and Anna whom he had adored in those early years but who didn't need him now at all, and the police department, and Gigi, with whom it seemed to him he had reached in only a few hours an almost perfect understanding. This had never happened to him before, so perhaps he had loved Gigi most of all, a new start for them both might have been possible. A moot point now, of course.

All these thoughts and others went through his head in a confused jumble. A New York police captain dead inside an avalanche in the Alps?

It made no sense to him. It almost made him laugh or perhaps cry; it mustn't happen. He could find Gigi, if he could get out of here. He didn't know what had gone wrong between them, only that he had not fought hard enough, and had lost her. But he could find her again, try again, he told himself.

All of the avalanche had stopped, all noise suddenly shut off. The world had become absolute stillness, in which he was immobilized.

So he kept reaching upward, what he hoped was upward, in any case the only direction available to him. If it was down not up then all was lost, he was lost. Punching, straining against snow that was incredibly hard, he broke through. A patch of snow fell in on his face and the sky appeared. This seemed the greatest triumph of his life. He saw not only sky but clouds, and as he watched them sail by he wept with delight. He thought he had never seen such beautiful clouds. Tears ran down his face, they were so beautiful.

So he wasn't buried very deeply. I've got a chance, he thought. The avalanche had very nearly spit him out altogether.

Deeply or not, he was still buried, already he was nearly exhausted, and there was no guarantee his strength would come back. There were terrors all around him. He sat entombed like a member of one of those primitive tribes who buried their dead sitting up. He rested, breathing as quietly as he could, and listened for sounds of the avalanche starting up again, and for voices of Augustin's men who would be looking for him.

He listened hard, but the mountain made no sound.

In his white coffin he was cold. Resting, he was cold, and he thought about hypothermia, and that was a terror too. How much time did he have? How long before hypothermia set in, took away all his strength, and he went to sleep and died?

Gradually these subsidiary terrors merged, until there was only the one terror, that he would not be able to dig himself the rest of the way out. He had work to do that was possibly beyond his strength, but he was not going to just lie here and die; he was determined to stand up again somehow. He was going to get out of here.

To start he would hammer at the snow on his upper body, giving himself more breathing room, clearing the weight around his chest, his stomach, his shoulders, enlarging his personal space. He worked as fast as he could.

He was cold, very cold. His clothes were soaked. His whole being ached. But the work was so strenuous that his upper body stayed warm enough, though not his legs which felt frozen, and were beginning to cramp, and not his hands either, and he had to stop often, not only to rest but also to blow on them, to warm them under his arms, sometimes staring at his murdered knuckles, for if his hands stopped working he would die. He remembered his necktie, a Christmas gift from his mother, silk, very expensive, and he ripped it off his neck and wrapped it around his right hand. It made a pitiful excuse for a mitten but was better than nothing, and from then on his right hand froze more slowly than his left. He tried to rip the pockets off his suit coat to use them similarly, but they resisted him, causing him to waste energy he could not afford, so he stopped. The fingers of both hands were so cold he could not feel them.

Bit by bit he enlarged the area around him, over him, compacting snow, making room. Time passed, how much he did not know. Exhaustion was gaining on him. He knew this. So was the cold. How much longer could he last? he asked himself. The answer that came back terrorized him anew: not long.

When he had enlarged his hole sufficiently, he tried to stand up, but had very little strength, and for a moment feared that his clothes were frozen into the snow and would not come unstuck. But with increased effort they did, and squatting, still partially imprisoned, he waved his arms around over his head, enlarging the sky. When he had cleared enough to reach his feet, which were still buried, he dug around them. They had to be cleared but seemed an enormous distance away, and he began to cry because his strength was gone, he wasn't going to be able to do it. You are a stupid man, he told himself. You lost your wife, you lost Gigi, you lost the police department, you have probably lost your present job, and now you have lost your life as well. To have lost so much was unbearable, and tears ran down his cheeks. He thought of just giving up, allowing himself to die, it would be so easy to die.

He rested. The tears stopped. He went back to work. He cleared snow and rested, cleared snow and rested.

It took many more rests, many more minutes. But at last he managed to squeeze himself into an upright position. He felt an explosion of joy, and he thought: I've licked this thing, me, I did it!

He stood in a tight little hole that came almost to mid-chest, but underfoot was something that felt solid, and he looked back up the mountain to where the avalanche had started, remembering the other two men, who with their guns could be on top of him any second. But there was no sign of either that he could see. The remains of the avalanche were below him, masses and masses of snow, shelf piled upon shelf. He had no idea where the two men might be, and the snow around him, as he rested, looked too unstable to go searching. Alone, and considering the shape he was in, he could not have dug them out anyway, even if he could find them. Even if he had a mind to, which he did not.

Into the side of the hole he stomped steps, and then an exit ramp, excruciating work because his feet were numb, his legs cramped, and his entire body was shaking. Having climbed half out of the hole he sat on the rim, and shook with cold, with residual fear as well, to an extent he had never experienced before. He forced himself to his feet. I've got to move, he told himself. Then came a new panic. His wallet, his passport. If they were gone, what did he do then? And he slapped at his pockets trying to locate them. A miracle, he still had both.

Shaking and staggering, he resumed his downhill stroll, a 35-year-old man who was wet, sore, nearly exhausted, shivering, limping. He was terribly thirsty as well, and he sucked from time to time on handfuls of snow. Even when his legs began to work again, he moved hesitantly, avoiding brusque movements lest he rouse the mountain from its sleep, stopping every few steps to listen in case it had begun to stir. As life came back into his fingers and toes, the pain made him whimper.

He came to where the bare earth showed through, and shortly afterward reached the unmoving chairlift. It was easier to breathe here, and less cold, the altitude being less severe, the danger of avalanche was over, and after resting again he continued down under the suspended chairs. At the bottom he came to a road, a restaurant beside it, and he went in. The dining room was closed, but he found an office where a man sat at a desk, and stood before him and invented a story. He had been out hiking, Conte said. Suddenly, far above him he had seen two men caught in an avalanche.

He had spoken in English, which, he saw, was not among this man's accomplishments, so he repeated the story in Italian. Could a search party be organized?

The man held up his hands. In any language the gesture that meant incomprehension. Conte tried a third time using what French he knew. A search party. Possible, yes?

With no language in common it was hard.

Smiling up at him, the man spoke, Conte trying to guess at what the words might mean. "Yes, there are always avalanches up there," he seemed to be saying. Something like that. "That's why there are no lifts on our side." He was puzzled by Conte's bedraggled appearance, and asked about it, but showed no concern about the missing men. Or perhaps he didn't believe in them. Had he understood at all?

"Do you have a rescue team here?" Conte asked him. "You must have. Can you alert them?"

The man made a short speech in his own language, Conte grasping at words here and there. To find them, the man said, a guide was needed: "How will we know where to go?"

Conte said: "You ought to be able to find an avalanche, for crissake."

He wanted to get his wet clothes off, get something to eat, lie a long time in a hot bath, but thought he had to report the accident first, make somebody understand.

"Two men," he said, "you going to search for them, or not?"

He saw that if he didn't press this search, perhaps actively join it, then there might be no search.

"Call the search team," he said. "Call the tourist office. Call somebody."

Augustin's two men were no longer goons to Conte, just employees who had been doing their job, men with families most likely, men buried now under snow, maybe alive, scarcely able to breathe, hoping rescuers would find them.

The man across the desk had lifted his telephone, on which he dialed a number. While waiting for the connection, he nodded up at his American visitor and asked a question. Conte was pretty sure he understood this time. Could Conte lead a party up the mountain to where the men were last seen?

"No, I can't," Conte said. He owed the two men nothing. They were probably already dead. He had felt obliged to report the avalanche, and now he had done so. Or at least he thought he had. He himself was at the end of his strength. He could do no more.

"Search for them," he muttered, and turned away.

He caught a ride in a service truck the rest of the way down.

It was a town of timbered houses and chalet roofs, a well-known ski resort catering like all of them at this time of the year to hikers and honeymooners. Once in the streets he walked along buying himself clothing. He bought underwear, corduroys, loafers, a shirt, a tie, a sweater, toilet gear, and, finally, a small satchel.

He checked into the best hotel in the town and in his room drank two cognacs out of the minibar. They seemed to take some of the pain away, they made him giddy and warmed him, and a hot bath warmed him further. He lay in it up to his neck and touched his various bruises while trying not to fall asleep. Every part of him hurt, and his knuckles were raw. He dressed in the ill-fitting new clothes, and when he looked at himself in the mirror he thought he looked like a hayseed. His dress shoes and expensive suit went into the satchel, the ruined tie as well, for it meant more to him now than it ever had. Back in America perhaps one thing or another could be saved.

He was too early for dinner but he limped into the restaurant where they were just setting up and prevailed upon them to bring him a tureen of soup. It was all he wanted anyway, and he drank it all, two and a half bowls full, ate some bread and butter, and emptied a bottle of mineral water.

At the front desk he rented a car and, when it came, checked out. He thought the local police, alerted by Augustin's office, would be here in the morning or sooner, and maybe other police as well. He could not afford to be grilled by anyone, for his story would not hold up. Better that he get as far away as he could, as fast as he could.

He drove to the airport in Zurich, where he caught a plane to the one place he did want to be, which was Amsterdam, though he could not be sure if Gigi would even be there. Nor how she would receive him.

On the plane he fell asleep at once.

It was nearly midnight when he knocked on her door. He heard movement inside, someone appraising him through the peephole, a moment of tension for him, perhaps it was someone else, not Gigi at all, he could not be sure even what country she might be in by now, another woman might open, another man. Then the door swung back and she was standing before him looking sleepy, wearing only a nightgown, and then she came into his arms, and he forgot this ugly case, forgot the whole harrowing day and week. He embraced Gigi, his face in her neck. She became his only reality, and he held her. He had got past all of it, he was still alive, and he had made it home.